WHERE
THE CURLEW FLIES

MARGARET R SNOWDON

First Published in 2010
by New Generation Publishing

Second Edition

**ISBN-13: 978 -1493560493
ISBN-10: 1493560492**

Also by this author:

The Promise of Heaven
The Edge of Heaven
The Allure Of The Wild
Cockermouth Farm

✳ ✳ ✳

**FOR COLIN
WITH LOVE**

The Call of The Curlew

The distant horizons glisten and shimmer,
stretching for miles to the edge of the sea;
the curlew calls, its song rising and falling,
its flight fearless, its soul wild and free;
swooping, soaring, its tuneful imploring,
I follow its journey, watching it fly high;
it twists and turns, fills me with yearning
and finally fades, a mere speck in the sky.

Margaret Snowdon

PART ONE

ONE

Jessica Sheridan's adoration she bore her husband absorbed her very soul and existence. He was the centre of her world. She had nothing of herself left, no corner of her spirit that was not his. Sighing dreamily, she glanced around the bedroom again, a glance of satisfaction and sheer pleasure. She had the most delightful suite of rooms.

The carpet under foot was thick and luxurious, in a mixture of different shades of cream with the slightest hint of pale green here and there; her favourite colour. The curtains at the window reached right down to the ground and were of the same matching green in the carpet. Ivory flock paper and lovely water colours of Lake Windermere where they had spent their honeymoon, covered the walls.

Two moss green soft velvet chairs stood before the fireplace with a small circular polished table by each. A low fire burned in the grate, and in front of the hearth there lay a thick pile ivory rug. Jessica's hand went to her chest as she took in a deep breath... she still could not believe that all these wonderful things were for her to enjoy. She had expected comfort, but nothing in her imagination had prepared her for all this.

She slipped off her shoes and sinking into one of the chairs stretched out her legs, running her feet over the softness of the rug, as she glanced about the room. Against one wall there stood the most beautiful kidney-shaped dressing table. A small glass vase filled with a variety of delicate wild flowers stood to one side, and in the mirror she could see the reflection of the great double bed behind her. Getting up, she went to sit on its edge, running her hand over the smooth silk ivory bedspread. All these beautiful things were hers ...hers and Luke's.

She thought about the excitement of their love-making as she took the exquisite lace frill between her fingers-tips. A fresh urge washed over her as she recalled how so easily he was able to make her quiver. It always seemed so perfect and yet, for her each time proved better than the time before. The trend of social feeling mistakenly encouraged the idea that sex-life was a low, physical and degrading necessity which a pure woman was above enjoying. How wrong they were. The only thing she dreaded was the possibility of having as large a family as her friend, April Ramsey, had.

In the room adjoining there were two great wide matching mahogany cupboards that housed all her gowns and cloaks, with full length mirrors on the outside, standing side by side against the wall. A high mahogany chest of drawers, containing a profusion of bonnets: gloves, handkerchiefs, stockings, reticules, and undergarments. A washstand, a miracle of elabor-ate ingenuity, made of the finest mahogany and marble, furnished with one large and one smaller jug for hot and cold water, two porcelain basins, and a glass jar full of coloured soaps of different shapes and sizes. Jessica had never seen anything quite like it.

In addition there was a large shallow zinc hipbath and a towel-horse with several soft towels of different sizes, all carefully folded and placed over the rails. But the most intimate piece of furniture of all was a high-backed chair with intricately carved arms and a hinged lattice seat that lifted, her own personal commode.

Standing in front of the mirror she looked at herself to see if she had changed now she was a married woman, the back view of her reflecting from the cupboard mirrors. Her gown was of pale green tulle with lace flounces of deeper green at a low curved neck, the bodice smooth and tight, emphasizing the curves of her body, with lace ruffles sweeping down from the waist to the hem. The back led the eye to a small frothy train, and around her shoulders was a cream cashmere shawl, with trimmings of cord and elaborate embroidery of gold thread, which Luke had bought her on their honeymoon. Smoothing down the front of the skirt, she smiled at her reflection. Yes! She certainly did look different she decided. Quite sophisticated, even if she did say so herself. - Mrs Luke Sheridan.

She wanted so much to be a lady, to please him. She was so happy. Happy and satisfied, with one exception; the housekeeper, the starchy Mrs Osborne. How she had detested meeting the staff that very first time, particularly the housekeeper, with her cold hard stare. She had only seen the woman once before, on the day she had called at the house to speak to Luke about April Ramsey's dilemma of losing her home.

When she returned to the house as the new Mrs

Sheridan, the woman's look had said it all, resentment showing clearly on her face. 'Fancy a gentleman like Mr Sheridan choosing a miner's daughter, a low-class girl, when there were well-bred young ladies to choose from.'

Jessica had held out her hand in greeting, but the woman had not taken it. The contempt had showed clearly in her eyes, but in spite of that she had smiled bravely and greeted her politely in her very best voice. She could not help but smile when she thought of the three girls standing there, so erect, dressed exactly alike, in awful grey dresses, stiff white aprons and those silly caps. They looked quite comical. The very sight of them was enough to make anyone smile.

There was Amy, who was as short and plump as the one called Maggie was tall and thin. So cold and unfriendly, the pair of them. Then there was Alice, a tiny fragile looking creature who appeared to be no more than a child, as if a puff of wind might blow her over. She had stood there with her head lowered all through Luke's introductions, obviously extremely shy.

Thank goodness they were not all like the stern faced Mrs Osborne. Mrs Miles, the cook, seemed a kind enough woman, the only one who had actually given her a welcoming smile. Her husband Ned was gardener and general handyman - Jack-of-all-trades, he had called himself. He and Tom Saunders, who, being a friend of her brother Joe, she already knew, worked together, keeping the stables and gardens in tip-top order.

At least there had been one who showed real pleasure in seeing her again – the dear little terrier, Toby. He had been quite ecstatic, wriggling about and wagging his tail, what there was of it, so hard it was a wonder it hadn't fallen off. Mrs Osborne had grabbed hold of his collar and shut him in the study until he calmed down.

'He's best off there. The late Mrs Sheridan didn't care t'have him running loose about the house,' she had said, her eyes locked with her own all the time she was speaking. 'It doesn't do t'let him have all his own way.'

There had been few kind words spoken to her since. And if she really thought about it, even Luke seemed different somehow, now they were home. Not tender, not as attentive as he had been. A little cold, distant even. The only time he showed any real affection was in the privacy of the bedroom. Even then he seemed to hold back, careful not to reveal his feelings.

And all these rules: don't eat with your mouth open; walk, don't run; don't interfere in the kitchen or upset the maids routine, and Heaven forbid if she left a few books scattered about the house to help her feel more at home. Anything to take away the artificial look of the rooms.

Apart from the usual bright liveliness of fires in the grates, it seemed as if no one ever used them. No sooner did she put her cup and saucer down it was whisked away. A book she hadn't finished reading, was put back in its place on the shelf. Everything kept in its place. Nothing disturbed, so thoroughly neat, so provokingly in order. And all this changing of clothes. She had changed into more gowns in the last few weeks than she had during her entire lifetime. What did it matter if she wore the same gown through -out the day?

To be at all times absolutely impeccable seemed to be an obsession with her husband. Not as much as a speck ever marred the white surface of his shirt, no crease ever sullied the perfection of his suit, and as for his shoes and boots, they were always polished until they shone. Not a fleck, not a smudge on them. His jackets and topcoats were made by one tailor, his shirts and waistcoats by another and breeches by a third; each a specialist in his own field.

Her deepest desire was to please him and her conception of happiness was to know that she had succeeded in doing so, but she had never quite succeeded beyond a certain point. With all this stored-up happiness to sustain her, it was curious that she found herself yielding to a nervous apprehension. But there the apprehension was. Perhaps it was because she was more tired than normal? Or for some other ridiculously trivial reason, moral or physical, she found herself unable to react against the feeling?

With a sigh, she turned and walked through into a fair-sized sitting room, just as lovely as the bedroom, the carpet the colour of faded moss, the curtains a rich gold. The room was tastefully furnished with two-seater sofas, one of beige and one a harvest gold, placed to each side of a large fire place, exactly facing each other, with several soft moss-green cushions, blending with the shade of the carpet.

A long, low polished table had been placed be-tween the two sofas, with a variety of fresh fruit arranged in a large oval bowl, placed precisely in the centre. The walls were covered in the same ivory flock paper as that of the bedroom, and several more water colours of swans on a lake and birds with the background of the fells. By the long window stood a large high-backed, gold velvet chair and a small round polished table on which stood an arrangement of bright yellow roses.

The view from the window was quite breathtaking. Emerald grass sloped downwards to a belt of tall elms, shimmering birches and proud conifers that rose up to meet the clear blue sky and, beyond, a sudden wild sweep of bracken slopes that ran up to tall regal oaks.

The mellow beauty of Wildacres lay like a spell on its new mistress. She loved the old house - an enchanting place in a perfect setting. On one side grew a plantation of chestnut and fir, on the other was the yard that led to the stables, and at the back was an old fashioned garden. It was formally arranged with a turf walk bordered by strawberry beds, leading to the garden's focal point; a sun dial, where there were boarders of flowers and long benches to sit and relax on. She sighed with the wonder of it all. All this …and Heaven too.

'Excuse me, Madam. I did knock.'

So lost was Jessica in admiring the beauty of the view that she had not heard the maid enter and the voice startled her. It was the girl, Alice.

'Tell me, Alice, who put the flowers in the rooms? Do you know?'

The girl's face flushed. 'I did, Madam. Rose, I …I mean Miss Bradley, the first Mrs Sheridan's personal maid, once told me you liked wild flowers.'

'Yes, I know who Rose is. Thank you, Alice. The flowers were very thoughtful of you.'

The girl's hand went nervously to her mouth. 'Oh, Madam, I …I almost forgot. The master said you were t'join him for tea in the drawing room.'

'Oh, I didn't realise the time,' Jessica said. 'Would you mind if I had tea here? I'm feeling rather tired.'

'As you wish, Madam, but what shalla say t'the master?'

'Tell my husband that I intend to take a rest.'

'Very well, Madam.' Alice gave a curtsy and left, closing the door quietly behind her.

Jessica went back into the bedroom, took off her shawl and laid it carefully on a chair. She undid the buttons on the tight bodice, pushed aside the silk cover on the bed, and then laid down, wondering if Luke would come to join her. Day-dreaming of the first joys of their union, of their future happiness, feeling confident that she had at last found the one who would give eternal understanding and tenderness, her eyelids drooped ... and she slept.

TWO

Jessica liked her assured position, her husband's constant generosity, and took happily to her new life. She had read somewhere that a woman was supposed to have no spontaneous sex-impulses, but to feel his warm lips on hers was heavenly bliss, melting her in mists of tenderness.

Although there was always some part of him detached, some part he held back, exercising rigid control, still she was intoxicated by the magic and was hopelessly devoted. Their marriage proved to be a happy one, their happiness of the radiant kind that nothing, least of all differences of opinion, could disturb. Their relationship was securely anchored in a deep need each had of the other. Or so she believed.

The stillness in Wildacres, which Jessica could not fail to notice, seemed to hold echoes of events long past and voices that were silent. In those first weeks she prowled about the silent house, as curious as a cat. The drawing room was still more brilliant, a rich world of painted butterflies, animals and flowers, elegant upright chairs of black ebonised wood, with flower designs of aesthetic Oriental flavour, and a grand marble fireplace, an array of deep comfortable sofas, footstools, small tables scattered here and there, a writing desk and a splendid glass-fronted chest holding the most exquisite porcelain ornaments.

The windows that reached from ceiling to floor looked west, down to the enormous stillness of the conifers and were hung with heavy curtains, the colour of ruby wine. There were dividing carved oaken doors into the dining room that could be opened to allow more space. The dining room itself was long, with a two-tier Jacobean chimneypiece, the top half dominated by a great gilt-edged mirror.

Twelve elegant rococo chairs covered in claret leather surrounded a highly polished, long oval table. A sideboard stood in a recess lined with claret velvet, and against the wall was an ornately bulging wine cooler and a long dresser with bulbous legs, displaying numerous silver serving dishes and trays.

But the finest room of all was, without a doubt, the study - her husband's study that was rather impressive and attracted her more than any other room. The whole area had a masculine touch about it. There were prints of hounds and horses, and great pictures of war battles covering the panelled walls, rifles and a sword in a glass-fronted cabinet, a low bookcase full with ledgers, and shelves well stocked with books. An entire shelf was filled with books on mining, mathe-matics, geography and art.

Awe filled her as she read some of the titles, names of philosophers she had never heard of. The entire room was flooded with light, the sun coming through long windows that overlooked the yard, lighting up the warm honey-brown of the oak panelling and the soft red of the capacious high-backed leather chairs. Two were set by the fireplace, another in which she loved to sit, behind a great leather-topped desk.

A gold frame hanging above the high mantelshelf caught and reflected the sunlight, drawing Jessica's attention. She uttered a little impatient exclamation. It was a painting of a young pale blonde woman, looking down with a sad smile ... Annie Sheridan, Luke's first wife, who had died in childbirth, along with the child. Jessica just couldn't seem to avoid looking at it. The eyes appeared to follow her about the room. What it was doing still hanging in her husband's study was a mystery to her. In fact, it positively annoyed her.

She spent an enjoyable hour reading a curious old book, which she had taken from one of the shelves and was leaning back against the cushion with her eyes closed, thinking of what she had just read, when suddenly she felt she was no longer on her own. She opened her eyelids, knowing without a doubt, she would see someone, but there was no one ... she was quite alone.

For some reason she felt compelled to glance up at the haunting portrait. To make sure of not seeing it, she had deliberately seated herself just beneath it. Rising from the chair, she stood for a while looking up at it. The strange light of early evening could hardly account for the extraordinary pallor of the young woman's face. The bluey-green eyes seemed to stare straight back at her.

Jessica considered eyes to be of strong spiritual power. She noticed then that one of the eyes was slightly lower than the other. A person with one eye lower than the other was said to have the Evil Eye, and Jessica's faith in the Evil Eye was strong. It could bring misfortune or illness to another.

She moved closer and looked real hard at them to assure herself it was no fancy, and then she perceived, standing out distinctly on the pale cheeks were two tear drops. In that timeless tranquillity it required little effort of the imagination to see her there - the delicate, pale faced, first Mrs Sheridan. Jessica crossed her fingers and fled from the room.

Upstairs, along the landing was the housekeeper's bedroom and adjoining sitting room, which Jessica steered clear of. But there were other chambers and dressing rooms she explored, each with chintz drapes of various colours to the windows and immense four-poster beds. All the rooms were furnished with a wardrobe, washstand, a writing table and a chair, also a small sofa covered with the same colour of the curtains. All the perfection of comfort.

In one of the rooms where the furniture was shrouded with dustsheets, she came across a partly splendidly done tapestry stretched on its frame; a scene of ducks and swans on a lake, with trees in the background. It was obvious the woman whose work it was had not been content with anything less than perfection. Jessica lifted one of the dustsheets.

Underneath was a Queen Anne walnut bureau of superb colour, raised on bun feet, and a walnut stool with slightly curved sides and rounded corners, on cabriole legs carved at the knees with shells and bellflowers, ending in diamond toes. The drop-in seat was covered with period needlework, with petit point panels depicting hounds in a landscape surrounded by multi-coloured arabesques on a dark brown ground. It was really quite exquisite. The interior of the desk was fitted with an inkwell, pigeonholes and small drawers inlaid with stringing. She discovered what she thought was a leather-covered book at the back of one of the drawers. She opened it at the first page. It turned out to be a journal, but only in note form, making it possible for her to have a glimpse of the first Mrs Sheridan's life during the time of her marriage to Luke.

Name - Annie Jane Sheridan. In case of my death please inform my parents

James and Agatha Merchant of Hawkeshead.

Why an earth would one so young write such a thing? It was almost as if she had known she would die at a very early age. Jessica turned over the page. The first entry was dated January 1824:

Jan 5th - I still feel weak after losing the child. Weather dull and frosty.

Jan 6th - No letters. How I long for some news. A high wind has blown up and it has turned dreadfully cold. Rose and I spent most of the day sewing and reading, close to the fire.

Jessica flicked the pages over until she came to July.

July 1st - Luke still away. Went for a short walk by the lake in the afternoon.

July 2nd - Sick and ill. Lay in bed until three. When I arose, I was far from well, but grew slightly better after tea. Rose read to me. I retired early.

Then there was a whole page of writing:

July 3rd - Not at all well. Breakfasted in bed. Doctor paid a visit. We had a long talk. In my own life, comparatively short and lacking in experience though it might be, I have known both personally and vicariously so much anguish that might have been prevented by knowledge. Yet again I am with child. I cannot bear it. The thought of going through all the agony again leaves me feeling utterly depressed.

July 4th - I feel trapped. I pray this time I can give my husband the son he so desires and that he will then leave me in peace. Please God ...I beseech you ...let *me bear this one healthy male child.*

Outside it is not at all like a summer's day. Raining quite steadily. Stayed in my sitting room and wrote to Mama, telling her the news of the child and asking her if she could come to visit.

July 5th – So weary and depressed. How I wish I could be with Mama and Papa and my dear sister Mary. If it was not for Rose keeping me company. I am sure I would go out of my mind in this lonely place.

July 6th - Letter from Mama. Unable to come. She, Papa and Mary are to be away in London. They will not return home for almost two weeks. How I wish I could go with them. Escape this place.

Jessica sighed. What a humdrum life the woman had led. It all sounded so monotonous to her. She shut the journal with a snap and placed it back in the drawer. After reading what she had she felt quite sorry for the poor woman. It was evident she had not been happy here at Wildacres and would have much rather been back with her family. She closed the lid to the desk and replaced the dustsheet over it and the stool, leaving everything just as she had found it.

A steep flight of stairs lead to the attic rooms where the servants slept, going up at night with their candles and rising shivering on bitter winter mornings, when ice had formed on the water in the wash jug ...Jessica suspected. The sight of the bare floorboards and iron bedsteads, not to mention the cast-off pockmarked mirrors and cracked washbasins, and towels that were so worn they were practically rags, was enough to depress even the most placid of natures. And placid she was not! It was junk - the lot of it. There was not even a strip of carpet to step on.

No doubt, even the chamber pots were cracked. She took a look. They were cracked and chipped. Was it any wonder the girls always looked so miserable?

She closed the door on the lot of it and went back down the stairs, her mind ticking over one to the dozen. No one should be expected to live under such conditions when there was all that decent furniture covered over by dustsheets - most likely forgotten. She intended to do something about it and would have her way. She decided to reorganize her household in her own time and in her own way, whatever the sour-faced Mrs Osborne might say.

THREE

The house was overly silent. Soft-footed servants went quietly about their duties with heads down and eyes averted. The very air breathed tension. A lovely, sweet smell of baking drew Jessica to the kitchen and silly though it might seem, she suddenly felt home-sick, as it reminded her of the kitchen at Fells View …and she wondered for the umpteenth time just where Betsy Randall was, the woman who had been like a mother to her.

Mrs Miles, the cook - a true household treasure - reigned supreme over the kitchen. It was a huge room with the fire in the centre of one wall, and two large ovens, one to each side of the fireplace, which made it extremely hot. Jessica wondered how an earth the staff stood it in there.

There were two dressers full of crockery standing side by side against the wall, and. a great table in the middle of the floor, with racks above that were fixed to the low ceiling from which hung brightly polished copper pots and pans of all shapes and sizes.

'Is everything all right, Madame? Are you wanting something? There's always a nice cup o' tea,' Mrs Miles offered with a sunny smile.

Jessica smiled back at the woman, grateful for her kindliness.

'No thank you, Mrs Miles. I'm just browsing around, getting to know the house.'

Jessica glanced down at Toby at her feet. The little terrier wagged his stub of a tail, pleased that he was being noticed.

All of a sudden the door was flung open.

'Out! Out!' someone shrieked.

Jessica turned to the woman in shocked surprise, quite thinking she herself was being ordered out of the kitchen, but then it came to her that it was Toby that the housekeeper was ordering out.

The poor little thing cowered at her feet, with his ears and stubby tail down. Mrs Osborne looked at her in a casual, uninterested way in which strangers might regard each other. The woman never lost her temper; she became icy calm which, as Cook often said, wasn't natural and enough to put the wind up any-body. However, Cook's temper flashed across the blue sky of her sunny nature and just as quickly fizzled out, because before she could say anything to Mrs Osborne, the young mistress spoke.

'Ah, Mrs Osborne. Just the person I wanted to see.' Jessica's initial reaction was to refuse to put the dog out. And how dare she treat her so indifferently ...but listening to her inner voice, common sense prevailed and she decided to let it pass.

'Oh, just what would you want with me, Madam? I'm very busy. I've a hundred an' one things t'see to.'

'Then it can wait. We can't have you over-worked now, can we?'

The housekeeper's look was one of puzzlement. 'Well, if it's not important....'

'It is important, but I'll talk to you when you are less busy,' Jessica said lightly, confident that she had the housekeeper wondering. She would let the woman come to her. 'Now, if you'll excuse me, I need to get some fresh air.'

Before Mrs Osborne could say another word,

Jessica stepped out of the kitchen door, followed by Toby, out into the yard and breathed in the fresh air. She smiled then.

The place was alive with chickens wandering freely. She marvelled that the little terrier showed no interest to chase them, but stayed close to her skirts. This was more like it - her kind of world, outside where things were alive and moving and friendlier. With Toby at her heels, she took off in the direction of the lake, and walked for an hour or more.

FOUR

Mid-January brought the snow, covering everything with a vast white blanket, throwing great drifts against hedges and walls, over four feet in places, reaching up the front walls of the house, and still falling from the skies like a heavy colourless curtain.

Jessica felt so restless she could scream. This could last for weeks. Weeks! She would never survive being shut in all that time without seeing her father and Clara, and not visiting Megan and Joe. And how would April cope with the children without her help? She had come to enjoy being with April Ramsey and her lively young bunch. It helped to fill the empty moments in her life, when Luke was constantly away on business.

By the time two o'clock came the snow had reached the top of the garden wall. She had attempted to cross the yard to the stable, wanting to see Luke's roan, but her long skirts had hindered her, holding her back, making it too much of a struggle and she had had to turn back.

'We're in for it now,' she said aloud to herself, gazing out of the drawing room window that over looked the front garden. She had best see that the fires were kept banked up. Luke must surely be close to home by now. He had said he would be back by mid-day and it was now gone three.

It had taken Luke the best part of an hour to wallow through the snowdrifts that reached up to his thighs and much higher in places - to get from the main road where Ed Morley had dropped him off. The cart would soon have got stuck if it had left the main route. He made the rest of the journey on foot. As it was, he wondered if the man would get through to Roughton. His clothes had gone stiff, dragging him down time and time again and now, with the snow falling fast and furious, he was soaked through to the skin, his hat and shoulders completely covered, the snow even settling on his eye-brows, giving him the appearance of an old man.

Jessica saw him through the window, struggling and half crawling across the white blanket of the garden. She moved as quickly as her skirts would allow, across the soft carpet of the drawing room, out through the door.

Calling for the housekeeper, she made her way through the hall, reaching the front door first, opening it wide, the snow spilling in everywhere with Luke stumbling after it.

The two of them hovered in front of him.

'F..for pity's s..sake, s..shut the d..damn door,' he stuttered, gasping for breath.

He could hardly move, so stiff was he. He stood shivering on the spot where a pool of slush had formed on the flagged floor. Bringing his arm up stiffly, he removed his hat and the snow from it fell to join the pool of slush. One to either side of him, the women helped him off with his topcoat.

'I'm as ...as s..stiff as a ...b..board. I can ...can h..hardly ... move my arms,' he gasped.

'Hot rum, don't you think, Mrs Osborne?' Jessica said quietly, careful to put the idea to the housekeeper in the way of a suggestion rather than an order. For wasn't there a truce between them? She did not want to risk spoiling the peaceable relationship, if you could call it that. The woman was liable to change moods without reason. 'It will help thaw him out, don't you think?' she added tactfully.

Luke was too preoccupied with his discomfort to notice the sudden harmony between his wife and housekeeper. His teeth were chattering. 'Bring ...the ...b..bloody bottle. I'll need it.'

'Send it upstairs, please, Mrs Osborne,' Jessica added.

If her husband objected to her manoeuvring him, he did not say so, for he allowed her to help him up the stairs to her own private sitting room where the door shuts behind one and one is transferred to a separate existence, where the fire had been banked up high and was roaring merrily up the chimney. In the privacy of her room she helped him remove every stitch of his clothing, rubbing him down with a soft scented towel, as he stood naked in front of the fire, chatting away as she did so, her voice mellifluous and soothing.

Hearing a gentle tap, Jessica dropped the towel at his feet and quickly crossed to the door and opening it just a little, reached to take the tray from Maggie, thanking her and pushing the door shut behind her. Luke took the mug of rum and hot water from the tray she held out to him and swallowed it in one gulp. She placed the tray down on the little rosewood table close to the sofa, and poured him another, but neat. He sipped this one slowly. She watched the colour slowly return to his cheeks and the stiffness leave his long hard body. Taking up the towel, she returned to rubbing his skin.

'That ... that's enough, my pet.' His voice sounded

husky and low.

Jessica dropped the towel to the floor and with gentle loving hands smoothed his chest, her soft lips planting little kisses on his skin, light teasing kisses, her hands gradually moving further down his body. He felt his stomach quiver, his breath quicken in his throat. He whispered her name, his arms creeping round her tiny waist, pulling her against his hard naked body. She smiled, a wicked mischievous smile, but wriggled free.

His dark eyes were soft and musing as they followed her across the room where she turned the key in the lock. She was suddenly back by his side. His discomfort for-gotten, he drew down the bodice of her gown, lingering in absorbed concentration on her throat, her breasts, stripping her right there in front of the fire, the occasional soft hiss and splutter serving to emphasise the room's peace, quite marvelling at her loveliness, the smooth soft texture of her skin. He lowered her to the floor and she clung to him as they lay together in the warmth from the flames, her mass of silken hair spread over the rug, her lips warm and eager against his own.

Luke studied at great length the hard peaks of her almond nipples, the rounded quivering of her smooth belly to the soft curve of her inner thigh and the crisp, copper spring of curls in between. She reached out and wound her arms about his neck, drawing his mouth down to her distended nipple, throwing back he head in ecstasy as his lips took first one, then the other, sucking and teasing it with his tongue. She stretched and groaned in delight, her hands moving through the damp dark curls of his hair, as she arched her back and strained against him as if she could not get enough of him, her voice rising jubilantly.

'Luke. Oh, Luke...'

He chuckled softly and spoke against her skin. 'Patience, my pet.'

But feeling his own excitement rising, he knew he must not wait and gently pushed her back, and as he entered her, she curled her legs about his hips... their desire for one another not to be denied, their passion bursting from them at the same time, both shuddering to a climax.

Nothing outside the enchanted circle of firelight in the quiet room existed for them during that afternoon. And that night they lay in each other's arms, like two young lovers entwined, her head against her husband's arm, with a contented smile and his name on her rosy lips.

With a peaceful night's sleep behind him, Luke woke feeling refreshed. He gently removed his arm from under his wife's head, trying not to disturb her. He looked at her lying there, peacefully sleeping, looking so innocent and young, with strands of her hair stuck to the dampness of her forehead, long lashes resting on flushed cheeks, her lips full and pink, and he felt strangely stirred, which surprised him, for he was not a man who believed in romantic love. But he found a certain kind of contentment in this second marriage, which he had never found in the first.

From the very beginning he had vowed he would take good care of her and make her the first object of his life. It had helped that she was young with fire in her body, but he had married her only because she was strong, with plenty of spirit and could give him the fine sons he longed for. For that reason and no other. And after that little episode yesterday afternoon and again that night, he would be surprised if she was not already pregnant with his child.

He studied her face a little longer. She was certainly a prize to grace any man's home. She deserved to be pampered. He would take her away somewhere for a few days once the snow had cleared. He slipped into his dressing gown and quietly left the room, crossing to his own at the other side of the landing, where he bathed and put on fresh clothes and then went in search of a good breakfast, before he put his mind to tackling what needed to be done.

Great drifts of snow lay everywhere, burying walls and gates, making it impossible to know where one field began or another ended; even the hedges had dis-appeared in places. Only the tops of trees peeped out above the white smooth landscape. Luke wonder-ed if the men would manage to dig a way out of their cottages. He shrugged - that wasn't his concern. He paid others a fair wage to see that his mines were kept running and were productive. It was each man for himself, to see he got to his job, whatever the weather. He stood at the window in the drawing room, his hands pushed deep into the pockets of his working cords, his eyes screwed up against the blind-ing brightness, gazing across the silent fells.

Tom would take care of the animals in the stable, the rest of the staff carrying out their duties as usual, but the problem of getting himself to Keswick for his appointments was his, and by the looks of it he wouldn't get far in this; the appointments would have to wait. There were plenty of other things he could be doing. He turned away, making for his study, where he shut himself in.

Surrounded by ledgers and plans, Luke stretched his long limbs in the great leather chair, looking at the clock on the mantel. Almost eleven thirty. Where was everyone? It was about time a drink was brought in. There seemed to be a bit of a commotion going on outside. He rose from the chair, crossed to the window and raised an arm to rub away the mist, and looked out. He could see Tom and two of the maids, wrapped in layers of clothing, out there clearing the yard. Rather them than me, he thought to himself. Just as he was about to turn away, Tom straightened up and lifted an arm to wave.

Good Grief! It wasn't Tom as he had thought. It was Jessica, dressed in what looked to be an old pair of tweed trousers and a grey baggy jacket tied in the middle with a much too long leather belt. His wife was out there, out there with the hired staff ... *shovelling snow!* He couldn't believe his eyes and had to look again, watching with disbelief as she attempted to push her unruly hair back up underneath the cap she had on.

'For Heaven's sake! Will that girl never learn?' he cried aloud, striding across the room to the door, flinging it wide and shouting at the top of his voice, 'Mrs Osborne ...Mrs Osborne!'

In a matter of seconds the housekeeper appeared in the doorway, looking quite flustered. 'What is it, Sir? What's happened?'

'What is it? I'll tell you what it is. My wife is out there clearing the bloody snow. Are you aware of this?' he enquired angrily, his jaw hardened with displeasure.

'Yes, I'm aware, Sir, an' I'm sorry. I did try t'stop her, but you know Madam has a mind o' her own,' Dora said, relieved it was not her that was at fault. When she had heard his thunderous roar, she quite thought something was seriously wrong.

Luke drew in a deep breath. 'Well, kindly inform her that I want to see her in my study ...at once!'

Dora opened her mouth to say something more, but thought better of it and hurriedly retreated, closing the door quietly behind her. She had found Mrs Sheridan much more co-operative these last few weeks and didn't want to cause any bad feelings. But on the other hand ...an order was an order and had to be obeyed.

It was some minutes before Jessica came through the study door. She had removed her boots, the jacket and cap, revealing her bodice, which was tucked into the old tweeds that were pulled up high just below her breasts, the belt holding them there, the bottoms dragging on the floor. Her hair tumbled about her shoulders, a thick mass curling loosely at its ends, her face flushed and happy, her nose tipped with red and her eyes sparkling. Looking absolutely radiant... but for the clothes. Luke hesitated just for a moment, as she looked across the room at him, holding his stern gaze.

'Luke darling, what's so important that I had to come at once?' Her long lashes fluttered, her smile sweet and innocent.

'Don't Luke darling me! And stop flashing those eyes at me.' His voice was sharp.

Jessica winced. He was clearly angry. Was this the same man who had held her in his arms last night and had made her so happy? 'Heaven forbid! Where would you have me flash them?' she questioned audaciously, feeling a little hurt.

'And don't be clever. Sit down.' He stood by the desk, stiff and erect, his face a mask of anger, as he motioned to the chair in front of the fire. 'I have something to say to you.'

'I don't want to sit down, thank you,' she said defiantly. 'I don't know what has put you in this foul mood, but until you can be civil, I intend to leave you to it.'

She turned to leave, pulling the legs of the cords up off the floor, as without the boots to tuck the bottoms in to they were ridiculously long, making it difficult for her to walk. The very sight of her made him forget his fury. She did look ridiculous. God ...she could make him so furious one minute, then light-headed the next.

'Jessica, sit down.' he said more calmly. 'Please,' he added reluctantly, in an effort to keep the peace, trying hard to conceal his frustration.

'That's much better, Luke. I won't be spoken to in any way you choose.' There was a quarrelsome edge to her voice.

'Won't you sit down?' he asked, his face losing its hardness.

She appeared to be considering the request, choosing to stay where she was, standing very straight, thrusting out her chin indignantly, her expression clearly stating that she would not be treated like a child. His face darkened again. 'Jessica, I did not marry you to be my servant or one of the yard hands. It's Tom's place to clear the snow.'

'But Tom has a bad chill, and...' she started, without taking her eyes off him. Her voice suddenly softened. 'Oh, Luke, really! I was just having a little fun. Haven't you ever enjoyed the snow when you were a child?' she spoke with the enthusiasm of youth.

'Yes, but that was a very long time ago,' he said impatiently. 'And you're hardly a child. You're my wife. It's not your place to mix with the servants. I won't have it!'

Her face put on a look of distaste. 'Oh, for Heaven's sake, Luke. Mix with the servants! Why, they're people just the same as us. How was I to know you would take on so?'

'Mrs Osborne warned you that...'

'Oh, Mrs Osborne! That woman resents me even being here. The frustrated old....' she trailed off, unable to think of a suitable word to call the woman.

'Now, watch your tongue,' Luke warned.

'Heaven forbid that I should criticise the wonderful Mrs Osborne.'

'Mrs Osborne has been with this family for a great many years. I have a good deal of respect for her.'

She stared rebelliously at him before answering. 'And don't I know it. I've heard you sing her praise so many times since I came to this house that I'm beginning to wonder why you didn't marry the woman, instead of me,' she stated flippantly.

'Don't talk foolish.' He counted silently to retain his patience. 'It's a pity you couldn't learn from her. She could be of great help to you in the running of the house.'

'But she runs it perfectly well herself. She and the servants do a marvellous job. You've made that quite clear often enough and she's told me as much herself. So, what would you have me do with myself, shut in here day after day?' Her lip dropped in a pout, and she pulled at the legs of the old tweeds, shuffling across the floor towards him.

'You do look a mess, woman. If you could only see yourself.' He could barely stop himself from laughing, but it wouldn't do to laugh. She should remember just who she was. As his wife she should keep herself more presentable. As a show of his dis- approval he would not visit her room tonight.

Jessica giggled girlishly and stretched up, balance- ing on her toes, placing her hands about his neck and pulling his face down to hers to plant a warm tender kiss on his lips. She sighed overdramatically, deliber- ately fluttering long lashes at him and when she spoke her tone was mocking.

'Darling, I'm off to change into something more fitting for the wife of Mr Luke Sheridan,' she purred. 'Then I will have one of the maids serve us tea and toasted muffins in my suite. That's if I might have the pleasure of your company, Sir?' She curtsied then, fluttering an imaginary fan, her eyes dancing mischievously.

She left the room with an exaggerated sway to her hips, struggling with the legs of the tweeds, pulling them up to reveal the soft curve of her buttocks just below the mass of her brilliant hair which hung down her straight back. He heard her muffled laughter as she made for the stairs. What was he going to do with her?

She had to move with a hop and a jump, always full of youthful spirit, generous and impulsive, a fresh natural charm that seemed to captivate everyone. But she must learn to settle down. He could not remember ever having experienced the careless gaiety of youth himself. He sighed deeply and turned back to his books to put his desk in order, but could still picture the lovely enticing curve of her buttocks. A wicked smile lit up his face.

Leaving the study, he followed after her, and entering her bedroom turned the key. He was just in time to catch her stepping into her petticoats, but she let them drop to the floor as his arms slid about her small waist, pulling her roughly to him. The radiance of her smile banished all trace of annoyance.

'What am I to do with you?' he whispered, picking her up easily and laying her on the bed. Smiling contentedly, she watched him remove his own clothing, opening her arms to receive him as he lowered himself onto the bed beside her.

The tea and muffins could wait!

Another week went by, a slow tedious week; still Luke could not get away. Winter seemed reluctant to leave. Every morning they rose to find the house surrounded by a mantle of glistening white. Silent and cold.

When Luke was in the study he expected to be left in peace, undisturbed, but Jessica, feeling shut in, was restless and had quite expected her husband to spend more time with her during the long hours of daylight, other than when in the privacy of the bedroom.

She was on edge, irritable over nothing, bored and inclined to sigh with tedious regularity. 'I must get across the fells,' she said, collecting her boots and hurrying to get ready.

Luke stood with his back to the roaring fire, an expression on his face that said he had no intentions of allowing her to go anywhere, not in this weather.

'It's not yet clear enough to get through.'

'Tom got through to the farm. He said there were men abroad rescuing the sheep.'

'Yes, strong sturdy farm hands. The drifts have blocked all the lanes. So deep in places it reaches a grown man's waist. Such conditions must render the taking of the daily feed to the beasts difficult and time consuming. I don't know how the farmers' manage.' He said, trying to make her see it would be senseless to venture out. 'If you can't think of the danger to yourself, then think of the poor animal you're so fond of. You'll both get stuck and then what!'

'Oh, Luke.'

'I said no! And that's final.'

'I'm not a child to be told what to do,' Jessica cried indignantly.

'Then stop acting like one. If you were in your right mind, you would know that I'm right.'

She slumped down on to the sofa. 'I just have to get out, to get some fresh air at least. I feel I could scream.'

'Patience has never been one of your strong points. Tomorrow I hope to attend a meeting at the bank in Keswick. Weather permitting, I'll leave at eleven sharp. You can come along for the ride if you wish.'

The pleasure of the prospects of getting out of the house, in which she was imprisoned, lit up her face.

'Oh, can I?'

'Yes, but I don't want any interference on your part.'

'I'll be a perfect angel, I promise.'

He threw his head back and laughed. 'You? A

perfect angel? I can't picture you as an angel some-how. All I ask is that you won't get carried away and air your views on matters that don't concern you.'

'I won't. You have my word.'

'Well, I haven't promised anything, but we'll see. It's still too cold to be outside for long. Now go and find something to occupy your mind.'

The snowdrifts were covered with a thin coating of ice; tears quivered on them and on the trees; a dark slush of mud and melting snow flowed along the roads and paths. In short, it was thawing, but through the dark nights the heavens failed to see it and flung flakes of fresh snow upon the melting earth at a terrific rate. In a frenzied dance it whirled in the wind that would not let the snow settle on the ground.

It was four more days before winter begun to release its icy grip. They spent cheerful evenings by the fireside, while the snow whirled wildly outside, and even the hooting of the owl was hushed, doing nothing at all but just sitting and reading. On the fifth morning Luke had risen early and gone without her, for he feared there might be another fall of snow. Jessica did not know the restlessness of her husband's nature, the underlying melancholy that might spring out at any moment when the bloom was gone from his first passion for her. She did not know that the only thing that could hold such a man was the sense that nothing held him except his own will; for restraint drives such natures mad, and they will be over every fence. She was absolutely furious, stomp-ing about all day, her face stiff and expressionless, unable to settle to anything for long.

FIVE

The thaw set in with that first south-west wind, which brings each February a feeling of Spring such as is never again recaptured, and men's senses, like sleepy bees in the sun, go roving. There began in Luke again that restless, unreasonable aching; it awakened in him more violently than ever the craving for something new. He was marking time, just waiting, but for what, he had no notion.

He lingered undecidedly in the pleasant lobby of Pulteney Hotel in Piccadilly. In summer it was always cool and restful, but on wintry days like today it was a cosy place, the tread of feet hushed with thick soft carpeting, its polished panelled walls reflecting the gleam of the flames from the logs that burnt cheer-fully in the great open fireplace, and the mellow tick of an ancient clock on the mantel above. There were shining oak settles that invited relaxation or a place to gossip, china bowls on low casual tables frothing over with the flowers of a belated autumn, to charm the eye. He had spent the last two days at business meetings, the evenings in ease and idleness at his club, and was in two minds whether to be on his way or put off the journey home and stay a day or two longer.

'Bonjour Monsieur.'

He knew that soft musical voice as soon as she spoke. He swung round to face her and a pair of eyes, as blue as sapphires, smiled in to his.

'Good Lord, Madame Duprez! This is a surprise.'

Without warning he felt that old familiar tug of attraction. She was even more stunning than he remembered her. She was attired in a pelisse of rich dark brown velvet, that reached to her feet, clasped at regular distances from the throat to the bottom, tightly over the bosom and pinched in at the waist giving her an hourglass look, and trimmed with a deep band of ermine at the hem and around the wrist of the long tight-fitting sleeves. A pert little ermine trimmed bonnet to match, perched at a rakish angle on top of her golden head. In her gloved hands she held a small purse in the shape of a shell.

Amel extended a gloved hand, which he took delicately. 'Monsieur Sheridan. How wonderful to see you again.'

'Likewise. I thought you had moved back to Paris?'

She tilted her head and smiled. 'So I did, for a while.'

'When did you get back?'

'We docked in Brighton early this morning.'

She eyed him up and down. He was impeccably dressed in a long dark grey frock coat and tight fitting trousers, a snow-white frilled shirt and cravat, with a green satin waistcoat embroidered in peacock colours with iridescent threads. Clothes designed to draw attention to his slim waist and accent the muscles of his thighs, those strong wonderful thighs that she remembered well. So smart and extremely attractive.

'Just look at you. I had forgotten just how handsome you are,' she flattered, her eyes meeting his.

'You've changed.'

'I have?' A gloved hand went self-consciously to

her perfectly groomed hair, pushing an imaginary loose strand under her bonnet. 'I must look absolutely ghastly.'

'Not at all,' Luke said too quickly. 'You're even more beautiful than I remember, if that's at all possible.'

'Oh Luke, you always were a flatterer,' she said, fluttering long gold-tipped lashes. 'And are you well?'

'Well enough thank you. What are you doing here anyway?'

'Waiting for my maid to unpack. She always takes an age.'

'I meant back in London.'

'Oh, that's a long story.'

'I have time. Perhaps you would care to join me for a drink?' he offered.

'Why not indeed? Bridget knows where to find me.'

They settled side by side on a sofa, in a quiet corner. 'I heard you've broken at least two hearts since we parted,' he said teasingly, as he turned to face her.

'Oh, at least!' she agreed, smiling good-naturedly.

'Now then, tell me what you have been up to in Paris.'

'Visiting my son.'

'But of course. I trust he is well?'

'He's a picture of health.'

'And besides seeing your son?'

'Oh, playing the fool.'

'Playing the fool? What exactly does that mean?'

'I formed an attachment, but it didn't quite work out the way I expected.'

'So it all come to nothing?'

'I was dumped would you believe!' she said, with merriment showing in her eyes.

His widened in surprise. 'Good grief! Dumped you say?'

'Yes ...dumped for a wealthier woman. Isn't that unbelievable?'

His face broke in to an amused smile.

'I thought that might amuse you.'

'It does indeed! I seem to remember going through that self-same thing myself.'

He had wanted her, had asked her to marry him and she had refused. He was a rich, powerful man, a man used to getting exactly what he wanted and he had not taken the rejection well.

'Do you remember our parting? The night you proposed? How you stormed off with your wounded ego?'

Luke tilted his dark head back and laughed along with her. 'How could I forget? I must have been out of my mind.'

She laid a hand on his arm, pressing it intimately, resting it there. 'Oh, Monsieur, please, leave a lady some illusions. I quite thought you were madly in love with me at the time,' she teased, with her unforgettable crystalline laugh.

'It all seems so ridiculous now.'

'That's all in the past.' She leant towards him 'Can't we still be friends?'

'There's no reason why not.'

'Well, tell me about yourself,' She straightened up and withdrew her hand. 'Are you still looking for a suitable wife?'

'Good heavens no! I've been married some time now.'

She smiled wickedly. 'I know. I was only teasing. You're still so serious.'

'And harder,' he added.

'The same old Luke, with so many faces.'

A young woman approached and bobbed a curtsey. 'Pardon, Madame ...Monsieur.'

Amel looked up at her. 'Oui, Bridget?'

'Tout prêt, Madame.'

'Merci, Bridget. Je sérai la bientót.'

'Merci, Madame.' The maid gave another bob.

'Tell me, what are you doing this evening? Perhaps we can meet for dinner?' Amel suggested, when the maid had taken her leave.

Temptation stared Luke in the face. He hesitated, but only for a split second. 'Why not? I've nothing better to do.'

She gave a little sigh. 'The same tactless Luke. Still, never mind; I hate to eat alone.'

'Here in the hotel?' he asked.

'Yes, if you have no objections. I'm too tired to go further afield.' She lifted a gloved hand and whispered behind it. 'Will you be wanting to part me from my panties afterwards?'

'Hell no!' he replied, grinning with hilarity, his mind filling with the most pleasing expectations of future pleasure. 'Just dinner. Panties are optional.'

Amel laughed softly. 'Oh, how amusing you are. Do forgive me. I could not help myself. I could do with a little cheering up. Now, if you'll excuse me...' She rose to her feet. 'I must find something halfway decent to wear this evening.' Her blue eyes lifted to his and she gave him a most brilliant smile, offering him her hand. 'Au revoir, Monsieur ...until tonight.'

He took it, bowing slightly and bringing it to his

lips. 'I look forward to it.'

Luke watched her go, gliding across the floor gracefully, her head held high and her back perfectly straight. Several pairs of eyes suitably dazzled were turned upon her, a human magnet who gathered to her unfailingly the observance of those around. A year had elapsed since he had seen her last and he had hardly noticed. Had he been of a fanciful turn of mind he would have imagined that fate had drawn him to her. What a surprise, meeting her now just when things seemed dull, mundane, along comes that unexpected opportunity. That's what he counted on in life. Opportunities, like eggs come one at a time. And he was always one to grasp an opportunity when it presented itself.

It was late when Luke arrived home three days later. He went upstairs to find Jessica on the sofa in her private sitting room. She looked so peaceful, her face rosy in sleep, lips slightly parted, her hair in a radiant tumble about her shoulders, shimmering in the candlelight. Quite lovely in fact. The thought of seeing her again was always one of the most pleasant things about coming home. Her very presence seemed to light the place up. He had married her for breeding purposes only, but to his surprise he found that the more he saw of her the more he liked her.

Although he had to admit he never experienced the same brilliant rapture in their union as he did with the alluring Amel Duprez whose kiss, whose very touch was a zest and exhilaration that stirred the blood, intoxicating like precious wine and satisfying that yearning for fresh experiences. But Jessica did possess a rare combination of strength and gentleness, with a natural generous, affectionate spirit that somehow breathed new life into him; a meek and passive instrument for his indulgence, filling him with a sense of what he thought to be contentment. He could not tell her, of course, his pride would not allow it.

It was not a thing to say out loud. He had an inbred fear of looking her in the eyes and talking of his feelings. It didn't do to get too close. Feelings control you and needed to be crushed before they could grow. What he had in the way of emotion was an occasional fitful sentiment that sometimes caused him as much inconvenience as emotion of a stronger kind.

Now, would begin the gruesome process of deception and brazening of visage. He aroused her with a gentle kiss, bringing a twinkling smile to her lips and eyes. Her arms went about his neck, pulling him to her spontaneously. Her devotion was quite extraordinary. The familiar reaction of welcome engulfed him, and all tiredness and aggravations were forgotten.

A spark, a glow of burning light arose between them, a warm flush of understanding and they went amicably to her bed. She was as feverish for his embrace as he was for hers, quick to learn just as he was eager to teach. He enjoyed teasing the neat, discreet little cleft and then abandoning it, until the animal within was aroused, drawing aside its silken curtain for more. Only by fusion of two can a human life come into being.

SIX

Amelia's skin glowed pale and translucent in the lamplight. Her shining hair was parted in the middle with exact precision, plaited at the sides and wound in a circle over each small perfect ear. Luke took her hand gently in his. No foolish convention had prevented him, had interfered with what impelled, even commanded him to see her.

'I've never said this before, not to anyone, until now. I need you, Amel. I need to be near you. Being away from you has made me see things differently. I don't begrudge you anything and I certainly don't resent you your freedom. I only want you to be happy.'

Amel met his gaze. 'You mean it?'

'Yes, I mean it.'

'Oh Luke, what can I say?' she crooned.

'There's no need for you to say anything.' He released her hand and from his pocket drew a small blue velvet box and carefully opened it. 'I have something for you.' He held out a ring, an exquisite sparkling diamond. 'I intended you to have it on the night I proposed.'

Her fine and curiously oblique eyebrows rose in marvel at what she saw, her eyes widening with surprise and utter delight. From that moment he ceased to gnaw at her nerves. 'And you kept it all this time?' She fluttered long golden lashes. 'Oh, Mon amour, how romantic.'

If anyone had called him romantic he would have laughed aloud at the idea. His need of her was not for romantic reasons, not in the least, but if it pleased her to think so, then let her. He had two relationships, each with their own value, and he knew exactly what he wanted from this one and was prepared to pay for it, but had no intentions of being kept waiting in line. As simple as that! An ideal arrangement.

'Yes, take it as a token of my adoration,' he said smoothly.

Amel drew in her breath, momentarily speechless. It was just the thing to raise her spirits.

'Well, do you like it?' he asked

'Like it! I simply love it. It's absolutely beautiful,' she crooned.

'Not nearly as beautiful as you, my darling. Put it on.'

'You put it on for me.'

He placed the ring carefully on the third finger of her left hand, the marriage finger. His dark eyes met hers. 'Do you mind?'

She shrugged appealingly, all smiles as she held out her small slender hand, admiring the exquisite jewel, turning it this way and that. 'How could I? But tell me Monsieur, are you going to expect special favours?'

He grinned wickedly. 'Absolutely!'

'Then you will surely receive them. I promise you.' She looked once more at the sparkling ring. 'Now, are you going to tell me about your wife?'

'What does she matter? I'm here with you, that's all that matters.'

'Oh, come now, she must matter. Otherwise, why

would you have married her?'

'I married for no other reason than to beget a son,' he said, which was the truth. 'In return I give her everything she could possibly want.'

'The poor girl. Marriage is the supreme blunder that so many women make.'

'She'll survive. A discreet wife has neither eyes nor ears.'

'Why do you say that? You think she knows? About us, I mean.'

'How could she possibly know?'

'What if she finds out? She's bound to be hurt.'

'Then I will make certain she doesn't find out. I wouldn't want to hurt her.'

'Poor naive girl,' Amel said again.

Luke frowned. 'Will you stop saying poor girl! There's nothing poor about her. She doesn't want for anything.'

'There is no perfect marriage for there are no perfect men.'

'That's not very flattering.' His smile was derisive.

'Tell me, is she as good as I am?' she asked with interest

'No one's as good as you are, my darling.'

'You are such a charming liar. But please, do tell me what she's like.'

'Why would you want to know?'

She shrugged prettily. 'I'm curious, that's all.'

'Well, if you insist.' he raised his eyebrows in concentration. 'Let me see, what can I tell you about her?'

'What her name is, for a start.'

'Jessica. Her name is Jessica.'

'Is she fair or dark?'

"Her hair is more of a chestnut colour.'

'The opposite to mine.'

'The exact opposite. It's wild and unruly like her nature.'

'Really? How interesting. What else?'

'She's young, healthy....'

'Younger than I am?' she interrupted.

'Yes, by eight years.'

Amel raised fine eyebrows. 'As young as that! And is she beautiful?'

'I wouldn't say beautiful, but she's attractive and has character.'

'Is she intelligent?'

'I suppose she's bright enough.'

'Bright enough! What does that mean?'

'That in conversation she's lively and pleasant, without being very remarkable. Now let me see, what else? She's gentle by nature and popular with just about everyone. Oh, and she's strong-willed, very strong-willed and passionate about everything.'

'You mean, she has a conscience?'

'Exactly.' He grinned. 'And a quick temper to go with it.'

'You sound as if you care for her.'

'I suppose I do in a way, although she can be infuriating at times.'

'You do get on with her though?'

He looked doubtful.

'Well, do you?'

'Not for any length of time.'

'But you are fond of her?'

'I have to admit I like her. She grows on you after a while,' he said thoughtfully. 'I suppose I'm comfortable with her.'

'Then what are you doing here with me?'

'I'm here with you because I don't feel the same for her as I do for you. You must know that,' he replied, which was the truth. He reached to take her hand again, bringing it to his lips. 'I happen to adore you.'

'Oh Luke, you can be so charming sometimes,' she whispered.

'And what about you?' he asked, his look serious.

She withdrew her hand. 'What about me?'

'Are you fond of me?'

'But of course.' She gave him her most charming smile.

'You've never said you are.'

'Well, it goes without saying,' she answered as honestly as she could. 'You know I enjoy our time together.'

'But that is not quite the same thing. Tell me what you feel for me.'

Long lashes drooped to veil the eyes, hiding whatever look lay in those azure depths. She was attracted to most every man she met, but had no conception of serious feelings. 'Luke ...please ...I have already told you I enjoy being with you.'

'Then do you mind if I ask you something which is absolutely none of my business?'

'About my marriage, you mean?'

He looked surprised. 'Yes. How did you guess?'

'I think I know you well enough to know just what's on your mind.'

'Heaven forbid!' the words came easily to his lips, words he had picked up from Jessica. 'Am I so predictable?'

'Not always.'

'Tell me then, were you in love with him?'

'Love? What is love? I truly don't know what people mean when they say they are "in love". How do you define it? Is it the same feeling that drugs or alcohol gives you? No, we were not "in love" as they call it, but strangely enough we were happy together, compatible, until he became ill. Then everything changed.'

'In what way?'

'His moods mainly. He had terrible mood swings. He became a different person. Before he took ill he would take either girls or boys, as long as they were pretty and untouched.'

Luke's brow wrinkled with distaste. 'You're not serious? You once mentioned he preferred masculine company, but young boys and girls...'

'It's the truth. He was willing to pay a good price to satisfy his appetite.'

'And that disgusted you?'

'After a while one became used to it. He went his way and I went mine, discreetly of course.'

'Then what?'

'I didn't feel I knew him anymore. It was like living with a complete stranger.'

'But wasn't all that to do with his illness?'

'Yes, I understood that well enough, but it didn't make it any easier. He was on medication of some kind, but couldn't function properly, could no longer lead a normal life. Thus the frustration.'

'It must have been a very difficult time for you both.'

'Oh, it was. Indeed it was. I can't remember how I got through those last months. To tell the truth, I was relieved when it was over.' She looked at him without

registering any emotion. 'Luke...'

'What is it, my darling?'

'I've wanted to tell you that, how I feel about marriage has nothing to do with you personally. I just don't want to be a wife or mother again, to be left alone while my husband goes off to his mistress.'

'That would never have happened.'

'It's happening now, at this very moment, isn't it? You're here with me, while your naive little wife sits at home alone, wondering where you are, who you're with and what you're up to.'

'That's entirely different.'

She raised fine eyebrows in question. 'Oh, how is it different?'

'Because she is not you.'

'All the same, I know how she must feel. I've been in that very situation. You can't appreciate just how marvellous it is for a woman to have her own money and independence.'

'I understand that now. I suggest we come to a mutual understanding to which we can agree.'

'That would please me, Mon amour. But you won't stifle me with your possessiveness?'

'I'll do my utmost not to. I don't want to risk losing you.'

She met his eyes and sighed. 'I have to admit you're right. You and I are well suited, perfectly matched. Both spoilt, selfish and demanding in every way.'

He chuckled. 'That's not very flattering.'

'But true. I knew right from the start that we were two of a kind.'

'Perhaps it's our imperfections that make us so perfect for one another.'

Her look was serious. 'Perhaps.'

'Well, you can be as demanding as you wish, my darling and, I in turn, will have the pleasure of spoiling you.'

She softened again. 'Oh Luke, you are so good to me. And I did miss you. Truly I did. I thought you might have forgotten me.'

'How could I forget you?' He smiled. 'I no longer expect you to be as a dutiful little wife, waiting patiently for my return, each time I leave.'

'Does she wait patiently?'

His smile broadened. 'Perhaps not patiently, but she has no option but to wait.'

'She must feel a prisoner.'

'Hush now! Enough about her. I'm here with you and my only thought is to make you happy. You shall have everything your heart desires and money to top up your account.'

'Oh, Mon amour, you are so good to me,' she repeated.

'Don't think you've caught yourself a fool though. You're going to earn it several times over.'

'That will be my pleasure, Monsieur,' she said amiably.

'Mine too, Madam.'

So eager were they to lie in each other's arms, their feet hardly touched the ground on the journey to her apartment. Completely uninhibited, she readily assented to whatever he pleased, to be at his disposal without the least reserve, rekindling the fire of boundless pleasure into which they both plunged together in a transport of lust.

Later, much later, when he saw the bills for her latest shopping excursion, he was tempted to modify

his promise that she could spend money on whatever her heart desired, but such minor imperfections in her no longer troubled him. "Need" had become an inadequate word to describe what he felt for her. The past two weeks had been the happiest of his life.

SEVEN

Jessica sat toying with the food on her plate. She felt terribly wounded by the scant attention her husband showed her. She yearned daily for the tender companionship and nearness they had shared in the first weeks of their marriage, but the only real affection he showed her was, on the rare occasions he came to her bed where they were equal, otherwise he treated her no better than a child, never allowing her to have opinions of her own. And he was always criticising, even more so lately, with that mocking smile which seemed to say he was always right and she was wrong. Why did he do this to her? Surely he cared for her? Why else had he married her?

Secretly, passion burnt through her body as if some tormenting devil had taken possession of her, until it became a pain nagging mercilessly at the base of her abdomen, pulsating and aching deep within; a madness from which she could find no release. In an effort to cool her thoughts and refresh her spirits, she walked, some-times covering considerable distances and purposely tiring herself so that she would no longer be able to feel anything but exhaustion.

Luke glanced across the table at his young wife. He had to admit that being with child suited her. She had grown slightly more rounded and in spite of her pouting expression, looked absolutely radiant in satin. Her face glowed with good health, and her shining hair was drawn back from her face and tied with an ivory bow, the same shade as the gown, which was cut low at the front, showing the curve of her breasts.

Feeling his penetrating eyes upon her, Jessica raised her head.

'You're unusually quiet tonight, my pet.'

'I'm practicing.'

'Practicing what?'

'Keeping silent. I've been doing it a lot lately,' she said sulkily. 'I've had ample time while you were away goodness knows where.'

'Well now, we are in a strange mood. Do cheer up and eat your fish. It will do you good.'

She pushed the plate away with a look of distaste. 'You know I can never eat anything with a face. How anyone can eat something that stares back at you, I don't know.'

He threw his head back and laughed. 'You really are the sweetest thing.' There was no response. She was not her usual cheerful self. 'Is something else bothering you, my pet?'

She met his steady gaze. 'Well, this is my home, isn't it?'

'But of course. Why an earth should you think otherwise?'

'I've fallen in with your wishes not to interfere in the stables and not to interfere in the kitchen where the staff have at least a say in things. And I'm not to ride when I want or walk the fells when I want....'

'Come now, you exaggerate,' he interrupted impatiently.

'But you said yourself I'm not to interfere, that I must leave all arrangements to Mrs Osborne.'

'Why bring this up now? Has something happened to upset you?'

'I just want to be able to do as I please for

once. I'm not used to being shut in all the time.'

He smiled at her, trying to humour her. She was still strong-willed, not yet submissive, still fighting against the rules.

'I've told you before the mare is at your disposal. Tom can have the carriage ready for you whenever you want. You have only to ask. He will accompany you wherever you wish to go.'

'I don't want Tom to damn well accompany me wherever I go,' she protested.

'Now then, Jessica, watch what you say. It doesn't do for the lady of the house to use bad language. The servants might hear.'

'I don't give a tinker's curse.'

'Will you stop that or...'

'Or what?' she interrupted, challenging him with fiery eyes. 'Will you forbid me to speak next?'

'Had I known you would be in such a foul mood I'd have stayed in the city where the company is more agreeable.'

'Well, I can't help it. I feel like one of those …those trained bears in a circus, having to do everything you want.'

'Come now, it's not as bad as all that,' he reasoned. 'You know my sentiments about going out alone during pregnancy. Having Tom drive you is necessary for your safety and your comfort. Do you know, that mare's the best you can buy? She should be, she cost me forty guineas. Have you thought of a suitable name for her yet?' He thought perhaps if he humoured her a little, her mood might change, as he felt quite aroused just by looking at her.

'Bramble.'

'Bramble. I like that. A good choice. Now, do

cheer up, my pet. You know all my efforts are directed to one end; the preservation of your health and to save you from fatigue.'

'That's very thoughtful of you, but I'm not a china doll, I feel perfectly well,' she insisted

'No, but you're a married woman and a pregnant one at that,' he said, feeling pleased with the fact. 'You know what the birth of this child means to me. I shall be consoled for all the disappointments with which my life has been marked.'

'Your disappointments! What about mine?'

'God damn it, Jessica, I had hoped we would have a pleasant evening together, but it seems you are determined to spoil it.' His patience was beginning to fray, and his tone said as much.

'Now who's using bad language?' she asked scornfully.

He had plans. Now that she was well into the fourth month, he felt sure it would be safe to resume the intimate side of their relationship. Her voice brought him from the thoughts that were running through his mind.

'Tell me, why does everything have to revolve around you and what you want?'

'Because I'm the one who pays all the bills,' he stated. 'I would just ask that until you have our son you allow Tom to accompany you, that's all. It's not as if I'm asking you not to go out at all.' I suppose I ought to spend more time with her ... he told himself silently. He smiled then, determined she was not going to spoil what he had in mind. 'Come Friday I'll be going to Keswick on business. Perhaps you would like to come along? You can take the reins while I sit back and relax.'

Her face brightened then. 'Oh Luke, can I?'

It was obvious he was trying to please her and she supposed he was right not to want her to go about alone in her condition, although she felt perfectly well and would be careful. There was nothing for her to do in the long hours he was away doing whatever it was he did business-wise.

'I have an appointment at the bank. You could browse round the shops perhaps, and then we could have lunch together. What do you think?'

'I'd like that,' Jessica said with enthusiasm.

She was as easy to please as a child might be. For the life of him he could not prevent himself from going to her side and stooping to kiss her on the cheek. There is a world of poetic beauty in the longing of a loving woman.

'I must say, you look particularly charming this evening, my pet.'

Jessica felt a stirring of pleasure, but regarded him with puzzled awe. She could never quite comprehend him. He was so distant at times and then suddenly, like now, he was the exact opposite, all attention and ready to please. How long was it since they had lain together? Too long! Perhaps that's what was wrong with her? She needed to be loved. The need ran through her veins, tightening the pit of her stomach and tormenting her with its lack of fulfilment. She could have doubled up and nursed herself in anguish with it as she had often done alone in her bed. There was a widespread view that it was only depraved women who had such feelings, that most women would rather die than confess that they do at times feel a physical yearning as profound as hunger for food. Every night she pleaded with God to purge her of her wicked longings and unladylike hungers. But God never answered her prayers and she was left to struggle alone …fighting a losing battle.

Luke took both her hands and drew her up from the chair just as a tap came at the door. He frowned with annoyance at the interruption. 'Come in.'

Maggie entered and gave a curtsy. 'May I clear the table now, Sir?'

It was Jessica who answered. 'Yes, Maggie, please do. We'll have our coffee in the drawing room.'

Luke stood back to let his wife pass through the door before him and followed her into the drawing room, the most comfortable room in the house, setting himself down in his usual place, in a chair to one side of the cheerful crackling fire. He sighed and settled back, watching the lively dance of the flames. He felt content. Things were going well again at the mines. He was warm and fed ...and once they were left un-disturbed, he would have the one other thing on his mind that would relax him even more. As soon as it was certain they were alone, he would turn the key in the lock and have his fill. He gazed at his wife sitting opposite, spreading and smoothing the skirt of her gown.

'There's no point in smoothing down your skirt, my pet. It will soon be crumpled again,' he told her, his smile wicked.

Jessica's eyes widened. 'Here? You wouldn't dare! The servants might walk in on us,' she said, feeling the excitement rise in anticipation of what was to come.

'A little suspense will set a keener edge to the pleasure.'

They sat together in friendly intimacy, she looking

at him with adoration, wondering at the feelings he aroused in her. She felt a burning impatience for the renewal of joy, wishing now she had not asked Maggie to bring them coffee. Well, it was here now and they would soon be alone, she thought as Maggie came into the room with a laden tray.

'The tray can be left until morning. We don't want to be disturbed,' Luke instructed the maid.

'As you wish, Sir,' Maggie replied, quietly closing the door behind her.

Luke crossed over the soft carpet and turned the key in the lock. They now had the utmost privacy. He dropped to his knees in front of his wife where she lounged on the sofa and reaching to unfasten the bodice to her gown, exposed her ample breasts, all fragrance and warmth, letting them spill out.

Lips upon her breasts was one of the surest ways to melt her to tenderness and make her physically ready for complete union. He snuggled his face in the hollow between them. Jessica lay back without complaint, abandoning herself entirely to the delights she swam in.

When he came up on the sofa beside her, he pulled her skirt up around the tops of her thighs to reveal long shapely stocking-clad legs. Elated beyond measure, he gently patted her slightly rounded stomach. By autumn, when the leaves on the trees had turned to gold, he would be a father ...at last.

'You're just beginning to show,' he said softly. 'We must be careful.' The pleasure that dawned in his dark eyes gave her infinite delight.

He skillfully relieved her of her drawers, dropping them on the carpet at her feet, leaving her stockings in place. She did not protest, but lay back obediently, impatient for him to continue. He lowered his head again to her breasts and took a nipple gently between his teeth. His hands, which knew how to give her pleasure, began to glide over the smooth snow white skin of her inner thighs, applying her with a thousand little tender caresses, to that little warm place between, lusciously exploring the sweet secret of nature. He continually stroked and teased, making her quiver with anticipation and moan with sheer pleasure as the feeling gradually moved through her body.

She moistened her lips with her tongue and when she spoke her voice was but a whisper. 'Luke …oh, Luke, please...' She fumbled awkwardly with the front of his breeches as she spoke, feeling his hard erection, but he eased her hand away.

'Just lay back and enjoy.'

'But I want you...' she moaned.

He chuckled. 'Don't be so impatient, you hussy.'

With the gentle, skillful hands of an experienced lover, he soon brought her to the peak of her feelings, joy bursting from her. His lips found hers as she moaned and clung to him breathlessly. She was lost to everything but the enjoyment of her favourite feelings, holding him tightly as though she wished never to let go. He eased himself free, stood up and quickly removed his boots and breeches. The sight of his proud erection brought a wicked smile to her lips.

'Oh, that was wonderful. I want to give you the same feeling,' she said softly, her eyes glowing, her cheeks flushed with fulfilment.

'You will, my pet, you will.' He laid his hand on her soft flushed cheek, displaying a tenderness that was new to her. 'You are not too hot?'

'No, I feel absolutely marvellous.'

'Then lay back and relax. I don't want to hurt you.'

She did as she was told, spreading herself to the best advantage, giving him full view of that delicious little cleft that was ready for action. He was quick to enter her, but it was with a tenderness he had not shown before, taking time to slowly arouse her again and when they come to the peak of their pleasure it was at the same moment ...together. It did not occur to him to feel surprised that the other woman in his life scarcely touched his thoughts.

Jessica felt certain that by this tender show of passion he must surely love her, but little did she realise his main concern was for the child she carried inside her ...an infant of the utmost importance. That night she slept with the ease of an innocent child. And the next day she had Tom Saunders drive her in the carriage, according to her husband's wishes, to Fells View to visit her family.

EIGHT

Alice Little was a small and delicate looking girl of fifteen years, who spoke softly, almost apologetically. Good-tempered, but shy, as timorous as a little mouse she was, desirous to escape observation. She had the fairest of eyebrows, so pale they were only noticeable when you looked really close, over large blue wondering eyes in a colourless face, and the stubbiest little nose that looked as if it had not been finished off properly. Her hair was fine and wispy, the colour of ripe corn, on a funny little scrap of a thing, so that one was apt to overlook the fact that she was actually quite pretty. The little maid-of-all-work she was, to clean the grates and light the fires. With bucket, brush and soap, she dragged herself about.

Jessica caught her continually sniffing. 'Have you caught a chill?' she asked.

'No, Mistress.'

Alice looked so sorrowful that the young mistress caught her sadness. When she looked more closely at the girl, she saw that her eyes were red-rimmed. 'Have you been crying?' she asked kindly. 'You don't have to pretend with me, Alice. Is it because you're worried about your mother? I heard she was poorly.'

A sad expression shadowed the girl's face. 'No, Mistress, I mean yes …I do worry about her, but...'

Jessica could not help but melt a little when a pair of tearful eyes were turned appealingly towards her. 'What is it Alice? You can tell me. No one need know. Tell me what's troubling you.'

The girl sniffed and turned her eyes to the door, as if expecting someone to walk in at any moment. 'Oh ...I daren't, Mistress.'

Sensing her nervousness, Jessica closed the door quietly and came back to stand in front of the distressed girl. She touched her gently on the shoulder. 'Now then, we're on our own and won't be interrupted. No one will hear,' she said gently, willing to listen.

But Alice still looked uncertain.

'Are you afraid of someone?'

'Yes ...I ...I mean ...mean no...' Alice stammered.

Jessica took a lace edged handkerchief from her pocket, unfolded it and offered it to her, looking at her with an expression of ineffable tenderness. 'Here, blow your nose.

'Oh, no, I couldn't. It wouldn't be right.' Alice spoke with pious resignation.

'Nonsense! It's only a handkerchief. And who's to know? Now come along, Alice, I insist, and if you want, you can return it when it's been laundered.'

Alice gave her a shy smile. 'Thank you, Mistress.'

She took the handkerchief from Jessica's out-stretched hand and blew hard on it, but as she did so, overcome by the mistress's kindness, tears filled her eyes again and overflowed on to her pale cheeks. Gentle hands held her close, patting and rocking her as if she were a baby, just as her mother sometimes did and for a few moments she forgot that this was the mistress of the house and she was a mere scullery maid. The lowest of them all, the skivvy at everyone's beck and call, given the worse jobs, from scrubbing floors to emptying chamber pots and cleaning the closets outside. Oh God ...the closets! She hadn't done the closets and it would be dark soon.

Jessica felt her stiffen in the circle of her arms. She loosened her hold and the girl stepped back and straightened herself up as she wiped her face with the handkerchief

'Thank you, Mistress. I don't know what come over me.'

'It's better to let it out, Alice. That's what my father always tells me. Alice...' Jessica hesitated for just a moment, for she didn't want to start her off crying again, but it was obvious something had upset her in the first place and she hoped to get to the bottom of it. 'won't you tell me what's troubling you? I might be able to help.'

The girl shook her head from side to side. 'I don't think so, Mistress.'

'You'll feel better for talking about it. I promise you. That's another thing my father always says.' She could not help but smile, as talking her problems over with her father more often than not ended in a bit of an argument. They could rarely agree now she was grown.

Alice bit into her bottom lip and looked towards the door again. 'Well, it's everything really.' She kept her voice low. 'Me mother being poorly is such a worry, her being on her own an' all. An' then there's … well … there's Maggie….'

'What about Maggie?'

'Well, she's been saying things....'

'What sort of things?'

'She tells lies about me an' makes all sorts of nasty remarks. She told Mrs Osborne I'd been stealing food to take to me mother an' you know that's not true, Madam ...I mean, Mistress.' Her face clouded and she sniffed again. 'I'd never do anything dishonest.'

'Is that what's upsetting you?'

The girl stared at her with wide moist eyes. 'Well, it's not just that...'

'Tell me what else?'

'Well, Mrs Osborne...' Alice stopped abruptly, hesitant to talk about whatever it was distressing her. She had a meek, patient expression on her face, and her voice like her face expressed weariness and resignation.

'What Alice? What about Mrs Osborne?'

It all kept tumbling out then, with smiles and blushes coming and going. 'Well, everything can be sparkling clean with not a mark anywhere, but she ...Mrs Osborne, that is, makes me do things over an' over again. She deliberately knocked the bucket of dirty water over the hall yesterday an' made me clean it up after I'd spent an hour or more getting it clean in the first place.' Now she had started there seemed to be no stopping her. Her little jaw was set rigid, her voice excitable. 'An' ...an' do you know what she did when I wasn't quick enough collecting the chamber pots?'

'No! What did she do?' Jessica asked with curiosity.

'She took the pot from me hands an' emptied the piddle...' her hand covered her mouth as she realised what she had said in front of the mistress of the house. 'Oh, I'm sorry, Mistress, I didn't mean to swear.'

Jessica covered her mouth in an effort to control the bubble of laughter that come up from her throat. 'Oh Alice, I know I shouldn't laugh, but your face is such a picture. You look as if you could murder someone.'

Seeing the young mistress laugh, Alice forgot her embarrassment and pressed her hand harder over her mouth, unable to control her girlish giggles. For the second time in the last few minutes she forgot that she was just a lowly maid in the company of the Mistress. They were just two young girls enjoying a joke together.

'Tell me what happened,' laughed Jessica.

'Well, I just stood there with ...you know ...*that* all over me cap an' running down me face an' all over me clean clothes.'

Jessica put on a look of shock. 'Goodness! Didn't you say anything?'

Alice suddenly looked serious again. She straightened herself up, wiped her eyes, which were now moist from laughter. 'Oh no, I couldn't, Mistress. I daren't. You know what old tin…' she faltered. 'I …I mean, Mrs Osborne's like when she gets a bee in her bonnet?'

'What was that you were about to call her?'

The girl blushed a deep scarlet. 'I couldn't say, Mistress...'

'Old tin ...you said. Tell me, Alice,' she insisted.

'Well, promise not to breathe a word.'

Jessica nodded. 'Cross my heart.'

'Well, I heard Maggie muttering it to herself one day after receiving the sharp edge of Mrs Osborne's tongue.' Alice leant towards her and whispered close to her ear. 'Old tin drawers ...she called her.'

'Eeh!' Jessica let out a squeal of delight. 'Old tin drawers! How I'd like to call her that to her face.'

'Oh no ...please, Mistress. I shouldn't've told you.'

Jessica laid a comforting hand on Alice's arm.

'Don't worry. I won't breathe a word, not to anyone. But you must admit it suits her.'

'It does, doesn't it, Mistress? But if she knew ...well, life's unbearable as it is an' if she finds out I've been complaining I dread to think what might happen. I didn't think it funny at the time mind ...I can tell you.' she spoke without pause. 'Before I could go to change she made me mop up the kitchen floor, though there was nothing to see. It had all gone over me, hadn't it! Lucky there wasn't much in the pot.'

'She's a terrible woman,' Jessica said, now recovered from her fit of laughter.

'She is an' all. I had to wash all me clothes before I went to bed that night, as I've only the one change. The other lot was in the wash waiting for me to do them. I had to wear damp clothes all the next day.'

'And that's how you caught a chill?'

'Suppose so an' I fell behind with things. Now she's making me work from five instead of six in the morning 'til ten at night.'

'Oh, that's not right!'

'I can't stand much more, Mistress. I'm telling you! I'm so tired of a night I can't get off to sleep for hurting all over an' when I do drop off it's time to get up again.'

'Oh, Alice, you poor soul. I had no idea,' Jessica crooned, all sympathy.

'I'm used to hard work, Mistress, but no matter what I do ...well, there's just no pleasing some people. Just look at me hands.' She held out small chapped hands for Jessica to see. In some places the skin had broken open, and was red raw and festered.

'Good gracious! You poor thing!'

'I can hardly hold the bucket let alone bear to put
them in water.'

'They'll never heal if you don't keep them dry.'

'That's what worries me an' with them so bad-like,
I'm not allowed to help in the kitchen. So instead of
having a few easier jobs as I used to, I just get the
dirty ones which makes them even worse.'

'You must let me talk to her, Alice. You can't go
on like this.'

'Oh, no! She'll dismiss me an' then what would I
do? Please don't say anything ...please,' the girl
begged. 'You won't, will you?'

Jessica could see the fear in her eyes. 'All right! If
you don't want me to then I won't, but we must do
something.'

'But what? If she finds out I've been talking about
it, going behind her back ...an' to you of all people,
she'll dismiss me. I know she will. What would I do
then, with hands like this?' She shrugged her thin
shoulders. 'Who would want me? You won't say
anything, will you?'

'I won't say a word.'

'Oh, thank you, Mistress, thank you.'

'Now don't give up. I've not known you long, but I
do know you try your best and work hard.'

'Yes, Miss ...I mean Mistress, but...' she broke off,
tears filling her eyes again. She quickly wiped them
away with the handkerchief she still clutched in her
hand.

'Now Alice, people like her are not worth crying
over. It will all seem better tomorrow.'

'Will it?' Alice murmured, unconvinced.

'Yes. You'll see! I'm going to work something

out,' she promised. Then seeing the girl's anxious face, added, 'Now don't worry. No one will know we've discussed anything. It will be our secret. First, I'll give you something to put on your poor hands to sooth them, and then we'll see. Even if I have to help you with the work myself, then that's what I'll do.'

'Oh no! That wouldn't be right.' Alice smiled then, a sweet smile of friendship. 'But thank you all the same, Mistress.'

But it was the same the next day and the next, each time Jessica came across her. Alice grew more with-drawn and by the appearance of her eyes she had been crying again. And when things seemed they could not get worse, the poor girl's mother passed away.

Very few people are actually so cynical as to marry without the hope of happiness. Fantasy is always better than reality, when visions of romance fade disappointedly in the light of every day existence. The heart of every young woman yearns with a great longing for the fulfillment of the beautiful dream of a lifetime union with the perfect mate. Jessica gazed across the table at her husband, a secret disappointment clouding her inward peace. She had entered the marriage with optimism and hope. She lived in a fine house, had money enough for whatever she might need, and yet she was wretchedly lonely and unhappy in a world that held her securely bound and caged.

Life had been straightforward and simple before she had married. Loved and protected she had been, with the simple belief that what you put into life you received back, and yet it didn't feel that way, not with

Luke. She had married as an ignorant girl, but often vaguely felt a sense of something lacking in her husband's intimacy. Their union had somehow lost its early bloom. It was difficult to recapture that first rapture, the consideration and the irradiating joy that had followed their wedding day, which to her had been priceless. So dazzled she had been by the witchery of that first passion she had not seen that her love was not returned with equal intensity.

Luke was a man with many shades to his nature and much of that was hidden. Even in the most rousing embraces, his mind seemed to be somewhere else. There were myriad subtleties in the adjustment of any two individuals, she knew that, but affectionate as she was and wanting to do right, she found it impossible to achieve any real closeness with this controlled, unemotional man who had chosen her for his wife. Always he held back, appearing slightly indifferent, most adept at concealing emotions, at hiding his feelings. A man of the world who spent so much time away from home, robbing himself of a greatness that their dual unity might reach.

Her love was his, there was no doubt about that, but there were times it seemed to her that it was not enough. She wanted him to crave for her the way she craved for him, but even during their most intimate moments together there was part of him that was never totally committed to her. When she asked him if he was happy he would always reply he was, and yet she sensed a change in him, a certain restlessness. She contributed it to the continual pressure of work, supposing his business affairs were always on his mind.

She raised her arm to rest on the table, keeping

time with her fingers to the tick of the clock, wondering with despair if she would ever find a way of bringing real happiness to him.

'Must you do that?' Luke remarked from behind the newspaper he was reading.

She removed her hand from the table and laid them both together on her lap, sighing heavily, with a touch of melancholy. He lowered the newspaper and looked straight at her. She was usually full of fun and smart sayings that made him smile, but now she seemed petulant, resentful even without reason.

'Is something wrong?' he asked, his tone belying the concern he felt.

'You and me need to talk,' she said sullenly, the loneliness that was past, and still to come flooding up within her.

'You and I.' he corrected. 'I've told you before it's you and I need to talk.'

She shrugged impatiently. 'Whatever!'

'Just what is it you want to talk about?'

'I want to know what you're planning to do. When you're out all the time, always away, we don't get to be a family.' She grumbled, resenting whatever kept them apart. Suspicion would always rear its ugly head whenever he stayed away too long. 'To marry, to be a good wife, that's all I ever dreamed of, but you are hardly ever here.'

He raised the paper again and spoke from behind it. 'I'm here now, aren't I?'

She gave a tut of annoyance. 'Oh, you know what I mean! How long have you been here over the past six months? There's always something that keeps you away from home. I've been more alone than I've been ever before. Our life together started out well enough, every day was special, and then one day suddenly we couldn't talk anymore.'

Tears stung the back of her eyes, but she blinked them away, setting her lips like a pouting child.

'You've time for everything except me. You used to hang on my every word. Now you don't even look at me when I'm talking to you. May I ask why?'

'You're imagining things,' was all he said, since he himself, the only person who might explain it, found no positive answer to give her.

True he had his mistress to curb his appetite, but he also enjoyed nothing better than to return home to Wildacres ...his haven where there was peace and quiet away from the bustle of the City.

'I don't think so. You have to admit you're rarely here for more than a day or two at a time. Three at the most. Then you're always busy. You barely give me the time of day. You promised to show me around London, a promise you broke ...yet again,' she complained accusingly. 'What sort of person would keep breaking promises?'

He lowered the paper with a crackle of annoyance, his face creasing into a deep frown. 'A person with responsibilities, who works damn hard to keep several businesses running smoothly. That's what kind of person.'

She did her best to curb her tongue, but it was not easy, not at all. It took all her self-control, which wasn't much at the best of times. 'But you've reliable men working for you. Surely you're entitled to a little time here with me ... your wife?'

'I intend to do that very thing. Take a few days off.'

'When?' she asked, studying the fierce dip of his

dark brows.

'Soon.' He lifted the paper again, burying his head in it.

'When is soon? Luke, I'm asking when is soon?'

'Soon, when I've settled a few urgent business matters,' he said for the want of something to say. 'I promise.'

She sighed in an exaggerated way. 'I suppose that's much better than later. In the meantime, perhaps you would be good enough to have your portrait painted, so I will recognize you when you do come home.'

He could not help but smile at her wit. 'I think, my pet, you have a lot of energy, but not much focus. You need to find an interest outside yourself through the pursuit of charitable endeavours.'

She became quiet again, a silence that held unspoken questions, questions she had the good sense not to ask. And she did not say anything about the portrait in his study, for she did not care to enter into an explanation, since he was inclined to laugh at her for being so superstitious.

NINE

Jessica was close on six months pregnant and feeling reasonably well, but couldn't describe herself as truly happy. The nights were the worse, she couldn't sleep, she would lie between the fine soft sheets and covers in the big empty bed, missing Luke and wondering what was keeping him away so long. There had been no word from him. He had not joined her in her bed for some time - didn't want to risk it - was his excuse, but she felt so lonely and frustrated, longing to lie in his arms. He always kept her at arm's length now, lest she should arouse him, he said. Well, she had quizzed April Ramsey about whether it was safe or not, and she had said that being pregnant had never stopped her and Owen.

The feeling of resentment was driving her wild. She had hoped to talk to her father alone. It seemed so long since she had spoken to him with that affectionate humour they had once known between them. She had always been able to discuss everything with him. Not personal things, of course, but most things. Now there was Clara, which made it impossible.

The housekeeper was the direct representative of her mistress. She had no female equal. Her day was full of duties, of constant supervision, each hour having its task; giving out stores, seeing to every detail to do with housework, looking to the condition of the linen, furniture and hangings. In addition to doing the accounts, she had to make inventories, organise all arrangements for entertaining, and spring-cleaning when everywhere from cellar to attic was thoroughly cleaned and polished. And most important of all, respecting the master's slightest whim and obeying it as law.

Order and method were necessary, but she did not have to soil her hands with anything approaching heavy or dirty work, and she was waited on, her meals brought to her in her room. Jessica allowed her to go about her business in whatever way she wished, she never interfered in any other sphere of the housework. There was never any need - Mrs Osborne kept everything running with admirable smoothness. But she had started to notice evidence of an inner loneliness in the older woman, finding her bark to be worse than her bite. She needed to relax a little and not take everything so serious.

Jessica's own day began with a bath, soaking in exotic oils. She used rose and lemon water to cleanse her face, witch hazel to keep it soft, and chamomile to bring out the shine in her hair. After breakfast she discussed the day's meals with Dora Osborne, who then passed on instructions to Mrs Miles. Not that she minded what was served, for Mrs Miles was an excellent cook, but it was the principle of the thing. She must start as she meant to go on, let it be known that she was the mistress of the house.

She then dealt with any correspondence. And after a light lunch, in the early afternoon she generally took a walk, bringing home with her a variety of wild flowers she had picked, arranging them in bowls and placing them where shafts of sunlight coming through the windows could catch their lovely colours. Afterwards, she might lounge on the sofa and read - her form of relaxation. She did a fair amount of reading, of both the serious and the popular literature of the day.

Luke had submitted a list of books that might interest her and she also liked to read the newspapers regularly to keep up with current affairs. She was very familiar with eighteenth century novelists, Fielding and Richardson, but if asked, she would have to say her favourite was the female novelist Jane Austin, who had written many successful novels, but had died at the early age of 41 in 1817. Wordsworth was still her favourite poet. She found his poems soothing. She read them to quieten her mind during the days Luke was away, which were many.

It required courage, though she had her share of that, to summon the housekeeper to her drawing room. Truculent and hatchet-faced was Mrs Osborne, in unrelieved black taffetas, hissing to her entrance as if she lodged beneath her petticoats a colony of snakes. Jessica listened as patiently as her nature allowed to her sound advice as they drank tea and gorged themselves on Mrs Mile's freshly baked biscuits.

Without the housekeeper's shrewd advice it was un-likely that she could have conducted herself in the most difficult situation with such stead. To step out of the decorum role her marriage had cast her in was to commit social suicide …or so she had been told.

'We have certain rules, Madam. The lady o' the house does not do things for herself; she tells other people what t'do,' Mrs Osborne told her for what must have been the umpteenth time.

'I have rules of my own, Mrs Osborne. Combined they should more than ensure a happy correlation for us all. And with your expertise, you can guide me,' was Jessica's clever reply.

'Afternoons are the best time t'receive callers. An' it's not advisable t'allow the dog int'the drawing-room, Madam, particularly when receiving callers.'

'Why an earth not?'

'Some people have a dislike t'animals in the house.'

'But he's a friendly little soul. Aren't you, Toby?' The dog's eyes were fastened intently on Jessica. 'Yes, it's you I'm talking to.'

'It just doesn't do! There is always a chance o' breakage through his leaping an' bounding about.'

'Don't worry, Mrs Osborne, we'll be especially careful.' She did not give a fig for the conventions of the day.

'Just as you like, Madam,' the housekeeper said haughtily.

'What about the evenings?' Jessica asked, tactfully changing the subject.

'Musical evenings are specially commended. Music can be a great hindrance t'conversation, but it can break the ice while you're meeting strangers, an' puts the guests int'the right mood an' makes them all the more willing t'talk.'

'But I don't play.'

'Then you could hire a musician, Madam. Such occasions require studious planning. Menus have t'be discussed, supplies checked, special items ordered, an' o' course, seating arrangements considered,' Dora Osborne explained patiently, in the tone of someone speaking to an idiot.

'It all sounds like a lot of hard work to me,' Jessica said thoughtfully.

'We'll manage well enough. We always have in the past. If you're not keen on a musical evening, you might prefer to read aloud '

'Oh, no, I couldn't.'

'But you read very nicely t'Mr Sheridan. I've heard you.'

'That's different. I couldn't possibly read aloud among strangers.'

'Then a musical evening it will be. The dinner invitations should be sent at least two weeks, preferably a month before the date an' care should be taken t'suit the guests t'each other.'

'Oh dear! It's getting more complicated by the minute.' Jessica said with a sigh.

'We'll manage.'

'I'm sure you will, Mrs Osborne. I know just how capable you are.' I ought to...I've been told often enough ...Jessica said silently to herself. 'How many do you think we should invite?'

'Eight makes a convenient number for pairing down each side o' the table.'

This seemed an eminently intelligent decision, and it was so decided. Next came the question of what to give the guests for dinner. After some deliberation, Dora thought it would be best to offer them cream of mushroom soup to start with, followed by Haunch of Venison or Buttered Lobster with a choice of fresh vegetables, followed by a light desert, sweetmeats and then coffee. Then there was the final problem. Who to invite?

'To me most of them are only names. But by the grace of good fortune, Mrs Osborne, I have you.

Perhaps you would be kind enough to write a list and a short account of who they are and what they do? A short and concise summing up of their antecedents and accomplishments,' Jessica suggested.

Dora Osborne knew well enough that part of her job was to listen to her mistress's instructions, but afterwards she always did exactly what she had intended to do. But the game was played by both sides. Jessica shrewdly got on to the subject of Alice.

'Tell me, Mrs Osborne, what exactly are a lady's maid's duties?'

'Well, she would look after your clothes an' person, as well as your bedroom an' dressing room. Dress your hair, read to you whoever you wish an' accompany you wherever you go. O' course, you must insist on a neat appearance an' good manners. An' she needs t'be young, for no lady would want an elderly maid as a personal attendant.'

'I was seriously thinking of Alice. She qualifies well enough, don't you think?'

The housekeeper looked astounded. 'Our Alice?'

'Yes, our Alice. I've noticed she hasn't been herself lately.'

'Has she had reason t'complain, Madam?' Mrs Osborne asked hurriedly.

'Good Heavens ...no! What would she have to complain about? It's just that she has the right temperament, don't you think? She's gentle and patient, which she would need to be.'

'But a personal attendant o' the lady o' the house has t'be well spoken. Alice has many little habits an' faults o' speech.'

'Oh, I am sure that with both our guidance she will soon improve.'

'But the girl has no experience.'

'All she needs is a bit of practice. Of course, I would not even consider Alice if you did not approve, Mrs Osborne. I was thinking that perhaps you would prefer to hire someone more suitable to replace her, someone stronger, who would take some of the worries off your shoulders. Even two persons perhaps, to share the work more evenly, so you would have more time to relax. Surely, you must yearn to have a little more free time of your own?'

'If you yearn for nothing then you can't be disappointed,' the housekeeper remarked stiffly.

'Oh, but you work so hard, Mrs Osborne. You should not be over-burdened.'

'Thank you, Madam. It's nice o' you t'say so,' Dora said grudgingly.

'You're welcome,' Jessica replied politely, wanting to keep the woman sweet. She wanted to approach her on the subject of the maids' rooms next, but one thing at a time. 'Of course, Alice must have her own room and a lower maid to clean for her.'

'You realise that by taking Alice for your personal maid will cause unrest amongst the others?'

'I'm sure you can deal with that. After all, you are in charge of running the household,' Jessica said with care, concentrating hard on her grammar, wanting to make a good impression. 'Do you know, I have really enjoyed our talk, Mrs Osborne.'

'Thank you, Madam. If I might say so, I think you should rest now. A woman in your condition needs her rest.'

'But I don't feel tired at all. I feel absolutely fine.'

'I had two children o' my own, you know. Lost both t'fever. It took my husband first.'

Jessica's response was sympathetic. 'I'm so sorry. I had no idea. Why did you not mention this before?'

'It happened a long time ago,' Dora said sullenly.

'But such a loss must've caused you a great deal of heartache. May I ask what made you tell me now?' Jessica enquired.

The older woman shrugged. 'I don't really know. I suppose just t'let you know I'm not the heartless ole woman everyone thinks me t'be.'

'Oh, I'm sure no one thinks that, Mrs Osborne'

'There's no need t'be kind, lass.' she said, forgetting she was talking to the mistress of the house for just a minute. 'I know exactly what the others think o' me.'

A sultry gloom seemed to have settled over them. For a full minute they stared at one another. Dora Osborne studied the young girl's pale face. Her eyes were startling and her beautiful fiery hair hung loosely down her back. Her own daughter would have been about the same age had she lived.

'This house has been a sad place these past two years.' Her pale eyes widened as she stared wistfully back in to the past. Nothing must go wrong, or the master would never forgive her. There had to be a fine healthy child this time. 'You really must take care, Madam. A child is very precious.'

'I will. I'll do as you suggest. Take a short rest. Perhaps we could do this more often, you and I? Spend a few pleasant moments together, I mean,' Jessica said kindly.

TEN

Jessica helped herself to toast and marmalade, but her tongue did not taste it when she put it in her mouth. She sat staring down at her plate without appetite.

There was now a more serious barrier to her joy, a strong streak of jealousy, one of the most frequent shadows cast by the blight of love that is apt to sow the seeds of distrust. There lurked a doubt no deliberate effort could stifle, a note of interrogation, like a hidden flame it glowed and just would not fade.

'Something is going on in that mind of yours, Jessica,' Luke remarked thoughtfully. 'You seem so distant.'

She met his steady gaze with a look of distrust.

'What was that look for?'

'I don't know what you mean,' she said sullenly.

'Come now! I know a look when I see one.'

She toyed with her napkin. 'Well, if you must know, you've been talking in your sleep. You've mentioned a name. Amy, it sounded like.'

Luke shrugged, his eyes meeting hers, giving nothing away. 'I can hardly be held responsible for my dreams.'

'You've repeated the name more than once.'

'Just what is it you're insinuating?' He raised one eyebrow in question, his gaze fixed and unblinking. 'You truly believe I'm carrying on with some other woman? You can just get that notion out of your head. I'm really not in the mood for this kind of nonsense.'

'I just needed to know, that's all,' she said quietly. The doubt suggested itself like a whisper from some evil spirit, and she strove not to listen. 'I'll never mention it again.'

'It seems I am disturbing your sleep. It would be best if we revert to sleeping in our own rooms again, don't you think? You must have your rest,' he said quietly.

She was hurt by his coolness and baffled by the change in their relationship. An overwhelming dread took possession of her. She couldn't understand what was happening. Why this sudden change towards her?

Just when it had all changed she could not say, but she knew there was something wrong between them, something that was gradually growing. Having separate rooms meant that he only came to her when he had some demand to make upon her. But those visits had become quite rare. She felt insecure, wanting to keep him there, to bring back some of the magic they had shared in the earlier days, to lie in his arms as she was entitled to as his wife. He was a stern disciplinarian, with a stringently enforced set of rules that she was expected to observe, a typical self-opinionated male with an absurd fondness for tradition and routine.

At nineteen she had been wholly passive in his hands; he her sole arbiter of right and wrong, her conscience, but as her character matured she begun to judge things for herself. Her independent spirit constantly clashed with his traditional views and they had occasional differences, differences wholly on abstract points of truth and justice that begun in shy humanity and continued with vague doubts. He took her passionate arguments in his passionless hold, turning and twisting them, then producing them so different that she failed to recognize their meaning or even her own words. She ceased to think at all of her hopes and dreams, over which this man's influence hung like an accursed shadow.

She loved him, of that there was no doubt, but love could not blind her objective eyes to his faults. She knew him to be an idealist, but an idealist of narrow vision, endeavouring not only to choose her books and her friends for her, but prohibited her from going near the mines, among people she had known most all of her life, quite unaware that he was encroaching on her very personality.

He did not care to see her associating with miners and the likes of April Ramsey, or Liam O'Malley and the other farm hands that he considered to be rough men. She had wanted to argue, but had held her peace. She should be free to go unchallenged on solitary excursions. What could happen to her? She knew most of the men better than he did. She enjoyed her visits to the farm that drew her like a magnet, but they could only be undertaken when Luke was not about to ask where she had been. She felt edgy with guilt at undermining his authority, going behind his back and yet at the same time irritated that he should order her about like one of the servants.

'Luke, make love to me,' she murmured without the slightest embarrassment.

He met her unabashed gaze. 'What …now?'

'Yes! Let's go up to my room.'

She needed sweet words and caresses. But her pleas withered in her throat as she saw something like fury contorting his face.

'Do you know, you are really quite incredible?

You deliberately try to provoke an argument, and then expect me to make love to you.'

Her heart sank at his harsh expression. 'I said I'll never mention it again. If anyone deserves a little of your time, surely it's me! You can't just keep me here in a box and take me out whenever you feel like playing with me.'

'Oh, for heaven's sake! What are you jabbering on about?'

'I'm just saying you rarely give me any attention anymore. Haven't I fallen in with your wishes and dealt with the servants as you suggested?'

'Yes, and I'm impressed how effortlessly you've made them do your bidding.'

'You are?' She was pleased with his response.

'I said so didn't I? But there's no reason you need burden yourself with mundane things. It will only put wrinkles on your lovely face.'

'But I want everything to be perfect, just as you like it to be. By the way, Mrs Osborne suggested Alice as my personal maid,' she lied, crossing her fingers and blushing, as she always did when she lied.

'Splendid!'

Her eyes widened in surprise. 'You mean you don't mind?' He usually told her to stop bothering him with such trivial matters. That Mrs Osborne dealt with such things.

'It's what you want, isn't it? I'm sure Mrs Osborne knows what she's doing.'

Jessica almost laughed out loud, but stifled it. Needing to touch and be touched in return she rose to her feet and come to plant a kiss on his cheek, a tender kiss of love, her hands exploring and caressing.

He put up a restraining hand. 'Jessica, not now.'

A fresh wave of resentment hit her. 'Why do you keep pushing me away?'

He looked up at her. 'I don't keep pushing you away.'

'Well, it certainly feels that way. I don't know what's wrong with you. You're like a different person. You were away for two weeks and yet, instead of being pleased to see me, you acted rather cold and distant. You hardly talk. I know you're not happy, but I don't know…' she trailed off, her look forlorn.

'You're just imagining things,' he interrupted impatiently.

Her eyes narrowed. 'Then tell me, when's the last time we did anything spontaneous? I know this kind of talk makes you feel uncomfortable, but do you know, you haven't touched me in weeks? I miss the affection.'

If he had been really listening he would have heard the adoration in her voice, but his mind was else-where, on other things; more important things. He checked his pocket-watch.

'Jessica, I haven't the time or the energy for this right now.'

But she wouldn't be put off. 'Tell me, do you care for me at all?'

'Do you doubt it?'

'That's not an answer. Tell me …do you even like me?'

'Most of the time,' he said, trying to make light of it.

'Don't make fun of me, Luke. I'm serious. You really ought to think about how your treat people?'

'Meaning you, I presume?'

'Well, you're always finding fault. It makes me feel I'm a disappointment to you.'

'Have I said you're a disappointment?'

'Not exactly, but there's none as deaf as those who will not hear. Meaning, when I talk you rarely listen.'

'I know what you mean,' he said tetchily. 'You talk the damnedest nonsense sometimes.'

'Well, it's true. When you do listen you criticise whatever I say and you're always chiding me for acting and dressing inappropriately. I'm not to read the books I like, not to mix with my friends.'

'Friends! People who use you for their own ends, you mean. You have no obligation to them. You owe them nothing.'

'Oh, you don't know diddly. True friends ask for nothing.'

'You have a different life-style now. You can't go on living with one foot in each world.'

'And I'm certainly not allowed opinions of my own,' she went on regardless.

'Only because you seem incapable of obeying the simplest of orders.'

'Perhaps it's because they're orders rather than requests? I even feel I have to continually conceal my views when they differ from yours. Who do you think you are? Moses handing down the commandments?' Her face deadly serious. 'But what I really mean is all people, particularly those that work for you. Politeness is a small price to pay for the good will of others. You can't rule everybody. Others have rights you know, but you just won't listen.'

She could not bear anyone to think ill of her. But Luke did not care a toss whether people liked him or not.

'For goodness sake stop your whining. It doesn't become you,' he told her sternly. Women! If they didn't have anything to worry about, they invent something. 'Sometimes I think you make these dramas up to test me. One reason why I find the dog such a likeable creature is that his tail wags instead of his tongue.'

She looked at him long and hard, wounded by his disdain. 'Animosity breeds, you know.'

'I don't want to hear such talk. I don't hire people to like me. I hire them to work. If they don't care for the way I treat them, then they should stay away.'

But Jessica was too worked up to let the matter rest. The breath of jealousy and suspicion sprang up in her heart. It was no good …she had to ask. 'Is there someone else?'

The question was asked so suddenly it took him off guard for just a moment, but he quickly checked himself and when he spoke, he was on the defensive, raising his hands in the air in exasperation, and then letting them drop again. 'Do you know, you're unbelievable! Where do you get such an idea? And don't tell me it's from hearing me murmur something in my sleep. Who has been talking? What bastard's been upsetting you?'

'No one's been upsetting me. There are two things a woman doesn't need to be told. When she's pregnant and when her husband has tired of her.'

'The youthful pearls of wisdom!'

'I'm serious, Luke. Maybe you've had enough of me?'

They fell silent as light-footed servants removed the dirty plates and replaced them with clean.

'I'll tell you this...' she continued as soon as they

were alone again. 'I won't live out the rest of my life being humiliated.'

Exasperated, he sighed heavily. She could be so infuriating at times. 'There's nothing going on, I assure you. Why won't you believe me?'

'Maybe it's the way you look at me when you say you're telling the truth.'

'And just how do I look at you?'

'With a holier-than-thou attitude. That expression you have that says Luke Sheridan can do no wrong.'

'I'm sorry. It's certainly not intentional,' he said resignedly, weary of the discussion.

'You say that a lot lately, but it doesn't answer my question.'

His hand came down hard on the table making the cutlery dance and Jessica flinch.

'Jessica ...my patience is wearing thin. You have an over-active imagination. I repeat ...*there is no other woman*,' he insisted fiercely, hostility rising automatically when anything of this kind was mentioned. 'There have been other women in the past; you know that, but not since our marriage. What else can I say? Your jealousy and distrust is beginning to get tiresome. Just what is it you want of me?'

She badly needed reassurance. 'What do I want of you? Well, you're healthy and I'm quite aware you have your ...your needs, yet we haven't been together for ...well...' she lifted her shoulders and raised her hands, 'since God knows when. Why not? Tell me that.'

'I know I've been neglecting you of late, but a man in my position carries a great deal of responsibility on his shoulders,' he said shrewdly.

'It isn't me then?'

He raised his eyes to the ceiling, but when he looked at her the words he spoke were reassuring. 'Of course it isn't you.'

But the doubt, the note of interrogation nonetheless persisted. 'So, if it isn't me and you swear you've no one else, what is it then?'

The truth was she demanded of him more than he was willing to give. He had to admit his desire for her was beginning to dwindle, that he had come to resent her failure to excite him as much as she used to. There was no magnetism, no mystery to discover. Amel was always full of surprises, adventurous and less inhibited. Her image flooded his thoughts. He reluctantly pushed her to the back of his mind.

'It's simply I get tired, that's all. I lose feeling for everything. I suppose it's natural enough when you consider I'm up at six in the morning and rarely go to my bed before midnight. Everyone wants some part of me. There seems to be no time for myself.'

Jessica was now relieved of that anxiety. 'I'm not in the mood to apologise, but as I misjudged you, I will,' she said, almost grudgingly.

She was unbelievable at times. He did not permit himself to smile, but when he answered there was in his eyes a kindly, tolerant look. 'And I'm not in the mood to accept, but I will. Just look at the time. I'd hoped to be in London before dark.'

Jessica gave an exaggerated sigh. 'All our life seems to consist of is saying goodbye. How long will you be away this time?'

'Not long, my pet. I'll try to get business over within a few days,' he promised in an effort to soothe her. 'Now, I want you to take good care of yourself.

Anything you need just ask Dora. Stay near to home. If you get too restless have Tom drive you over to visit your father, but don't overdo it. If you're a good girl I'll bring you back a present, something nice.'

She crossed the room to pull the bell-rope to order a fresh pot of tea, the solution to all the problems of the world.

ELEVEN

Beset by debts, George lV was in a weak position in relation to his Cabinet of ministers. His concern for royal prerogative was sporadic; much against his will and his interpretation of his coronation oath, he was forced by his ministers to agree to Catholic Emancipation. By reducing religious discrimination, this emancipation enabled the monarchy to play a more national role. The papers reported that in addition to the usual gout and rheumatism, His Majesty had suffered feverish attacks and violent irritation that could only be subdued by laudanum, but always returned when the effect of the opiate wore off. In addition to this, he was now blind in one eye and it was believed he would lose sight in the other.

George Shillibeer - coachbuilder and livery stable keeper in Bury Street, Bloomsbury, had started London's first regular horse-drawn omnibus service. Shillibeer had seen the omnibus operating successfully in Paris and was inspired to do the same in London. It was said that the omnibus could carry up to twenty passengers and was drawn by three horses. Shillibeer boasted it offered a safer and more comfortable ride than ordinary stage coaches, as all passengers would ride inside. The fare of one shilling was far beyond the means of the average worker in London yet less than the price of most short stage coach rides.

Luke folded the newspaper and placed it down on

the table beside the chair. He felt an unusual satisfaction. Here they were, already half way through 1829 - time seemed to go by with a blink. His businesses were flourishing; he had the company of a doting wife when at home in the country and the excitement of an enticing mistress here in the city. They were virtually living as husband and wife. All in all, things were going well. Life was good.

He turned and looked Amel up and down. Her golden hair had been cleverly arranged in curls on top of her magnificent head and separated with a band of pearls across the forehead and round the back of her head, with a long springing ringlet hanging down each side of her lovely face. She had on a white satin dress with a train, in the most elaborate style. The front was plain apart from the bottom which was finished with a large pearl tassel. The train and short puffy sleeves were covered with blue spider net showered with tiny French pearls. The height of fashion! Indeed, she was quite exquisite. Her name curled across his tongue. His smile was challenging and his brown eyes caressing as she went willingly into his arms. He covered her mouth with his own, devouring her lips like a man starved of affection.

'How long are you staying, Mon amour?' she whispered breathlessly.

'Two nights.'

She stiffened in his arms. 'Only two nights? No longer?'

'I'm afraid not. It's my wife,' he said, seeing her eyes cloud with disappointment. 'Something is upsetting her.'

'She hasn't said what?'

'Well, not exactly, except she complains that I

neglect her. I don't want to be away from her too long. She's easily upset.'

Amel pulled away from him with an exaggerated sigh. 'You seem unduly concerned about her.'

'What affects her could well affect my unborn son, I don't want her fretting. It's not good for her to be emotionally disturbed.'

Amel felt a sudden rush of resentment. 'Oh, for goodness sake, can't you see she's playing on this pregnancy.'

Despite her best efforts she couldn't conceal the anger in her voice. She hadn't seen him for well over a week and now he was here, all he could think about was his silly pregnant wife, when he should rightly be thinking of her. 'Children are born into the world every day.'

'Not mine. What threatens her, threatens the child. I cannot risk losing the child.'

'My word, she certainly has you dangling. Give a wolf a taste and keep him hungry.'

'Now, don't let's get spiteful, darling. It doesn't become you.'

She fluttered gold tipped lashes and pouted her rosy lips. 'Like any other woman who would take you away from me, Mon amour, she is my enemy.'

'No one could take me away from you. Come now, at least we have two whole days and nights to look forward to.'

She nodded in acceptance. 'Then don't let's waste time. We must make the most of what little we have.'

And those very words set the tone for what followed. They pleasured themselves in playful antics, chasing each other about the bedroom where twinkling lamps and candles gave the scene an air of unreality. When they undressed, she did not remove her high-heeled kid shoes or the white stockings fastened at her knees with embroidered garters. Then she insisted on rubbing his body all over with exotic oils, provoking irrepressible laughter and arousing him until the fever consuming him was totally unleashed.

He lifted her bodily and stood her down before one of the long gold-framed mirrors, gazing at her reflection. He was convinced she was the most beautiful woman in the universe. A golden Goddess superbly fashioned to give pleasure. The fact that she took her change of lovers like a change in the weather no longer perturbed him. He had even began to ask himself if it were not better to own part of her as a mistress who knew how to make a man happy, than all of her who lacked opportunity to acquire the art. For it was an art, along with the fantasies she invented. And he knew exactly to what training she owed her skill, but he had passed into that of complete acceptance, ceasing to satirise himself because time had dulled the irony of the situation.

He started to kiss her on the side of the neck as he greedily fondled her breasts, all the time observing their reflections in the mirror, flaring an incendiary passion. Their shameful escapade lived on in the limbo of things not given words. When they could bear to pull them-selves apart and return to reality, darkness ruled outside.

TWELVE

It was almost dusk, just a sliver of moon could be seen in the sky as Alice Little entered the woods amongst a belt of dark pines and tall elms, each one a scheme of clustered columns that upheld the massive black-green foliage, so that the wood seemed like a low chamber with a heavy carven roof, under which twilight always brooded. A short-cut that led through to emerald green slopes that ran down to the gardens and the house.

It was her afternoon off and she had been to Ireby churchyard to put flowers on her mother's grave, but had lingered too long in the teashop chatting to Mrs Chandler, telling her how eternally grateful she was for the good luck that had brought her so kind a mistress, who had promoted her from a lowly skivvy to ladies' maid - a giant step. And all about her duties, which were to wait on the mistress in menial capacity in a confusion of tasks, to fetch and carry, as it were. She had learned the best way to clean and press delicate materials from the mistress's wardrobe, keep her shoes and boots in pristine order, and how to dress her hair, studying and copying the styles from the latest fashion magazines.

It was a great chance for her and she meant to make the most of it. Her own timid nature was the opposite side of the coin to the young mistress's passionate nature, her fiery defiance of polite society and its demands, but during the past few weeks which they had begun as virtual strangers, they had become constant companions. She was happy. She had never been so happy, and yet it saddened her when she thought of the hard life her mother had had, struggling to bring her up on her own, and now her own life had been made so much easier her beloved mother was not here to share her good fortune.

The tall trees towered above her and through all the topmost branches there ran a low, mournful sound, as if every tree was whispering. She advanced with short swift steps, all the time looking nervously about as though expecting to see someone. She could not shake off the feeling that her every move was being watched.

The figure of a man stole along in the darkest shadows he could find and, at some distance accommodated his pace to that of the young girl's; treading cautiously lest he should make any noise, but the floor of this place was deep with the leaves of many centuries, which had gathered with the thickening years till they muffled the tread. He crept stealthily on, never allowing himself in the ardour of his pursuit to gain upon her footsteps.

Suddenly stopping, Alice turned slowly, fearfully tilting her head and listening, then called out. 'Who's there? Is someone there?'

She walked on again, quickening her pace, moving as fast as her short little legs could carry her, eager to get out of the woods before it turned dark.

When the girl was about the same distance in advance as she had been before, the man crept quietly on in the shadows, following her again. Alice was first aware of his presence when she heard the distinct rustle of leaves, sending a chill tingle up the nape of her neck. All of a sudden he stepped out from behind a tree, looming over her and blocking her path.

At first sight of him she felt she should turn and run, but took a step backwards, staring up at him vacantly as though the angel of death stood before her. Beady eyes looked slyly out above a big, sharp, protruding nose with wide-open nostrils; his hair combed neatly back from a smoothly shaven round bloated face. His clothes looked to be expensive, although not a good fit, the waistcoat straining across his projecting belly, and he noticeably smelt of stale sweat. He wheezed a greeting at her, trying to engage her in conversation, but Alice was shy and felt uneasy.

'You're a lively little thing, aren't you? As fast as a ferret, you are. So fast, I could hardly keep up,' George Roebling said with a smirk.

Alice willed herself to speak, but the tremor to her quiet, gentle voice told of her nervousness. 'You gave me such a fright. Please let me pass or I'll be late at me post.'

'Not before you give me a kiss,' he said, taking one step nearer.

Alice instantly stepped back. 'Your advances are not … not welcome, Sir,'

She wanted to say she would rather kiss a pig than his hideous face, but common sense prevailed, for fear it might provoke him to violence. At that moment she was completely at his mercy and the thought genuinely troubled her.

'A girl like you should be flattered. Give me a kiss an' I'll let you go.'

'If …if you don't let me pass I …I'll scream,' Alice cried nervously.

George Roebling shrugged his shoulders. 'Scream

all you want. Who is there t'hear?' He took another step toward her and Alice stepped back again. 'I bet you're a pretty little thing underneath those skirts.'

She felt her cheeks burning. 'You …you're very insulting.'

'An' you're at my mercy,' he said, with a scornful smile on his lips. But the girl's unfriendliness was beginning to annoy him. He decided to amuse himself, teach her a lesson. Distractions were somewhat scarce lately.

Podgy hands suddenly caught Alice by the shoulders and pulled her roughly towards him. Her heart constricted in alarm, his touch affecting her badly. It was so unpleasant it made her flesh creep.

He abruptly released his grip and slipped an arm about her tiny waist, holding her chin with sweaty fingers and stooping to bring a mouth full of saliva close to her face. Her reaction was one of revulsion; she strained her head back to escape his sour breath and placing her hands on his chest she pushed with all her might, trying frantically to thrust him away, but it was futile for she was a tiny slip of a girl and he a strong full-grown man.

'Come on now, give me a kiss if you don't want t'get hurt,' George hissed beneath his breath, looking around as if he thought he could be overheard.

His mouth fastened on hers before she had time to turn her head away. His teeth sank into her bottom lip and she tasted blood. Unversed in the ways of the world, tiny innocent Alice Little could never have predicted what was to happen to her or that those moments alone with George Roebling would be her last. From the instant she had entered those woods her fate had been sealed.

The girl was completely in his power. He liked them young, the younger the better. He was shaking with an inward burning excitement at the thought of what he might do to her. Anticipation flooded his body and swelled the crotch of his breeches into a bulge of enormous proportions.

Alice was now all too aware of his evil intent. Although an innocent girl, she was not completely naive as she had heard Maggie and Amy whispering together about such things; what men liked to do to women. She was in terrible danger here. The realisation sent a cold shudder down her spine. Terror prickled through her veins. She started to beat against his chest with tiny clenched fists. He lifted her bodily and shook her like a dog shaking a rabbit, her small head jerking back and forward, sending her senses reeling. Knowing her very life depended on it, she struggled frantically against him as he carried her into the bushes. But it was no use; she was no match against his strength.

A scream raced around in her head, but it couldn't escape. Not until he flung her on the ground did her terror escape in one high-pitched shriek, cut off as fingers like steel clamped over her mouth almost smothering her.

George Roebling licked his lips and grunted with pleasure. Her cries only added spice to the grappling, exciting him further.

'High-spirited little filly, aren't you? Now, hold still.'

But she wouldn't stay still. Like a live eel she wriggled all over the place; he could hardly hold her.

'Stop your damn struggling, you stupid bitch if you don't want t'get hurt.'

The nauseating reek of his breath sickened her as he leant over her, spewing oaths at her. 'Now … let's see what …what we have here. I'm going t'enjoy this.' He yanked up her skirts, exposing the soft white flesh of her thin legs, forcing them roughly apart, 'Not much o' you, but you'll do.'

His hold slackened slightly as he fumbled awkwardly with her drawers, pulling them off. The buttons on his breeches were just as difficult to undo with one hand; his moist lips were constantly moving and shaping them-selves into a sickly smile as he released that which gave him the greatest pleasure. It had grown rock-hard and grandly erect, demanding what it meant to have. It was a red ugly bit of a thing.

The thought of what he was going to do with it horrified Alice. She shuddered with revulsion, turning her face away, but not before she had seen the savage glint in his evil pig-like eyes. Then he was right on top of her, knocking what breath she had left from out of her fragile body, crushing and almost suffocating her, pinning her fast beneath him with his immense weight. Without hesitation he forced a painful insertion, thrusting unmercifully at the most private part of her body, his vileness eating into her. She grew rigid with shock, floundering helplessly without direction in a sea of pain.

Driven by the forces of nature, he moved on top of her, snorting like a pig, exerting himself without restraint, ripping the poor tender young girl apart, all the while with his clammy hand held in a tight grip over her mouth. His thrusts became more and more furious, cruel and merciless, jolting her body with the very force, in a hideous orgy of agony, his sweaty hand pushing against her nose. She couldn't breathe.

She was going to die. Her life rushed before her, the lightning experience abruptly lasting no more than a few split seconds and yet the flash seemed timeless, her existence ending through suffocation.

The luckless young girl lay quiet long before he had finished with her. And when he had, he took her limp fingers in his and let them drop again. He adjusted his clothes hurriedly, muttering beneath his breath as he did so.

'Stupid girl; if you'd just laid still.'

He dragged her farther into the bushes and covered the slight, lifeless body with twigs and dead leaves, then slunk away in the shadows.

It wasn't like Alice to be late. Jessica felt a vague unease, something she could not put her finger on. She spent a restless night, tossing and turning, and almost before the first faint sign of dawn appeared she arose and opened the window to let in the fresh morning air; the panes were still wet with trembling tears left by the night rain.

She dressed hurriedly and went down stairs only to discover that Alice still had not returned. So sick with worry was she that after a light breakfast she put on her bonnet and voluminous cloak to hide her increasing size and strode off across the fells in the direction of Ireby, in search of the girl she had grown quite fond of.

A morning mist hung over the fields and the yellowing ferns with their feathery arms, an effusive yet magnificent silvery veil full of light from the sun as yet semi-opaque. The village of Ireby squats on the small rise behind that benevolent, old giant Skiddaw, about a little over a mile or so north of Uldale. The entrance to the village is a narrow road between two ancient houses that lean towards each other like confident sentries. A truly unspoilt village of no more than eighty people at the most, a village you could walk through in just a few minutes, consisting of a church, a hall, the Sun Inn, a few scattered houses and rows of little white-washed cottages. The first place Jessica checked was the graveyard where Alice's mother was buried and inside the church, but she couldn't say why because Alice would have long gone from there. As it was, they were deserted.

At a loss where to check next, she walked back through the main street and stopped outside the teashop, the only shop of any sort, in fact, that doubled up as a butcher and general store. Jessica popped her head inside the door to enquire if Alice Little had been seen. Noticing the beautiful though pale face of the young woman, Mrs Chandler, who served there, insisted she come inside and sit herself down to rest a while. She knew who she was. Well, she would, wouldn't she? Young Alice had had nothing but praise for her mistress, the kind Mrs Sheridan.

Jessica sat down thankfully. There was a pain in her back, like a dull ache. Within minutes a refreshing cup of tea was placed down on the table before her. Alice had apparently popped in for a cup of tea yesterday afternoon after visiting her mother's grave, so Mrs Chandler told her, and had left for home. She couldn't rightly say the exact time but it was still light.

With a troubled mind and heavy steps, Jessica started a slow walk back. In the fields sheep moved slowly, heads down and intent on keeping the grass clipped short. A fox, curled up asleep in a ditch under thick overhanging greenery, awakened at her approach and quickly disappeared. The tired feeling increased in intensity, until her steps began to falter. She stopped to rest against a low stone wall. She should have had Tom drive her in the carriage, as he had suggested, but she would not listen. She thought the exercise would do her good. Cows came ponderously jostling towards the wall in order to have a closer look at her. But blind now to the beauty of her surroundings, divorced from any sensitivity to the animals, she straightened herself and stumbled onwards.

When she finally arrived home, she felt totally exhausted. She wandered into the kitchen, brushing past Maggie without really noticing her. The girl stood with her mouth agape, her eyes on Mrs Osborne, waiting for the onslaught when she saw the young mistress barging into the kitchen. As that was what she did, barged past like she was in a great hurry, pushing by anyone who stood in her way. She waited for the sharp voice - Mrs Osborne demanding that the mistress had no business coming in to the kitchen ... but to her surprise it did not come.

'Where is she?' Jessica enquired.

'Who, Madam?' Maggie asked, as she hovered in the doorway with the bucket in her hand. 'If it's Cook you are wanting, Madam, it's her day off.'

'No, Alice, where is she? She must be back by now.'

'She's not here, Madam,' was Maggie's response.

It wasn't for her to say, but she didn't like the look of the young mistress, so pale was she and her hair clung against the dampness of her forehead. She didn't look at all well. If anyone wanted her opinion ...the young mistress should be off to her bed. If the master came home and found her dashing about in this state, all hell would break loose, him so anxious to have this child and all.

'Are you feeling all right, Madam?'

She was astonished that the dark-clad figure of Mrs Osborne carried on moving about the kitchen as if the young mistress wasn't there. It was her usual routine on Cook's day off to carry out an inspection to check that everything was clean and to her liking, and if it wasn't, then she would say so. Maggie had never yet known her to find anything that was not sparkling clean. Cook was just as particular in keeping them on their toes during kitchen duties as she was, having them clean everything that didn't move. Now here was the mistress in the kitchen again, after "old tin drawers" as she thought of her, had openly boasted to Cook that the master had said to her straight that she was in charge of the house and who she allowed in the kitchen was entirely up to her. Hadn't she overheard it with her own ears? She'd been so sure that the mistress wouldn't dare bother to show her face in there again, not after the master had put her in her place. Well, it hadn't done any good, had it? Maggie jumped as the harsh voice broke into her thoughts.

'Don't just stand there gawking, girl. Get on with your work an' be quick about it. I'll deal with this.'

Well ...Maggie thought ...she must have eyes in the back of her bloody head to know she was still there. All the same, she had best get on if she knew what was good for her. Pushing open the door she scurried out, mumbling under her breath about having to do the work of two while that lazy bitch Alice Little was off goodness knows where. There had been no message from her; she would be in for it when she showed her face.

'Where can she be? It's so unlike her,' Jessica said half to herself.

'If you mean Alice, Madam, then she's not here, as you can see.'

'She hasn't returned from her afternoon off. She told me she was going to visit her mother's grave and would be back before dark, but all night long she's been gone. Something must have happened.'

Jessica sat down heavily on a chair, leaning forward to rest on the edge of the table. She felt her temples were about to explode as a wave of blood rushed to her face. What was the matter with her? She felt totally exhausted, damp and uncomfortable all over. Her back hurt and she was experiencing hot flushes that left her breathless, and her heart seemed to be hammering in her chest as if it might burst. For the first time in her life, she thought she was going to faint.

Panic rose inside of her. She held her hands out in front of her. They were shaking. She had done too much, walked all the way over to the Ireby and back, convinced she would find Alice there …perhaps taken poorly and not able to let them know. She put her weight on her elbows, supporting her head with her hands.

'Would you fetch me a glass of water, please?'

Mrs Osborne turned on her then. 'I beg your pardon? Are you talking t'me?'

'Yes. I'd like a glass of water please.'

'It's not my place...'

'Oh, for goodness sake, fetch me a glass of water,' Jessica demanded crossly.

'Well, really! I'm not used t'being spoken to in such a manner, but then what can one expect.' Nevertheless, the housekeeper filled a glass with water and placed it on the table in front of the young mistress.

'Thank you. I didn't mean to snap,' Jessica murmured apologetically, embarrassed by her display of anger. 'I'm sorry, really I am. It's just that I'm feeling rather strange, unwell.'

'It's no wonder, the way you gad about, traipsing all over the fells an' in your condition. It's not fitting.'

Jessica could hear her talking with a ceaseless monotony of self-expression. She who preserved all day an iron control of word and look.

'It's just not fitting...' the housekeeper repeated moodily. '...but then it's not for me t'say. I'll be back when you've gone from the kitchen.'

Jessica flinched at the sound of the door banging behind her. Oh God! Her nerves were on edge and she felt sure she was about to be sick. A throbbing pain encircled her head like a crown of thorns and nervous tremors shook her from head to foot. She must get to her room to rest; perhaps then she would feel better. She pushed herself up by her hands ... feeling strangely weak and dizzy, as if her legs did not really belong to her.

'Please ...won't someone help me?' she called. But there was no one there to hear her or see her slip in to blackness on to the cold stone floor.

Maggie, who had just finished washing the hall floor, got to her feet and stretched her aching back. Picking up the bucket of dirty water, she took it into the kitchen to tip it away down the sink. That's when she found the mistress, unconscious on the floor. She put down the bucket, lifted her skirts and ran up the stairs, two at a time, to knock on the door of Mrs Osborne's private sitting room at the far end of the landing.

'Come in.'

She peeped nervously around the door. 'Sorry t'disturb you, Mrs Osborne, really I am...'

'Well, what is it?' Dora asked irritably. A body couldn't have a moment's peace.

'There's something wrong with the mistress.'

'Something wrong? What do you mean, something wrong?'

'Well, she's on the kitchen floor. An' I think she's unconscious.'

Dora Osborne's heart did a somersault. 'Then we had best go an' have a look, hadn't we?' she rejoined, sounding calmer than she actually felt.

She moved as quickly as she could without knocking any of the china ornaments, her own personal treasures, from the beautifully polished table in the cluttered little sitting room. She was secretly worried about the young mistress. No docile young miss who would sit and rest, she had been used to striding out upon the fells lately with young Alice Little to accompany her.

'Now, calm yourself girl an' don't run. I've told you before about running.'

'Yes, but...' Maggie began.

'An' don't answer back,' Dora snapped.

Maggie clamped her mouth shut. God Almighty! There was the mistress lying unconscious, maybe dead even, on the cold floor in the kitchen and the silly old cow tells me not to run. Whatever next!

A sudden pain racked Jessica's body and brought her eyes wide open in alarm. She glanced hazily about. She was lying on her soft bed in her room. Her clothes had been removed and Dora Osborne was standing over her, gently washing her body with a cool wet cloth.

When Dora saw the young mistress had regained consciousness she swiftly covered her naked body with a soft towel, patting her on the hand like a concerned mother.

Jessica looked up at her, confused and surprised. 'What ...what happened?'

'Now, now, don't you worry about anything. You're safe an' I'm here t'look after you.'

Was she still dreaming? Was this the Dora Osborne she knew? The same hostile woman who made the lives of all who worked under her a misery?

'But ...but what happened?' she asked again, her hand going to rest protectively on her swollen belly.

'You passed out, Madam. Now try not t'worry. I'm right here should you need me,' Dora said soothingly, praying silently to God for the doctor to arrive. 'Everything will be all right, I'm sure.'

'But how did I get here? Who brought me upstairs?' Jessica asked, calmed by the woman's words.

'Tom an' I carried you. It wasn't easy mind, but

we managed. Do you feel more comfortable now? I bathed you down with cool water.'

'Yes …yes, thank you.'

'Tom's gone for the doctor. I just hope he finds him at home.'

'Dora, why are you being so kind?'

'Well, you've been talking while you were unconscious. You sounded troubled. I didn't realise how unfair I've been an' yet not once have you turned on me. Warm-hearted an' kind, that's what you are. Never the once have you uttered any complaint or criticism. I feel thoroughly ashamed o' myself, really I do.'

'Oh, Dora, there's no need...'

'It's just that I thought you were trying t'take my place, you see. What I mean is ...I've run Wildacres for so many years, I didn't want any interference …not from anyone.'

'But I just wanted to be friends.'

'I know that now, my dear. No one's ever wanted anything more from me than a well-run house. The first Mrs Sheridan was a quiet little woman, nothing t'say about anything an' before that I'd run the place just as Mr Sheridan liked it. I suppose I harboured some resentment, you coming here an' being so popular with everyone. I've come t'realise that getting what you want at the expense o' others isn't at all satisfying. As I said, I'm right ashamed o' myself. I was wrong.'

'Dora ...oohh, my …my back.' Jessica grasped the older woman's hand tightly, holding on to the bedclothes with the other as pain suddenly racked her body.

'Goodness …I shouldn't be talking like this with

you the way you are. How long have you been getting pain in the back?'

'For the last couple of days.' The pain altered, it moved from her back and gripped at her stomach like a great vice. She screamed, twisting and writhing with agony. She couldn't help it. 'Oh God …oh God!'

'Dear, oh dear. Let's get you int'your nightgown.'

Jessica took a long shuddering breath as the pain gradually subsided. Surprisingly gentle hands raised her to a sitting position and she lifted her arms obediently to receive the soft fresh garment over her head, and then lay back thankfully on the pillows, lifting her buttocks to allow Dora to pull it down to cover the lower part of her swollen body. It was then Dora saw the dark stain on the bedclothes. Her heart flipped as she felt the beginning of fear. Something was wrong, seriously wrong. The young Mistress was bleeding. She knew that the most common symptom of threatened abortion was vaginal bleeding, with or without intermittent pain

'Oh, I think I've wet myself,' Jessica mumbled, as she felt the warm fluid escape from between her legs. 'What can be wrong?'

'I really don't know, my dear,' Dora said steadily, although she was at her wit's end. Wildacres was isolated, miles from the nearest large town where additional medical help might be obtained in an emergency.

'You don't think the baby's coming, do you?' The corners of the girl's mouth quivered slightly as she spoke. 'But it can't be. It's not time yet. The …the doctor said I had another six weeks to go.'

'Babies don't have calendars. Here, let me put this

towel between …down here t'soak up the wet,' Dora said, hastily thrusting a towel between the poor girl's legs to soak up the blood. 'Now, try not t'worry. I'll have Maggie brew up some herbal tea t'help you relax. It might be some time before the doctor gets here.'

Jessica tried hard to relax and to master the fright, but she couldn't stop trembling with nervousness. 'Will it? Oh, Dora, I'm so worried about Alice. It's not like her to stay away. What could have happened to her?'

'Now, now, stop your worrying, my dear. When Tom comes back, I'll have him go look for her. You just lay back an' think o' good things.'

Jessica did as she was told and settled back on the pillows, but just as Dora got to the door, she came abruptly to life, the pain tearing her flesh to shreds.

'Oohh …don't leave me.'

She clutched at the sheets, her eyes full of fear, pleading desperately to Dora for help, fighting a panic that almost choked her. The pain began to retract, with-drawing its thorns. Long lashes fluttered as she sank back on the pillows again.

The pain came again and again, striking without mercy, then slowly diminishing, retreating to the point of its birth in her stomach. Nothing could ever have prepared her for this.

'I wish …wish Luke were here.'

She must have lost consciousness, because when she opened her eyes again both the doctor and the midwife were in the room, exchanging words in low murmuring voices. Their concern was apparent. Half propped up, with towels about and beneath her, her face was contorted in a spasm of pain, and wisps of her glorious hair that Dora had loosened to make her more comfortable, lay damp against her temple.

'I just don't understand. I only examined her a little over a week ago an' everything was just as it should be. She seemed well an' thoroughly happy in her condition. Why things should suddenly go wrong at this stage is a mystery, but these things happen,' the doctor said resignedly, his voice tinged with regret. 'Treatment for threatened abortion usually consists o' continuous bed rest throughout the remainder o' the pregnancy, but I fear in this case things have gone too far. The contractions're getting stronger, but it could be hours yet.'

'What?' Jessica cried, gulping in horror. She had only caught the last words he had spoken …it could be hours yet.

And the very thought that this …this horrendous torture could go on and on filled her with terror. She writhed as a new contraction took hold of her body. 'I can't …can't bear it.'

Doctor Morrison's kind face and large, sad eyes looked down upon her. He slid his hands beneath the blankets and with firm gentle movements began to knead the young mother's abdomen. 'There now, try t'relax, my dear. Push only when the pain comes,' he advised with an air of calm, quiet authority. For her own safety she had to bear the child soon.

Doris was still there, encouraging her through the severe contractions that left her exhausted and weeping. A strange wave of pity swept over the woman at the sight of the young mistress's face. 'Push, my dear … push!' she encouraged.

'I am bloody pushing,' Jessica screeched through clenched teeth.

She knew labour was supposed to be painful, but surely not as agonizing as the extended contractions that she endured for so long. Her mother had not spoken about such things; they had been strictly taboo, so how could she have known just what to expect?

'Don't give up, my dear,' Doris whispered, all concern. 'It's coming.'

Wiping Jessica's forehead with a cool damp cloth and murmuring soothingly, Dora managed to achieve a few moments of calm for her between the racking pains. But the moments became fewer as the mighty heaving pain tore at the girl. She gave a long agonized scream. It was only then that Dora's hands started to shake. Jessica's eyes were filled with fear. She felt the walls were closing in on her.

'Oh God help me ...I'm dying...' she sobbed, as yet another piercing, wrenching pain tore and ripped through her poor body, working itself up to a crescendo and then, after what seemed like an eternity, lessened, leaving her panting, shaken and weak.

The housekeeper caught her infectious rising panic and much to the midwife's displeasure, she hung on tightly to the girl's hand. 'I'm right here. Hold ont'me an' push when the pain comes ...my poor, dear girl.'

'Oh God grant me this ...this one indulgence. Make ...this a ... a son. Because I ...I'm telling you now, God ...this ...this will be the last.'

Shriek after shriek followed, her screams becoming louder. The noise cut through everyone present, like a sharp blade of a knife.

'Well done, Jessica, almost there,' the doctor announced with an edge of relief in his voice.

'Another good long push might just do the trick. As soon as the pain comes …push.'

Then came one last shriek, long and piercing, agonizingly loud. Jessica fell back on the pillows, her pain-racked body utterly exhausted. There followed a death-like silence.

Dora was the first to speak. Her voice was flat, scarcely above a whisper. 'There now, you poor, dear girl.' Sympathy and anguish were the expressions that showed in her eyes.

Those words cut through Jessica like a blade, but clouds of merciful sleep overcame her. The loss of the child she carried was only the beginning of her sorrows; gradually they would grow until they blackened her entire world.

A note was sent to her husband, urging him to return home.

THIRTEEN

She could see a row of tombstones all in a straight line, bearing the names of those she loved. One for each of her beloved brothers, John and Adam, standing side by side, and next to theirs was her mothers who she had loved from a distance. Another for Owen Ramsey and sweet little Holly, that special little girl she had once nursed on her knee, and her dear brother Rufus. She could make out the name of Samuel Miller - Uncle Sam, who had been so dear to her and his son, Will. And right at the very end was the tiniest of tombstones, but she couldn't see a name on it. No …no …it couldn't be …there's been a mistake…

She opened her mouth to scream, but hadn't the strength. She simply could not bear the pain of the loss of any of them and her loneliness was quite insupportable. Tears run silently down each side of her face and dripped just as silently onto the crisp whiteness of her pillow.

Gentle hands held her and a reassuring voice whispered in her ear. Forms and faces closed in about her. Sometimes it was the doctor's face that swam into view; sometimes it was Dora's and sometimes it was his face, white and drawn. Where had he been when she had needed him most? She didn't want him now - just peace, a long, long peace. But he was trying to coax her to sip the warm sweet tea of camomile to help her relax, he said. She cast aside his hand and wept bitterly.

Unable to endure the sound of her suffering, Luke paced restlessly about the house. He finally went out into the garden, breathing in the cold air. Doctor Morrison, who had called to check on his patient, came out to join him.

'She's very distressed, but is in good hands.'

'What happened?' Luke asked lamely.

'Spontaneous abortion. The child was still-born.'

Luke gave him a puzzled look. 'I don't understand. My wife seemed so healthy, so well when I left. There must be some explanation.'

The doctor shrugged his shoulders helplessly. 'There's no explanation. It's a complete mystery. The embryo may die an' be retained in the uterus for weeks, even months sometimes, in a so-called missed abortion.'

'The main thing is, my wife. Will she be all right?'

'Yes …yes. She will recover. Nature will take its course. She's had a bad shock, but mercifully has done no real damage. I would recommend that she remain in bed for a week at least. A light, nourishing diet devoid of stimulants an' plenty of fluids will do the trick. Oh, an' plenty o' sleep. Sleep's a great healer.'

'Tell me … was it a boy?'

'Yes, it was a boy. After the loss o' this first child, the health o' the mother demands that there should be no hurried beginning o' another, for at least six months before a second life is allowed t'begin its unfolding.'

A vein of indefinable sorrow threaded the air of the house, affecting everyone within. The dreadful ordeal

had left the young mistress physically and emotionally drained. Depression snatched at her heart.

Dora took to fussing over her like a mother hen,
taking her a glass of minced up raspberry leaves and
ginger, cloves and cinnamon, first thing every
morning to help build up her energy. Organising her
light nourishing meals to tempt her appetite. The
warming pan that hung conveniently near the kitchen
fire was constantly filled with hot cinders and pushed
in at the side or foot of the bed, swung up and down
and to and fro, until every inch of the bed was heated
and the sheets ironed hot and smooth, while the
young mistress soaked in a bath of warm water and
salt, in case of infection, and to soothe and heal her
tortured body.

At night, before bed, a hot brick taken from the
oven was wrapped in a blanket and placed carefully at
her feet. Nothing was too much trouble for the young
mistress. Well, hadn't she suffered a tragic loss now?

Jessica saw the shock and disappointment on her
husband's face, when he looked in to see her. He
moved further into the room, awkward and stiff as
she had never seen him before. Somehow the sight of
him increased her distress. His dark eyes were steady
as they rested gravely on her and his mouth clenched
rigidly, as though he was afraid he might say the
wrong thing. He swallowed and she saw his Adam's
apple rise convulsively in his throat. He spoke her
name hoarsely, before clearing his throat.

'Jessica, how are you feeling?'

'How do you think?' she replied bitterly, wanting
to hurt him, punish him for not being here when she

had needed him most. Pain and indignation had her in their grip. She had not fully realised the danger childbirth entailed. She might have died. 'Where were you when I needed you?'

'I came as fast as I could. As soon as I received the message.'

Emotions dragged her down like a heavy weight, tears filling her eyes, hovering in the corners and then escaping to streak across her pale cheeks. She gazed at him through her tears. 'It's said you can bear the pain of childbirth because you …you have something to hold afterwards, but my arms are empty. Why are my arms empty? What did I do wrong?'

'The baby came before its time.'

'But I don't understand. What happened? I felt so well…'

'Now, don't distress yourself. It's all over. You're young. When you've recovered, there'll be others when you're well enough. Until then Nurse is taking orders from Dora,' he said, bravely endeavouring to calm the frayed edges of her nerves.

She turned her head away wearily, as if to escape the sound of his words. His disappointment was unmistakable. It was in his voice, in those dark eyes and the stoop of his shoulders. Everything he suffered, she suffered too. She felt the great sorrowing beat of his heart inside her own breast, the pain in his head drumming into hers. Her inner turmoil, from which she could find no respite, increased, and her weeping filled the room and became a source of agony to him. Sometimes there was nothing to hear at all as she held her breath, and then her sobs forced their release, pouring forth her anguish.

'Don't take on so. You'll only make yourself ill.'

His hand went out to touch her, but she knocked it away. Taking it as a sign of rejection, his face hardened. After that one unguarded moment, his whole being was clenched in silence. An expression came into his eyes that was like a shutter between them.

Her sobbing gradually eased and she lay quiet again, staring fixedly at the ceiling, her face wet and her eyes all puffy and stinging. She turned them to where he was sitting with his head in his hands, clutching at his thick dark hair. She attempted to say something, but the words stuck in her dry throat.

Once downstairs, Luke poured himself a stiff drink and swallowed it back in one gulp. He picked up the poker and rammed it into the fire, scattering a shower of clear bright sparks, all the time cursing silently to himself that still he did not have the son he had hoped for. To give birth to an heir was the major service of a wife. He pulled at the cord for the maid. The voice that was usually so coolly modulated raged with intolerable pain. 'What the hell am I paying you for? Get this damn fire banked up at once.'

The poor maid bobbed a curtsy. 'Y..yes, Sir.' The corners of her mouth quivered slightly as she fell to her knees and placed several pieces of coal from the shuttle into the flames.

'Now ...get the hell out and leave me alone,' he snarled. A weariness and faint despair overcame him.

Once the door was closed, he sunk down in a chair, bent forward and put his elbows on his knees and buried his head in his hands. Yet again fate had dealt him a cruel blow.

FOURTEEN

The first time Jessica brought her feet over the side of the bed, her body felt so light; it seemed as though she was about to float away. She ordered the maid to draw a warm bath, after which she had a light lunch brought up to her room. Then she sat by the window till sunset, sometimes attempting to read, at other times watching every movement outside without much purpose. The sun went down almost blood red that night and a livid cloud received its rays in the east. Up against the dark background the only shapes visible from the window were the trees that rose distinct and lustrous, their peaks bristling with rays.

Luke looked in to see her after supper and found her still sitting by the window, her eyes fixed intently on something in the darkness outside. Thick shadows clung to the ceiling like hovering night birds, eliminating the corners and all furniture not within the light from the fire's radius, obscuring detail and giving the room a measure of gloomy dignity.

'Why are you sitting there in the dark?'

'I like to watch the sunset. Anyway, there's light enough from the fire.'

He dutifully kissed her on the cheek. 'I thought the doctor had forbidden you to move? Mrs Osborne had no right to get you out of bed.'

Jessica jumped to Dora's defense, confessing it had been her own idea - that she felt much better. As Luke drew up a chair beside her, she turned and held his gaze with dull eyes. She could not bear to speak of the child she had lost and dreaded the thought of him bringing it up.

'I've bought you a book.'

'How kind. Thank you,' she said automatically, her sullen expression not changing.

'It's Persuasion. One of Jane Austen's novels.'

'I thought you didn't approve of me reading romantic novels? You said they were full of nonsense.'

'Well, I thought there no harm in it if it helps cheer you up,' he answered matter-of-factly. He sat in silence for a few minutes. 'Jessica, there is something I must tell you. It's bad news, I'm afraid.'

'What is it? What's happened?' She met his dark eyes and instantly knew, as though her instincts, the warning sense that lies buried deep beneath all her other senses, was telling her that some other devastation was to come. 'It's Alice, isn't it?'

Dear sweet-tempered Alice, shy at first in the new post to which she had been promoted, but so eager to please. Alice, who made her forget her own loneliness when Luke was constantly away.

'I knew it! I knew something was wrong. Has she taken poorly?'

'I fear it's much worse than that. Now, I don't want you to get upset.'

'What an earth has happened? Tell me!'

She let out a wordless cry of grief, stifled almost to silence before it began, as he told her without a flicker of emotion on his face that Alice had been found in the woods, less than half a mile away from the house, brutally murdered by persons unknown. His voice seemed to hack the air and leave it jagged.

It was like being bereaved twice, just as though a

knife was being thrust into a newly savaged laceration, in a wound which could barely stand the agony of the first. There was a moment of stunned shock, and then, when realisation had come, of tearing, anguished grief. She began to weep, great, long shuddering cries of grief and pain, and when he knelt at her feet to take her in his arms, she clung to him.

There would come a day when horror, stark and terrible, hideous and ghoulish, to add its tortures to the load of misery she now carried.

PART TWO

FIFTEEN

Dan Greenward laid down his pen and glanced at the clock on the mantel. He had managed to work undisrupted for almost three hours and felt due for a break. He had been busy on the ledgers, accounting for all financial transactions and labour costs of the mines for the regular labour force, and salaries paid out on separate time sheets for contracted or temporary labour, taking stock and drawing up his orders for fresh supplies. Pleased with himself, he sat back in the great leather chair, looking round the office in quiet contemplation.

It was certainly a change from the old days. It had been newly built, with twice the room he used to have. There were blinds at the windows, comfortable chairs, a great leather-topped desk, several shelves and even a small drinks cabinet. A few scattered rugs covered the floor, a mirror and a couple of watercolours of the countryside decorated the walls, and a cheerful fire burnt in the grate. Home from home! It was all Clara's doing ... this and the lift in life she had given him. What was it she had said? "Success is a bright sun that obscures and makes ridiculously unimportant all those little shadowy flecks of failure."

Life was certainly at its best. There was a new strength about him that seemed to come from his very core. He had long pushed away the thoughts of old age and had never felt better or more vigorous, never so happy as he felt now. And he had mellowed in the last months, his attitude now more carefree, patient and tolerant toward his fellow men, particularly towards his son, Joe. They were closer than they had ever been before, with a greater understanding of each other, both having suffered similar emotional traumas - the death of their wives. Joe's wife, Kitty, drowned in the swollen, raging river during a storm. The bags of sovereigns she had stolen from old man Thornton, which she carried in the pockets of her skirts, dragging and anchoring her down. A terrible shock to them all.

His own wife, Sara, had faded away before his very eyes after the death of their two younger sons in a mining accident. She lost the will to live. But finding out that she had had an affair, his grief for her loss had come abruptly to an end. Meeting and marrying Clara had been the best thing to happen to him. A new lease of life: a second chance.

He supported his son in whatever he wanted to do, and, in turn, Joe listened to his ideas and problems to do with the mines, often giving valuable advice. He sometimes felt guilty that he should be so happy when Joe was still alone, without anyone to comfort him and share his life.

Dan sighed and stretched his limbs. "Ah, well, you can't arrange other people's lives,' he said aloud to himself.

On Sunday afternoons that often stretched into evenings, his house, Fells View, was a haven of good company, intelligent talk and good food. Today being his birthday - fifty-seventh - mind, he never felt it, Clara had arranged a gathering of family and friends, as a celebration, for four o'clock this afternoon. He had never been a particularly social animal himself, but his Clara greatly enjoyed the company.

She enjoyed teaching the little 'uns too. She was a woman remarkable for her piety and common sense, with very strong views on the importance of education, an admirable teacher, with a rock-like determination to educate all those who came under her wing. And she possessed an extraordinary patience that won the devotion of all the children. She insisted that they all wash their faces and particularly their hands before sitting down to their lessons, not wanting mucky fingerprints all over her priceless books. And the girls were made to wear clean white pinafores to hide their shabby dresses.

Both boys and girls were taught together: reading, writing and arithmetic were the main lessons. And the older girls, if interested, were taught to sew, knit and even to make lace. But first they were all taught to write their name. Clara worked to a regular timetable, teaching lessons from nine thirty until mid-day, stopping for lunch at one, and then from two to four there were more lessons. Saturday from nine thirty until eleven thirty they went over the lessons they had been taught during the week and were encouraged to read aloud. There were to be two weeks off at Christmas, one week at Easter and Whitsuntide.

All this for one penny a week, which was collected on a Monday morning, to be spent on more slates and books, chalks and pencils, and the necessary materials needed for sewing, knitting and lace making.

Dan rose to his feet and pulled on his smart tweed jacket, glancing at himself in the mirror, smoothing his mop of thick silvery hair back from his forehead. It had been cut short, but still it wouldn't lie down. Well, at least he had a full head, even if it did have a mind of its own. He turned his face this way and that, examining his reflection in the mirror.

His gaze was steady and friendly, his figure quite youthful, and he was dressed clean and smart, hair well groomed and even his nails manicured. Clara saw to all that, the polishing of his rough edges, and he indulged her. But then, where would he be without her? He smiled at his image in the mirror. Not bad for fifty-seven, he complimented himself. Growing old was no more than a bad habit which a busy person such as himself had no time to form. He had never been happier in his life, as in these last six months since Clara had become his wife.

The wedding had been a very quiet affair, setting the tongues wagging one to the dozen. But they hadn't cared. She loved him and he absolutely doted on her. They were so compatible, both mentally and physically. He had found her to be a charmer whose languid, highbred manner concealed a most sensuous nature. When she loved it was with overwhelming solemnity. Whenever he came to her in the dark privacy of their great double bed, she made no protest: her arms always opened wide. He was blessed with the most wonderful woman who knew how to awaken the tenderness in a man, raising him out of that self-centred state of mind in which he had wallowed unhappily for so many years.

The party was well on the way when he arrived home. He moved about the room, greeting the familiar faces, but there was no place more delightful than your own fireside and as soon as it was polite to do so that was where he sat, in his usual place near the fire, in the chair, his hands caressing where John's busy hands had once grasped it. It was as much a living thing to him as the tree it had come from. Whenever he settled in it, the chair would impart something of the old life of the tree into him. There was a restfulness about it that invited both meditation and recuperation.

Fells View had somewhat changed since Clarinda Faye Gaskell had become the new mistress, the new Mrs Greenward. Cosy and friendly was the house's atmosphere since she had moved in and taken charge. Dan had made the mistake of giving her a free hand, to do as she pleased regarding the house. It had been freshly decorated throughout, and apart from the kitchen, each and every room had been carpeted. Every piece of dowdy old-fashioned furniture discarded and replaced with new and several pieces of her own from the cottage.

There were new good quality curtains at all the windows, paintings and gilt-edged mirrors on the walls, new bed linen for each of the beds, and a variety of cheerful cushions for the sofas. Pieces of lace were scattered about the parlour, now called "the sitting-room", at Clara's request. It was a complete transformation. The amount of money that had been spent by his new wife, who had impeccable taste, absolutely astounded him, and yet he did not begrudge her the indulgence. Money was made to be spent he told himself. Whatever made his Clara happy, made him happy. He would continue to earn money for as long as his health and strength held out.

He glanced up at Joe. 'Have you noticed how Megan's come out from her shell since she's been attending lessons?'

'Yes, an' I'm astonished how her personality's changed. She loves her lessons. I can hardly tear her away from her Aunt Clara, when they're over,' Joe answered.

'Well, that's a good thing, isn't it?' Dan said, smiling up at him. 'You know she's in safe hands here.'

'I suppose so, but it's getting I hardly see her. If she's not here she's trailing round after young Miles. She follows him round like a shadow, but the lad doesn't seem t'mind.'

'That's life, I'm afraid. They grow up an' leave anyway, so you best get used t'it.'

'That's a long way off yet.'

Dan lit his pipe, shook the match and flicked it on the hearth.

Joe bent to retrieve it and threw it in the fire. 'Those matches stink o' sulphur,' he complained.

'They're more convenient than the tinder-box.'

'They may be, but you're likely t'burn the upholstery, flicking them about like that. You'll have Clara after you.'

Dan shrugged. 'She's too preoccupied t'notice what I'm up to.'

'You have t'admit, she knows how t'look after people. Gives nothing but her best.'

'Yes, she's in her glory. She's afraid o' less than

perfection,' Dan said proudly.

They watched Clara moving around the room, offering assorted sandwiches and plates of her home-made cakes and biscuits. Dan noticed there was something different about her, a kind of soft radiance that had not been there before.

Millie caught his attention as she came into the room, carrying a tray laden with tea for the adults and milk for the children present. She was the eldest of Eric Master's girls, the pump-man at Roughton, who was now a widower. Clara had invited him along, thinking it would be nice for him to be with his girls, but he stood alone, looking awkward and quite out of place in a room which would be considered luxurious by a working man's standards. At seventeen, Millie had grown into a fine young woman, and had recently become engaged to one of the labourers on the Hawthorne Estate.

She, and her younger sister, Edna, now fourteen, had been persuaded to return to work at Fells View and had settled in nicely. Dan followed Eric Master's gaze to April Ramsey and wondered what the man was thinking, what was going through his mind. April had put a bit of meat on her bones since taking the position as housekeeper at Chapel House Farm, looking more like her old self, and was as happy as could be expected without her man.

A woman hired to assist in the farmhouse itself was considered lucky by some. But was she? In addition to the usual chores of lighting fires, cleaning the house and preparing meals, she had, before breakfast, to skim the milk and pour it into copper pans to heat over the fire, for the cowman to feed the calves. After breakfast, utensils, milk pans and buckets had to be cleaned and the dairy swilled.

April Ramsey drove herself hard. The Greenwards had been good to her and her little ones, in their time of need. So full of gratitude was she, she worked herself to the bone. When dinner was over, the afternoons brought their own particular jobs - the churning and making of butter, cleaning the brass, copper and silver whenever it needed doing, bringing in the fuel for the fires, and looking after the poultry. In addition to these chores, at the busiest season of the year, she even helped in the fields. But April never complained. How could she? Joe had brought her along, with two of her youngest, little Violet and Poppy, leaving Daisy at the farmhouse in the capable hands of Liam O'Malley. She offered to help by handing out the drinks, and when she came to Eric Masters he suddenly came to life and kept her talking.

Parson Drew Appleby and his wife, Lydia, stood talking to Brooke and Brent, the Henly twins. The twins had returned from the Continent just a little more than a year ago, to settle here in Cumbria, after the sudden death of their father, Jonathan Henly, who had never really got over the shock of his young wife deserting him. He died of a heart attack shortly after she had left. The twins had inherited the family home, or at least Brent Henly had, being the only surviving son. Clara had met Brooke through her lace making and they had become good friends. Neither twin had married and seemed to accompany each other every-where. Jeannie Miller stood next to them, looking lost, her eyes wondering over to Dan, meeting his across the room. She smiled, but the smile didn't reach her eyes.

'Joe, do your ole father a favour, will you?'

'Anything! What is it?'

'Rescue Jeannie. The poor lass looks lost. I don't think she'll ever get over losing all the men in her life. Try t'cheer her up, will you?'

'I'm hardly the best o' company myself.'

'Missing ole man Thornton, are you?'

'I am. I'd become fond o' the ole fellow. Still, he went peacefully in his sleep. I never dreamt he'd leave the lot t'me.'

'Well, he obviously thought a lot o' you. Go cheer up Jeannie, will you?'

'I'll give it my best shot.'

'I know you will, Son.'

Ed Morley was present. As Deputy he had taken a great deal of work off Dan's shoulders over the last year or so, which he was more than glad to bid adieu, and would one day take the reins when Dan retired. And Frank Maidment, as overman at Roughton, had taken on a whole realm of duties too, making life much easier.

Ed had also become a great favourite with the children, and had Joe's daughter, Megan, balanced on one knee and little Poppy Ramsey on the other, but his watchful eyes were on Clara. He was completely entranced with the dazzling woman, who floated gracefully about the room waiting on her guests. She held herself with such dignity, a true lady ...he thought, his eyes boldly admiring her.

Clara felt his eyes upon her and with the rustle of silk, crossed the room to where he sat. 'I hope you are going to eat a few of these, Mr Morley, or Daniel will be eating them all next week.'

Ed Morley focused on the smooth hand she placed gently on Megan's shoulder. Next to the plain gold band was a ring set to form a flower of radiant loveliness, a glow with a delicate hue of colour - six glittering sapphires accenting the circle of petals, with a glorious larger single sapphire set in the very centre. It must have cost a fortune.

'Down you get, children. Leave Mr Morley in peace now,' Clara said softly, smiling all the time. The two little girls obediently climbed down and wandered off to play together. 'I've noticed you have a way with children, Mr Morley.'

'I like children, Mrs Greenward. I regret not having a family o' my own, but it's too late now. I'm getting ole.'

'A man is not old until his regrets take the place of dreams, Mr Morley.'

He looked up at her. Her disposition was sweet and her manners excellent. 'I'll have t'remember that. An' please call me Edward.'

'As you wish.' She held the plate of sandwiches out to him. 'Do help yourself, Edward,' she said in a voice so different to the true dales women. 'And do call me Clara. I think you will agree we know each other well enough by now.'

Ed smiled broadly at her. 'Thank you kindly, Clara.' He lowered his voice to just a whisper. 'Do you know, if I was fortunate enough t'have a woman like your good self, I wouldn't want t'let her out o' my sight, not for a single minute. The very sight o' you is enough t'make a man happy just t'be alive.'

Clara was secretly flattered. 'Edward Morley, are you deliberately flirting with me?'

'Oh, I didn't mean t'offend,' Ed said quickly, his face colouring up.

She touched him gently on the shoulder, her face

radiant. 'I'm not offended in the least.'

'Married life obviously suits you. You're absolutely blooming,' he dared say, her friendliness making him bold.

'Why, thank you, Edward. A woman of my age could only be dazzled with such compliments. Especially from a handsome man such as yourself.'

He looked embarrassed then. 'I'd hardly say I was handsome.'

'Oh, but you are, I assure you,' she said softly. 'Tell me, why have you never married?'

'Life's been too busy for romance.'

'Nonsense. You just haven't met the right woman, that's all.'

'I have, but all too late.'

'It's never too late, Edward,' Clara said smoothly, choosing to ignore the flirtatious remark. 'Love can come at any age.'

'I realise that. The problem is, the woman I want is unfortunately out o' reach.' He popped a tiny, perfect sandwich into his mouth, washing it down with a mouthful of tea.

'Then you must find another before it is too late,' she said quickly.

'What chance have I o' meeting someone now? I don't go anywhere.'

'But there's no need. Dan and I met outside the church in Caldbeck. We just happened to bump into each other and it developed from there. Now, low and behold, I belong to him.' She tilted her head and smiled charmingly. 'So you see, there's no need for you to go looking. Why, in this very room alone, here today, there are unmarried women, just longing for a man such as yourself to sweep them off their feet.'

Ed looked at her with amusement.

'Now, don't you look at me like that, Edward Morley. I'm serious. Really I am. What about Miss Henly?' she suggested.

Ed raised his eyebrows and grimaced. 'Very nice, but out o' my league, wouldn't you say?'

'Miss Miller then? Or perhaps she is a bit too young for you?'

'I've known Jeannie Miller since she was a little 'un. I used t'bounce her on my knee.'

'Widow Ramsey? April is a delightful woman.'

'Too late! I've heard her head's been turned by the Irishman.'

'The one who works for Joseph?'

'That's the one! O'Malley, I think his name is.'

Clara beamed. 'Really? That's wonderful news.'

'Nothing's for certain mind, so keep it under your bonnet.'

'I will. But there, don't you see they had not far to look? You'll find someone. I'm sure,' she said with certainty.

'It's all a bit o' a risk though. What if we don't suit?'

'Without risk, there's no gain.'

'I suppose you're right, but it's one risk I'm not willing t'take. I'd sooner stay as I am.'

He gulped down the rest of the tea, and then stood up, saying he was ready to leave.

'Oh, must you go so soon? I do enjoy a good chat. The children's lessons keep me so busy these days, I rarely have time to keep up with the news.'

She held out a hand to him and he took it in his, holding onto it a little longer than was decently necessary.

Dan sat tapping the end of his fingers together, watching them from across the room. Each time he saw Ed Morley's good looks and youthful confidence it made him feel old, and feeling threatened by the younger man, jealousy reared its ugly head for the first time in his life. He experienced a deep burning resentment. Ridiculous to feel this way ...he told himself. Ed Morley is a decent sort, honest and loyal. He had gained everyone's admiration and complete acceptance, including his own. He didn't know what he'd do without him. Why, I would trust him with my life. And as for my Clara, well, she's no less than perfect - an angel.

'I don't believe in over-staying my welcome,' Ed said quietly, his eyes soft as he studied Clara's lovely face.

'You must come again. To supper, perhaps,' she offered politely.

'You certainly know how t'look after a person, Clara,' he said quietly, glancing across the room at Dan, and noticing his eyes on them dropped her soft warm hand quite suddenly. 'Thank you for the offer. I do appreciate it, really I do, but I think you'll understand if I don't accept. I can see by the look on Dan's face he's missing your attention an' would prefer t'have you t'himself. I can't say I blame him. I'll just say my good-byes an' will be on my way.'

Just inside of an hour the rest of the guests were gone, everything had been cleared away by the two girls, Millie & Edna, who had now gone to their home along with their father, leaving Dan and Clara alone once more.

'I was telling Edward how we met, about our short courtship. It's a shame he couldn't stay longer. If I wasn't already spoken for, I could quite easily have my head turned by such a nice man as him,' Clara said, only speaking teasingly.

Dan felt alarmed. His whole world revolved around her now. 'Oh, an' just how long have you been on first name terms?' he asked abruptly.

'Only since today. Why? Do you object?' She looked at his long face. 'Daniel, my dear, why the doldrums? Today of all days?'

'I'll thank you not t'discuss our personal affairs with strangers.'

'Edward is hardly a stranger. And I was only telling him how we met.'

'That's private, between you an' me.'

She shrugged. 'But I only mentioned it casually. He happened to say how blooming I looked. How married life suited me.'

'He has no damn right t'flirt with another man's wife,' Dan retorted sharply.

'I would hardly call it flirting. He was merely paying me a compliment, which I in turn thanked him for. After all, a woman of my age needs all the compliments she can get.'

'Don't I pay you enough compliments?'

'Really, Daniel, I don't know what's got into you. If you're going to make a fuss every time I have a conversation with another man, I will be afraid to open my mouth to one in future. It's really too much.'

Under her disapproving gaze, he took a grip of his mind and of his tongue. He might have told her of his feelings, of his fears, but realizing he was the worse for the amount of brandy he had consumed, apprehension rendered him wordless. Often the difference between a successful marriage and a mediocre one consists of leaving some things unsaid. In his opinion it was better to keep your mouth shut and be thought a fool than to open it and prove it.

'Daniel, what is it?' Clara asked, with genuine concern.

'Nothing. I'm sorry.'

'Tell me what's really troubling you.'

'I suppose I just felt left out, that's all,' he said gloomily.

'Goodness, you've no need to feel that way. I always have you in mind, wherever I am, whatever I may be doing.'

His face brightened. 'You have?'

'But of course! You're everything to me,' she assured him.

'An' you are t'me, my lovely lass. More than you'll ever know.' He pulled her to him. 'Come here. I need t'be held.'

'We all do at times,' she said softly, resting her head against his broad chest.

'You're the best thing that ever happened t'me. Before you came int'my life each day resembled the other. But then I've told you that often enough, haven't I?' he whispered against her hair. 'Deciding t'marry you is one o' the few decisions I'll never regret. I do love you, Clara.'

'And I love you, you old silly,' she said fondly. 'Now, let's sit down, relax a while before we go to our bed. I'm suddenly feeling very tired.'

They sat on the sofa, side by side. He took her hand in his. 'I didn't really know what love was before I met you.'

'But surely you loved your wife in the beginning?'

'I thought I did. I was certainly ready t'marry an'

was content in a way, but then things changed between us. I couldn't find a trace o' who I'd started out loving. We just drifted apart. It was never quite right between us. We were never really suited I suppose. The physical side o' things I mean, not like it is with us. It was more o' a habit with her, just an act o' relief.'

Clara squeezed his hand. 'Well, that's all in the past now and best forgotten.'

'You're right. Do you know, when I looked around the room t'day, there were very few faces from the past, faces I really know.'

'That's nonsense! Joseph was here, and Megan. Most all of the others I invited were friends of yours, apart from Brooke and her brother, Brent.'

'They're a strange twosome, I must say.'

'Brooke Henly is a very dear friend of mine. She has been a great help to me in the past.'

'I realise that, but why does that brother o' hers accompany her everywhere?'

Clara shrugged. 'Perhaps he feels it his duty to chaperon her? After all, she is an unmarried woman.'

'An' likely t'stay that way if he doesn't allow her t'break free. She reminds me of Jonathan Henley's young wife. Henley was never the same after she left him.'

'Didn't she run off with the butler? Such a sad affair,' Clara said morosely.

'What did you expect? She was young enough t'be his daughter.'

'Oh, well, let's forget about them. It's you I'm worried about.'

'I don't want you worrying. That's the last thing I want,' he told her.

'I think perhaps you were more disappointed than you let on, over Jessica not being able to come.'

'I did miss her presence,' Dan said thoughtfully. 'Poor lass. What with the loss o' the child an' then the shocking news o' her maid ...well, you can wonder the lass is ailing.'

'Jessica's young. She can have another child, but as for that poor young girl ...well, and the murderer still running loose! Who could have done such a thing?'

'Who indeed! Whoever it was, will be long gone by now. Likely one o' those travellers passing through. My God, there's some wicked people in this world. There were rumours of Ned Cartwright being the culprit, but I have my doubts. Whatever else Cartwright was, I can't see him murdering an innocent lass. No one has set eyes on him. He seems t'have disappeared from the face of the earth. Not that anyone misses him. He was hardly the most popular overman.'

'I was thinking, Daniel, why don't you drive over and visit Jessica tomorrow? It will help cheer you both up.'

'I've too much t'do t'morrow.'

'Oh, the meetings. Of course. I'd forgotten.'

'Do you know, sometimes I wonder what I'm doing mixing with all the big wigs, Sheridan's lot: Pendle, Bilton, Charlton...'

'Edward Charlton? He supplies the machinery for the mines, doesn't he?'

'That's right. You met him once.'

'Yes. And Pendle, the banker. Did you say he owns the wool mill now?'

'That's right.'

Having heard so much, Clara wanted to hear more. 'But what will happen to poor Mr Roebling?'

'As far as I know, he's t'be kept on as manager. He's a good sort. Mind, he must be due for retirement before long.'

'That's more than I can say for his son. Has anyone heard anything more of him?'

Dan shook his head. 'All I know is he's got himself lost in London. It's just as well. He's a bad lot, that lad. If you'd seen the sight o' those poor little lasses in that cottage. It brought tears t'my eyes, I can tell you. An' Ed wasn't a lot better.'

Clara shuddered. 'Oh, I can hardly bear thinking about it.'

'There would've been murder done that day if we had come across George Roebling. No doubt he'll be back. A bad penny always turns up.'

'At least those girls are in good homes now. If it wasn't for you and Mr Morley, it would still be going on.'

'Ah, well, you can only do your best. It seems you just solve one problem then there's another. You know Ralph Cullan's moved on?'

'So you mentioned.'

'Well, we've a new manager at the timber company now. That's causing a few headaches, I can tell you.'

'For Luke?'

'Huh! For me! Who else! Sheridan's never around when you need him. No wonder my Jessie gets so down, with her husband away goodness knows where, from one week t'the next. All these men with their big names an' connections. They all have plenty o' money, that's for sure.'

'But you have beauty, my dear,' Clara said kindly.

Dan met her gaze. 'That's a funny thing t'say o' a man.'

'But it's true. You see things and are kind to people, giving them so much more than you take. You have compassion and understanding. That's what I admire most about you.'

'That's a grand thing t'say.'

'I only speak the truth.' She stifled a yawn. 'Oh, my goodness, excuse me. I'm so tired.'

'Then come t'bed, my love.'

They got to their feet both at the same time, and she stood by his side, slipping an arm through his, but he pulled her to him, possessively, holding her tightly in his strong arms, burying his face in her hair that smelt of fresh lavender. They stayed that way for several minutes, simply holding each other close, their hearts and bodies blending into one.

'A warm fire when it's freezing, good food in my stomach when I'm hungry ... an' the most important thing o' all, the love o' a good woman. What more could a man want?' But climbing the stairs robbed him of his breath. 'I'm growing ole.'

'Nonsense. You're only as old as you feel.'

'Funny, that's just what I used t'tell my ole friend, Samuel Miller.' Dan said breathlessly. 'An' look what happened t'him. He was younger than me when he died.' He sighed heavily. 'The cemetery's full o' people younger than me. Two of my sons even. Who would've thought I'd outlive my children?'

'Daniel, dearest, what's making you so morbid? No one ever hurt their eyesight by looking on the bright side of things.'

'I'm sorry; I'm being a perfect ass.'

'Nobody's perfect,' she teased, bringing a shadow of a smile to his lips. 'That's more like it. You have such a wicked smile.'

'It's because you bring out the beast in me. There might be snow on the roof, but there's still fire in the furnace.'

'I'm glad to hear it. And now you're in a better frame of mind, I have something special to tell you, something that will change your way of thinking, I guarantee.'

'What is it?'

'A surprise. I've been saving it especially for your birthday.'

'What kind o' surprise? A nice surprise, I hope. There's nothing like good news t'patch up a lover's quarrel.'

'That was hardly a quarrel, Daniel.'

'Tell me then! What is it?'

'Just you wait and see.'

SIXTEEN

Feeling sensitive to pressure, Clara had instantly discarded her corset and all clothes with any definite bands or tight fastenings. She had gone through the months of pregnancy with no handicap other than the expected morning sickness during those early weeks, which was looked upon as perfectly normal and to be endured as a matter of course, although why this nauseating experience should accompany what to her were the most rapturous months of her entire life - was a mystery. There is no joy or pride greater than that of a woman who is bearing the child, carrying the sacred burden, of the man she adored.

Dan Greenward was one happy man. As winter's snow gave way to relentless rain, he could see not a cloud on his horizon. The knell of their joy had struck. The disturbance to their lovemaking, which had become less frequent since Clara had told him the wonderful news of their child, was in no sense a danger to the unruffled surface of their happiness, but its crown and completion.

Love is fed not by what it takes, but by what it gives, she had a habit of saying. He was beside himself with utter joy. The shock of pleased wonder never left him. He would sit in his chair in the evenings, puffing away at his pipe with the newspaper on his lap, whilst his Clara, his love, busied herself making lace antimacassars to protect the back and the arms of the upholstered chairs, but never so busy to catch each other's eye and smile contentedly. She was an exceptional woman, was his Clara; a tender, loving wife who found some means of giving him the physical relief that his nature needed, by careful and gentle caressing.

In the hearts of all who have known true love lies the realisation of the sacredness that is theirs when they are in the very act of creation, giving the most intense physical pleasure the body can experience, a mutual not selfish pleasure that draws out an unspeakable tenderness and understanding in both partakers. The exquisite, unselfish tenderness that is aroused in a man by the means of mental and spiritual harmony with a wife who understands his needs was one of the loveliest things in their marriage.

Her aim was to satisfy his needs, and his first need was to make her pant with sheer pleasure, for relief to take place without any physical connection. It was sufficient for him to be near her, to lie side by side, holding her in his arms, embracing her and with unflagging patient tenderness caressing the little crest which lies interiorly between the inner lips until it is intensely roused, transmitting this stimulus to every nerve in her body - always bringing them both in turn to a height of sheer bliss.

SEVENTEEN

Luke stood at the reception desk of the Londonderry Hotel in Park Lane. 'I've booked you a suite, Mr Sheridan. Suite twenty-two, Sir. If you would care to sign the register, the porter will take up your luggage. Oh …and there's a message from Madame Duprez, Sir, to say she will be a little late.'

Amel came sweeping in to the room looking absolutely stunning in an elegant pelisse of green cloth trimmed with ermine tails, over a simple ivory gown. In contrast to the gown, the pelisse, and a turban fashioned from a silk scarf woven in multiple colours, she wore, were exotic and indicated wealth. A true tribute to the skills of the dressmaker.

He welcomed her with a smile of real pleasure, encircling her with his arms and pressing his lips to hers. She stirred a passion in him he'd never known before - that sensual tie that binds a man to a woman.

Releasing her, he stepped back. 'Let me look at you, my darling.' His dark eyes moved over her appreciatively. 'I must say you look absolutely stunning.'

'Merci, Mon amour.'

He guided her further into the room with its ostentatious gilding and displays of antique furniture, and cut glass lustre's hung with faceted beads and pendants that cast a warm, welcoming glow. 'Where have you been? I arrived well over an hour ago.'

'I had an appointment with the doctor.'

'Are you unwell?'

'Non! Just women's problems. Nothing to be concerned about.' She had been to have the usual periodic genital examination, but of course, it was not something she could admit to anyone.

'I cannot say I'm anything but relieved to be back. It has been so depressing at home, what with one thing and another.'

Standing in front of the dressing table mirror, Amel removed the turban from her head and placed it down on a chair, then turned to face him as she patted a few stray golden hairs into place. 'You've been gone so long. I suppose I should be flattered that you did at least bother to write, although it was all doom and gloom. I was truly sorry to hear of your sad loss.'

'Not only was it a terrible shock, but a great disappointment.'

'I've no doubt there will be others.' She started to unbutton the pelisse.

'Here, let me help you with that.'

'I take it your wife has recovered?'

'Not fully, but she's in good hands.'

He took the pelisse from her and carefully hung it on the back of a chair, then stooped to kiss her on the side of the neck, breathing in the fragrance of her.

Amel sighed. 'Ah, Monsieur, you haven't stopped caring for me?'

'How could I?'

'You didn't wonder if I've fallen in love with someone while you were away?' she questioned, smoothing her gown over slender hips.

'Have you?' he enquired with a lop-sided smile.

'Non! I'm not in love.'

'I hope you admire my self-restraint?'

'Your self-restraint?'

'By not asking awkward questions. I must say I've been tormented by what you might get up to in my absence, but was determined not to ask ...and won't.'

'I must say, Monsieur, I don't think being jealous is quite you.'

'That's past history. Over and forgotten. I'll be on my best behaviour in future. I give you my word.'

'That suits me fine,' she said with relief. Although he was sometimes intolerable, still it was impossible to do without him. She settled in one of the deep soft chairs close to the fire. 'I didn't realise just how I would miss your company.'

'Well, I'm here now.'

'Aren't you going to offer me a glass of wine?'

Luke's dark eyes turned towards the enormous canopied bed. 'I had something else in mind, but if you prefer...'

'Just one glass, perhaps,' Amel interrupted.

Luke gave an exaggerated sigh and crossed to the drinks cabinet, where he selected a bottle of chardonnay and popped the cork. He held up a stemmed crystal glass for inspection, then another to assure they were perfectly clean; he filled them, placing a full glass in Amel's outstretched hand.

He lifted his glass in a toast. 'Good health.'

'Bon la santé,' Amel repeated, sipping the rich liquid slowly, savouring it. 'Mon amour...'

'Yes, my darling.'

'I've been thinking, I might purchase a house here in London. One I can entertain in. London society offers more prestige and entertainment than the provinces. What do you think?'

He crossed to where she sat and bent to kiss her lightly on the cheek. 'Some day ...perhaps.'

'London is growing. There is so much to do here, so much to see.'

He could see her point. It was a thought worth considering. But right now, at this moment in time, he had other things on his mind. They had wasted enough time. He emptied his glass, then took hers from her and placed them both on the small table by the side of the chair, and, taking both her hands in his raised her gently to her feet and enfolded her in his arms, savouring the melting, acquiescent way she cradled close to him.

'Come now, no more talk of houses and politics.'

'But Luke...'

'I take your point, but here in this room pleasure comes before business.'

She hid her annoyance. This was no mewling school boy she could lead about on a chain and expect him to obey her every whim. But she wouldn't be beaten. She tried another ploy.

'It would be so much more convenient when we want to be together. We would have much more privacy,' she whispered close to his chest, using the "we" as her bait.

But Luke did not take the bait. He had dreamt of this moment. No other was as lovely, as alluring as she. Bending his head, he covered her mouth with his own, silencing her, devouring her lips, making up for the time they had been apart.

EIGHTEEN

The weeks passed and soon the Spirit of Spring touched the whole of the countryside. The rustle of her robes could be heard in the woods and fields, her whispers running through the trees and hedgerows, calling to the hedgehogs and badgers that caught the sound from deep in their winter dens. When the evening shadows fell they scrambled out into the open and went about their business hurriedly and noiselessly, hunting through the woods.

The earth stirred from her sleep, ready to awake, bringing sound and movement to the muted land. In the fields, through dew-drenched grass rabbits scampered, to leave dark trails behind. There was sighing in the branches of the trees and the chuckling song of running water. A melancholy whistle fluted eerily in the air. A curlew was astir. Its silver clear call aroused the pewit host, and upon a hawthorn breaking into leaf a blackbird with an orange bill sang delectably.

Then all the birds were moved to chorus in an anthem to a day as yet unborn, though pulsing from the womb of night. A lark climbed in the blueness and carolled as it rose. Blackbirds sang, thrushes too, while finches and other small birds twittered joyfully. From tree and hedge, from field and river bank, the tide of song swelled as the shadows paled and the sky grew light, until at last the sun's rim peeped shyly above the fells. Gradually, the songsters ceased their carolling. They ran and probed and pecked, going about the task of finding food.

Having previously been living in a state of suspended feeling, Jessica now lived in a mood of fragile calmness, relieved of that wayward heaviness of the past several weeks that had dragged upon leaden feet and quenched the vitality of youth in her without substituting the philosophy of mature years.

Outside, in the bluest of skies, the air was wonderfully fresh and laden with the fragrances of the morning; honeysuckle over the porch, wild roses in the hedgerows, and sweet-scented flowers laid out in beds in the neat garden. Gay gladioli, spikes of puce and white, and the red of yielding fuchsias. With mosses garnishing their fountains of bloom, and a patch of balm, the sweetest thyme, and green caressing films of parsley fern. All of which helped blank out morbid thoughts over the child she had sadly lost, and the brutal murder of poor, sweet Alice, who had been no more than a child herself - just sixteen - and was now laid to rest alongside her mother. She felt a tear form in the lashes on her lower lid, and lifted her hand to dash it away. She must not cry again. The time for crying was past.

Yet in the hushed and mystic glamour of those springtide mornings alien thoughts and emotions enmeshed her senses and she saw life and its creatures as something beautiful and sweet. She saw beauty in all things of everyday life … the wonderful diversity of birds, green swelling hills and wide woodlands, and acre upon acre of smooth rich pastures. The bilberry with its hanging bell-shaped blooms, the sharp prickly stems of the bramble, the fox-glove with its shy drooping flowers, and the heathers leafy spikes of pink and white. Birches in their silver radiance, the sharply pointed junipers, the rowan with its clusters of white blossom, and the king of all deciduous trees - the magnificent towering oaks with their ripening acorns.

But the greatest attraction of all was the vast giant across the water. The gloriously breath-taking views of Skiddaw, empurpled with scree, rifted with ravines, and small crags sheering skyward aloof from the bulk of the magnificent mountain. Bands of green and brown and golden yellow, in purple streak and white, tree-fringed, with clumps of bramble and bush, it rises rock upon rock, slope upon slope, towering up and up to the heavens above - combining all into an idyllic picture that cheered and restored her spirits and the pain gradually began to fade.

She could not stay still. She felt so full of energy. There was a sudden decisiveness to her step, a glint of purpose in her eyes, as she followed the mood of the day, with the sun shining and a warm whispering breeze gently caressing her body. She took the mountain track, a path of glory, winding in bracken and wild tangles of heather. Hardy sheep grazing on the shelving hillside among the boulders, timorously rushed off at her approach, picking their way accurately over the debris.

The way twisted up through the boulders, climbing steeply and ruggedly, every few yards giving a fresh view, a new angle of vision to the fells and lake below. Thin green shadows of the ghyll where rivulets slip down to the lake through piles of emerald moss, the breeze lifting it along, to burst on boulders, throwing a shimmering spray into the air in a glorious medley of soaring water, to fall on shiny fangs of rock, giving a sparkle to both grass and fern alike.

She had climbed far enough. From there she could see forever.

Standing perfectly still, she watched the softening glow of the sun throw giant shadows across the fells. She could just make out folk toiling in the fields almost ready for the mowers; so far away they looked merely the size of dolls. The crops would not be sufficiently grown to be cut until late August or early September, when the weather was apt to be so unsettled that once the grass was mown almost superhuman efforts would be made to house it. A few hours lost could mean the farmer would watch his crop wasting away. This, the only harvest, was of great importance; unless it was well secured the supplies of winter forage for the flocks would be scant and much suffering caused.

The soft breeze ruffled the lake's surface, sending ripples frolicking across the water in play. Where were there waters more sparkling or meadows greener than these? But the supreme marvel, which had the power to wash life's troubles away, the power to heal, was the sky above, as the day melts away and evening gradually grows nearer and the drama of sunset ebbs on the rocky heights. A wafer of cloud draws away from the flaming west, curling and rolling its course, its brilliance fading to crimson, to soft purple, then out of all glory gone from the sight at the Zenith, streaks of nightglow appear in its stead, serving the magnificence of the moment. A sight that froze her into instant immobility. She was utterly mesmerised. But she could not risk being caught out. Miss your footing and it could be fatal. It took her a good hour to descend, picking her way with caution, for life was suddenly precious again.

Spring merged into summer waxed with hot and cloudless days, when nature itself puts on a lavish show; a favourite time for Jessica. Not that she really knew when she loved the fells the most. In the austere and majestic purity of the winter snows when the fell country is in its deepest sleep? Or the rich and golden glory of the autumn tints when falling leaves whispered her name? A time of real magic. Or as now, in the full-blown glories of summer when warm winds wave the green ocean of bracken and the sky is as blue as the sea. The finest weather under Heaven, when the shimmering heat turns the wheat to gold, when all was vibrant with life and the joy of living. When heights are tinged with pink and the glow of gold, when the musical cry of the curlew comes sweet and clear through the warm air, and the call of the cuckoo in some far-off place rings like a silver gong. Each season held for her its own charm, each morning, each noon and each and every night.

No sooner had she reached the breast of the fell than she saw a lark spring in the air. She watched it climb in the pale blue sky as though drawn by an invisible cord, just a tiny dot that spilled a stream of liquid sweetness through the unsullied air. But to those who truly love the fells there is no stronger attachment than the streams that leap and gurgle from crest to base, mere soft trickles in the heat of summer, white furies when the rains have swelled them, filling their rocky channels to the brim so it appears as though the mountains gush forth milk. Day after day, she roamed on those very slopes, amongst the heather and by the tumbling beck where the dipper nested, the grey wagtail also, an elusive sylph that flitted up and down the stream, a vision of grey and black and pure canary-yellow.

In the ghyll she stood idly by the water's edge watching a trout dart from the shallows in to the depths of the pool. One minute there, the next minute gone. It was the water that lured her constantly to the ghyll, where the beck rushes down, flinging itself from one ledge to the next, swirling and splashing against boulders in its path, rippling over gravelled, sun-flecked froth-fringed shallow pools. Here and there were sallow bushes on the bank, their pliant twigs tinged with red, and little hazels decked with dangling, pollen-laden catkins and tiny crimson flowerets, emerald mosses and ferns, and clumps of dwarf gorse with bright yellow blossoms on their prickly stems. She had loved this place from the very beginning.

Many a long hour in all weathers, did she spend on a ledge halfway up the bank where she could watch the water thrusting itself over the lip of the biggest fall of all, dropping in to a dark pool some thirty feet below. There was a companionship in the tumbling water which did much to support her in that time of great loneliness and anguish. Dry-eyed and hopeless, she sat on the mossy bank hour after hour and bleakly watched the tumbling beck, the dipping, sparkling, spray-drenched ferns, the chattering squirrels which, all unconscious of her presence, frisked and gambolled and searched for food above and about her.

Sometimes she scrambled up the bank, climbing the ledge and from that vantage point watched a buzzard soar and circle in the steel-blue sky until it became just a speck merging with other specks, dancing before her straining eyes. From time to time a pair of dippers came and went, charming little birds with perked-up tails and prominent white bib with a chestnut patch below.

Utterly regardless of her presence, they explored every nook and cranny, diving in to the pool, hunting for grubs and crustaceans, which made her wonder if they had made their nest behind the solid mass of tumbling water. They were so alert, so alive, true spirits of the fast flowing streams, flying through the curtain of spray flung up ceaselessly; a curtain that towards sunset shimmers with all the colours of a rainbow. It was fascinating to watch them dart through the spray; see them bobbing on the boulders in mid-stream, their sweet warble blending delightfully with the splashing gurgling of the beck. She never wearied of watching them.

If only Luke was here to share such privileges. He had been gone so long. Surely he would return soon? She wouldn't be able to just walk out of the house without saying where she was going then. She realised that what she had been doing was well beyond the bounds of propriety.

Mrs Osborne indulged her, although she didn't approve of her gallivanting about the countryside on her own, especially after what had happened to poor Alice. Reluctantly she had to face the fact that the delight of her stolen freedom must be surrendered if trouble was to be avoided.

Dora Osborne was as irritable as a nursemaid with a wayward child, suspicious too, for you never knew with this one what she was up to, gallivanting all over the place when the master was away, and by herself. Dora knew the master would not like it should he find out. And there she was off again on some bloody jaunt, the very air about her vibrating with the energy she created. Not telling her where she was going, merely tapping her nose and smiling in that daft way she had when she wanted to keep a person guessing. She was a rare one right enough and you could understand why the Master had taken to her and tried to keep her so hedged in. She had that quality few young women her age had, attracting both men and women alike to her like bees to honey.

There was no resisting the charm of her blushing youthfulness, her pleading voice, her ready confession of error, no withstanding her sweetness and simplicity. Her spirits seemed inexhaustible and the thought of danger never seemed to enter her head. She was Luke Sheridan's wife and people respected that, for he was not a man to be trifled with, not if you wanted to keep your health. He was a man with some influence as wealthy men usually have, but there was always one fool who might be reckless enough or mad enough to approach her, and if Jessica Sheridan came to any harm or was insulted, which was much the same as offering insult the master would want to know how Dora had let it happen. The responsibility she had been given was an onerous one.

NINETEEN

As London expanded the whole question of maintaining law and order become a matter of public concern. During 1829, the Duke of Wellington accomplished some useful changes, including assisting Sir Robert Peel in his efforts to reorganize the Metropolitan Police. Sir Charles Rowan & Richard Mayne were appointed as Justices of the Peace in charge of the Force, the first two Commissioners of Police at their headquarters at Scotland Yard.

The first Metropolitan Police patrols went on to the streets on 29th September 1829, three months after the Metropolitan Police Act, after much planning and other work performed by the first joint Commissioners. Peel, the chairman of the committee, stressed that the principal duty of the police was to be crime prevention rather than detection. The force was organised into divisions and planned like an army, with superintendents, inspectors, sergeants and constables. All were paid a wage and wore blue coats and top hats. At first, judges, magistrates, juries, soldiers and Londoners alike, to say nothing of criminals, detested them. But good discipline, a soft but vigilant approach, good humour and a decline in the crime rate, soon won them respect and support.

The directors of the soon to be completed Liverpool and Manchester Railway Company were unsure whether to use locomotives or stationary engines on their line. To help them reach a decision, it was decided to hold a competition in October where the winning locomotive would be awarded £500. The idea being that if the locomotive was good enough, it would be the one used on the new railway. Designers were invited to submit their locomotives to a test. The three judges of the competition were John Rastrick, Nicholas Wood and John Kennedy. Each locomotive had to run twenty times up and down the track at Rainhill, hauling a load of three times its own weight at a speed of at least 10 mph, which made the distance roughly equivalent to a return trip between Liverpool and Manchester.

On the first day over 10,000 people turned up to watch the competitors, Luke and Amel among them. Ten locomotives were originally entered, but only five turned up and two of these were withdrawn because of mechanical problems, leaving the three remaining machines to compete: Stephenson's Rocket, Hackworth's Sans Pareil, and Novelty, built by Braithwaite and Ericsson. The Novelty was much smaller than the other entries, but it was the quickest and reached speeds of 28 mph during the trials that took place on the first day. It was extremely popular with the large crowd that attended and was a hot favourite to win the competition. However, on the second day the boiler pipe became overheated and was damaged. To reach it for repairs, John Braithwaite and John Ericsson had to partially dismantle the boiler.

At first there were doubts whether Sans Pareil would compete as the judges claimed that it was overweight. However, it was eventually agreed to let its inventor, Timothy Hackworth, show what his new locomotive could do. The Sans Pareil carried out eight trips and reached a top speed of just over 16 mph, but after the promising start the locomotive suffered a cracked cylinder. The next day, when the Novelty reached 15 mph, the joints started to blow. The damage was considerable and the Novelty was forced to retire from the competition.

The final entry was the Rocket entered by Robert Stephenson. Two men, who worked for the Liverpool & Manchester Railway, Henry Booth the Secretary and George Stephenson the chief engineer, were also involved in developing the Rocket.

On the third day it covered 35 miles in 3 hours 12 minutes, hauling 13 tons of loaded wagons, averaging over 12 mph. On one trip it reached 25 mph and on a locomotive-only run 29 mph. After studying all the evidence judges awarded the £500 first prize to the owners of the Rocket, the boiler of which would become the prototype for every conventional steam locomotive built.

TWENTY

The house Madame Duprez chose was a magnificent, three-storey, stone-fronted building, consisting of a central block with forecourt and balancing wings connected by curving walls that screened corridors. In the 1770's the west front had been extended, two bow-shaped projections added in order to provide three connecting rooms comprising of a drawing room, a music room and a fifty-foot-long saloon. The property, said to be one of the finest pieces of architecture in Europe, had originally been sold in 1815 by the 6th Duke of Devonshire for fifty seven thousand pounds to his uncle, Lord George Cavenish, the grandson of the famous patron of the arts, the 3rd Earl of Burlington. It was said that at one time Lord George had both Handel and William Kent to stay under its very roof.

Burlington House stood back from the road in about two acres of land, looking over Piccadilly to Green Park where the grass slopes into the valley to Tyburn Stream, affectively screened and protected from the street by a high grey-stone wall surmounted by ornamental lamps, and two vast wrought-iron gates with a tall, classical, pedimented arch between them. The interior showed the work of different stylistic periods - magnificent reception rooms on the ground floor overlooking the gardens at the back of the house. Certain rooms were completely re-designed to meet new needs and keep up with the fashion.

London craftsmen had added decorative flourishes to the cornices and shutters, picked out in soft shades of cream, vanishing mahogany sashes, as well as gilding plasterwork of leaves, grain and honeysuckle. Each room in turn, enriched with everything money could buy; heavy moulded wainscoting, magnificent carved doors, crystal chandeliers, monstrous marble fireplaces, beautifully draped curtains with the sheen of silk and new silk wallpapers, and handsome patterned carpets supplied by Lapworth Brothers of Old Bond Street no less, the carpet manufacturers to the Royal Family. And naturally - French furniture, only the very best - gilded chairs upholstered in a rich creamy damask, with deep comfortable sofas to match.

French, Italian and English arts, amongst them three impressive paintings of scenes of Paris by Amel's young friend Richard Parkes Bonington, a multitude of hangings - embroideries, gilt framed mirrors, plain and fancy clocks, decorative Oil lamps of all shapes and sizes - all presenting wealth. Alterations and furnishings had been extensive, eating up the better part of Madame Duprez's personal fortune, but she was not one to worry about the cost. Her object was to produce a magnificent setting for the entertainments she proposed to give.

The walls to the saloon were decorated with landscapes, with a frieze of blue and gold, at one end an enormous fireplace with freestanding columns and a plaque with a relief of shepherd boys, at the other end a huge bay window that took up most all of the wall and overlooked the gardens. The music room was richly hung with the palest of green silk and the fireplace inlaid with green marble. Between the music room and dining room to the left of the entrance hall, runs a narrow corridor that had been given the vaulted treatment of semi-circular arches. Ivory painted panels lined the library with its large collection of books, all of which looked quite new; books which undoubtedly would never be opened... there only to impress.

The staircase was the principal feature of the house, with its wrought-iron balustrade lit by a tall round-headed window gracing the landing. The surprise was startling when one raised one's eyes and found oneself looking up at the intricate decoration of the walls, which were of the French style known as rocaille that was very popular with the English. In the larger panels an eagle and a lion rampant were modelled in relief above a design of scrolls, with the other panels framing elaborate vases of flowers.

Madame Duprez was obviously more interested in atmosphere than a convenient house to live in. A house where the fashionable world of London could be entertained in the utmost splendour. To create such an atmosphere needed a large purse and an inch-by-inch attention to detail. She had thought of everything, rooms to suit every occasion and every mood, even a room housing an elaborately inlaid billiard table, with cues and a score-board to match, and leather-padded raised benches for the spectators, where a game of billiards could be played, whilst the ladies occupied themselves in quiet gossip. No expense was spared.

The bedroom floors were divided into self-contained suites, each with its own bedroom with carved and painted chimneypieces, dressing room and bathroom, all richly furnished and decorated. The house also boasted the latest comforts, not least, of which were no less than five Bramah water closets, a new form of flushing toilet.

Immediately beneath the dome was Madame Duprez's boudoir, the circular ceiling painted a dark blue and sprinkled with hundreds of tiny silver stars to resemble the sky at night, and gilt framed mirrors from floor to ceiling. The room was dominated by a great exotic bed with a gilt canopy hung with clouds of soft white tulle, dazzled with silver and gold decoration, and scattered with deep comfortable velvet chairs and a chaise lounge of equal elegance.

On the hood of the fireplace a winged Goddess of Love, was seated above a carved frieze depicting the summer amusements of lovers; a showiness of opulence, grandeur and more than a touch of fanciful decorative confectionery. In an alcove off the bedroom was the most magnificent Roman marble bath, inlaid with metal figures of fish and mermaids, and a long washstand fashioned in the shape of a castle with two towers, each containing a tank of water, piped to the central tap made in the shape of a fish; from here it spouts into a large fancy china basin.

Less impressively, below ground floors, were the servants' quarters, kitchens, washhouse, drying room and ironing room, and an office, which looked out onto an area as dark and narrow as anything built in the eighteenth century. A large complement of servants was a status symbol. At the top - the butler, king over all; not hired as a mere servitor, but "engaged" - an expression Butlers' felt to be more dignified and in keeping with their station in life.

Also at the top, was the housekeeper, her duties

mainly ceremonial, supervisory and administrative. Then came the footmen; the peacocks among domestics, with their brightly coloured coats with brass crested buttons, plush breeches, gleaming boots and silk stockings, and their hats with cockades in them.

Madame Duprez believed that appearances were vital. They were one of the most vital parts of their mistress's equipment of display. Then there was the Lady's maid, who was not only the personal attendant to the lady of the house but also an expert needle-woman, and Cook, queen of her own domain, who presided over the kitchen maids; both brought from France at enormous expense. Immigrant chefs from the noble houses of France were settling into the wealthy houses of England and their services, though expensive, were much sought after.

At the bottom were the lower domestics: house-maids, kitchen maids, the gardeners and the laundress, right down to the lowest of the lowest - a ten-year-old yard boy and a twelve-year-old tweeny, the little maid of all work.

Mon amour, how I miss you. To while away the hours until we can be together again, I have kept myself occupied by sorting out the furnishing and am able, I feel confident, to do it all within the liberal limits which you have so generously allowed. I cannot thank you enough for your generosity, Mon amour, but can promise faithfully I will endeavour to do my utmost when you return.

Most all the furniture and drapes have been provided by Smalls of Oxford Street. All is settled to my satisfaction, but I have still to arrange the decoration of the dining room. I will run no risk, and have decided to employ those already at the top of their profession. Florentine Cipriani is my choice, the most expensive I fear, but the most fashionable. When I visited your home, I was most taken with the décor of your dining room and have decided on the same. Ivory for the woodwork and walls, and claret for the recesses, drapes and seat-coverings. I hope you have no objections. I have also accepted the contract for lighting the house with gas at the cost of £210 per annum, which I think you will agree, is quite reasonable.

I have been promised that the scaffolding will have been taken down by the end of this month and the forecourt cleared by the week after.

To write to you is the next greatest pleasure I feel to receiving word from you. When I think I won't see you again until next month, I feel quite wretched. Truly I do.

She ended the letter with a plea... *Won't you please... please come to me sooner, Mon amour? Amel.*

TWENTY-ONE

Luke deposited his travelling bag in the main bedroom, Amel's boudoir, where he would be spending most of his time. He had spent many nights of pleasure under its roof. He was to wonder later, much later, if he would not have been better served never to have set eyes on Amelia Duprez. She was a different person altogether in the bedroom, soft and yielding, at the same time an expert in the art of love-making. He certainly got a thrill out of their association; she awoke in him a hunger that consumed him night and day.

His greatest pleasure was to slide naked between the silk sheets, to feel the lithe sinuous strength of her body, in positions that no decent woman knew of, to please his fancy. He was well aware that she solicited custom elsewhere. He had no real objections. Why should he have, as long as she was available on his visits for him to take his pleasure, which was a bracing change from domestic dullness? He in turn took her to all the right places, showering her with expensive gifts, keeping her in the life-style she was accustomed to.

Amel had collected a stunning selection of beautiful things, expensive things. The coach-house and stables housed a barouche - a four wheeled carriage, with a protecting hood, a seat in the front for the driver and seats inside for four passengers, that was drawn by two matching white horses.

The dining room had a two-tier Jacobean

chimney-piece and a formidable sideboard recess lined with velvet in the rich colour of claret. The room had been furnished and curtained by A & L Small of Oxford Street, and decorated by no other than Florentine Cipriani, the most fashionable and, of course, the most expensive of interior decorators. Smalls supplied the Jacobean sideboard and side tables with bulbous legs, an ornately bulging wine cooler, a Jacobean plate warmer and twenty four elegant rococo chairs, their seats covered in claret Morocco leather.

Luke observed it all with an icy silence, realising that the entire performance of the previous night had been an elaborate subterfuge to persuade him to part with more of his money. The increase in her allowance he had given her had already been swallowed up by her extravagance. But he could not help but admire the Louis XV needlework table carpet, hung on the wall in the dining room.

It was worked in vibrant colours on a black background, with a central floral medallion surrounded by boldly scrolling leaves interspersed with flowers, the broad border with ribbon tied plumes and foliate arabesques, the inner and outer designs framed with gold borders entwined with oak leaves. At each of the corners was a heraldic heart emblem with flames, a symbol of Aphrodite and ardent love, while the arrows within it represented Eros's darts.

'I have to admit you're right. This is absolutely splendid,' Luke remarked thoughtfully, his dark eyes scanning the carpet appreciatively. 'It's an excellent piece of workmanship.'

'Isn't it!' Amel agreed, pleased with her find. 'It's

in remarkable condition. A variety of the dyes are especially rich and seems never to have been exposed to daylight.'

'So I've noticed. It's French, isn't it?'

'But of course. What else?' She pointed a well-manicured finger. 'You see it has a silk fringe that appears to be the original, matching exactly the wools of the needlework.'

'So I see. It really is superb. I wouldn't mind it myself. It must have cost you a small fortune.'

Amel did not volunteer the price. What did she care what it cost, since it was not her money in the first place? Luke followed her into the drawing room. She glided over to the mahogany bureau bookcase. Another piece of superb furniture that must have cost the earth. She opened one of the drawers, lifted out a pile of papers and handed them to him.

'What's this?' he asked, taking them from her.

'Accounts that are owing to Tradesmen.'

Luke sank into a chair and glanced through them, one at a time. He had great difficulty in not showing his irritation. 'A pianoforte at a cost of £1,500!' he read aloud. 'Perfume to the value of £85. Hats and millinery …£318.'

Amel sighed dramatically, smoothed her skirts and patted her hair. 'There's no need to read them out. I'm well aware of what is owing.'

Luke ignored her objection and carried on regardless, 'And what's this? A herbalist's bill for £28? Herbs costing £28!'

'Herbs for health, for women's problems.'

He sighed in exasperation and pursed his lips, twisting the mouth into an ugly grimace.

'Why such a glum face?' She asked in all

innocence. 'You told me to put them to one side until you arrived.'

He closed his eyes momentarily, fighting to keep his displeasure hidden. What she said was the truth, there was no denying. During one of his weaker moments, he had told her to charge whatever she needed to his name. By this undertaking he had made himself personally responsible if difficulties arose over payment. He opened his lids and a pair of fierce, dark eyes looked straight at her for some minutes, his gaze steady and piercing.

'You will, no doubt, think I'm speaking out of turn...' he said at last. 'but some things need to be said.'

'What an earth is it? Has someone died?'

'Don't be flippant,' he responded frostily.

'But the look on your face...'

'Can you wonder at it? Besides all this I've recently received yet another bill from your dress-maker, for the sum of...'

'Please don't be tiresome,' she interrupted, holding up a hand, refusing to look at him. 'I have a rule, a very civilized rule, never to discuss finances after dinner. You ought to know that by now.'

'That's all very well, but this is serious. I find your expenditure on clothing alone beyond belief. In fact, far too extravagant. Absolutely incredible!'

'I distinctly recall you telling me to charge what-ever I'm in need of to your account.'

'But the amounts you spend are absolutely incredible.'

'You're repeating yourself, Mon amour. You've already said that once.'

'And I'll say it again. These amounts are

incredible. You are over-spending,' he emphasised.

For a moment she felt angry and delivered a penetrating gaze. 'What you men don't seem to understand is a lady needs to keep up with the fashion to hold her own in society.'

'But I've already given you paraphernalia money for your own use, a separate income that I never touch. That should more than cover your personal needs.'

'Well, it was you who suggested the arrangement in the first place... "I've arranged matters so you need never worry about money again." ...is what you said. If it worries you I'll settle the bills myself.'

He laughed then, a laugh full of sarcasm. 'You will? With what? Have you any idea just how much you've been spending?'

'Oh, it's so vulgar to talk of money,' was all she said, greatly offended by the question.

'You've been eating into your capital at the rate of twenty thousand pounds a year at least,' he told her, determined to get the message over to her.

Her eyes widened in disbelief. 'Don't be ridiculous! It couldn't possibly be as much as that.'

'Then how is it you're in debt up to your neck?'

It was unnerving to realise that someone knew that much about her. 'You seem to know an awful lot about my private affairs.'

'You can hardly expect me to part with such large amounts without wanting to know where it is going,' he remarked coolly.

'You might contribute to my upkeep, but it's hardly enough to provide for me entirely,' she countered flippantly.

'There's no need to take that attitude. Economy is

an important virtue and debt is a danger to be feared. You're on very shaky ground.' Despite his best efforts he couldn't conceal a little anger in his voice.

'Oh, for goodness sake, don't lecture! I have every right to take that attitude. The last thing I need is...'

'I'm only asking you not to be so extravagant,' he interrupted impatiently. 'You should have married me when you had the chance. A husband is responsible for his wife's debts and obliged to support her all her life.'

She shrugged. 'But the ironic thing is that in the marriage service a man promises to endow his wife with all his worldly goods, yet in practice it is the wife who forfeits her property to him.'

'The gilded cage of bourgeois marriage is approved by those who idealise its comfort and security.'

'And hated by those who find it claustrophobic and frustrating. The law is that everything is in the property of the husband, and the wife is under his control. I would feel too constrained,' Amel said offhandedly.

She sighed then, closing her eyes briefly and pursing her lips. She could give as good as she got, not like that silly little mouse of a wife of his who was so utterly naive. 'I really have no idea how we got on to this subject. It's a sheer waste of breath. I for one have no intentions whatsoever of ever marrying again, to stand in the shadow of a man.'

'Then it's fortunate for you I am an industrious man. The cost of running this place must be enormous.' He spoke with the self-satisfied tone of the successful businessman he was. It must be confessed that fortune had favoured him and he had found the path to prosperity very soft to his tread. Everything he touched had turned to gold. 'The trouble with having money is everybody wants it.'

TWENTY-TWO

Dan Greenward paced the floor, wringing his hands with fear and guilt. The worry and sleepless nights had taken their toll. If anything were to happen to her, his Clara, because of him, he wouldn't be able to go on. He would be no good without her; he knew that as a certainty. She was his life ... his whole world.

He heard hardly a sound of complaint. If she would only cry out, curse him for his selfish bloody careless-ness. He knew he should be praying, but couldn't. Guilt forbade it, guilt that he had not been more careful. If there was a God let him be merciful.

He sank in the chair and bowing his head, he finally prayed; thanking Him for sending this wonder-ful, this precious woman to fill his empty life. He prayed for comfort, not for himself, but for the woman who lay upstairs twisting and writhing in agony in the great bed as the child, their child, fought to come into the world.

He must have slept then through sheer exhaustion, for when he opened his eyes, the room was dark and the house silent. He froze ...he could not move as a pang of fear gripped his pounding heart.

'She's dead. My Clara ...she's dead,' he croaked. 'Please God give me some sign. Tell me she's not dead.'

As if by some telepathic message, the stairs suddenly creaked. Dan looked towards the door, as the glow of a candle lit up the room.

'Oh God! Dear God!' he cried, his mouth agape and

his tired, strained eyes wide with dread.

Doctor Morrison came noiselessly into the room. 'Is that you, Dan? Why an earth're you sitting in the dark?'

Dan could not utter a word. He just sat there staring back at him, his eyes strangely unfocused, his face distorted by a mask of genuine terror.

The doctor placed the candleholder down on a side table, and as he did so Dan rose slowly to his feet, and with trembling hands gripped the weary man roughly by the shoulders, but no words came from his mouth.

'It's all right, man. It's all right,' the good doctor soothed. It was hard to believe this was the same strong man he had known for so many years. It was astonishing what the love for a woman could do to a man. 'You can relax now. You've a fine healthy son.'

'Clara? My Clara?' Dan managed to croak.

'You can breathe easy. Clara's doing just fine.'

There was nothing like a new child being born to charge the blood with hope and thankfulness, especially when it was one of your own. This mystical, wonderful fact has never yet found the poet to sing its full glory. He sank to his knees and there, right in front of the good doctor, Daniel Greenward, the man who had turned his back on God, thanked Him over and over again, and asked His forgiveness.

The scent of fresh flowers arranged in a great silver bowl filled the room, the sunniest room in the house. Clara had on a cream lacy peignoir, and was propped up against the pillows in the great bed they shared, bought when they had first married. Her dark hair, still damp with the sweat of her labour, was spread untidily over her shoulders, her face tired and strained, showing her age. But her eyes held a certain look ...a look of joy ...of pride for the awe-inspiring gift of life, the tiny bundle of humanity she held close against her heart.

'Our son, Mr Greenward,' she said in a choked whisper, holding the tiny form out carefully lest he should break, for Dan to see.

Dan moved forward as if in a dream and took the tiny bundle in his great, strong hands, carefully bringing his new-born son close to his own beating heart, his vision blurring with unashamed tears of overwhelming pride and elation.

'Clara, my sweet, clever lass.' He looked into her dear face. 'Are you sure you're all right, my love?'

'I'm fine, dearest. I managed without too much fuss, but I'm weary now, that's all. What is a little inconvenience compared to such a prize?' The corners of her mouth quivered slightly. She blinked away the threatening tears. 'Oh, Daniel, I'm so proud and happy.'

Her words were the words of a most contented woman, a woman who had been denied a child of her own to love. Now one had been delivered to her, she was overwhelmed by the wonder of it all.

'You've every right t'be. You've done well.' He gazed with enchantment at the pink crinkled bundle of humanity with his fine, long limbs and a mass of dark hair curling around his perfectly shaped skull. Fine lashes fanned his plump cheeks, and he had a button of a nose and a tiny jutting chin. So perfect. The vulnerability of the child moved Dan to such depths of protective love he was totally overwhelmed.

He gave a deep sigh and looked again into his wife's dear face.

'I've counted all his fingers an' toes. He's absolutely perfect, just like his mother.'

'Oh, thank you, my dearest,' Clara whispered.

'Don't thank me. Thank God, though I dare say it could not have been done without me,' he breathed, grinning boyishly. 'Our cup runneth over. He answered my prayers.'

'We are truly blessed.'

The little blooming face brought heart-rending memories of the sons he had once had and lost. He bent to kiss the warm plump cheek. 'Adam...' he whispered, his voice full of tenderness. 'It's Adam, all over again.'

'Then we shall call him Adam. Would you like that?'

'I would indeed! Adam John.' His eyes filled again, not with sorrow or pain, but with pure joy and relief.

'That sounds just perfect.'

The child opened his mouth and let out a tremulous yell. 'Just listen t'him. He's a Greenward right enough.'

'Here, give him to me.'

Dan placed their new-born son in her outstretched arms. Adoration shone from her eyes as she held him to her breast and watched the little rosebud mouth suck at the pink nipple. Nothing could have prepared her for this. She had not dreamed life could be so infinitely sweet. 'And all this time I thought I was barren,' she said triumphantly.

Dan gently touched the tiny, perfectly formed pink hand that spontaneously closed in a fist around his rough finger. The proud expression had not left his face and a smile still lingered on his lips. 'Then we must think o' this as an extra bonus, my love, a touch o' genius.'

'Yes, Daniel, a touch of genius,' she echoed, her eyes bright with joyful tears.

TWENTY-THREE

It was late in the day, cloudy, but not quite dark, the moon shining a little now and then, looking wasted and pale. Short-trunk beeches with their huge, grey spreading boughs, towering pines, birches and other deciduous trees, made a vast shadowy outline against the floating mists that lay about the fields. The emaciated individual shook in the frosty air like an aspen leaf, finding himself, with the night coming on, without a place to lay his head, but nothing …nothing could prevail on him to go back to the shelter of the workhouse.

Those without the means to support themselves; the helpless and the homeless, those who had nowhere else to go except the gutter, were consigned to the workhouse where rules were imposed with such strictness and food allocated with such economy no one in their right mind would go through the gates while work was to be had. Life was much tougher inside than out, even the buildings themselves were grim and intimidating, designed to look like prisons, full of illness and disease brought about by over-crowding and a starvation diet.

When admitted, you were stripped and washed down and made to wear a coarse prison-style uniform. He had been one of five admitted, and had left on the fourth day of discovering just what life in the workhouse was like. Inmates worked from seven o'clock in the morning till twelve, and from one till six in the afternoon; a ten-hour working day and then it was to bed at eight. He had been put to oakum picking - unravelling short lengths of rope and, crushing bones to make fertiliser. Sometimes the inmates were so hungry they would pick scraps of flesh off the bones and eat it. They were not all animal bones either!

Ned Cartwright was only half the man he used to be. His bloodshot eyes, sunken deep beneath the shaggy brows, held acute misery, giving no glimmer of the fire of life. Soured by misfortune, he was but a moving bundle of wretchedness. His clothes, if you could call the rags that covered his tall skinny frame, clothes, were coated with nasty decaying matter which was the residue of months of dribbling his ale, food, and his own phlegm which he continuously coughed up and wiped on the sleeve of his jacket. His hands and disfigured face were the colour of the filth in which he delved. The grey grizzled hair about his bull-like head fell on stooping shoulders, and that which covered the lower half of his face was a smoky yellow around the tight bitter mouth.

He was gasping for he was walking faster than he was fit for, driven by a raging bitterness, his stride contradicting the evidence of his sunken cheeks and deeply lined forehead. He stopped for a minute or two to get his breath, for the long walk, a walk that would have come easy at one time, had taken it out of him. Looking cautiously about, he felt for the crowbar shoved through his belt, to assure himself it was still there, and fingered the rope he had wrapped several times around his waist, hidden under his raggedy jacket.

No one had seen him, he was sure of that. It was doubtful anyone would have recognized him if they had seen him - so changed was he. All the same, he steered clear of Branthwaite village, tramping through the muddy, rutted tracks. It was one of those days when a chill moisture hangs over everything. No movement was noticeable among the branches of the trees, but from time to time drops fell from the pines that loomed dark through the drifting vapours. A faint, eddying breeze sighed softly through the curtain of drifting mist, blotting out the distance.

He had just decided to turn back when he noticed a glimmer of a light ahead, so hastened onward past High Greenrigg, following the trail like a hunter, stopping only to relieve himself.

The ground was damp and shadowy under the over-hanging trees and padded with a hoof-welded carpet of leaves. The stillness was now intense; the crunch of his boots on the stony way sounded hollow and muffled. A falling acorn clattered loudly through the withering leaves, making him stop in his tracks and cower nervously. He listened for a minute or two, and telling himself not to be a bloody fool, tramped on wearily.

Where the track narrowed, the high bank on one side was clothed with birch, prickly holly and garlands of wild vetch, united and interwoven by long wreaths of bramble and brier. So impenetrable were these thickets that even the sheep, although the bits of their snowy fleece left on the bushes bore witness to their attempts, could make no way through the thorny mass. Dusk thickened about him as the night tried to impress itself on the earth as a separate entity from the mist. The branches overhead suddenly opened out, but the channel was still bounded by low banks that gradually diminished and at last disappeared altogether. He was almost there.

Cartwright left the path, his stomach rumbling alarmingly as he thrashed between the trees. He suffered from a strange lightness in the head that he put down to lack of foodstuff, and a pain in his chest that was quite unaccountable. In fact, he felt positively ill, experiencing a chill and oppressive sensation, an undefined dread. His illness always seemed to worsen as night drew in.

Dreadful things were associated with darkness. The constant horror was becoming insufferable - he was loathe to close his eyes even, for fear of the rope. He could still feel it about his neck, squeezing the very breath from out of his body. Having been to hell and back, his preoccupation lay in keeping hell at bay, but in this unnerved, in this pitiable condition he felt that the time would sooner or later come when he must abandon life and reason together in the struggle with the grim phantasm - madness - that hovered impatiently to destroy him.

That very thought set him off trembling in every limb, and his grimy, calloused hand went to his throat that had never recovered from the torture inflicted on him well over a year ago. Dan Greenward had dragged him down, taken everything from him: his job as overman, his money and his strength; everything!

It started with Greenward blaming him for taking short cuts and causing the accident in Driggeth mine that had claimed several lives, two of them Greenward's sons. Greenward had threatened to bring him down, but too much of a coward to face him himself, he had got others to do the dirty deed for him.

Back then he'd had a reputation as a hard and vicious fighter, a man who had fought in a bare-knuckle boxing ring and had never been defeated, but there had been six of them that night, not one bugger stronger than himself, all advancing on him at once. He hadn't stood a bloody chance, although he felled one with the poker, breaking his neck and killing him instantly. They showed no mercy, incapacitating him and breaking his spirit - nearly finishing him off. First, by beating him to a pulp, then stringing him up by the neck, again and again, until he had lost his senses and passed out with sheer terror. His neck and throat had troubled him ever since, and left him in such agony he had nearly gone mad with it.

Like a wounded beast he had been forced to scamper away to hide himself from prying eyes, living less than half a life, and now, even the half he clung to seemed to be slipping through his fingers like crumbled winter leaves. He knew that he had gone down the wrong road when he first reached for a bottle. Drink was sucking him dry, pickling his brain, and when it was finished with him there would be nothing left but a shrivelled, useless old man. But inside him his hatred for Dan Greenward who had caused all his troubles, festered ferociously with a powerful force. His rage over what had been done to him, this very hunger for vengeance, seemed to generate its own peculiar strength and that very strength kept him going, had kept him alive all this time and enabled him to say to himself: 'I won't fail.' He had to succeed and to succeed he had to survive.

By God, he would make that man suffer. Destroy everything he owned before his very eyes, torture and slowly break him. He had worked himself up to do it, but his thoughts were confused to how he would bring it about, unclear as they wandered in and out of his mind, all over the place. But it would all come together when the time came, he was sure and he was going to enjoy every single minute.

His head was no longer accustomed to thought beyond food and ale and where they were to come from. He was certainly not inclined to planning ahead, since his life was nothing but slow drifting from one job to another. His brain began to thud with the effort.

Burrowing deeper into the shelter of the undergrowth, he removed the crowbar from his belt and laid it down on the damp leaves, and settled himself on a bed of feathery ferns, there in the dim dusk. With the brooding stillness all around, he brought his knees up to his chest and hugged them close, his muddled mind trying to work out what he would do once he gained entrance to Greenward's property.

He had been watching the comings and goings for more than two weeks - making a mental note of which upstairs rooms were occupied and which were not, by the evidence of the light through the windows of a night time. It being a weekend, the house would be quiet - just the two of them and that young slip of a girl - Eric Master's youngest - to take care of.

He stayed like this until late into the night, unable to move, the cold and dampness penetrating his bones, there amongst the trees where it was dark and plagued by creeping things. Something fluttered overhead and the breeze carried occasional screeching cries to his ears. A solitary, lonely man, he grew more frantic in his terror. But in spite of his fear, his misery and wretched discomfort, the fatigue of the journey gradually overcame the mind and body, and he sank into a deep death-like sleep - forgetting his troubles for a time - from which he was roused by the sound of wheezing - his own.

He rubbed his dirt-encrusted hand across his filthy, unshaven face, knuckling his eyes to remove the crusty matter that glued the lids together, and then wiped them down his grimy breeches. He then got slowly to his feet, leaning unsteadily against the rough bark of the tree. The time had come for the past to step on the heels of the present.

Cartwright lifted the crowbar and stumbled stiffly into the blackness of the night along the lane that led to Fells View - Greenward's place. It was bitterly cold, the ground beneath his feet crunchy with frost. The weight of the darkness pressed down on him, making him falter, but he forced himself to go on.

What he had come to do, needed doing ...he told himself over and over again. If he abandoned the plan now, he might lose his nerve and Greenward would have won. With the air of an animal, he peered cautiously in the direction of the house. He had no idea what time it was, but the place was in complete darkness.

He crept past the great barn, stopping only to pull off his worn, mud-caked boots, quickly moving on, stepping on silent, bare feet across the yard to the side door of the house. In another minute he was at work easing the crowbar down the side, gradually applying what strength he had to force it open. After a few attempts there came a long, drawn-out groan as it gave way under pressure. He stood a while and listened. There wasn't a sound.

He stole silently into the kitchen where a fire

blushed a rosy red in the grate and the lingering smell of baked bread filled his nostrils. He would help himself to something to eat, but there would be time enough for that later. First things first - he had to do what he had come to do. Creeping as lightly as a soft-pawed cat across the kitchen, he went through the door into the hall.

It was then that he sneezed, cursing himself silently, tempted to turn tail and run, but he willed himself to remain completely still for several minutes until he was certain that the sound had passed unnoticed.

Clara Greenward's eyes shot open. Her heart seemed to stop and then beat again furiously in her breast, like a wild thing set free. She had dreamed a fearful dream of Daniel dying and leaving her all alone. But what had awakened her from her dream into the dark confusion of the night? She was a very light sleeper and heard every sound, yet the house was quiet - only her own breath made whisperings in her ears.

The dream was still fresh on her mind. How morbid she was, foolishly fretting over nothing. She sat up, shivering slightly, for the fire had died sulkily into grey clinkers tinged with red that had no more warmth to it than a splash of paint. Reaching for the tinderbox, she lit a candle and peeked into the cradle that stood by the side of the bed where a little bundle of humanity, her precious little angel, slept peace-fully. Soft, glossy dark curls lay across the pulsing fontanelle to the crown and in swirls about his perfect little pink ears and his baby-smooth neck. He had the soft button nose and the pouting rosebud lips of a new baby, and long fine lashes nestled on his satin cheeks that were rosy with good health.

Holding the candle high, she glanced at the clock on the bed-side table and sighed fretfully - it was only twenty past two - she had barely slept an hour since he had settled after taking him to her breast. It was her own fault really, since she had refused the help of a wet-nurse or a nanny, insisting on caring for the child herself. As he was the only one she was likely to have, she wanted to savour every waking moment with him, which was proving to be more exhausting than she had anticipated.

Edna did her best to help, of course, but the girl had enough to do with the chores and couldn't be everywhere at once. Because of the baby's restlessness, and, of course, he needed his rest, Daniel had taken to sleeping in the room adjacent to theirs, just until she recovered from the birth and Adam settled. She missed his presence, the closeness of him, the feel of him next to her, but had to admit it made sense to sleep apart until she was fully recovered.

Her Daniel could be a very demanding man, but was wonderfully kind, thoughtful and generous, everything she had ever dreamed of in a husband. In truth, she was blissfully happy, glowing with an inner fulfilment and finding life quite wonderful. Not just the physical loving but the strong emotional bonds that is the mark of true love. Yet a single dread they shared in common; lest one should be taken and the other left. That the final harvest might come for both together was their intense desire.

Daniel's rhythmic snoring could usually be heard through the adjoining wall, but there was no sound - the house was tomb-like in its silence. Edna slept in the small room at the end of the passage, but the girl slept soundly and never seemed to hear a thing. Still, she shouldn't complain, Edna did her best, albeit half-heartedly and never without a grumble. Edna wasn't used to working alone. The girl missed her elder sister, Millie, who was now married and living with her husband in one of the labourer's cottages on the Hawthorne Estate.

Clara smiled to herself. Once she was back on her feet she would find another girl, someone a little older and more responsible, who could work without super-vision, guide young Edna and ease her workload. That should put a stop to the girl's grumbling.

She became serious again when she heard Daniel cry out, a lost voice coming from along the passage, uplifted as if in protest in some dream of terror. Her own dream had faded and in its place came a nagging feeling that something was amiss. She felt it. She swung her long, slender legs over the side of bed, and as she was still feeling a bit unsteady, sat there for a while. After a few minutes she lifted the candleholder and crept noiselessly over the carpet from the room and along the passageway. The door to the room where Daniel slept was slightly ajar; she pushed it open. The fire was still alive, casting a soft glow over the room.

'Daniel...?' she whispered.

Clara stood just inside the doorway, enfolded in a long, white nightgown, with her hair lying like a dark shadow about her shoulders, holding up the candle with one hand and the other clasped fearfully over her mouth as she took in the scene that paralysed her with crushing fright. She did not see the intruder until a tall shadow on the wall moved. She started violently, her white, moth-like hand fluttering nervously from her mouth to her breast.

The form was that of a man, a tall, mad-looking skeleton of a man, miserably clad and begrimed, and in his hand he held some sort of weapon, but she couldn't make out what it was. Her heart doubled its beat in a sudden spurt of panic. She could literally feel the blood draining from her face as her mind filled with racing, half-coherent thoughts, but the one that was uppermost was the safety of her child ...her precious son, Adam.

Something within her, something that is in all women who are mothers, sprang to life in defence of her child and she turned to go to him, to run with speed along the passage to the cradle where he lay, to snatch him up in her arms and protect him like the spitting cat into which this evil intruder had turned her. But all too late. She just wasn't fast enough.

Cartwright gave a sudden lunge towards her. Grabbing her violently by her mane of shining, dark hair, he dragged her viciously backwards to the bed where Dan, his hair and face matted with blood, lay trussed with rope about his wrists and tight about his neck, with a knot at his throat. He was securely tied to the iron bedpost, his eyes darting and watchful like two fearful birds side by side in a nest. It was impossible for him to speak even, to reason with this mad man who had broken into his home and was threatening his wife.

Clara's head was brutally forced back, her mouth was wide and straining in a rictus of agony. Shock turned to terror and she began to scream, but so weakly that she could not have been heard by anyone who was not within immediate earshot - and who was there to hear but Edna who slept the sleep of the dead? Dan struggled frantically to be free to go to the aid of his beloved wife. But it was futile. The more he struggled the more he gagged ...he could hardly catch his breath.

Cartwright let go of her hair and clamped a great, grimy calloused hand across her mouth, grasping her cruelly about the jaw, instantly silencing her. He was as dangerous as a maddened bull. His temper had always been short and fierce. In fact, those who had once worked in his vicinity had walked about him virtually on tiptoes lest they disturbed the uncertain stability of his nature. A wrong word or a look even, could set him off. Mad Dog's temper - that being his nickname the men had given him - was a legend around the mines of Cumbria where he had once worked as overman, before his mysterious disappearance well over a year ago.

He banged the crowbar down on the small bedside table and grabbed the candleholder that Clara still clung onto for dear life, from her hand, setting it down alongside the crowbar. The second he took his hand away from her mouth she started to scream again, and he gave her a good whack across the face to shut her up, snapping her head back with such force her hair fell in a wildly flying whirl about her face as she went sprawling backwards across the bed.

'I'm warnin' yer ...yer stupid bitch, keep yer bloody gob shut or I'll shurrit for yer ...permanently,' he threatened in a strange, dry gruff voice, his face a distorted mask of red fury.

Clara knew they were all in deadly peril. Fear trickled through her veins, overwhelming her with a giddy sickness as he loomed over her like the devil himself. Filthy raggedy clothes hung on him with pitiful looseness. Blood-shot eyes peered from under slanting, puffy lids. His hands, and face, what you could see of it, were the colour of mould, encrusted with dirt like a tombstone. She didn't recognize him. She didn't know him at all.

Cartwright's attention was now on Dan. Surprise had been his weapon. Asleep in his bed, Dan hadn't known what hit him. ''Ow does it feel? 'Ow does it feel, yer bloody coward?'

He turned on Clara again, his lips twisted in a snarl, his cutting words belying the white-hot fury which burned inside him.

'This so-called man o' yers 'ad me bloody beaten, almost t'death, 'ung from a tree 'till I was senseless. Did yer know that? Did yer?' he screeched right into her face, his spittle spraying over her.

Clara was so unnerved she could only shake her head dumbly. She could feel the blood in her veins become sluggish and her heart stilled.

'No ...I don't suppose yer bloody did. Well, tis 'is turn. I want 'im t'suffer, t'know what tis like. The breath bein' squeezed from outta yer body.' His lips writhed, as if the words were coals between them, revealing all his loathing, all his bitter, pent-up antagonism for the man who had flung him into the nightmare world in which he now lived. All the time his head moved in a strange jerking manner, as if his neck were on a steel spring.

Dan attempted to shake his head in denial, for he had had nothing to do with the attack, but the rope gripped tight, the knot straining against his Adam's apple, choking him.

'No one messes with Ned Cartwright an' gets

away with it. I've dreamed o' this moment an' now tis 'ere I mean t'enjoy every bloody minute o' it. I'm goin' t'distroy everything yer value, Greenward. Do yer 'ear me? Do yer bloody 'ear? Everything yer own, every bloody thing. This 'ouse, this fine 'ouse …I'm goin' t'burn it down ...an'…an'…'

His hand went to his great head. The ache that lay in the base of his skull had sprang to full life, biting at him ferociously. He couldn't think straight. His face contorted in the fearful effort to concentrate, to get it straight and clear in his mind. He only knew that he had to finish what he had started, make the bastard pay, make him suffer, wreck his home …and …and his woman …yes …the bastard's woman.

For the first time in all her life that evil thing called terror grabbed hold of Clara Greenward, clawing at her very backbone with sharp icy fingers, lifting her hair with its freezing breath. She put out a trembling hand in a gesture of appeal, thinking to reason with him, not on her own behalf but on behalf of her precious baby son, since he was surely in terrible danger.

'Take what you want. There's money…jewellery …my rings …take them. Take it all, but don't… don't hurt my son. I beg you …spare my son. I'll do any …anything … but please …spare my son,' she pleaded.

But Ned Cartwright was beyond reason. He gave a hoarse, cracked laugh, defying hell to do its worst as he hit her again. Never before had he felt the extent of his power. His piercing eyes fell on the shapely figure sprawled on the bed, at the well-formed breasts peaked at the nipples clearly visible through her thin nightgown and his gaze was nailed there. His face suddenly suffused with lust, the eyes hot and wild, and the ghastly cracked lips parted in a wicked smile presenting the yellow stumps of his decayed teeth. Feeling his manhood stir as his imagination took hold, with a practiced hand he gave his crotch a fondle to encourage its growth. He had taken such pride in his manhood, bigger than any man's he had ever seen. He had been quite a lion among the ladies at one time, but it was a while since he had had a woman to thrust it into. Since things had turned sour for him he had had very little use for it other than to take a piss.

Dan's eyes were wide and murderous as he watched Cartwright undo his belt to let his filthy breeches fall to the floor and step right out of them. It did not take a crystal ball to tell what was on the maniac's sick, evil mind. He felt the pain tear at him, split him, rip him apart, the hellish tattoo of his heart increasing, faster and even faster as if it might burst. He began to groan; a kind of rasping that came from deep in his throat, a low stifled sound that arises from the bottom of the soul when overcharged with burning red-hot rage. The shadow of death was already brooding.

Cartwright knew that sound, knew it well. Many a night, when all the world slept, it welled up from deep inside him, with its dreadful echo of terror that came to haunt him, again and again.

Clara's quivering lips moved in a silent prayer as a plea for help. The horror was upon her before she had time to brace herself. The beast yanked up her nightgown, lowered itself to kneeling position on the edge of the bed, with the lower part of his grimy body horribly exposed, like a maggot that had crawled out of the earth …hideous …repulsive …she could even smell it. She began to whimper helplessly. His vile, slithering hands were all over her, groping in a brutish fashion about her creamy white body, crawling, clutching and pinching. His fingers prying into the most intimate, still tender part of her that had not yet healed from the birth of her child. Then came the fierce penetration that split her asunder, invading her very soul, prompting a frenzied wail. An agony not to be borne.

It went on for some time, as Cartwright wasn't a well man, but he was in no rush. As long as he was gone from here before dawn. As he pounded away at the woman beneath him, he swivelled his stabbing eyes until he looked directly into Dan Greenward's, telling the defeated man that he, Ned Cartwright, was the victor and had always known he would win. All the time his dried up, leathery lips smiled horribly. He felt triumphantly in charge, claiming the spoils of victory.

Dan felt the darkness of that sickening smile, a smile like the shadow of death, and the seal of damnation upon his own face reflected that very fear. But Cartwright was not moved by the agony on the older man's face. His smile widened in an expression of profound self-satisfaction, blended with hatred and scorn. And as the beast heaved on top of her, Clara Greenward turned her head towards the raging form of her husband, locking her eyes with his as he writhed and bucked, which only served to tighten the rope about his neck. His breath rattled in his throat and his eyes begun to bulge horribly as death crept in like a snake to choke him.

Clara felt the scream start somewhere deep inside

her, in that dark place where nightmares live, bubbling up through her tortured body until it reached her throat to erupt in a most heart-rending screech, a piercing shriek of despair.

Her hysterics only incited her attacker to make a greater effort to reach his goal. But when she started clawing madly at his evil face, ready to tear out his eyes, fighting like a mad woman escaped from an asylum, disrupting his concentration and cutting short his enjoyment, his manhood rapidly shrunk. It turned soft and limp, rendering it useless. His eyes narrowed to slits of frustrated fury, and making a fist, he gave her one hard blow full in the face, knocking her out cold.

Young Edna Masters came abruptly awake, wondering what all the bloody commotion was about. She lit a candle and shuffled along the passage to find out. Half asleep and bleary-eyed, she stood in the doorway, blinking in the candlelight in a helpless way, like a young barn owl. Her eyes locked on the half-naked fiend hovering over the missus in the most hideously threatening way. From her lips came a sound that freezes the living flesh, a low groaning noise that started in the back of her throat that rose from a groan to a wail, from a wail to a shriek of mortal terror. She dropped the candleholder and turned to flee, but Cartwright was upon her in a flash, heaving her into the room and flinging her with what strength he had left, against the wall, cracking the back of her skull like an eggshell. The girl was dead before she slid to the floor.

Cartwright grunted and shrugged, telling himself she wasn't important, turning his attention back to the figure on the bed. Feeling the eyes of the departed upon him, he forced himself not to perceive the bitterness of their expression and, gazing down into their depths told himself aloud how clever he was. He placed his filthy hand in the region of the older man's heart and kept it there for a minute or so, just to make sure he was definitely dead. Greenward was dead right enough, stone dead, gone into the region of shadows.

But what of the woman? She might be out cold now, but would soon come round and could identify him. Then Greenward would win. He must get rid of her. That's what he must do, finish her off …he told himself, talking aloud. He frowned, cursing himself for not thinking of finishing her off earlier when Greenward was alive to see it.

He lifted the crowbar with both hands just as Clara opened her eyes. They widened in heart-stopping fright as he brought it down hard on the side of her head, the force of the blow crunching bone, opening the side of her skull and shifting the top half of her body jerkingly sideways, making him start.

Cartwright calmly reviewed every incident of the night, every vivid detail, but with less satisfaction he thought of the recurring faintness, the curious sense of weightlessness that had once or twice come over him. Now the score had been settled he was feeling as listless as a sick dog, as if he was on the edge of some mental breakdown and might collapse at any minute. Getting even with the old man had been embedded in his mind, the festering hatred part of him, like a limb, an arm or a leg, and had kept him alive during those long, hard months tramping about the countryside.

He struggled to imagine a life where vengeance no longer mattered. But he mustn't think about that right now ...he told himself. He could only think of one thing at a time. First he would collect his trophies. There was sure to be a few riches about the house, jewellery, silver candlesticks and suchlike, things of some value; anything saleable would do.

Chuckling to himself, he picked up the shovel from the hearth and lifted the glowing embers from the fire, scattering them over the bed - Clara and Dan Greenward's deathbed. The woollen bedding started to smoulder at once. Another shovel full he laid on Edna Master's outspread lap, setting the fine material of her nightgown alight instantly.

But Cartwright wasn't satisfied. He lifted the candle and set light to the girl's hair, then to make sure that nothing would be missed, he opened the door to the great oak cupboard that stood against the wall and placed the flaming candle inside against the hanging clothes, telling himself how clever he was. Filled with food for the flames, the inside of the cupboard flared up within seconds, and in less than ten minutes it was blazing, the hungry flames missing nothing. The great cupboard itself, being very dry and rendered more combustible by wax and oil, was eagerly eaten into.

Cartwright stood outside on the grass, watching like one fascinated by a power he could not resist, the great ocean of smoke pouring from every outlet of the upstairs rooms. The sparrows in the eaves blindly took wing, and rendered giddy by the smoke, fell fluttering down to earth. The fire would spread soon enough and destroy the whole house. As he stood there, he told himself time after time that he was right. Of course, the law would condemn him, but morally he was right and had only punished

Greenward as he deserved to be punished.

Now, he must get away, make his way to London maybe, where he could get lost in the crowds. His mood had changed now to one of jubilation. With the roll of banknotes, the watch and rings, and all the silverware he had collected, he would soon grow content again. His imagination saw the future stretch before him in a golden glow.

All of a sudden there was an almighty roar as a fireball ripped through the top of the house, ballooning high in a huge flower with orange, crimson and gold petals, giving him such a fright he scrambled backwards and landed on the ground, still clutching his bulging bundle of trophies and the crowbar. Cursing, he struggled to his feet and throwing the bundle over his shoulder, crossed the yard. As he hastily pulled on his old boots, he heard a shrill whinnying coming from inside the barn. The smell of the smoke had drifted in, alarming the horse …he supposed. The horse! His means of escape! He would be well away before daybreak.

Pulling open the barn door, he stepped inside, standing for a minute or two until he grew used to the gloom. His first mistake was in dropping his bundle on the ground, right in front of the horse's stall. For some reason, unobserved by Cartwright whose only thought was to coax the beast out of the stall and get away from there as fast as he could, the already fretful animal took the sudden clatter as a further threat. There was a great scraping of hooves and kicking up of the straw that covered the ground.

'Whoa! Whoa there!' Cartwright cried as he opened the makeshift gate to the front of the stall and moved to the mare's side. She rolled her eyes fearfully, ready to snap at the stranger's hand. He ran a rough hand over her shoulder and reached to grab her by the mane, to lead her out of the stall, but the animal danced nervously backwards, blowing through flaring nostrils.

'Bloody lunatic 'orse,' Cartwright grumbled as he made another attempt to grab her by the mane.

This time he was successful. But the horse reared up, straining every nerve, and Cartwright hung on perilously, his arm almost pulled out of its socket. He was forced to let go. Raving and swearing, he made a fist and whacked the beast brutally on its sensitive muzzle. His second mistake.

'That'll bloody teach yer,' he yelled. The animal snorted and snapped savagely at him, lunging wildly. Cartwright was knocked backward and flattened agonizingly against the wall.

'Damn yer. Damn yer t'ell.' He struck the horse another blow, thinking to teach the stupid beast a lesson. This was his undoing.

The mare's ears flattened with fright as she whickered shrilly in the back of her throat, and, as her fear grew, she crashed against her attacker. Cartwright let out a long, thin scream as he felt his ribs crack.

Cartwright kept perfectly still, suspended in space, hardly daring to breathe as he saw the future go spiralling downwards into the dark. The deed he came for was done, but despair was in his very triumph; wild, uncontrollable, raging despair, for the hopelessness of the peril into which he had plunged, maddening him and setting his teeth chattering uncontrollably.

He started to edge slowly and cautiously sideways

along the wall of the stall in an effort to escape, but again the throbbing animal crashed against the now petrified man, battering him with its superior strength. Cartwright went down under the shock, howling like a mad man. In the dim light the animal loomed over him. Fearing for his life, Cartwright made the final mistake - a fatal mistake.

He lashed out with the crowbar at the threatening animal's vulnerable legs, crunching iron on bone. The frenzied, quivering beast screeched piercingly, bounding wildly about in the restricted space, then quite suddenly keeled over, snorted the once and was still, its enormous, deadweight trapping and crushing the doomed man's legs.

The pain was excruciating, unbearable. Cartwright drew in his breath and held it for several seconds before letting it go jerkily. He was alone, marked and singled out for his wickedness, a Lucifer among devils. He had been in danger a good many times in the course of his life, but almost always when he could warm the sense of peril by action. Now he felt his time had come and nothing he could do would avert it.

He started to sob loudly like a child, his whole life rushing before him, across the abyss of the past to the wall of the present that now imprisoned him, a lightning experience lasting no more than a few seconds and yet a flash that seemed timeless, ending with a long drawn-out shuddering sigh as he fell into a state of blessed oblivion.

TWENTY-FOUR

The sky above was dull and the earth was of a still darker tint. There had been frost, then rain. Although the rain had now ceased, pools of water lay about the yard. Joe entered the woods from the hillside pasture, lounging a moment against the old lichen grey stone wall, which like the house had become worn and mellowed by the tempestuous years, to note the play of early light and shadow on the birches. His eyes lingered restfully on the wonderful mixture of soft colours that no brush has ever yet imitated, the rich old gold of autumn tapestries, the glimmering grey-green of the mouldering stumps that the fungi had painted.

His walk was the walk of a strong, confident man, each step long, steady and firm, quite devoid of haste. Although the furrows were full of water, the path, a mere narrow cart track, was firm under foot, protected by the towering archway of the trees, leafy shadows closing into perspective like the roof and columns of a cathedral. A harsh wind followed him along the chill, shadowy tunnel, driving the fallen leaves that had been lying beside the way rustling and dancing after him. But wind, rain or storm did not affect Joe Greenward, nor the bitter frost or snow. This was a man who digs and delves in the earth and sometimes lies on the bare ground in the night.

The love for the countryside that persisted in his heart sprang from the fact that however much political, economic or social conditions change, nature and her laws remain.

The crunch of his sturdy work boots startled a blackbird roosting in the hedge, seeking the warmth it could not find. It flurried out and flew away across the field. Further along, on the sheltered bank lie maple leaves, fallen from the bushes that form a kind of barricade against the wind, to nestle on the ivy that covered the bank. He strolled on, wading through the moist grass, climbing with almost feverish eagerness. There was a path of sorts with rocky outcrops, and from every bit of ground where sustenance might be saplings of rowan and sycamore grew. A curlew cried overhead, shaking its sweet, long-drawn whistle into silver drops, shouting defiance at the hills.

The serrated soles to Joe's boots, which were impervious to the muddy ground, gripped the wet stones as he mounted the slippery slopes to his eyrie on the bare crag. It was a perfect place to be at this time of day, when the world was waking and everything was bright and fresh with dew. He loved to watch the coming of the dawn. There was always enchantment in its approach, in that fading of the darkness and the glowing of the clouds; magic in that moment when all creation stirs. And from here he could view down the whole length of the valley, noting with a farmer's eye, his cattle and sheep scattered over the fells below, browsing the frosty grass, going to and fro in the unreserved way that animals have in the early hours before the restraint of human society is imposed on them.

Undulating fields extended on either hand, brown from the late passage of the plough, a pale yellow where the short stubble yet remains. It was a familiar sight to Joe, but it filled him none the less with a great sense of satisfaction, as always. He had money invested in the soil, seed lying waiting the genial warm rain that would cause it to germinate, capital in every furrow traced by the plough. On the other hand, he had money in his stock; sheep, pigs, cattle and poultry. A double anxiety was his; first that his crops may prosper, secondly, that his stock may flourish. In his view, nothing conveys so strong an impression of substantial wealth as the view of golden wheat-fields. A diamond, a sparkling gem may be worth a fortune, but the sum it represents seems abstract rather than real. But wheat, a field of golden wheat is a great fact that seizes hold of the mind, symbolizing real wealth.

Joe Greenward was in the very prime of life when youth and experience meet, tall and built proportionately wide across the shoulders, and a chest so broad that he was compelled to wear his shabby jacket unbuttoned. His dress was somewhat disorderly and drab, but his linen always spotless. His features were handsome with a good-humoured expression, the face, neck and hands a healthy brown. There was an air of restless, feverish energy about him, but he was calm and happy, and yet, just at that moment his forehead was marked with the lines caused by involuntary contraction of the muscles when thinking, as he turned over in his mind the hundred and one things that had to be dealt with. A pair of new wheels had to be fitted on the cart and a few fresh tiles on the roof of the house. The work on arable land is never finished. Even in winter there is still something doing - continuous work for a fixed number of hands - grain to be carted to market, the ploughing in of the stubbles for root crops, cattle and sheep to attend to, and stone walls to repair.

Miles Ramsey was a good lad. A bit on the quiet side and inclined to be a bit sulky if things did not go his way, but nonetheless, an honest, hard-working lad and, above all, a useful one. It was amazing how versatile he was. Grooming the horses, cutting wood, drawing water and cleaning the yard - all done without being ordered. Never was there a handier lad with a kindness and thoughtfulness, which none but those who know the careful ways to which necessity trains country children would think believable. If he keeps steady, he will do well.

A satisfied smile replaced the serious expression on Joe's face. The Ramsey family had made a vast difference to his and his daughter, Megan's life; they had brought the house alive again. In spite of losing her husband, Owen, to the mines at such an early age, April Ramsey was a woman of strong affections, who lived for the sake of her children - Miles, the light of her life, and her three surviving daughters. He was delighted with her cheerfulness, her good humour and the total absence of selfishness. She worked exceedingly hard, showing an evident desire to please, and was already teaching her eldest girl Daisy and his Megan, the rudiments of household work.

Over all there was an atmosphere of welcome, a genial brightness about the house. It was spotlessly clean; furniture and floors highly polished, windows gleaming, curtains and bed linen immaculate, and the kitchen was a model of neatness. She seemed to anticipate everything he could possibly want; hot water ready the moment he put his foot in the door, fresh, clean linen always at hand and as if by magic, a tasty meal set on the table at the precise moment he was ready. And as for the butter and the cheese, they were excellent and so, too, was the home-baked bread and meat pies, the more so because only touched in the processes of preparing by the cleanest of hands. Such simple things brought to perfection by a caring nature.

Joe's green eyes were thoughtful. To show his appreciation he would have the two cottages knocked into one and fit a new stove for her and Liam. Now they were married there was sure to be more children. April's girls had taken to Liam O'Malley well enough, but young Miles was inclined to be resentful of his mother remarrying and made it known. But if anyone could bring him round, O'Malley could; he had more ease of manner than any one he knew. A kind, tolerant Irishman with all the patience in the world, and another good worker. He wouldn't want to lose him or April.

O'Malley worked hard as a shepherd, continuously taking an interest in his charges and often in the face of the most inclement weather. It was hard to find good hands that you could trust. They certainly deserved to be happy, the pair of them. He was genuinely pleased for them, watching them in their newfound love, and yet seeing them together some-how made him feel lonely. He had everything that the heart of a man could desire, except a wife, and that commodity had been offered to him from many quarters in various delicate and diplomatic ways, only to be as delicately and diplomatically rejected. It was the little events of everyday life that fixate a man at the last; the commonplace, circular come and go that runs between the cradle and the grave. Not all these new-fangled inventions, the coming of the railroads or even the upheavals of great wars; but marriage, birth and death, and the making of new friends. Binding all is the rich thread of the seasons, with its many-coloured strands and, backing all, the increase-ing knowledge of Nature and her ways, that revolving wheel of beauty growing ever more complex and yet more clear, more splendid and yet more simple as the pulses slow to a close.

Gone was the mood of the moment. If he was honest with himself he had to admit he had his maudlin moments when thinking of the lovely Rose Bradley and what might have been, but those thoughts seldom survived sunrise and breakfast. He had too much to think about, too much on his mind. Only at night when he lay alone in his bed he would allow himself sweet remembrance, recalling her fresh fragrance and every detail of that sweet, innocent face, those lovely lavender eyes, the soft, smooth creaminess of her skin and every single curve of her fine, slender body. It was then he ached for the feel of her - when he was forced to attend to himself due to the lack of sexual fulfilment. The thought of her still affected him. His heart jerked involuntary as desire soared, to sink back like a weary dove, bearing only the bittersweet of unforgettable memories. She was quite unlike anyone he had ever met.

Only once could a man feel the love that passed all things, the love that, whatever grief and unrest it might come through, alone had in it the heart of peace and joy. He doubted he would ever feel that way for anyone again. When he looked back and tried to understand how it happened, he could say only that he felt pierced by the sight of her. He had fallen in love with Rose Bradley from the first time he had clapped eyes on her, but it had been hopeless right from the start. Fate had torn that love from him, nipped it off as a sharp wind nips off a perfect flower. And after Kitty's tragic death, he had been riddled with conscience and guilt. If he had not hardened his heart, he could not say what he might have done. He supposed that recovering from an ill-fated romance is, after all, to anyone of sufficient will power, purely an attitude of mind. Besides, a lovely young girl like Rose Bradley was more than likely married by now.

Oh, well, you can't have everything in life …he told himself. After all, he had his land and land lasts. Land from which he drew his wealth. Land that rewarded him strictly according to his ability as a farmer. You take care of it and it will take care of you. In his mind working the land was no exertion. He worked towards an end, but it was a worthy end, for ambition, if not too extravagant, is a virtue. To rise socially requires as great or greater work than for a poor man to achieve a fortune. It was, in fact, a period of inflation. Like stocks and shares everything was going up; everybody hastening to get rich. Herdwicks' fetched fancy prices and corn crops ruled high.

He pursed his lips and nodded his head in full self-satisfied agreement with himself, then turned around. It did no good to stand brooding - there was work waiting; it might be Sunday, but the cattle still had to be attended to - cows milked as well as foddered, pigs' and chickens' fed, and the eggs had to be collected.

The land sloped upwards in a patchwork of brown and green fields, divided by grey stone walls, some still in need of repair, stubbles stretching far beyond, where the land rose and fell in undulations. On the distant horizon a great, grey column of smoke curled briskly up into the air and floated off in a banner over the hillside. Someone has a bonfire …a hell of a big one at that! Who was there to have such a fire way past Branthwaite? It appeared to come from High Greenrigg or from …a curious sensation passed over him as if a cold hand had grasped at his heart …from …sweet Jesus! He was suddenly very afraid. Of what he could not have said.

He dropped hastily off the crag; down into the eerie mist he plunged and set off with a fast fellman's stride across the intervening heath between Uldale and Branthwaite. It was rough going, with many little hills and hollows and narrow steep ravines where little moorland streams ran down from the watershed of the hills. Across them he hurriedly picked his way, using sheep tracks that he knew until he could cut across to an old bridle path where the going was easier, running like a man possessed. Across the springy turf he went, skirting half-buried rocks from behind which sheep got clumsily to their feet and leaped away in alarm. He stumbled a couple of times, but was soon back up on his feet. A curlew sobbed its cry somewhere in the silence, and the trees reared their great long arms heavenwards in mockery as he ran on, his breath coming in short gasps, knowing nothing but the blind necessity to be in time.

As he hastened past High Greenrigg, he could see the immense expanse of smoke rising high above the trees. He muttered a prayer that died in his throat. Something told him he was too late. He began to slip slowly into the pit that his own active mind dug for him, his imagination dragging him to the very depths of it, thoughts that seized his brain and cramped it until no feeling came to him other than intense alarm.

He met shouts and cries of confusion as he reached the yard. Half a dozen men and women were already there. Three of the men he instantly recognized - Reg Dibble, Todd Beech and Bob Fisch. They had formed themselves in to a line, dashing back and forward to the water pump with buckets and saucepans or whatever they had been able to find that would hold water. They passed them from one person to another, spilling half the contents on the ground, the men taking turns to run with it into the smoke-filled house in a feeble effort to douse the flames in the upstairs rooms.

Joe bent double to catch his breath.

'Side door's been forced an' the 'ouse's bin deliberately fired if yer ask me,' Bob Fisch shouted above the raised voices and clatter of buckets and pans. 'I've sent for Constable Radford. An' the doctor, if 'e can be found. 'Ope I did the right thing.'

All Joe could do was nod.

'Good thing we got 'ere when we did or the whole bloody 'ouse might've gone up. Our Nell saw the smoke when she was throwin' out the slops. It bein' the Sabbath I was still in bloody bed.'

Joe straightened up just at the moment someone carrying a bucket came staggering out of the front doorway, bent over double and vomited over the grass. Another silhouette appeared, this time carrying a small bundle... his clothes like a smoking hayrick, bringing the active line of people to a paralysing stillness. Joe darted forward to meet him. It was Bert Lithgow with a towel wrapped about his mouth. What you could see of his face was as black as soot, streaked by the tears that streamed from his tortured eyes. He held out the bundle. He had found the child …he had perished in the smoke.

Joe flinched in alarm. 'Sweet Jesus!' He felt the ability to think slip away as his disordered mind plunged in horror. He clung desperately to the hope that his father might have survived. He gripped Bert's arm fiercely. 'M..my father? Clara...?'

One of the women came forward to take the small bundle from Bert's arms. Another to throw a wet cloth over his smouldering shoulders. Bert squeezed his stinging eyes shut. All he could do was shake his head stiffly from side to side. The smoke had almost certainly affected his throat and he was more than likely rigid with shock at finding the small child lifeless. He bent double with a sudden fit of coughing.

Joe looked up at the top storey of the house. One of the upstairs windows shone like burnished gold with glowing brightness. 'I'm …I'm going in.' He pulled off his jacket and was about to cover his head when someone thrust something wet at him.

''Ere …take one o' these wet towels. Yer'll need it.' It was a woman's voice.

Bert Lithgow straightened up, shaking his head from side to side, but fiercely this time. 'No …no man! Let one …one o' the others...' he cried hoarsely.

He'd always thought of himself as a strong man, but the ghastly sight he had witnessed in that house had shaken him to the very core. A sight he would never forget as long as he lived.

'I'm going in,' Joe repeated stubbornly.

Bob Fisch laid a hand on his shoulder. 'Then I'll come with yer. Dan's bin good t'me an' mine.'

Bert grabbed his arm in an attempt to hold him

back, but Joe pulled away. Each of the two men draped a wet towel over his head and held it around the lower half of his face. Then they were away, carrying a bucket of water in each hand, caring little for the danger as they bounded up the stairs, which surprisingly were virtually untouched by the blaze. On the landing the smoke that met them was dense. Their eyes streamed as they made their way into the first of the bedrooms, which seemed to be untouched by the fire, but the smoke was thick and dense. There was no apparent damage; furniture and the cradle that stood near the bed appeared unblemished. The room was unoccupied. Coughing and spluttering, the two men went farther along the passage through the wall of smoke. Joe stood one of the buckets on the floor, throwing the water from the other into the room.

The heat was so intense that the paint on the door had swelled into boils, blistering the incautious hand that touched them. But Joe didn't even flinch. In those remaining seconds all his efforts were focused on that one spark of hope - that his father and Clara might be in the room, unconscious, maybe trapped and waiting for help to come. But sorrows, like joys, fall swift as thunderbolts from heaven.

The worst of the fire seemed to be out, just smouldering remains, but there were flames still licking like a serpent's tongue at the heavy oak cupboard. They saturated it with what water they had left in the buckets, dousing the last of the blaze, rendering themselves giddy from the hissing, steaming smoke. The smell in the room was pungent, overpowering, the evil power of it paralysing them in an instant. Joe dropped the empty bucket on the floor to squeeze both his eyelids shut with his fingers, blinked several times and peered hard through smoke-tortured eyes. Both men remained motionless where they stood - horror-struck.

There bore upon Joe Greenward's brain a sense of violation too sickening to be endured. As strong a man that he was, he was not prepared for this; the most sickening sight that struck cold as winter's ice against his heart.

A vision of hell: two charred corpses. Both still recognizable. Scenes of wickedness, of murder, of treachery and of lust fell dismally upon his sight, as he was brought face to face with the vilest results of man's evil.

In sheer soul-splitting despair he ground his teeth ferociously together lest he should shriek out loud. Bob's strong hands gripped him and pulled him away, following behind as Joe staggered along the passage-way and back down the stairs, taking one unsteady step at a time. It was a miracle he reached the bottom without falling or spewing up. Still holding the banister in a death-like grip, he hovered with teeth clenched, trying to keep the bile from rising in his throat. The effort hurt his jaw.

Outside, daylight had grown strong, shining upon the heap of furniture from the downstairs rooms that had been piled upon the down-trodden grass. Ironically, it started to rain, stinging his cheeks as he stood rooted to the spot in a trance of agony, grasping each of his arms by the elbow tightly to his heaving chest.

The chaos had eased and there was a long, painful silence, the women clutching at each other in obvious distress. Words failed them. Bert Lithgow had told them what the score was, what he had seen.

Bob Fisch took charge. As long as it wasn't one of his own, he could stand anything. Sheets were brought to cover the bodies. Dan Greenward had evidently been strangled. There were the remains of a thick rope about his neck. His eyes seemed to jut out from their sockets, the tongue swollen and protruding from a mouth stretched wide. So vile a death.

Strangely, the flames hadn't reached either of their faces. Clara Greenward wore a look of terror, her eyes wide open; you could still see the scream in them. She must have lived to taste the bitterness of death before it took her, killed by a blow of a blunt instrument, an axe or a hammer maybe, that had split open the side of her head. There was a deep hollow, an oozing gap across the side of her skull.

Joe shuddered when he saw the wound, and a sharp pain tore at his heart. He cast down his eyes for a moment, stifling a sob, his body shaking uncontrollably, asking himself silently ...how a day that had started in such tranquillity, could change in such a short space of time into an indescribable nightmare.

He sank to his knees on the hard ground and muttered aloud that he would never get over this, while the rain drifted in a cold, steady stream upon his horror-stricken face.

The yard by this time was full of men and women from nearby villages and a couple of wailing children, all watching the horrific scene with mounting dread. The crime of murder has always exercised a horrid fascination over the minds of men. An extra chill is added if the crime remains unsolved. Would the murderer strike again? The most shocking thought of all was that they might even know the brutal fiend.

The upstairs of the house was a disaster. The fire

had burnt through two of the rooms, but the other two were mainly smoke damaged, pathetic in their empty desertion. They found poor, young Edna Masters, slumped against the far wall where she had been hurled. She was barely recognisable from the ghastly burns to her body and face - an appalling addition to the horrors of the scene. The back of the girl's skull had been shattered - hopefully she had died before she was set alight. The shocking sight of her made even the boldest tremble. Everyone was on edge.

'Bad do this. A bad do,' Todd Beech reflected. 'The little 'un perishin' in the smoke like that.'

'The 'ouse must've been fired in the early hours,' Reg Dibble commented. 'Otherwise it could be a lot worse.'

''Ow could it be a lot worse?' Bert Lithgow uttered. 'Four bloody deaths! What could be worse than that?'

'You know what I mean. The 'ouse would've burnt right through,' Reg explained in exasperation. 'Not just the upstairs rooms, but the whole bloody lot. That's what I mean.'

'Why didn't yer say so then?' Bert grumbled.

'I just did.'

'Cut it out, you two,' Bob Fisch yelled. 'There's work t'be done. We'll need somethin' t'bring the bodies out on. A plank or somethin'. Take a look in the barn, will yer? See what yer can find.'

The two men leapt into action. The door of the barn was already ajar. A shaft of light like an arrow pierced the old boarded walls. Their timbers and the roof soared aloft in venerable regularity drawn from some long forgotten forest. A fragrant carpet of sawdust covered the ground underfoot, and the air was charged with the smell of smoke mingled with wood. Todd pushed the door farther open to let in more light as Reg stepped inside and took a good look about. Todd followed him in. It was Reg who found him. He started in fright.

'Bloody hell! Look 'ere!'

Cartwright was trapped by his legs under the lifeless horse, with the bloodied crowbar still grasped in his hand.

'It's bloody Cartwright,' Todd gasped fearfully. No one had set eyes on the overman since the night they had set upon him.

'I know that, yer bloody fool. But're yer thinkin' what I'm thinkin'?' Reg asked.

'Reckon I am,' said Todd, his lean face looking uneasy.

'Then yer best get Bob an' Bert in 'ere, an' quick about it. But mind nobody else follows.'

It was soon realised why Cartwright had made the brutal attack on Dan Greenward and his wife. All four men had been involved on the night they had beaten and strung him up on a branch of a tree. They had meant only to teach him a lesson he would never forget. Cartwright had obviously convinced himself that the attack on him had been ordered by Dan, but it was not so. The men had taken it upon themselves to punish the man for his greed and negligence that had caused the loss of lives.

Cartwright was still breathing, but they couldn't tell the extent of his injuries. Nor could they say why the horse had keeled over and died, trapping Cartwright's legs beneath its great bulk. It was a complete mystery.

Bob sighed resignedly. 'Well, tis no good standin'

'ere gawkin'. Joe'll 'ave t'be told.'

''Ow much are we t'tell 'im?' Todd questioned anxiously.

'No more'n 'e need know. It'll only make matters worse if 'e were t'find out the truth. It's more than our lives're worth. 'E'd likely want t'kill the lot o' us,' Bob whispered, riddled with guilt. 'An' I can't say I'd blame 'im. For all our sakes, we best act ignorant. Agreed, lads?'

'Agreed!' the other three chorused.

'Right then! Bring 'im in. But watch what yer say an' go easy on 'im. The poor sod's still in a state o' shock.'

'What shalla I tell 'im then?'

'Just tell 'im 'e's wanted in the barn. That's all. Now, you lot, let's get this 'ere 'orse off this bastard, so as t'see what damage 'as been done.'

Joe was led into the barn. He gazed helplessly about him, as if for someone to direct and guide him. Bob Fisch had the task of telling him just what they had found.

For a fraction of a second Joe's stunned brain was unable to decipher what Bob had just said. The words had no meaning, they were incomprehensible, floating in the air, but gradually, very slowly, they sank in until he grasped their meaning. He felt the ice-cold fury start somewhere in his chest, seeping through every inch of his body, and yet, it was as though his thoughts were so hot and maddened they would set fire to his mind. A mist swam before his eyes and the blood pounded in his head.

With murder in his heart, and a roar that turned everyone's head, he launched himself at Cartwright. But the men thrust themselves in front of the would-be combatant, barring his way.

Joe's eyes blazed with blood-curdling hate, his mouth twisting into a vicious snarl, like that of an enraged bull. He felt his blood run hot and fast in the need to maim, the need to kill this man, this animal that had brutally tortured and murdered his father, the one man he loved.

'Let me at him. Let me at the bastard.'

Bob clamped a restraining hand on his arm. 'Steady. Steady now, Joe. 'E's in a bad way.'

But Joe snatched his arm away with a violence that astonished Bob. 'In a bad way! In a bad way! I'll slaughter the fucking bastard. He's robbed me o' those I love an' all you can say is … is *steady*. I'll make him wish he'd never been bloody born.' His hands clenched into fists so tight he could feel his fingernails cut into his palms. Never in his life had he felt such savage, killing fury. 'Let me at him. I'll kill the bastard. I'll fucking kill the bastard!'

There was a riot in his head. He wanted to crash his fists into Cartwright's ugly face, pummel the man to death. But strong arms were flung around him, hustling him backward, pulling him clear.

Bob could see the hate in those remarkable, transparent green eyes, a rage that was terrifyingly awesome. 'The scum's not worth 'anging for.'

'Let me at him. For pity's sake …let me at the bastard.'

The men had no shadow of a doubt that there would be more murder done should they let Joe get to Cartwright. There was a scuffling of feet; then the struggling man's bruised mind slowed from its racing explosion of rage and gradually cleared as he struggled to consider the consequence his murderous, bloodthirsty intentions might bring.

Joe quietened and the danger was past. A strange alteration had passed over him. When they let him go, he was shaking violently with heart-rending emotion. It spun out of control. He dropped to his knees and threw back his head, with his eyes squeezed shut. The men around him watched the spectacle in total helplessness. All of a sudden his mouth begun to quiver, and for the second time in his adult life, Joseph Greenward wept for the loss of his loved-ones. It sounded like the wail of a badly wounded animal, a thin agonized sound, echoing about the great barn for several minutes - a cry to make one shudder.

Cartwright had not been able to resist the temptation to steal; the bundle still lay where he had dropped it. In his jacket pockets they found a roll of banknotes amounting to forty five pounds, some loose change to the value of twelve shillings, a gold fob watch and chain, a plain gold wedding band, and a ring set to form a flower with six glittering sapphires accenting the circle of petals and a glorious larger single sapphire set in the very centre - a token of love given to his beloved wife by Dan Greenward. The contents of his pockets, together with the crowbar, and the sack of stolen property all proved Cartwright's guilt conclusively.

A tumult of talk burst forth.

'I say leave 'im for the gallows. What 'e deserves. 'E's likely the one that raped an' murdered that poor lass from Wildacres,' Todd Beech stated.

'Huh! Yer probably right, but I don't think 'e'll live that long,' Reg Dibble put in. 'We ought t'ang 'im 'ere an' now from the 'ighest tree.'

Bob Fisch threw him a disbelieving look. ''Ave yer 'eard yerself? We could 'ang 'im 'ere an' now with pleasure, but where would that leave us, aye? 'Ave yer thought o' that? 'Ave yer? No, I didn't think yer 'ad.'

'I say put 'im in some dark dungeon underground,' Bert Lithgow suggested. 'Let the bloody bastard rot an' the rats feed on 'im.'

As the parish constable, Murphy Radford was to make the arrest. After a heated discussion between him and Joe, he reluctantly agreed to the prisoner being kept at the farmhouse. Just until he was in a fit state to travel, when he would be transported to Newgate Goal to await trial for crimes that would most certainly receive the death penalty.

The Old Bailey was the court for nearby Newgate. A Jury of twelve men would hear the accusations and evidence brought to them by the constable, to decide whether the accused was innocent or guilty. If the prisoner survived, that is. And, of course, he had to be watched at all times. Not that he was likely to be going anywhere by the look of him. All the same, it was best to be on the safe side, Murphy added.

The community was stunned, shaken to the very core by the news of the shocking, brutal murders. Daniel Greenward was a good man, a man of illustrious and unblemished character, well-respected by those who had cause to be thankful for what he had done for them in the past. He had always stood up for the weak, kept his word and never kicked a man when he was down. He would be sadly missed. And equally respected, his wife, Clara Greenward;

she was a pearl among women some said, known for her warmth of heart, who had winkled him out of his shell after the loss of his two sons and his first wife. Indecently hasty, some might say, when it came to the mourning of a dead wife. They talked of nothing else. Hard living did not allow much softness in these people, but their hearts were warm with kindness and a caring which was shown in true neighbourliness.

As was the custom, a constant succession of men and women alike sat in Joseph Greenward's parlour at Chapel House Farm, throughout the days and nights beside the already sealed coffins that held the badly disfigured bodies of Daniel and Clara Greenward, and their infant child who appeared to be peacefully sleeping.

TWENTY-FIVE

The great, scrawny frame lay on a wooden bed in one of the old-fashioned rooms of the farmhouse. Although it was not fully dark outside, the curtains were drawn, and the room was dimly illumined by the faint rays of a wood fire and the light of a single candle which reflected on the highly polished floor of dark oak. A pair of old worn boots and some of his ragged clothing had been removed, but he still wore his shirt that had been torn open to free his chest for examination. The pallor of his deeply marked face was death-like, the sunken eyes closed, his whole stance that of exhaustion and semi-stupor, and his breathing very heavy and arduous.

Joe stood at the foot of the bed, looking as he always did, freshly shaven and his shirt well laundered, for life in the house went on as normal despite what had happened. His hair was a tumble of uncombed curls, his cheeks gaunt, his face stern, teeth tight-clenched, as though he was holding something in that he would dearly love to let out. But it was in his eyes that the real depth of his suffering was revealed. The glow, the sparkle in them, was no longer there.

Deftly, but non-too gently, Dr Morrison set about his examination. The patient was in a state of oblivion, neither moving nor speaking, although from time to time a moan escaped from between tight-pressed lips. He was not even recognizable as the strong, tough Ned Cartwright, the overman who had once made the life of every man, woman and child who worked under him, a misery, with his penny-pinching methods and reckless ambition. This wreck, this six-foot-odd skeleton, this mumbling stranger who had come back from goodness knows where.

Dr Morrison gazed at the man with vacant eyes, felt the pulse and found it very jerky and feeble. 'So this is what the devil looks like, is it?'

Deft though he might be, he was well aware that his probing was not without agony to the injured man, but he was burdened by too many patients to waste too much time on such a low-life. And he felt no sympathy, not an ounce of compassion after witnessing the result of Cartwright's merciless brutality to humanity - crimes that lifted the hair and shook the soul. His very name was a synonym for hate and wrath.

'There's several ribs broken an' with the poor condition o' his breathing, I suspect there's something worse inside, but we should know more in a day or two. That's if he survives.'

'Is he in danger then?' Joe enquired sullenly.

'Maybe yes, maybe no,' said the doctor. 'Considering the state o' his general health I'm surprised he's lasted this long.'

'The bastard was strong enough t'break int'my father's house, overpower him an' commit bloody murder.'

'Well, all I can say is he must've taken Dan by surprise, because by the look o' him he's wasting away. He's nothing but a bag o' bones.'

Cartwright was shaken into consciousness by some rough hand, but he kept his eyes tightly closed as he listened. He distinctly heard an uplifted voice with a faraway, emotionless intonation. The sudden pressure of those hands, hands that were incredibly powerful, brought on the burning agony in his side, as if Death itself was fingering him. He was not in his own power; he was under the spell of some other control.

'Just see that he's well enough t'stand trial. That's all I ask.'

The doctor sighed resignedly. 'I can't work miracles. With plenty o' bed rest the ribs would normally heal, but taking into account his other injuries …the fractured leg an' his poor condition …well… '

Joe passed a trembling hand over his strained eyes. 'How long?'

Doctor Morrison shrugged. 'Who can say! He's well-nigh spent an' if he lives through the night, I shall be more'n a little surprised. He breathes an' that is all. He might never wake up. It's my opinion he'll go out like a light, as quiet as you see him now. I've made him comfortable. All we can do now is wait.'

Comfortable! Cartwright repeated mutely. Bleeding comfortable! Suffering the agonies of the damned and he calls it comfortable. Everything hurt and he was so tired, so weary. He slept, giving up everything.

He lived on, in a kind of daze, opening his eyes languidly to examine a strange world upon which he had not yet focused his mind. His head was throbbing painfully as if it would blow up, but that was not the only wave of pain that swept over him. If he as much as moved a muscle, a terrible stabbing shot through his side and a strange burning pain, a pain that he was unable to account for, in the region of his chest that seemed to be growing more acute. So he stayed perfectly still …like one who was dead. There he lay, drowsiness still heavy on his eyelids, breathing faintly, otherwise stirring neither hand nor limb, feeling his power gradually ebbing away,

He slept and woke and slept in a semi-conscious numbness of cold and silence, deathly pain and fatigue. Always in the same confused victimised state, as though he was drifting on some consummation that he had no will to avoid, yet which seemed heavy and terrible to him.

Sometimes a shadow of a man would come and sit in the room, in absolute silence, casting his menacing spell over him by his very presence, his silent, powerfully physical presence. Always he was treated with this curious impersonal attentiveness, this utterly impersonal benevolence, as an old man might treat a small child. But underneath it he felt there was something threatening, as if he were a victim and all the attention given him was the work of oppressing him.

When his visitor had gone, in his quiet, insidious fashion, a shock of fear came over him; though fear of what he did not know. The room gradually grew darker and colder, and there was that dreadful silence, a silence that is heard, a silence ominous and strange, in which the very beating of the heart is audible. He closed his eyes and felt the horror of the spell relax, and his consciousness left him like one who is drugged.

The wind moaned in gusts about the building, making strange, restless noises, which Cartwright's strained mind twisted into the semblance of a voice calling his name. He blinked and opened his eyes. The room was dimly lit by the flames from the fire. A shadow stirred in the doorway, setting the door to the jamb with a firm, decisive push.

His nerves were unstrung and ready to shape the shadow into a ghost. It seemed to glide across the open space to where he lay. The blood froze in his veins, and his heart stood still at the sight of the face that hung in the air above him. So great was his fear that what teeth he had left were chattering. Even in the dim light he recognized it - the face of Dan Greenward, spectral and horrible, risen from the dead, wearing a dreadful expression of mental suffering.

The eyes were staring and penetrating, looking into his with a sort of intent fury, as though he were about to spring upon him. Then came a sound, a sound that was low and yet charged with power, like the groaning of a man in grievous pain. A sweat of icy coldness sprang on his brow, his reeling brain telling him he was safe where he was, but how he could resist the power of the ghostly face he did not know. A strange weight like a millstone pressed upon his heart, and his limbs felt like lead, heavy and weighed down; his flesh seemed to be diffusing into a sort of mist in which his consciousness hovered like some dark cloud. The face began to waver and grow dim, and then faded away altogether.

'Tis just a dream, a 'ideous dream,' he told himself aloud. But the vision had seemed so real, so vivid that he could not set it down as only a dream. He was certain it was the man's spirit that had come to haunt him. His scheme of vengeance had been in vain. He closed his heavy lids and lost consciousness in utter abandonment to exhaustion.

It happened at last in the grey of dawn on the Wednesday, as the stars paled and the whitened grass was still stiff with hoar frost, and rime coated the branches of the tall elms. The evil demon, Ned Cartwright, departed - giving the registrar of deaths some additional business - cheating the hangman.

It was the pain that roused him; his side was throbbing most violently, like a knife cutting him in two and there was a great tightness in his chest that was making him feel breathless. He became conscious that he was not alone. The shadow was there in the room with him, but he never stirred, nor did his breathing change. The sensation of fear he had felt when the face first appeared upon the scene returned, but with much greater force. It hovered above him, the eyes fixed with a rigid unwavering gleam, an unrelenting sort of hate, the lips closed in a sinister, sad grimness, in a fixity of revenge and the growing jubilance of one who was going to triumph. These things he could read in the face - the face of a man who had plainly died and yet still he lived. But how was it he looked so young?

'Gr..Greenward?' he murmured from between dry, cracked lips. Just at that moment, a great log shifted in the grate, and as the sparks flew up the chimney as thick as bees from out of a hive, the candle flared high in the last moments of its life. Cartwright's pain-misted eyes looked straight before him at something only he could see - staring at the image which he had fixed in his confused mind. 'Am …am I in 'ell?'

The question was scarcely more than a hoarse whisper, barely audible, but Joe caught the pitiful intensity of it. Cartwright was out of his mind. He knew the man was dying and the very thought of him this …this animal …escaping punishment for his vile crimes, churned up his emotions into a wild chaos of pain and loathing. For a moment the mask was raised and Joe smiled, but the smile merely contorted the lower part of his face, his eyes taking no share in that smile. Before he could answer he passed a trembling hand over his strained eyes. His nerves were under this intolerable strain.

For two whole nights he had not closed his eyes in sleep; his brain seemed to be on fire. His sense of outrage, his anger, was curiously stilled, but left in its place was something worse - a cold thirst for revenge - to make the bastard pay. To make him suffer, squirm with fear, feel the very terror that his father must have suffered before he finally breathed his last agonizing breath. An ugly thought, but consumed by the need for revenge and finding self-control impossible in his weary condition, he decided to "go the whole hog" as he phrased it to himself later, set about tormenting the already tortured mind. His reply was brusque and vicious, whispered close to Cartwright's ear, with his lips set to an ugly snarl.

'No, but you soon will be, Cartwright. The hangman's rope is waiting.'

A whisper that set panic loose to shiver through the damned man's emaciated, pain-racked body. Clutching fingers crept about the dying man's neck, locking themselves, white-knuckled around the throat. It was this that finally unhinged him. His steady breathing was cut short with a gasp, the last shred of self-control leaving him as terror poured into his befuddled mind in the form of the rope. The hangman's rope.

'You might've escaped the rope for robbery, but murder for murder you'll hang. Do you understand, you bastard? An execution's a public spectacle for all t'see. You'll be blindfolded an' the noose'll be placed round your neck. Just picture it, Cartwright. It'll draw a huge crowd. When the trap door opens, the rope'll tighten an' slowly, very slowly squeeze …squeeze the breath from out o' your body. A slow, agonizing death by strangulation. You'll piss yourself with fright, scream for mercy, but no matter how loud you scream, no one will help you, Cartwright. Nobody will put you out o' your misery by pulling your legs, because nobody bloody cares. You'll hang there, swinging from the rope...'

The petrified man started twisting and writhing on the bed, his shrill cry like that of an anguished animal in agony, the sound harsh and broken, fierce and terrible and strangely hollow; the hideous whole indescribable, for the simple reason that no similar sound had ever jarred upon the ears of humanity. His gnarled hands clutched frantically at his neck so fiercely that the nails were driven in deep, and blood seeped down his collar of his shirt, every fibre of him trembling with terror.

For a moment Joe was completely unnerved; the hairs on the back of his neck bristled, and his heart leapt with superstitious fear. He watched with mingled astonishment and alarm, an involuntary shudder running through him from head to foot as Cartwright arched his back, his one good leg flailing widely. At the same time, the upper lip writhed itself away from the discoloured rotten teeth, while the lower jaw fell with an audible jerk, leaving the mouth widely extended and disclosing in full view the swollen, black-coated tongue, quivering violently. He went with all his sins upon him, his whole body jerking with a convulsive effort. So hideous beyond conception was the appearance of Ned Cartwright at this moment, in this deathbed frenzy that Joe shrunk back from the bed. A long, vile rattle escaped from the tormented man's throat, and he was suddenly still and limp, the muscles relaxed in death - in the power of Satan.

Joe could feel the cold run through his veins, and the frozen feather of ice trail across his flesh. The hairs on the back of his neck rose stiffly, and he vomited. Afterwards, he still felt ill, but he was mentally calmer, as if his mind had rebelled against the violence of his emotions and forced his body to make a gesture of expulsion.

Cartwright's face was stamped with an expression of fright and mortal pain, the eyes bulging, the tongue swollen and protruding from a mouth strained wide open. On his neck there were marks, dull blue marks grooved in his skin. In his terror, he must have caught at his own throat. On the death certificate the cause of death was given as heart failure.

TWENTY-SIX

Joe had arranged his father's, Clara's and the child's funeral to take place on the Friday, which presented itself as a dull, dark, soundless day when clouds hung oppressively low in the heavens. It was well attended. A great crowd, all of them mourning those who had gone, gathered closely together in the yard and when the coffins were carried from the farmhouse along the "corpse-way", they followed all the way to the churchyard. The "passing-bells" tolled nine times for each of the dead, and the spirit of the people sank, as the eyelids of the old sink on a twilit afternoon.

Even the church seemed bowed to the earth with the weight of the prayers that clung to her arched roof. The bearers stopped at the lych-gate, resting the coffins on trestles. In the midst of the heavy breathing of the bearers came the timely words - 'I am the resurrection and the life.'

The coffins were then carried to another trestle by the open gravesides. The silence was complete as the crowd, many of the heads bowed beneath shawls and cloth caps, parted for the relatives of the dead to pass - the only two left. As if they hadn't gone through enough! - they whispered to one another. In a state of dreadful shock was Jessica Greenward, Jessica Sheridan, they supposed they should call her now, engulfed in the horror into which she had been flung by her father's appalling death.

Underneath her passive exterior was a raw and painful anguish, a desperate, only just bearable agony of spirit which was harrowing to witness. It was a crying shame the girl's husband was not here to comfort and support her in this time of need. His absence fanned the flames of gossip even higher. Shrouded in black, with her glowing, copper hair hidden beneath a sombre black bonnet, except for a stray shining tendril that drifted against the side of her face that was as ashen as some strange apparition, she was held by the hand of that of her one remaining brother, Joseph Greenward - a young image of their father, looking as though she would not get through the day without him. A rock on which to lean. Her housekeeper, Dora Osborne, stood to the other side, there, should she be needed.

But Joe was feeling anything but strong. The picture of the disfigured corpses was burnt into his mind. He saw only the horror and the ghastliness of it all. Time and again there passed before his mental vision the events of the previous days. They were stamped upon his consciousness, seared on his memory with a clarity that time itself could never efface. Violent emotions over-whelmed his bruised and battered mind, and as they surged through open wounds to take root, deep in his soul, he knew for certain, Cartwright had damned everyone who had witnessed his barbarism.

In a pitiable attempt at self-control, Joe clenched his free trembling hand and shoved it deep into his pocket as he stood by his sister's side, his body beneath his dark clothes hard and powerful, shaped by the manual adversity of the work he had performed since he was a boy, first in the mines and then in the fields. The damp in the air caressed his overlong hair into tight, dark curls about his forehead and neck, putting spangles of mist in it, resembling tiny diamonds that sparkled like dew.

Savage devastation bowed him, sorrow and affliction bringing despair to his usually calm face that was like bleached bone, and a tightening of the lips that turned down in misery, his eyelashes drooping along the length of his heavy lids, curling and glossy brown. A strained fineness, which more than one woman in the churchyard thought tragically attractive. Although he had the manly firmness to keep the tears out of his brilliant, green eyes, his heart was paying the price. He lowered his head and drew in a deep, ragged breath, trying not to shudder with pain. Edward Morley, Dan's deputy and the obvious man to step into his shoes, stood close behind him, his head also bowed in despair. He had always looked up to Dan Greenward and held him in the highest esteem, but Clara Greenward, he had loved, loved from afar, and was haunted by her ghastly death. Frank Maidment and Garrett Wicks, both Overmen, stood by his side. And many of the miners who had worked alongside Dan for years, stood shoulder to shoulder, at the back. All men who had something to thank him for.

Jessica was aware of the crowd cramming the churchyard and the intense quality of the sad silence, broken only by the slow mournful drops that fell from the wet leaves of the motionless trees that stood beneath a heaven clad in weeds of sorrowful mist. Most of them were just ordinary folk, people her father had shown some kindness to, at their time of need, whose clogged feet sunk in the wet grass, and others whose lives he had touched. She was filled with a wondering sorrow that she had not known of the esteem in which her father, and stepmother, had been held. Jeannie Miller had always been fond of her father. She stood with April and Liam O'Malley; both had a lot to thank him for.

Frank and Lizzie Abbott and their adopted daughter, Emmy - the little workhouse girl Dan had brought to them. Mr Bilton, Mr Charlton and Mr Pendle, in their black suits and top hats; all men of business, connected with Sheridan's mines that Dan had supervised. Lewis Courtenay, now the Squire of Hawthorne Manor, was present, accompanied by his agent, Eric Wheeler. And Dr Morrison, the family doctor Jessica had known since childhood. Brooke Henly, a good friend to Clara, was there, supported by her brother, Brent. Just a few of the faces in the crowd.

Eric Masters, and his daughter, Millie, who wept for her younger sister, Edna, whose life had been tragically snatched from her along with the Greenward family, and had been buried the day before alongside her mother, Edith. Mrs Miles and her husband, Ned, gardener and general handyman at Wildacres. Tom Saunders and the three maids - Amy, Maggie and Tilly. Although they had not known Mr Greenward personally, they had come to support their young mistress.

It was an excruciating ordeal, a time of shock and horror, and of feelings something more intense for which there is no name upon this earth. Her throat was dry, and her soft sorrowful eyes, hot with unshed tears burning behind them. A voice droned on of everlasting life and the Kingdom of Heaven, the sound of which was no more than the buzzing of bees in her stricken brain. She felt her brother's powerful frame tremble as their father's coffin was lowered into the gaping hole.

April sobbed openly, to her Liam's distress. And Isaac Hencock, who had a sickly wife whom Clara had regularly visited, was so distressed he had to lean against the stone wall surrounding the church yard when her coffin was being lowered into the ground.

Every vestige of colour in Jessica's face, which was not a lot to begin with, drained away as it suddenly struck her that never again would she hear her father's voice or see his dear face, feel the touch of his hand, enjoy his warm embrace or know his love. He had been here but a moment ago. Now he was gone. Her heart hurt sorely, and the devastating truth of it was, she did not know how to ease it. A small agonized sound murmured in the back of her throat but she held it in, for it would not serve to fall apart now. If only Luke was here. His absence was a source of bitter disappointment to her. She felt completely let down. She needed him …now! When her aching, anguished heart needed him most.

For a moment she allowed self-pity to overwhelm her, forcing down her glossy head in utter despair. She seemed doomed to stagger through life beneath a multitude of misfortunes. No sooner had she over-come one than another came at her. But she must not allow herself to dwell on it now, she told herself, she would consider it later when she felt more able to cope.

When she lifted her head, the softness had gone and her girlhood with it, leaving only a young woman of cool beauty, impassive, composed, but empty of any-thing that could be described as warmth. Only an iciness, a sickening of the heart remained. She freed her hand and bent stiffly to scoop up a handful of soil, letting it trickle through her fingers to fall into her father's last resting place, throwing in the flowers she had gathered in the stillness of dawn, where they grew in the sheltered garden at Wildacres. Flowers that would lie forever under the earth with Daniel Greenward. She had read somewhere that when a good life was lived, flowers will grow on the deceased's grave, but if the deceased was evil, then only weeds would grow. When she straightened up, she looked upon the scene before her with an utter depression of the soul. The strange, dreamlike day had never really come awake.

There was a sigh from everybody then, like the wind in dry bents. It was over at long last. They made their way through the lych gate, to take the shortest route back to the farm. Joe, Jessica and Dora Osborne, crammed into the gig, which Joe had collected from his father's barn. A tidy few followed in their fine carriages, for most all that had been at the church, came back for the funeral feast. They were all there, their mouths agape at the sight of the glorious horses and the splendour of the carriages parked in the yard, as they crowded through the door of the farmhouse. Joe had asked two of the women to stay behind, to tend the fires and see to the posset - hot milk curdled with ale and wine and flavoured with spices - a glass handed to each of the mourners as they entered - for the air struck chill.

Jessica Sheridan was near the end of her endurance and it showed in the waxy pallor of her skin, the dark smudges beneath her eyes, and the soft and vulnerable droop of her mouth. She seemed to have lived many days in that single day. More than once she had been ready to collapse, but instead, had fallen into that terrible state of existence, which one experiences when the senses are living and awake, but the powers of thought lie dormant. She was conscious of shadowy figures about her, leading her away, and the sound of someone moaning, a thin anguished cry, as if it was some distance away, then she realised it was herself.

Much whispering was all about her, fragments of sentences, but she did not really hear anything of what was said; all noise fading until it was a mere murmur. She sipped tea from the cup, which mysteriously came into her hand, but her eyes continued to stare, unfocused and depthless, into some horror only she felt, and there was no expression on her ashen face. It was as if she was a spectator in an unreal play, living in a world of drifting shadows, trapped in unreality, and continually cold with the agony of her loss. A loss that was permanent.

Visions of her father's dear face kept rattling around in her head like pebbles rolling in a river, pictures rising sharply before her, covering all those years together. So clear were they, that they might have been splashed on a canvas that instant with a brush. They sprang into being as a white circle springs from a lamp when it is lit, flitting to and fro like exotic birds against a landscape with which they have nothing to do with, but it is the landscape itself that holds the eye from which, comes the silent magic, called memory. Even in the swift pictures flashing by her father, drifted slowly with steady purpose through life, and because of his slowness, he seemed to her more alive, and somehow, there was more time to look at him as he passed.

She was very still as she made that perfect transition into the past and the only sound in her ears was through the lips that laughed. The few journeys they had taken in life, she travelled over again and then, quite suddenly the pictures would become paler ...his dear face gradually fading before her very eyes until it was gone, out of reach, leaving her in a silent stillness in which no step moved or no voice called. She stiffened then, from being softly still, to becoming a rigid thing, stiller than sleep, because it was passionate will-power that held her still. It was already a moment or two since the laughter had passed and yet it still rang in her ears, flashing through her brain like a bright sword flung in a high arc through a night.

The truth that was behind it, she held rigidly from her, even as it tried to step within she tried to shut the knowledge out. She would not let herself think about it. But somehow it bubbled to the surface, and then the anger, that fierce, destructive rage would boil up to acknowledge the fact he was gone, gone forever ...and had suffered horribly in his going. And Clara ...kind, thoughtful Clara, who had always put everyone before herself and had made her father so happy. And little Adam; a sweet, innocent child that had barely breathed and lived, a child she herself, because of the loss of her own, had secretly and regrettably resented.

What kind of God had allowed them to die with so much suffering? Her mouth went slack and her eyes wide, as though she stared at some horror. Someone took the cup and saucer from her hands, just as she started to tremble. Her lips parted and shook so violently her teeth chattered in her head, and her restless hands plucked at her gown. Her breath came in quick gasps that were almost sobs as her eyes strained to find her father, her beloved father, her brain insisting that he was still here, her heart alone beating in hard, ponderous strokes, seeming as if it must shut out any further sound. And when the voice broke the silence so that it could not close again, her own power of restraint went by the board. Her hands lifted themselves theatrically and gripped each other across her breast, and her voice, shaken and full of tears, forced itself into her throat.

'There is no God, no Heaven …only hell …this hell on earth,' she murmured aloud, speaking only to herself. This shaken trust in God was little short of madness to such a loving nature.

'There now, dear. You're home again now,' a soft voice told her, while gentle hands smoothed her hair. 'Here, drink this. It will do you good.'

A glass with brandy in it was placed in her trembling hands; at least she thought it to be brandy, for the pungent smell of it and the burning sensation of it going down her throat made her gasp and her eyes water. It warmed her though and steadied the deep trembling, which had begun somewhere inside her, threatening to have her off her feet.

Outside, it was a grim night. A deep greyness dragged on the fields and lifted them to an unfamiliar horizon where a few dull stars sparkled feebly.

She was quiet now, she had reached the point at which the mind detaches itself resolutely from further emotional strain, but Dora, her face creased with concern, continued to smooth her hair, somewhat in the manner of a mother soothing her child. The sooner they got her undressed and into a hot bath, the better. Perhaps even another little sip of brandy in some hot milk, to help relax her and make her sleep? Ladies did not normally drink spirits, but just this once would not harm her, would it?

All this anxiety, this heartache, did no one any good. It had been one thing after another, a year of immense grief. First the loss of the child, then young Alice, and now, the shock of both her father and stepmother and their child's sudden and frightful death was enough to unhinge the strongest of minds. If only the master would come home to his grieving, young wife, to soothe the pain of her loss ...Dora said mutely to herself, for the umpteenth time. She did not much care for how the young mistress moved about the house like some shadowed ghost and sitting for hours in her own private drawing-room, without uttering a single word to anyone. Her mind was in a state of shock, not just that, but there was a weight on her spirits that overwhelmed her and locked her in the darkness of the depression in which she had curled. She had grown so thin and her cheeks had lost their healthy rosy bloom. A terrible thing to see, and she didn't like it, didn't like it one little bit, Dora repeated mutely, while she sat protectively by.

TWENTY-SEVEN

Jessica felt more alone than ever before, alone in spirit, alone in her unfeigned sorrow. At the back of her mind and in her heart, where it sat like a heavy load, was her longing for her husband - strong arms to hold her in her grieving for the kind wonderful man who had been her father, guarding her from the pain and desolation, sharing it with her. She could not expect Luke to regulate what he did because of her love for him. He was a member of the upper class and must go wherever his position in life takes him, of course, and it was her duty to wait patiently for him to come home to her …she knew that, but she could not help but feel bitterly aggrieved over his forever-increasing absences. He was never here when she needed him. A letter, a short note even, explaining what was happening, and telling her that he was safe and well, would have been most welcome. She was doing her best to make some sense of this frightful bewilderment, but when Luke …*when Luke comes home* - those words were a litany, a supplication she chanted over and over again.

She slowly turned her head. 'Dora! Oh, Dora!'

Her desperate cry was involuntary and she clapped her hand to her mouth to hold it in, and when she removed it the words she spoke were spoken anxiously, uttered many times before, 'Why does Luke not come home?'

Dora's answer was always the same. 'I really don't know, my dear. There must be some good reason.'

Those words whirled in Jessica's head like trapped birds in a cage. 'Tell me what reason a man can have that keeps him from his wife so long when she needs him?' she demanded, in a full-throated cry of resentment. 'He's always away. And he's changed over the last few months. He's so cold and distant. I don't think he loves me at all. I'm convinced he married me only to give him a son. He once called me a necessary creature. For one thing, he doesn't know the meaning of love, and for another, he doesn't have a heart.'

Shocked by the dreadful expression of suffering on the girl's face, a feather of unease ran down Dora's spine. Her own heart contracted in shared pain since she had grown fond of the young mistress. She didn't know which was worse …the cry of pain or the silence? She hovered like a ghost herself in her willingness to ease the poor lamb's suffering, clucking soothingly as one would to a child who had been badly injured and was in need of loving care and attention. It kept her strong enough to deal with this broken young woman, and sane enough to enable her to hold together the frayed strings of a household cloaked with sadness, its running, and the supervision of the servants, with a no-nonsense flow of words, which told everyone exactly what she considered to be right, never sparing correction when it was necessary that it should be used.

Dora sighed wearily, wondering for the umpteenth time if perhaps it might have been better if the girl could have wept - let go, shout and scream, burst into noisy tears, to release the tension. A good cry did the world of good at times like this. She wished the master would come home and fetch her out of the dark and shocked state in which her father's savage, brutal murder had thrown her. She would be glad of anything …*anything* to drag her out of the trance she was in. If she did not find some comfort soon she would surely go under. The doctor had been kind but insistent.

'Mrs Sheridan is suffering from a morbid acuteness of the senses, a mere nervous malady that will undoubtedly soon pass'…he had said, ordering the young mistress to stay in bed with the curtains drawn, and to swallow plenty of warm broth. Most of all she had to have absolute quiet so she could sleep. Stay in bed! Sleep! The girl didn't need sleep. A few words fitly spoken are what were needed. 'Time will heal.'…he had declared.

What good was that? Jessica needed firmness, a strong hand to guide her, but with care, made to see that life must go on, Dora was inclined to think. She had suffered sorrow and loss herself but had not been bowed by it. Well, not for long. Life had taught her that it didn't matter whether you believed in God or not, and followed the teachings of the church, the blows came just the same and there was only one way to deal with them when they knocked you off your feet. And that was to get back up again and get on with life. Only by fighting it and conquering it, would the young mistress come to terms with her own dreadful loss. She could not simply retire to her bed and give in …for heaven's sake.

It was not in Dora Osborne to let misfortune sweep the girl away helplessly like a leaf in a torrent. But to whom could she turn? Who could she ask to talk some sense into the girl? There was her brother …she supposed she could ask him. No, he had enough to contend with. His housekeeper …whatever her name was? No, she was a little on the rough side, not one the young mistress should rightly mix with. Besides, she would only bring her brood with her, the little scallywags. The one time they did visit, they had almost wrecked the place, knocking over one of the tables in the drawing room and climbing all over the furniture.

Maybe that young woman who had called on the mistress soon after she lost the child? What was her name? Brooke something or other? Henley! That was it …Miss Brooke Henley. But she was a bit on the quiet side. If she remembered rightly, what little conversation there was had been from Jessica herself.

Dora sighed despairingly. Oh dear, it was difficult to know what to do for the best. There was always Parson Appleby, of course. He was easy to talk to and a good listener - every woman's dream. He had a way of saying just the right thing. Of knowing exactly the nature of a person, so that, with kindliness and sensitivity, he drew a response, which was spontaneous. He would know what to say, find the right words to soothe the most rumpled of spirits.

Didn't he spend his life for the good of the parishioners? Hadn't he and his kindly wife found homes for those young orphans that Cartwright had had working in the mines? …and taken in that poor young girl when no one else would, given her a home until the baby had come? He was certain to be at hand at a time like this, a time of such deep sorrow.

Still, there was an air of deep and irredeemable gloom about the house - an atmosphere which had no affinity with the air of heaven. Insufferable melancholy pervaded Jessica's spirit - a hollow feeling that hurt and dragged her down, but she still could not weep. The tears which had sprung to her eyes with such humiliating ease these last months, now refused to come. She existed in a tearless agony. Yes, agony, excruciating and yet at the same time numbing, a numbness that held her like a rigid corpse frozen in ice, and nothing of what was happening about her now could touch her. All that was in her now was a desire to lie down and fall into a state of oblivion, a black hole in which she might, for a few hours, erase the torment, so deep she would feel nothing, suffer nothing, remember nothing.

Her thoughts turned to Joe, of the torment, the anguish he must be feeling, but there was nothing she could do. She could barely help herself. Her heart had been torn and bruised almost beyond repair, by what had been done to her father. The vision of his torture darkened her days and gave her sleepless nights. When she did sleep it was from sheer exhaustion, but she would wake up trembling, besieged by the raving spectres of her nightmares, the hours of wakefulness dragging on endlessly. Knowing that her father's and step-mother's death could be laid at no one's door now the evil person behind the killings - the executions - for that is what they were - had escaped retribution through premature death, devastated her to an anguish she could barely control.

From the moment she got out of bed in the morning until she got back into it again, she was wound up like a tight spring, her whole body aching with some strange malady. She was not to know that she was still deep in the shocked state the catastrophic events had thrust her. She had not prayed; she could not. Nor had she followed any tenet of the religion in which she had been raised. She seemed incapable of collecting her thoughts even. They wandered in her bewildered mind, trailing like wisps of grey cloud, going nowhere in the house of silence. How loud it sounded when you really listened to it? It had a quality she had never been aware of in any other silence, as though it were not merely an absence of sound, a thick barrier between the ear and the surging murmur of life just beyond, but an impenetrable substance made out of the world-wide cessation of all life and all movement. That was what laid a chill on her, the feeling that there was nothing beyond it, holding her in a state of paralysis, her brain numbed and empty and her body suspended in some merciful oblivion. She sat in the same place for long weary hours, gazing into the glowing embers of the fire, dressed in a rich, black satin gown trimmed at the high neck and around the cuffs with black lace. Her jaw was clenched, her hands clasped tensely together in her lap, her face expressionless and her eyes dead, hearing and heeding no one, until Parson Appleby came and sat down beside her - a light in the dark, never-ending tunnel of despair. She clenched her jaw even tighter, so tight she feared she might never be able to open it again when the time came, but it was the only way she could keep her composure.

TWENTY-EIGHT

Drew Appleby professed the highest regard for Daniel Greenward and the deepest sorrow at his sudden tragic death. To realise the pain of others, one must bear that pain oneself. He had a longing desire to say something to comfort his old friend's daughter. But what could he say? Hers was a deep tearing grief, a sorrow too great to be borne. It was a hard thing to think that such a tragedy should be so close to a creature so young and bright. She was in a sort of daze, in such a deep well of misery, all thought and speech was impossible. The only colour in her face was in her warm, coral lips. Her eyes were blank and lifeless still, just as though the flame of Jessica Greenward, now Jessica Sheridan, which had burned so brilliantly, so joyfully, had been snuffed out. He had seen it before.

Comfort was what she needed, loving tender care, which could only be administered by that absent husband of hers, wherever he may be - supposedly off checking on the progress of his timber company and visiting his mother in Hawkeshead, or somewhere in London perhaps? Although messages had been sent, no one had been able to locate him.

Jessica just sat there on the sofa, waiting, it seemed to him, for someone to tell her what to do. He merely placed his hands over hers in a moment of compassion. On the mantel the gold French clock chimed melodically.

As if the chime of the clock had awakened something in her, Jessica slowly turned her head and looked into Drew Appleby's face, her sorrowful, green eyes regarding him steadily, and he was left in no doubt that his presence was unwelcome to her. He himself looked pale and ghastly, his whole face pinched, from his recent struggle with ill health. Christian resignation and its consequent for fortitude were written on his brow.

Jessica gazed upon him with a feeling half of pity, half of awe. She had not seen him since his illness. Of course, he had taken the service for the funeral, but she couldn't say if she had seen him, in fact, she couldn't remember anything at all. He was by nature a jovial, friendly person, but now he looked some-what strained and tense. His gaze was sombre, the natural luminousness of his eyes had gone out, his face brooding, and the awful pallor of his skin startled her. Surely a man had never before so terribly altered in so brief a period, as Drew Appleby had? There was something in his wasted face that reached out and affected her ...unlocking something inside her, some-thing that had been tightly closed against invasion from outside forces.

For a second her calmness seemed ready to slither away into dozens of little pieces. Drew could see she was making a great effort to hang onto it. If she let one tiny tear fall, she might cry herself into a hundred shattered pieces. She snatched away her hands quite violently, doubling up in agony and gripping her arms fiercely at each elbow across her breast, her face working and her eyes blinking rapidly, desperate to blank out the ghastly flickering images that continued to blind her. She began to rock backwards and forwards, as though she was in great pain, and a faint moaning escaped from between her tight lips.

'Ohhh …why? Why does God let these things happen?' Her anguish lifted and pierced the stillness of the room, the sound of it flooding the place, making Drew Appleby wince involuntary. Somewhere, in another room the dog broke into hoarse barks and a voice rose to calm him.

'My dear girl, you have asked me a difficult question,' he answered solemnly. 'No one can understand God's ways. As the Heavens are higher than the earth, so are His ways than our ways.'

'Most everyone I loved has gone, buried beneath the ground. The earth on my brothers' graves had barely settled when my mother joined them.' Her words and her breath came with the leap of a mountain stream. 'And now …now, my father …my dear father and …and Clara …poor Clara, are both gone and …and little …dear little Adam …cold in their graves.'

Drew Appleby had the good sense and understanding not to interrupt. This was what the poor girl needed, to lose control for a few minutes, to lose that calm, unruffled control that had hidden beneath it a storm, a frenzied turmoil of pain and shock which, like a boil that needed lancing, will eventually burst and tear the flesh apart.

'Ohhh …I …I should have been there for Clara. Spent more time with her and the child. I deliberately stayed away, lost in my own …own selfish resentment, because she …she had a healthy son when mine …mine had been taken from me. How could I have been so selfish? How could I have known that …that those most dear would be snatched away …taken so soon. I feel as if I'm cursed. If only I had known I might have... ' She covered her mouth with her hand in anguish. Might of what? she asked herself mutely.

'The future is in no one's knowledge and I've often thought that a blessed thing, one t'be thankful for. If we could know what the future would bring forth, we should be profoundly mournful in anticipation of an event not yet guessed of. We swim in a sea of environment and heredity, are tossed to and fro by currents of Fate, and are tugged at by a thousand eddies of which we never dream. The sum of it all makes Life, of which we know so little and guess so much. Death is only a horizon, and, a horizon is only the limit of our sight.' His voice was ragged with tiredness and his own sorrow, but there was strength in it still, and a sense that what he said was right and true.

She lifted her trembling hands to her head and dragged them roughly through her hair, scattering the pins and letting it fall in wild disarray like a curtain of living flame about her drooping shoulders. 'But …but family is the heart of everything. Without them I'm …I'm nothing. My head hurts just to …just to think about it.'

'T'live in the hearts of those we love is not t'die.'

Her tormented heart was bursting in her breast, filling her with such desolation she did not know how to contain it. 'I can't seem to pull myself together. I feel so …so defeated.'

'Only one person in the whole wide world can defeat you. That is yourself! No one escapes life's tragedies. From them one can learn and grow. Admittedly, the past cannot be changed, but the future is still in your power.'

The words seemed to hang in the air between them. Drew Appleby was a kind man, generous to a fault, with a nature that could not stand to see a tear in any woman's eye. He gave her a sort of half smile as though to encourage her, and to let her see he meant to help her.

'You are from a strong family, Jessica. You just have t'look at your brother, Joseph, t'see that. When I paid him a visit he said two words …my name and that was all. There was no need for him t'say more, for no words could have expressed the bereavement reflected in his face. No words could have told me more clearly than the strong grasp of his hand, how absolutely we were connected by the loss. He's utterly devastated by the brutal manner in which your father and his wife died, but somehow, he has managed t'get on with his work on the farm. A tight-rope he has had t'learn t'balance.'

'We are not all made the same,' she said quietly.

'Oh, I know you've been too lost in your own pain t'see how your brother hurts. But in another month you'll be a little better, and the month after that a little better still, and one day you'll be able t'smile again. You'll see! Have faith. Faith adds surety t'the expect-ation of hope. It is not a material thing that can be seen, heard, smelt, tasted or touched, but is as real as anything that can be perceived with these senses.'

'The best and most beautiful things in the world cannot be seen or touched, but are felt here…' he placed the palm of his hand across his heart, 'in the heart. Faith is as sure as the existence of water, the fragrance of a rose, the sound of thunder, the feel of a loving touch...'

'Faith! How can I have faith, when that …that beast, that devil escaped punishment for his evil crimes? I feel nothing but pain and anger.' Her voice trembled with the injustice of it. Suddenly, it was all too much for her and to her horror she felt her eyes prick with tears. She swallowed hard. The moment was over and the temptation to let go behind her.

'All sins cast long shadows. There's no place t'hide a sin. God looks down from Heaven upon all our bitter conflicts; and weighs as a just Judge all the events that happen here on earth. Vengeance is mine; I will repay, saith the Lord. Did God not strike the sinner down?'

'Well …yes, but he should have been made to suffer.' The words were forced through clenched teeth. Jessica's whole body was clenched, her face a tight mask of pain.

'Now then, t'brood over wrongs we cannot put right is morbid and unhealthy. It saps our vitality. Your feelings are painful now, I know, but things will get better. It will pass in time and then you will see things more clearly. Because we don't know when we will die, we get t'think of life as an inexhaustible wealth. Yet everything only happens a certain number of times, a very small number really.'

Drew placed a comforting hand on the distraught girl's shoulder, a girl whose emotions had always lain very near the surface. He could remember having a similar conversation with her father not so very long ago, over the loss of his two boys.

'How many more times will you remember a certain exceptional incident that happened during your childhood, a memory that's so deeply a part of your being that you just can't conceive life without it? Perhaps three times or maybe even four? No more than that. Time will pass and the memory will fade. Live for the moment, because this is your life.'

The wounds of youth would quickly heal, and her father's memory would become a recollection of the happy incidents in time.

'Have you tried praying?'

Jessica shook her head dumbly and sighed heavily, continuing to shake her head as though to clear the cobwebs of anguish from her mind.

'You'll find praying helps. It will give you the strength and courage t'go on.' His face changed, a faint smile softening the tired lines, his eyes narrowing in that way which was so familiar to her. In the most curious way something in his demeanour touched a chord in her, something that spoke of tranquility, of a man of peace, of which she herself was in short supply. 'Jesus took our grief and bore our sorrows. He died for the chastisement of our peace, just as much as for deliverance from sin and healing of the physical body. You really must take care of yourself, my dear girl. The care of your health is, after all, a religious duty.'

Drew's eyes were suddenly bright and burning with living faith, and despite herself Jessica felt drawn towards him. So painfully affected had her mind been, and her spirit broken, but now, just as though this man, this kind, caring, sympathetic man, had pulled a switch, he dragged her from her misery. That gentle, pleasing manner, with the sense of intellectual power behind it, quite overcame the grieving girl, and for the first time in two weeks her sorrowful eyes showed some sign of interest. A tiny light shone there, and a muscle jumped in her clenched jaw as she felt a prick of hope, and a slight trace of colour painted her cheekbones.

She could feel the change in herself, feel the tension beginning to ease, lifting her out of herself, and she brought her head up and straightened her wilting back to its normal long and graceful curve.

Drew Appleby knew then he had taken an important step today in the healing of Jessica Sheridan.

'Use your religion. Use the Bible as a guidebook. The way t'master it is t'let it master you. Do the very best you can and leave the outcome t'God. God is as good t'us as we deserve. And remember …He never closes one door without opening another.'

The Parson's words floated straw-like past her as she floundered in a sea of pain, and since she was convinced she was drowning in it she made the gesture of grabbing the straw with both hands. The straw became a raft, and in that first flush of relief and gratitude, Parson Appleby became her saviour. The armour of numbness that had formed about her, shielding her to a degree, developed cracks in it that become great gaps and suddenly fell away, the fragile thread of control snapping. She closed her eyes but it did no good, the tears forced themselves from beneath her lids, clinging to her lashes, before rushing in waves down her face.

No further words were necessary. She felt as if God had called her, not with a whisper, but by a blast on a trumpet, and she felt ashamed to think that she could have been so deaf for so long. She knew now that He understood and that He was there to give her all the help He could. Although her face was still wet, the last of the tears had been shed. She took out a handkerchief to wipe her eyes, and a long, sighing relief shuddered from between her swollen, bitten lips.

It took Jessica several more weeks to master her grief, and even then control was a thin layer of brittle ice on a deep cold body of water. There were times when her lips quivered, when her heart cried out in agony, and anguish unspeakable came in the silence of the dusk, as the haunting cry of a lonely owl fell eerily across the land. When it would not allow her the relief of rest, the deep healing of sleep. But with the help of her God she began to look forward to bright and happier days to come.

PART THREE
1830

TWENTY-NINE

Luke was staying at the Londonderry Hotel in Park Lane that stood amongst a huddle of stables and innumerable taverns, the haunts of the drovers from the cattle-market in Brook Fields. Although most of his time was divided between Burlington House and his club. The hotel address was used for the purpose of anyone needing to get in touch with him, such as business-men or his wife.

He never came in his own carriage when visiting Burlington House, but in a hackney coach to avoid attention, although everyone must surely know there existed between Amelia Duprez and Luke Sheridan a passionate attachment. They would often be found together in a quiet corner of an obscure restaurant …or walking arm in arm in Hyde Park, and if anyone was shocked by the fact he was a married man, they had long since learnt to accept it with tolerance.

He would, in all probability, make much better progress on foot, but even in this busy thoroughfare one must be on their guard against pickpockets and the possibility of a more violent robbery. Bearing right out of Park Lane, the coach travelled along elegant Curzon Street, coming to Chesterfield Gardens, then on into Chesterfield Street, taking a left turn into Clarges Street, with its small dingy houses opening directly onto the street. The working–class district in which no man of wealth or position lived, with its mean, squalid streets, gloomy and forbidding.

A stinking narrow canal ran down its centre, into which evil smelling slops, waste, horse-manure, rotten vegetables and what looked to be the carcass of a dead cat, had been thrown. There was no drainage system in the city; even the most commodious houses were only beginning to install water closets. A chamber pot served well enough for most. There were no curtains at any of the windows; everyone looked to be broken and patched with paper or rags. Doorposts were blackened with dirt, the steps here and there occupied by women in shabby grey dresses and coarse black stockings, one washing what appeared to be bed linen in a large earthenware pot. Cunning not wisdom, sharpness not intelligence, were stamped on their wretched faces. Somewhere, someone was screaming abuse.

Here lived the poor, whose way of life was steeped in ignorance, dirt and crime. The countless broken outcasts of the industrial system, herded together in bug-ridden lodging houses and rotting tenements, let out to a dozen or fifteen families, according to the number of rooms. Pallid and gin-sodden, their ragged reeking clothes so vile that they left a stain wherever they rested. A reminder of what unemployment, sickness or any lapse from the straight and narrow path of social integrity might bring, like ghosts they rose out of a precipice into which every man might at any moment of his life fall.

It was a relief to get out of that vile little slum and to work one's way back into the light. It was a pity they could not avoid it, but Clarges Street runs south from Curzon Street to Piccadilly - "the magic mile" as it was known, with its tall and impressive buildings, stretching from Hyde Park Corner all the way along to Piccadilly Circus. Another of Piccadilly's tributaries was Berkeley Street, the street of mansions - number 94 belonging to Lord Palmerston - the Secretary of War, clubs, and a famous brothel, which had known many eminent guests. Here the clatter of wheels on cobbles was deafening, the crush of carriages in this part of Piccadilly so great that Luke made himself uncharacteristically late.

They eventually managed to thread the way through, and turning into Bond Street, the coach passed by the side of a high grey stone wall, where it turned under a pedimented arch between two vast wrought-iron gates, and amongst the noise of hooves, wheels, jangling harnesses and loud commands, came clattering to a standstill in a courtyard brightly illuminated with candle lamps, in front of Burlington House, one of the noble mansions of Piccadilly.

After Luke had disposed of his top hat and cloak, he entered the panelled dining room, splendidly lit by candlelight, quite full of company ...and insufferably hot.

Madame Duprez turned in her chair and held up her hand. 'Ah, Monsieur, I'm so pleased you've managed to come. We had quite given you up.'

She looked absolutely stunning, as always, dressed in a wonderful creation of pale green satin and lace, her golden hair shining and perfectly groomed into a neat bun, like a crown on the top of her head, worthy of the expression "crowning glory", with a single ringlet to the side of each of her perfect small ears.

Luke bent over the hand she offered, brushing it with his lips. 'My sincere apologies. I was held up.'

'But you're here now,' she said, smiling warmly. 'I'm afraid we had to start without you.'

'So I see. Ladies ...gentlemen.' He bowed slightly to those present, a height of good manners. These dinner parties were always crowded, mostly with males.

'I've saved you a place, here, next to me.' Amel gestured to the chair beside her.

He obediently settled down by her side. The maid hovered beside him, holding a great silver dish. 'Soup, Monsieur?'

'What is it?' he asked

'C'est artichaut, Monsieur,' the maid informed him.

'Thank you ....yes.' He opened his napkin and placed it on his lap, leaning sideways slightly to whisper to Amel. 'I'm happy to see how well things are going.'

'Yes, things are going well,' Amel replied. She was brimming over with her usual exuberance. Leaning towards him, she whispered over the top of her napkin. 'You're not too tired from your trip I trust, Mon amour? I have a gift for you ...later, when we are alone.' She placed her napkin on her lap, her free hand moving slowly under the table, gently closing about his crotch. Her smile was absolutely sinful. 'I must say ...you don't feel too tired?'

Luke chuckled deep in his throat, but his expression showed no surprise. 'You're positively wicked, tempting nonetheless. But do be careful. People are watching.'

'Which only serves to make it all the more exciting,' she whispered.

'You're in great form tonight.' He kept his voice low and intimate. 'And need I say, just how lovely you look. Even fully dressed you seem to be seductive.'

'Thank you for the compliments,' she murmured seductively, fluttering long gold-tipped lashes in play.

'You deserve them, every one,' he replied smoothly.

'Every woman wants to look seductive, daytime or at night.'

The meal was excellent, as always. Asparagus soup, followed by saddle of lamb and fresh asparagus in a creamy white sauce, and a dessert of ices and little heart-shaped French cakes soaked in rum. And of course, the usual procession of vintage wines.

Luke sat toying with his glass, leaning back in the chair and looking along the table. Amel chose her guests from a very cross-section of London Society, people of title, politicians, musicians, and more often than not, actors currently performing at The Theatre Royal in Druary Lane, which she frequented regularly.

Seated opposite him was Ellen Kean, wife of actor Charles Kean, looking very attractive and quite elegant in a gown of embroidered white muslin, trimmed round the neck with ivory lace; the short sleeves in half plaits, with ivory satin epaulettes and cuffs. Pearls graced her neck and hung from her ears. Ellen Kean was a very accomplished woman. Her performance in Covent Garden as Olivia in William Shakespeare's "Twelfth Night" had brought the most glowing reviews.

Seated next to her was Horace Twist, who was a constant source of amusement. On first appearance, one could not have said whether he was a man or a woman. His figure was undeniably curvaceous and he had the finest features imaginable, more beautiful than handsome, and the most remarkable pale blue eyes. The lids were beautifully bordered with long lashes, over which no pencil could have described two more regular arches than those that graced his forehead, which was high, perfectly white and smooth.

His small hands, with their long fingers and perfectly manicured nails, constantly fluttered about and were brilliant with rings. In short, he was one whom one would readily call a very pretty fellow, whose chiselled features and unblemished brow elevated him to a realm of male beauty that most women found irresistible and that most men, Luke among them, found repulsive.

Twist had lately abandoned his youthful dandyism, when he had worn feathered hats and fancy buckled shoes that were the distinguishing mark of privilege at the French Court, for black or grey coats with match-ing waistcoats, with buttons of solid gold, perfectly white starched shirts and white cravats. At least they were an improvement, in Luke's eyes.

Catherine Gurney - Duchess of Kingston, the widow of the late Duke of Kinston, sat to the other side of him, here visiting from Paris. When the Duke died, he had left her his entire estate, everything, on condition that she remained a widow; the reason of this restriction being her liability to be imposed upon by any adventurer who flattered her. A woman who now lived her life scandalously, she was remarkable for the freedom and indelicacy of her conduct, appearing on one occasion at a masked ball in the character of Iphigenia, so naked that you would have taken her for Andromeda. Self-indulgent and whimsical, her character was only redeemed from utter contempt by a certain generosity of temper.

Facing her was Waldoff Huskisson, who flattered her vanity in order to prey upon her, a notorious adventurer and gambler, who described himself as an Albanian prince, no less. As usual, the men outnumbered the women. Others around the table were two young officers of the 91st Argyllshire Regiment of Foot that Luke had never met before, John Walten, the owner of The Times newspaper and a strong advocate on independent reporting, and Archer Horne, a prosperous wool trader. Richard Parkes Bonington, the young artist who had come from Paris, where Amel had apparently met him when he was there as a student of Ecole des Beauz Arts.

Also, Charles Jersey was present, the eldest son of Lord Jersey, one of the leading radicals in Parliament, and beside him - his young bride, Elizabeth, the daughter of William Whitehead, the banker. She was a considerable heiress, and when both her family and Lord Jersey refused their consent to the marriage, the couple had eloped to Gretna Green, behaviour which was grounds for a lifetime of ostracism... had she been less rich and he less well-connected. The Duke and Duchess of York were present. The Duke was a dull but kindly man, and extremely wealthy. It was obvious he absolutely doted on his wife, and who could blame him, for she was an extremely beautiful woman, graceful and sophisticated. Luke had met them on two other occasions. Once at the ball held at Carlton House - their London home - on the night he had first been introduced to Amel, and the other at the Theatre Royal.

'You have the inestimable gift of making a party go,' Luke commented, addressing Amel.

'I do my best to make everyone happy,' she replied, pleased with the compliment.

'So I've noticed,' he said, a little too quickly, with a definite hint of sarcasm.

It didn't go unnoticed. 'Just what do you mean by that? I want each of my guest's visit to be memorable. Too often in this fast-paced world, the little pleasant-ries are forgotten. That is why I go out of my way to anticipate everyone's needs and fill them with warmth and graciousness one should expect from their hostess.'

'Why you should want to dangle yourself in front of every male present, looking so seductive...'

'I hope you're not going to make a scene?' she interrupted. 'Monsieur Walten is watching us like a hawk.'

'Mr Walten is hardly interested in who beds whom. I'm sure he has more important things on his mind.'

Amel sighed impatiently, all the time smiling sweetly, in spite of the annoyance he had provoked in her. His company could be a little sour at times, his mood swings becoming positively tedious and were beginning to get on her nerves. One minute he was the attentive devoted lover, the next, a possessive jealous bore. Just at that moment, someone addressed her from the other side of the table. Grateful for the distraction, she gave such a quick and apt reply that everyone around her burst into laughter. Everyone that was, except Luke.

With dinner over the ladies retired to the drawing room for coffee, leaving the men to their brandy and cigars. Talk was mainly about the railway. Building a railroad caught the interest of an entire generation. Trains meant commerce, development, and communications network across the nation. When William James first began to plan the building of the Liverpool & Manchester Railway back in 1824, he approached Joseph Sandars, a wealthy corn merchant and a Whig. He was well-known for his involvement in most of the progressive causes at the time, including parliamentary reform and the campaign to end slavery, and also a strong critic of the local canal and river monopolies. Sandars agreed to back the project, and with the support of other local Quakers that had a reputation as successful entrepreneurs, formed the Liverpool & Manchester Railway Company, recruiting George Stephenson as chief engineer.

The proposed Liverpool & Manchester Railway guaranteed more jobs, but on the other hand, was a serious economic threat to the Bridgewater Canal, which was making a fortune by shipping goods between Liverpool and Manchester. In 1825 shares in the company, originally purchased at £100, were now selling at £1,250 and paying an annual dividend of £35. The Marquis of Stafford, who became the principal owner of the canal after the death of the Duke of Bridgewater, was making an annual profit of

£100,000 from the venture, and understandably, led the fight against the planned railway. Turnpike Trusts, coach companies and farmers, also voiced their opposition and attempted to stop the Act of Parliament going through, but were in time defeated …Parliament finally gave the railway company the authority it needed to go ahead in 1826.

The main objective was to reduce the costs of transporting raw materials and finished goods, between Manchester, the centre of the textile industry and Liverpool, the most important port in the north of England. Manchester had extended extraordinarily in the last fifteen years, through its cotton manufactures. The rich manufacturers built large houses around the Mosley Street area. Factories had sprung up along the rivers Irk, Irwell and Medlock, and the Rochester Canal.

The homes of the working classes were scattered haphazardly around the factories, clustered together in narrow, dark, poorly drained and badly ventilated alleys and lanes, with more regard for the saving of ground rent than for the comfort and health of their inhabitants. Two or more families were crowded together into one small house, and often between twelve and sixteen persons were crammed in a dark damp cellar. The children were dirty and under-nourished, exposed to cold and neglect, and it was an appalling fact that more than half of these ill-fated off-springs died before reaching their fifth year; that is, before they could be engaged in factory labour. The town had no public park or other ground where the population could walk and breathe the fresh air. Every advantage had been sacrificed to the getting of money.

Stephenson was faced with a number of serious engineering problems. This included a nine-arched viaduct across the Sankey Valley, and a two-mile long rock cutting at Olive Mount. The greatest difficulty of all was crossing the immense unstable peat bog of Chat Moss, north of the River Irwell and five miles west of Manchester, part of which had to be drained and made solid with hundreds of tons of earth. John Dixon was recruited as resident engineer and together they devised a strategy for crossing Chat Moss. Unlike the bogs or swamps of Cambridge and Lincolnshire that consist principally of soft mud or silt, this bog was a vast mass of spongy vegetable pulp. Stephenson's idea was that a railroad might be made to float upon the bog. As a ship, or raft, capable of sustaining heavy loads floated in water, so in his opinion, might a light road be floated upon a bog.

The first thing done was to form a footpath of heather along the proposed route, on which a man might walk without risk of sinking. A single line of temporary railway was then laid down, formed of ordinary cross-bars about 3 feet long and an inch square, with holes punched through them at the ends and nailed down to temporary sleepers. This worked well and so it was broadened out to carry a contractor's line on which boys pushed the one-ton wagons of construction material. The boys became so expert that they would run the 4 miles at the rate of 7 or 8 miles an hour without missing a step.

Over 200 men were employed to lay drains on each side of the track area. Although this worked in the shallower parts, it made no impact on the deeper areas of the bog. Stephenson now had to change his plan. The drain was replaced with barrels and casks jointed together and coated with clay to create a form of pipe. This improved the situation but at an area known as the Blackpool Hole, the barrels continued to rise to the surface. But Stephenson refused to accept defeat. Work *had* to go on. An immense outlay had been incurred and a great loss would have been occasioned had the scheme been then abandoned. One of the men on the site suggested a plan that would produce a firm but pliable track of timber laid in herringbone fashion, combined with moss, heather and brushwood hurdles.

During the progress of these works the most ridiculous rumours were set afloat. The drivers of the stagecoaches, who feared for their jobs, brought the most alarming intelligence into Manchester from time to time that "Chat Moss was blown up!"

"Hundreds of men and horses had sunk and the works were abandoned!" The engineer himself was declared to have been swallowed up in the bog; and "railways were at an end forever!" But work continued, although progress was slow and the track across Chat Moss was not finished until December 1829, and on the 1st January of this New Year - 1830, the Rocket successfully hauled a one-ton carriage train across the four-mile section.

The cutting at Olive Mount was another major problem that Stephenson had to overcome on the Liverpool to Manchester line. The Olive Mount cutting was the first extensive stone cutting on any railway - two miles long, 20 foot wide and in some parts, 80 foot deep. It was said when describing it, that it looked as if it had been dug out by giants. Over 480,000 cubic yards of sandstone rock had to be removed to make the two mile long cutting, the rock blasted out and then used to build the Roby embankment and the Sankey Viaduct. Through the heart of the country a road was built and lines of shining steel laid.

The line had to cross the trench-like valley of Sankey Brook. The Sankey Brook Navigation Company objected to the building of the railway and made life difficult for George Stephenson and his team of engineers, by insisting on a 60 ft. clearance over their canal. William Allcard was given the responsibility of designing the Sankey Viaduct and came up with a nine arch structure, built of brick with stone facings. Each of the arches were of 50 foot span and rose from massive sandstone slabs quarried locally, including at Olive Mount. Thousands of tons of marl and moss, compacted with brushwood, were used to increase the height of the embankment. This alone cost the company over £45,000 to produce.

Later in the evening, Elizabeth Jersey, entertained them all with several songs, accompanied by Ellen Kean on the piano. Richard Parkes Bonington recited a number of poems and afterwards, Catherine - the Duchess of Kinston and Elizabeth sang a duet together. Towards midnight there was a light supper and champagne served in the dining room. The Duke and Duchess of York, Archer Horne the wool trader, the two young officers who were apparently friends of John Walten, and the newlyweds, had all made their excuses and left earlier. Those remaining were Richard Parkes Bonington and John Walten, the peculiar Horace Twist, Ellen Kean, Catherine Gurney and Waldoff Huskisson.

Luke's mood had lightened considerably, warmed by the champagne and the brandy that followed, and the thought of what was to come excited him, pumping adrenalin through his system. He stood back, allowing Amel, Ellen Kean and Catherine Gurney to enter the drawing room before him, deliberately barring Waldoff Huskisson's path. He did not like the fellow … there was something about him.

Luke stood with Amel and Mrs Kean, surrounded by all the magnificence, silently observing the conversation. They did not need much sagacity to perceive that the three men who had remained in the dining room, had the honour of being the target of Catherine Gurney's - or the Duchess, as she liked to be called - caustic wit. She was being very sarcastic on the subject of queers and bores. Her so-called Albanian Prince stood drooling over her, laughing heartily at whatever she said. After making a few very tasteless remarks, she suddenly lapsed into silence just as the men came into the drawing room.

Luke was not the only one to notice the atmosphere, so stifling to the mind. Failing to understand how anyone, particularly Amel and the delightful Ellen Kean, could listen to that kind of conversation, he excused himself and moved across the room to the fireplace, to light up a cigar.

Horace Twist came to stand immediately in front of Amel. No one admired Amelia Duprez more than he did. He had fallen in love with her when she was just a girl of fifteen. Rekindling the flame with the one that got away, he had pestered her for years, to marry him. She had refused him half a dozen times or more, and had married another, her Frenchman, yet still he continued to love her. It wounded him deeply that she did not take his proposals seriously. He made an exaggerated bow, and rising to take her hand in his, pressed it to his moist lips.

'Ah ...Mon la peche,' he crooned softly, keeping hold of her hand far too long and gazing deep into her eyes. 'Laisser nous faire l'amour.' In talking he used his free hand a great deal, moving it about theatrically.

Luke threw his unfinished cigar in the fire and moved forward, pushing between them, and taking Amel firmly by the elbow led her away, out into the hall, without as much as a polite "excuse me" to anyone. Horace's eyes followed them in amusement.

Luke let go of Amel's arm, turning to face her. 'What was that he called you?'

'Mon la peche ... my peach.'

'What the hell does he think he's playing at? He infuriates me, that fellow. There's just something about him.'

Amel slipped her arm through his, cocking her head prettily to one side. 'Oh, really, Luke, he means no harm.'

'I can't imagine why you invite him to these evenings. Who the hell is he, anyway?'

'You know very well who he is.'

'I mean where does he come from? Twist! That's not a French name.'

'Horace was born in Paris. His father was English, his mother French. Does that satisfy your curiosity?'

'What does he do?'

'He doesn't *do* anything. He has no need. He's the son of a very wealthy timber merchant,' she said. 'All the ladies simply adore him.'

'So I've noticed. The exhibitionist. Such a sight cures one of envy. I can't bear to look at him.'

'Then don't.'

'He's as vain as a peacock,' Luke sneered. 'What else did he say?'

She turned to face him. 'Oh, come now! Do you really want to know?'

'Yes, tell me.'

'As you wish. He said ...laisser nous faire l'amour ...let us make love.'

'The bastard!' Luke growled.

Amel sighed in exasperation. He could be so infuriating sometimes. 'Oh, can't you see he's just trying to ruffle your feathers?'

'Well, he had best watch out I don't ruffle his. In more ways than one.'

'Really, Horace is quite harmless. He has a heart of gold.'

'But a bit eccentric, you must admit.'

'Huh! You think he's eccentric! You ought to have known his father. He was a noted eccentric. He used to remove all his clothes and sit on them whenever it rained.'

Luke's eyes widened with disbelief. 'You jest?'

'I'm serious. It's true,' she said, a faint light of amusement in her eyes, her annoyance forgotten. 'Horace is such fun to be with. I am really quite fond of him.'

It was hard to imagine that she could care for that ...that puffed-up, soft dandy. It couldn't be for his manliness, so it had to be for his money.

'I find him such stimulating company. He makes me laugh,' Amel went on to say. 'I am all for having a good time.'

'A bit of hanky-panky, you mean?'

She giggled girlishly then. 'Oh, Mon amour, you

are so funny when you are angry.'

Damn her! She was making fun of him. 'I don't find it at all amusing. You can't tell me there's nothing going on between the two of you. There are many derogatory rumours in circulation.'

There was no certain ground for believing these stories, but then, there was no smoke without fire. He was certainly on very friendly terms with her, to see her almost every day.

Amel's eyes flashed. 'Take care, Monsieur.'

'He's hardly the sort to pay for those two magnificent carriage horses you have housed in the stable, unless he was getting something in return.'

Her lovely face flushed to poppy red, her mouth tightening with irritation. She withdrew her arm from his and looked at him directly. 'You cad! How do you presume to know what Horace feels for me?'

'Come now, you don't have to play games with me.'

'Really! This is too much,' she snapped.

'I'm fully aware those horses were a gift from him. And that he has proposed marriage. Can't you see you're leading him on? Giving him false hopes. Flirting with him before my very eyes. You can't be so obtuse as not to see I'm mad about you, insanely jealous...' He broke off abruptly. He could not believe he had said that. The brandy must have gone to his head. Him jealous? He had never been jealous of anyone in his entire life, except perhaps as a child - then he had felt jealous of the attention his mother had given her so-called companion - Dorothy Hawell, attention that rightly should have been his. 'Can't you see that ...that puffed up dandy is coming between us?'

'Don't be ridiculous! The country air seems to be turning your brain soft. You're stifling me with your possessiveness. Just because we've slept together, Monsieur, doesn't mean you own me,' she cried angrily. 'And you don't know how wrong you are. I've slept with a great many men, but not with Horace. Not the once! If you must know, he has an exaggerated interest in viewing sexual scenes.'

'You mean he watches?' Luke's dark eyes were wide with disbelief.

'Oui! That is exactly what I mean. He developed a taste for voyeurism in his adolescence. He wants no more than to watch and afterwards, be spanked.'

'You can't be serious?'

Amel closed her eyes momentarily and sighed in an exaggerated way.

'You are serious?'

'I said so, did I not,' she said impatiently.

'And you allow this?' He sounded shocked.

'But, of course,' she admitted, not seeing anything wrong in it.

Disgust curled Luke's lips. 'What do you think you're doing sharing the intimate side of your life with a total stranger?'

'I have no problem with that. And Horace is hardly a stranger. He is a friend. A very dear friend.'

'So it would seem. But friend or no friend, there are limits. Have you no sense of decency?'

'Where does one draw the line between lust and decency? What Horace wants he pays for. As simple as that!'

'The animal!' Luke hissed, with repugnance.

'In my experience I've found all men to be no better than animals.'

'Oh! Then what does that make you, Madam? I can't believe you would encourage anyone to watch when you're...?' he trailed off, unable to speak the words. He found the whole thing totally distasteful.

'What that makes me, Monsieur, is popular and well sought after.' He was by no means her only means of obtaining money. Far from it. She had other relationships to manage, platonic friendships and others not so platonic. Her friends were more often than not married, well-bred, *wealthy* men.

'No, Madam. What that makes you is, a common whore.'

Her eyes flashed dangerously. 'My God! How dare you call me names and question my conduct. Who do you think you are, my father?' Her voice, usually carefully modulated, had become shrill with indignation. 'My life is my own affair. Do you honestly expect me to wait around every time you disappear back to that silly, naive little wife of yours, mope about on my own until it suits you to put in an appearance? I think not, Monsieur! I have my own life and am entitled to enjoy myself.'

'I'm gone but a few days. Is it too much to ask of you to have a little patience?'

Her eyes narrowed. 'Patience! You're trying my patience to the limit this very minute, with your suffocating moods. I won't have you telling me whom I can and cannot see. I suggest you leave, Monsieur.'

'If I offended you, I apologise. It's just that your conduct sometimes...'

'It is too late for that now. I don't want to hear it,' she interrupted angrily. 'You have a certain animosity about you that pushes people away.'

It wasn't the first time he had made a scene. At one

time, not so long ago, he had forced her to promise never to see her dear friend Lord George again. She had had to agree at the time, in order to keep the peace, but of course, as she did all others, she broke that promise. Although she knew he suspected this, she took precautions to prevent him from discovering it for a fact. How easy it was to dupe a man. As it was, Lord George had moved on, as was his way, but with her usual tact and good humour she contrived that they should remain the best of friends. She found him to be an ideal confidante, discreet, a clever and unsentimental man who gave shrewd advice and accepted deceptions with a tolerant smile. The role of confidante and guide was always a favourite one with her and she exerted herself to bind him to her by every bond of affection.

'It's a mistake for you to suppose I am without friends, Monsieur. A cast-off mistress has little difficulty in finding another protector,' she informed him, self-confident to the point of smugness.

The truth was, she knew she would never rediscover the same excitement, the same passion with another living soul, but she found him so exasperating, so infuriating at times. He was generous, attentive and always good mannered and charming, she admitted ungrudgingly, but on the occasions they had spent several days together, she had found him to be far too argumentative, self-righteous, conceited even. These defects made him impossible to be with for any length of time, and she was often relieved when he took his leave.

But then, from the moment he departed, she missed him, and yet when he was around her too long, he maddened her with his faults. Of all the problems their affair had caused, she would not have missed it for the world. For the moments of pleasure, moments of sheer blissful ecstasy he had brought her, she would willingly live through it all over again. It had all been infinitely worthwhile, but now …she thought regretfully, with this tragic suddenness, it had come to an end.

He broke into her thoughts. 'Have you no sense of loyalty, no sense of decency?'

'I am merely being honest with you. Do you not remember the discussion we once had? No strings! Do you not remember?'

'I admit I was a little condescending,' he admitted grudgingly.

'More than just a little, Monsieur. You've gone too far this time. *C'est fini*,' she said with firmness.

'What does that mean?'

'It is finished …over,' she repeated.

He felt that he had something more he wanted to say, but could not bring himself to say it. A man was obliged to keep his feelings hidden. Completely enslaved he was, body and soul, by this ...this creature's dangerous charms. It was not so easy to tell what her exact feelings towards him were. It was plain that she liked his company, but did not seek it. Hostility towards him had been increasing with his every visit. On his last visit she had taken pains not to be alone with him.

'I mean it, Monsieur. Don't let me detain you.'

Luke stiffened. 'Meaning you would like me to leave?'

'Oui ...I want you to leave. You seem happy to let things drag, but not I. Why spoil a beautiful memory? We are only degrading each other. It is far better to part while we have a few shreds of dignity left.'

'But when something is good, don't you want it to last forever?'

She raised one fine eyebrow. 'Forever is a long time. I cannot think in those terms. I never could.'

'My God, you're a cold-hearted bitch. You make me sick.'

Amel shrugged, her stare icy. 'Then why are you still here? Please ...*go*! Crawl back to your matrimonial tomb.' She turned her back and glided away, leaving him staring after her. She was confident he would be back.

THIRTY

In his Castle at Windsor, a shadow of shadows, dwelled an old man, lost of his senses and forgotten by Death, who, remorselessly, had passed him by. But beyond his walls the stream of life flowed on, gathering momentum to turn the tide of change in the dawn of a New Age: an age of transition, of social and political revolt; of new forces rising, old shibboleths dying, and of new voices speaking for those who had never dared speak of their "rights" before.

King George lV's profligacy and marriage difficulties meant that he never gained much popularity and he now spent most of his days in seclusion at Windsor. As King he was scarcely known to his people, nor, during the last year had he been seen at Brighton, and that exuberant Folly of his, the Pavilion.

Earlier in the year, George's insomnia and mental confusion grew even worse, as did his breathlessness. Sir Henry Halford, who had attended the Royal Family for over three decades, registered that the present King's distress was worse than anything he had witnessed even when his brothers the Dukes of Clarence and Sussex were suffering attacks of spasmodic asthma. As the monarch struggled against attacks of breathlessness and was unable to lie down because of the fluid in his lungs, the doctors rigged up the pillows in his bed chair in such a way as to permit him to sleep holding his head in his hands.

He was still taking enormous quantities of laudanum.

As Halford put in his report of 3rd May to Wellington: 'In addition to the legs being very swollen, the breathlessness and fluid on the lungs, His Majesty now suffers from sores and watery blisters all over his body. He is black in the face and the ends of his fingers are also black. His Majesty's agitation is made worse by the realisation that his symptoms are identical to those from which his brother, the Duke of York, had died just three years earlier.'

Halford's diagnosis was that fluid, which had so far been directed outwards to the skin, was now finding its way into the King's chest and abdomen, with fatal consequences.

A week later Halford had better news to report. 'Benjamin Brodie has been called in to puncture the King's legs and the soles of his feet, so as to drain away the fluid that has accumulated there, and His Majesty's symptoms have been less severe. The paroxysms of difficulty of breathing are not recurring so frequently. His Majesty has eaten his food well and although he cannot command sleep to the extent he might wish, he obtains short, refreshing periods of it.'

Unhappily, the respite was not to last. It was reported that in spite of the new leg punctures and the fact that the King had stopped his frequent drinking, his waist was very swollen, which led them to conclude that the effusion continues. Further draining from the legs brought temporary relief, but Halford warned that the principal problem in the organs of the chest was as grave as before and that the King was manifestly growing weaker.

Windsor Castle: The reign of George IV has ended. His Majesty departed this life at the age of sixty seven years. The knowledge, from a very early period of his illness, which all persons well informed as to its nature possessed, that his recovery was not possible, has caused this event to be almost daily expected.

London Gazette: A Bulletin has been this morning received by Sir Robert Peel, one of his Majesty's Principal Secretaries of State.

The death of a King.

It has pleased Almighty God to take from this World the King's Most Excellent Majesty George IV. His Majesty expired at a quarter past three o'clock this morning, without pain.

Windsor Castle June 26, 1830.

The dining room of Burlington House was brightly lit, in contrast to the gloom outside. But the look on Amelia's face was far from bright. She seemed distant and reluctant to speak. There were only the two of them - a quiet evening at home. No foolish quarrel had kept them away from each other for too long. But it had cost Luke dearly.

'The death of King George was inevitable. He's been ailing for years, his symptoms identical to those his brother, the Duke of York, died of,' Luke said quietly. 'Mind, George was a good age. Well into his sixties. He will hardly be missed. He was never popular. I wonder what this one will be like? No better and no worse, I suspect.'

'Oh, why do you say that?'

'Well, they're a strange lot, to say the least.'

Amelia dismissed the comment with a somewhat careless shrug that was not at all like her. She was well read, he knew, and virtually interested in all matters of national, and even international importance, and capable of discussing most topics which were in the news.

'It's been said that the Duke of Wellington and his ministers only let him have his own way because they were concerned that his violence and irritability might have driven him over the edge.'

'Driven whom over the edge?'

'I was saying, my darling, how violent the late King was. That the Prime Minster only let him have his own way because he feared George might slip over the edge. It's said that he was quite mad and that his brother, the Duke of Clarence, is no better, as eccentric as he was. He must be in his mid-sixties by now.'

Amelia wasn't really listening. She had a lot on her mind. Her debts were piling up and with her health not being too good, it made it almost impossible to carry on. Sometimes she felt as though the tightrope she walked was none too securely fastened to its supports, the rope between threatening to tip her off into an abyss of disaster.

'You're unusually quiet tonight, my darling. What are you thinking?' Luke asked her quietly. 'What's going on in that mind of yours?'

'Oh, just private thoughts.'

'Won't you share them with me?'

'I think not,' she said moodily, looking at him with troubled eyes. 'I am feeling unwell. I think, perhaps, I
would be better left to myself tonight.'

He was silent for a few moments, studying her more closely. Then, when he spoke again, she sensed a note of sarcasm in his voice. 'Are you really feeling unwell or are you just making excuses?'

She retaliated quickly. 'Oh, believe what you want. I don't give a damn.'

She had such a sick headache that she could barely eat and was obliged to go to her room. Luke finished the meal alone. As Amel lay dozing, he, preoccupied with his own affairs, busied himself writing letters in the drawing room. By the time he had finished, she was awake and had recovered sufficiently for him to join her in her boudoir.

'You still look a little pale. I'll ring for the maid. A cup of tea will set you to rights.'

He settled in a deep comfortable chair by the fire, feeling relaxed after a splendid meal, a good cigar and two large brandies. He began to smile reminiscently as his thoughts turned to Jessica and her belief that tea was the cure of all the world's problems. He recalled her insistence that tealeaves strewn in front of the house kept away evil spirits. Or if the lid was accidentally left off the teapot, it foretold the coming of a stranger. And woe betide if two women poured out of the same pot; one would be sure to have a child within a year. All such nonsense really, but it made him smile. She made him smile about lots of things if he thought about it.

He remembered how anxious she had been when the new riding habit she had ordered had come to almost fifteen pounds. She had felt guilty in spending a mere fifteen pounds! Why, Amel's milliner's bills were always around four hundred pounds, the largest amounting to over eight hundred, totalling to almost thirteen hundred in the last two months alone. She was known to have spent as much as a thousand pounds on one shipment of elegant gowns, up-to-the-minute fashions from Paris. Her servants' liveries alone cost as much as their wages for the whole year. And the estimated yearly cost of keeping a single horse in London, inclusive of stabling and groom was around twelve hundred and twenty pounds. But then Amelia had the most extravagant tastes.

She possessed an unrestrained love of luxury: costly cashmeres, rich furs and brilliant showy ornaments; bracelets and brooches, feathers, flowers, decorative fans and beaded slippers, bejewelled combs, turbans and tiaras for the hair. She was also fond of red roses, as her florists' bills indicated; as much as she enjoyed expensive jewellery, fashion accessories: gloves, shoes, boots and belts. All of high quality, with price tags to match. Always the best of everything. The best plays, best restaurants …and gracious entertaining, filling the house with French furniture, eating French foods and drinking expensive French wines; setting a style for lavish hospitality and elegant dress. Living a gaudy, opulent lifestyle others could only dream of.

But Jessica …ah …now she was one of a kind, a breath of fresh air, a truly exquisite nature, honest and entirely selfless, a warm-hearted girl who believed in love and magic. First class qualities that Amel was without. A girl with that inclination to take bright views, who believed, with the optimism of youth that marriages were made in heaven and every cloud has a silver lining. Yet, not quite an Angel, with that streak of wildness about her that he so admired. Wild and audacious, with a fiercely independent spirit and the desire for freedom and experiences outside the sacred enclosure of home, forever straining against the confines of marriage.

He could not remember those first days without smiling to himself, the perfectly innocent admiration in her bright eyes at the sight of him when she had first seen him naked, her extreme bashfulness, how it's prodigious size made her shrink; the ignorance about her own body and his - that flower-like innocence. He recalled it taking patient persuasion to get her to let go of the bedclothes, to be taught those first lessons of pleasure. Moments that marks one's life. It was strange she should be so much on his mind - like a gemstone which glows at the perimeter of one's vision, the awareness of her forever there. There wasn't a day went by now when he didn't think of her, of the sparks and energy she gave off. He had found in her, not only a desirable mate, but a friend.

If only Amel was as open and affectionate as Jessica, he would be a much happier man, as although Mother-nature had done great matters for her on her outward form, especially in that superb piece of equipment she had so liberally enriched her with, still there was something more wanting …something sadly lacking.

One of the most obvious doors of escape into new experience was the prostitute, for that was what she was, a very expensive indulgence, but a prostitute none-the-less, supplying an element that was lacking in his relationship with his young wife.

The exquisitely beautiful Amel, an element of charm and mutual gaiety in pleasure, who knew many of the subtleties and peculiarities of the stimuli that gave him an added physical delight. Stooping to such a course was merely a craving for lust - no more strange than hunger. No matter how strange they were, given enough time they become normal. Well, a man, a healthy, normal man, had to have some fun in his life. Both females gave him what he needed, each in their different way. Jessica was being difficult now, insubordinate to her duties as a wife, but she would get over it. And yet, strangely enough he enjoyed her show of defiance.

He had to admit he had made a complete mess of things and had only himself to blame. He must be more careful and show her the attention that she craved. Age was apt to look upon the material side of the relationship to see its surface in the cold light of every day experience, whilst youth, dazzled by the bright glow of dreams seemed unaware how its unreal heavenly fantasies can be broken and shattered when unsuspectingly brought up against the hard facts of physical reality. She will have had ample time to cry her eyes out and should be ready to benefit by the consolation of common sense.

Nothing dries sooner than tears. All the same, he must remember to take more interest, give her more of his time, so she would be less likely to complain. And he would take her home a gift, something special, to make amends. He had to admit he looked forward to getting back to her and the country. His strength derived from the countryside in which, for all his absorption in moneymaking, his heart lay. London was but an encampment from which all that could afford it fled as soon as the Season and parliamentary sessions were over, when the hotels were half empty and clubs less crowded.

Amelia, who was feeling so much better and was now reclining lazily on the chaise-lounge, broke into his thoughts. 'I apologise, Mon amour, for my burst of temper earlier. I was truly not myself.'

Luke looked up at her then. Still, after all this time he admired her beauty. Her tantalizing form was draped loosely in a robe of purest white, arranged so as to suggest rather than conceal its exquisite outline, her head rested on cushions of the softest, snowiest satin, with her hair tumbling about her shoulders in soft golden waves. Her skin glowed pale and translucent in the candle light. A kind of magic seemed to radiate from her, a matchless piece of loveliness, wondrous as the ideal of a poet's dream.

The pleasure of enjoyment was the link she held him by. She had made him lose his taste for inconstancy and new faces. Again and again, an invisible hand forced him back to her, because she truly fascinated him. Her face still held a thousand mysteries, her body a thousand sweet promises, designed to please, to charm, as others were to breed. He often left her gifts of two, sometimes as much as three hundred pounds in bank notes on the table, for the privilege of spending the entire night with her, which she accepted without as much as the faintest blush.

A smile tilted the corner of his mouth. 'Apology accepted, my darling.'

'I want to ask you something,' she said after a few moments. 'Will you promise to answer me quite frankly?'

He promised, mystified, wondering just what the deuce was coming.

'I want you to tell me whether you've noticed anything strange about me lately,' she said. 'Have I said or done anything that seems odd?'

Her perturbation was so great that he smiled to hide his perception of it. 'Nothing more than usual. What makes you ask?'

But she was not to be shaken out of her fears, whatever they were. 'Do you not notice anything different at all about me?' She spoke impatiently, waving his politeness aside. 'In my appearance ...my complexion?'

Luke shrugged. 'You look a little paler than usual, that's all. Nothing more than that.'

'Merci. That's all I needed to know,' she replied, relief sounding in her voice.

With a surge of sudden energy, she swung long smooth slender legs over the side of the chaise-lounge and rose to her feet, the robe she had on falling open to expose her nakedness in full view, the whole region of delight, the soft light from the flickering flames moulding the deep hollows and peaks of her creamy flesh.

Luke's mood of nostalgia faltered, the radiant picture of his young wife fading from his mind. His blood warmed at the very sight of the woman before him, devouring everything with his dark appreciative eyes. The exquisite thighs, fashioned to the point of perfection, the smoothness of her softly curved belly ...so much sheer femininity. With that delicate and voluptuous emotion which she alone had the secret to excite, which constitutes the very life, the very essence of pleasure.

He was lost in the witchery of the spell she cast over him. He could almost feel the warmth of her flesh - almost taste her. Then, as if her impressive performance wasn't tantalising enough to raise his temperature, she cupped one of her ample firm breasts, running the other hand down over her smooth belly to the little triangle of soft fair fuzz between her legs.

Wild fire sprang up in his stomach …the whole of her an invitation to his senses that he scarcely knew how to resist. It would take the resolution of a saint to deny Amel Duprez. She really was, in every sense, a most exquisite companion, bewitching him with her sensuality. A supernal loveliness which no words short of poetic rapture could even hint.

She still had the power to draw him, drag him to her by his senses, as a magnet draws steel, and bind him with chains that he would not want to break! Her eyes glinted with humid fires, locking with his, reading his approval of anything she might have in mind. Unwell she might have been earlier, but she had not lost her powers of observation and could see how it was with him, below the belt, with the object of his desire.

Subdued light seeped through shuttered windows, making all seem distant and unreal. The bed, surrounded by clouds of white, seemed to be floating in the spangled light of the candles spread about the room. Here, one was transferred to a remote and separate existence, for the roundness of the room and the curved dome of the roof sprinkled with stars, the fragmented dull gold of the extraordinary furniture and the winged Goddess of Love above the fireplace, all had a quality of creating a little independent world. He was up on his feet, sweeping her in to his strong arms, driven by a passion too imperious for him to resist, crushing her body against him, holding her as if he would never release her.

'Well, my darling, some things do not change. You still have the talent to please me, which you know is a necessity in my life. I do believe we are well matched in our desire for pleasure.'

Sensing what he needed, she deliberately set out to please him, in the only way a woman could, which was what she was good at. Forgetting the fear of abandonment that forever lurked on the edge of consciousness, she pushed in effectually against his grip, putting pleasure effectively in motion, as ardent as he was himself, quivering with self-congratulatory bliss. She let her robe slip from her shoulders and helped him off with his clothes.

They sank to the floor, the soft luxurious carpet cushioning their naked bodies. She spoke very little, but made it up emphatically with action, pushing him back and straddling him, grasping his hard, erect manhood with velvet fingers and guiding him into her, lowering herself onto him. She was unstoppable, hell bent on pleasure. Supporting herself on her arms she began to move up and down, slowly at first, savouring the sensation, her warm soft breasts brushing tantalisingly against his skin, sending his spirits soaring in the dizzy heights of rapture. He was overpowered with the ecstasy, senseless of everything and in every part but those favourite ones of nature in which all sensation was concentrated, driving him wild. He threw back his head and gasped. The active energy of his eager upward thrusts, favoured by the fervid appetite of her motions stirred him beyond bearing, in a frenzy of passion that engulfed them both.

When the steamy session was over he was well satisfied and it seemed, so was she. To do her justice, she never gave him any reason to complain. He couldn't put a price on such experience. She really was a treasure, worth her weight in gold.

THIRTY-ONE

The passing of the old monarch and the accession of the new; on the death of George lV, his brother William, the eccentric Duke of Clarence, third son of George 111, became King. The scandal of his long association with the actress, Dorothy Jordon, who bore him ten children, was forgotten.

He too was scarcely known to his people, having lived these last few years in almost complete seclusion at Bushey, with his young Duchess, Adelaide, eldest daughter of the Duke of Saxe-Coburg. The couple had two daughters but they both died in infancy.

While few of his subjects had ever seen him, all knew what to expect. An amiable, somewhat eccentric old gentleman whose early youth and young manhood had been spent at sea. He had fought, but without distinction, in his father's wars and who, as Lord High Admiral, had been thrown out of office for unorthodox behaviour.

Yet there were some who saw, or hoped to see, in this Fourth William, the first monarch for over a century who did not bear the name of George; a cheerful omen. England had not been lucky with her Georges; this elderly King with his good humour, his rolling sailor's gait and his charming little wife, who so obligingly mothered his numerous bastards ranging from girls of her own age to nursery toddlers, might well be the best of a bad lot. Thus the verdict in the clubs of St James's, while bets among the blades ran high, that there would be another Regency before the year was out.

General opinion was that he was as crazy as his father. From the moment he left Bushey on his drive to St James's for the Proclamation, his craziness was only too apparent. Unrecognized along the way by the villagers of Twickenham, Putney and Hammersmith, he was hailed at Hyde Park turnpike by the tollgate keeper, who likewise, had no knowledge of this genial old gentleman's identity. William handed him a crown piece with the jovial injunction, 'Keep this, my good fellow. It will be the last silver coin you're ever likely to see stamped with George's head.'

At first he was reasonably popular, pleasing his subjects by announcing that he would keep royal expenditure to a minimum. When it was discovered that William's coronation only cost a tenth of the expense incurred by George IV's ceremony in 1821, people were convinced that he meant what he said. King George had spent the nation's money right and left, on his women, on drink, his houses and orgies, and on that Pavilion of his in Brighton, with its onion-shaped cupolas and towers.

Like his father and brother, William IV was prone to strange behaviour. On the day he became King he raced through London in an open carriage, frequently re-moving his hat and bowing to his subjects, Every so often he stopped and offered people a lift. And his habit of spitting in public also helped to obtain for him a reputation as an eccentric. The exaltation of coming to the throne at the age of sixty-five was so great that William nearly went mad, distinguishing himself by a thousand extravagances of language and conduct, to the alarm of all who witnessed his strange freaks.

One morning he inspected the Coldstream Guards, dressed in a military uniform for the first time in his life, and with a great pair of gold spurs halfway up his legs like a gamecock. Although he was shortly afterwards sobered down into more becoming behaviour, he always continued to be something of a clown.

William's near madness was a problem for all who had to deal with him. Seemingly unable to control his temper, he would grow literally purple with rage and hurl incoherent abuse at those around him. William was a Whig, and at one time even considered becoming a Member of Parliament. In the House of Lords he supported Catholic Emancipation and showed signs he favoured parliamentary reform. Shortly after his accession, he made a number of speeches so ridiculous and nonsensical, beyond all belief but to those who heard them, rambling from one subject to another, repeating the same thing over and over again, going much too fast, that it begun to alarm his Ministers.

The last round in the battle for Reform had reached its height, yet never had the season of parties, balls and dinners been more feverishly gay. The Tories and the Whigs met and intermingled, their swords, for the meantime, amicably sheathed.

The courtyard of Burlington House was full with carriages of all descriptions, the darkness spangled by their lamps and loud with the clatter of hooves and yells of drivers and grooms. Twelve wide steps led up to the vast double front doors, leading into a world of glitter and lights, music and laughter.

Madame Duprez's parties were now the best arranged and most fashionable in London. It was usual for her to give one about once a month, with music and dancing then supper afterwards, inviting all the performers from The Theatre Royal in Druary Lane. Everyone who was anyone was usually there; army officers, diplomats, anyone well-connected, the fashion-able set, all assembled at the house, attracted by its charming hostess who was considered a great beauty, an object of public awe and adoration, and the hospitality that might appear almost too lavish for good taste, but in which it was pleasant to share. Such occasions required studious planning on the part of the hostess. Menus had to be discussed with the housekeeper and cook, supplies checked, special items ordered, seating arrangements considered and musicians booked. Bedrooms that had been shut up were opened and aired, in readiness for those guests staying overnight.

A footman led Luke into the large central hall where ladies in elaborate gowns, glittering jewels and nodding feathers, stood whispering to each other of the latest scandal. Through an archway he could see the whole central space of the house to the roof filled by the great stair case adorned with classical statuettes standing in high curved recesses. Candel-abras were lit all around the house to supple-ment the fashionable but not very successful gas brackets that continually flickered; totally inadequate in dispelling the gloom. Candles proved far more dependable.

The saloon was fifty foot in length, with small tables and gilt upholstered seats aligning the walls, the centre being given up entirely to the dancers, who were waltzing to the by no means bad music of half-a-dozen players. Luke surveyed the room, or as much as he could see of it for the increasing crowd. Light struck rainbow sparks from crystal chandeliers on jewelled throats and heads, casting metallic gleams on scarves of gold and silver gauze, to die away amid the folds of multi-coloured satin, bathing shoulders in shadow and defining the feature of a face. The disharmony of women's voices, high and shrill as starlings, rose above the deep subdued murmur of their attendant men. More subdued, were the black and pastel greys of their swallow-tailed suits pleasantly blended with that fragmentary mosaic.

Luke caught the eye of Frederick Rolleston, the President of the Board of Trade, a somewhat elderly man now, but still handsome in a way, and strolled towards him. He saw that Amel and Horace Twist were already circling the floor. They made a dazzling pair with their striking looks and the graceful way they moved together. Twist was one of the most eligible bachelors in London, and two or three pairs of hopeful eyes were upon him, following him around the room. But his admiration seemed reserved only for the slender, enchanting and very lively Amel Duprez he held in his arms, who outshone every other woman present. Her complexion was brilliant and her eyes a sparkling blue, but the most attractive thing of all about her in his opinion, was her splendid zest for life, not in its spiritual or intellectual forms, but simply for living.

The music stopped and the dancers wandered off the floor, all eyes suddenly turning toward the door, all voices sinking to a murmur, when the footman announced the arrival of Albert Moore, the very wealthy cotton manufacturer. A most fortunate man, who could afford to indulge in his passion for books and paintings, works by Rembrandt and Rubens, which were kept on display in Melbourne House, his London home. His forceful, saturnine face with its shaggy, black eyebrows was frequently seen at Burlington House. With him came his friends, all much younger than he himself, drawn together by his magnetic leadership, his wit and charm, which made him a captivating companion, his manner a fascination for women and men alike; neither knew how to resist.

Amel moved swiftly towards them, this decisive manoeuvre noted by Luke. Tonight she was attired in a trained white silk evening gown of the classical style, high at the waist, falling smoothly down to her fine slender ankles and satin slippers richly entwined with silver. The gown was embroidered all over with the tiniest clear glass beads that caught the light and shimmered as she moved, the sleeves short and puffy, trimmed with ivory cording. Luke had never seen the gown before. There was no denying the effect was absolutely dazzling …and she knew it.

Men turned covertly to watch her, without making it too apparent. It was so daring; another fraction of an inch and her nipples would be showing, and it dipped to a low v at the back exposing her smooth creamy skin. She wore diamond earrings, and the tiara that crowned her golden head was hand crafted with multiple sized stones, pearls, and navettes. A spectacular costly piece certain to make a statement. He ought to know… it was a gift from him. He had purchased it himself when in one of his generous moods.

Among the group was Captain Rubin McLachlan

of the 91st Argyllshire Regiment of Foot. An officer, a gentleman and a gambler, with a melancholic nature that seemed to appeal to Amel Duprez. A fair stripling, somewhere between twenty-five and thirty, who was from somewhere up north and spoke in a strange way. He looked impressive in the full dress coat of scarlet cloth, double breasted, with a Prussian style collar a full three inches deep, the lapels buttoned back, and a very light skirt with kerseymere turn-backs, slash flaps with four twist holes and buttons wings, with a double row of gilt chains. White shirt and frill, and about a half inch of black silk cravat showed above the collar. All the regimental buttons were in gilt; collar, lapels and deep cuffs of regimental yellow. A crimson silk sash was wound twice around the waist, ending in cords and tassels. The three inch wide sword belt was of thick buff leather, pipe clayed white, fastened on the chest by the cross belt gilt plate decorated with silver ornaments and blue enamel surrounded by thistles in the centre.

He was also extremely good looking, positively hand-some in fact, his hair in tightly cropped fair curls, a face on which all the roseate bloom of youth and all the manly graces conspired to fix her eyes and fickle heart. She welcomed the newcomer, who fell at once under her spell as his eyes probed lower to the valley of her breasts.

Amel had always been popular at balls, being not only beautiful and a graceful dancer, but a lively conversationalist. She was never in danger of sitting out a dance, and indeed was so well supplied with partners that she was obliged to refuse one or two invitations at times. During the course of the evening she could be seen pivoting round and round the ballroom with one man after another.

Luke sought her out in a pause between dances to tell her that he was glad she was so popular and she was having such a splendid time, but what had been the point of inviting him if she intended spending all of her time with others? She simply shrugged her shoulders and gave him a bewitching smile. Throughout the entire evening she had promptly squelched him when he attempted conversation, the least contradiction seized upon, giving him disapproving looks, then had began talking to somebody else, which only succeeded in exasperating him further.

When his best sallies had fallen flat and his most provocative openings had been answered with insipid smiles, he relapsed into a baffled silence. Their relationship was delicate just lately to say the least and yet he had been happy to let things drag on. He cursed himself silently for allowing himself to ever having been drawn into such a relationship in the first place, with a woman who was so damn coquettish, pert, and thoroughly cold hearted.

It was all supposed to be so simple. You take what you want and afterwards just walk away. That was all he had wanted to do, but Amel Duprez wasn't a woman you could drop that easily. And she had not lost the power to excite him; the teasing, tantalising bitch. Even as he despised her, he longed for her. He had let it go on far too long and somewhere along the way it had got personal; she had become a vital part of his life, bewitching him beyond belief. It was not only her beauty that attracted him, but the vitality and that unquenchable sensuality. She could somehow move mens' emotions with her body, including his own. She had breeding, brains and beauty, and yet was incapable of real tenderness.

Amel's delight in her new friend was ecstatic. She was having a most enjoyable evening, the happiest she had had for a long time. He was so immensely attractive in his immaculate uniform that it was impossible to look at him without wanting him. She smiled to herself. An expert in the art of seduction, she would allow no dust to gather. Each time she looked in to one man's eyes she could see the reflection of the next, which was how she liked it. No more emotional entanglements for her. Rubin McLachlan in turn, was dazzled by Amel Duprez's astonishing sexuality, her goddess-like self-confidence and the way she flaunted herself; a woman so obviously proud of her body. Covert glances passed between them, shared looks, the surreptitious questioning appraisal of one another, expressions of mutual certainty that they would become more than just friends.

Frederick Rolleston, suddenly feeling unwell, had made his excuses and left earlier. In Luke's opinion, he had been the only male present worth talking to. He found him to be one of the best tempered men he had ever met, somewhat reserved in company but a fascinating companion and of course, immensely rich, as was most all Madame Duprez's friends, all of who continually showered her with expensive gifts.

Luke sat back in his chair in a secluded corner, toying with his glass of wine, stiff in formal wear and starched shirt, watching Amel's reactions closely. He damned her silently, despising her for so obviously enjoying being the centre of attraction.

Talk had become lively, the mood gay. Nitrous

oxide had been discovered way back in the year 1800 and when inhaled, was found to give a giddy, intoxicating feeling and released the emotions. People sat around inhaling its fumes, which made them laugh insanely ...much to Luke's disgust. He had gained very accurate notions of these men, scheming fellows, mostly of bad repute, but all of them men of intelligence who only made their way into drawing rooms either by their extreme skilfullness or by reason of fortunes shamefully acquired. He saw the set for what they were ...corrupt and loathsome.

Idle fools, generally calling attention to their insufferable manners, with their cock fighting, gambling for enormously high stakes and drinking themselves under the table - these were the diversions of men of wealth. He wasted no pity on them when their efforts ended in disaster. He was sufficiently well off to be able to indulge himself in such pleasures, but saw no sense in it. Let others live dangerously, let others stake their fortunes on the turn of a card, walk the tightrope that could lead to ruin. And as for the women! They were the most insufferable bores, mainly empty headed and ridiculously dressed creatures of fashion.

He had a notion that some of the people looked at him in rather a funny sort of way. And once when he strolled by two women who were sitting together he had the impression that they were talking about him and after he passed he was almost certain they tittered. But he couldn't quite make out what it meant. They were a strange lot. These so-called upper classes seemed to practice their own code of sexual morality, without anyone batting an eyelid, without it entering their small minds that there was nothing more insipid and worthless than their idle way of life. He some-times watched the speakers to see if they themselves were finding their own words ridiculous.

The fact was Amelia Duprez did not know what appertains to good society. He was never more than polite to any one of them. The smoke and drunken talk was getting on his nerves and already he was yawning with boredom. He needed to clear his head. He stood up and wandered casually out on to the terrace, away from the prodigious heat bred by numerous candles, out into the drifting mist that suited his mood and lit a cigar. He could see them from where he stood on the terrace, Amel and the Captain together on the dance floor.

Amel had a natural grace and feel for the rhythm, although the train to her gown made it a little awkward for dancing. For hours yet she would be there, going round and round in the arms of Youth! She practically had the young fool eating out of her hand. The two of them were completely out of control; he caught up by her gaiety and spirit, his eyes full of anticipation, fixed on her snowy-white orbs of nature, undisguised and heaving like the ocean. She was the cynosure of all eyes, as they swam in an aura of gaiety and excitement.

Luke watched with tight-lipped disapproval. He stubbed out his cigar with the tip of his shoe and marched right up to them and taking Amelia roughly by the arm, pushed her along the edge of the dance floor, through the double doors, out into the central hall, most every pair of eyes in the place following them.

'What is it, Monsieur? What in Heaven's name is

wrong?' she asked breathlessly. 'Let go of my arm. You're hurting me.'

Luke released his hold and turned on her, his face twisted with anger. 'I'm astonished at your conduct. I've never seen anything like it in my life,' he rebuked, his voice cutting through the commotion.

'What an earth do you mean?' She flicked open the fan that hung from her wrist and plied it vigorously to cool her burning cheeks. Dancing and the heat had given her rather too brilliant a colour.

'You know exactly what I mean, flaunting yourself in front of everyone here ...becoming a figure of fun. The drunkenness and the vulgarity is enough to turn one's stomach.'

The fixed smile slipped from her face. 'Vraiment Monsieur, je signifier non....' she started to say.

'I don't know what the devil you're talking about,' he interrupted impatiently. 'Speak English ...damn it!'

'I said ...I mean no harm,' she told him quietly, her voice perfectly steady and calm now, heedless of his approval or otherwise. 'I just happen to love the company of gay, interesting people.'

Both Horace Twist and Rubin McLachlan stepped out into the hall at the same time.

'Do you mind? This is a private matter, between Madame Duprez and myself,' Luke called with irritation.

Amel turned her head to glance at them. Horace asked her something in French, his voice full of concern.

'Non merci, Monsieur,' she replied calmly, smiling reassuringly at him. 'Deux un momento.'

'Is everything all right? Is this man bothering you?'

McLachlan asked in his North-country accent.

'Not at all,' Amel assured him. She didn't want a fight on her hands. 'Please wait in the ballroom.'

Both men turned on their heel and wandered back into the saloon.

'Can't you stop this vulgar pairing off?' Luke asked angrily as soon as they were out of earshot.

'Why should I? I see nothing wrong in it.'

'Oh, don't you?' he snapped.

Fierce tension cracked the air. But Amel showed no remorse for the torment she had inflicted on him. 'The trouble with you, Monsieur, is, you're far too serious. You always have been.'

'Then why did you invite me? Haven't you men enough to flaunt yourself in front of?'

She shrugged her bare shoulders. 'The more the merrier.' There was no sign of regret in those pale blue eyes.

'I take it from the frosty treatment you've given me all evening, you've been spinning your web? Making plans with your new admirer?'

'We're to have dinner together, if that's what you mean. It's not as if I was going to bed with him,' she lied expertly. 'I don't think he can afford me.'

His lips curled in a tigerish smile, his eyes watchful. He saw her making love with somebody else ...this ...this dressed up young pup and felt a surge of anger, the thoughts seething in his head. God! How the lies poured forth! He marvelled at the ease and rapidity with which they glided off her tongue.

'Come now, no doubt it will be a candle-lit dinner just for two, which always leads to the inevitable with you?'

She glared back at him but said nothing. He could be so exasperating at times.

'I won't allow you to go,' he said fiercely.

Amel closed her fan with a snap. 'Really? I can't see how you can stop me. Your possessiveness is just too much. I don't comprehend why I should be kept in slavery for your pleasure alone.' She would do as she pleased, go on pursuing her own interests without interference, as she always did, her look said.

He flexed his hands he held stiffly at his sides. He longed to give her a damn good shake. 'Damn it! All this dancing and drinking until dawn will send you to an early grave,' he warned.

'I think perhaps you are envious, Monsieur.'

'Envious! I think not, Madam. One is only envious of what one cannot have.' It was then he went on to accuse her of dishonourable behaviour, calling her a common whore. 'I really hate to be the one to break this to you, but no matter how you dress or how you act you'll always be exactly what you are ...a common whore that anyone can have if the price is right.'

'And you, Monsieur, are a bastard,' she retorted angrily.

His temper was completely out of control now. 'That's right! I'm a bastard and you're a whore. And what's more ...a whore in debt.'

'Ex..excuse me, Madam …Sir!' It was only when she spoke they realised the maid was standing in close proximity. Her cheeks were highly flushed with embarrassment. It was not a fit conversation for a young lady to hear.

'Fetch my hat and coat,' Luke ordered.

The poor red-faced girl scurried off as fast as her

legs could carry her.

'Do you know, I don't think I've ever truly seen you before. All you think about is what you can get from anyone whose fool enough to be taken in by your false charms. You have no morals, no principles whatsoever.'

'You sanctimonious cad! You're not talking about morals or principles. You're talking about money.'

'Money! You want to talk about money? Since you have none, let's talk about your debts.' Their voices rang down the hall.

'If you think I'm going to fall apart, you're very much mistaken. I don't care about any debts I might have. There are more important things than money.'

'I notice it's always the financially challenged who say that,' Luke commented acidly. 'It's no good burying your head in the sand, sitting at your long polished table with its pristine napkins and fine sparkling crystal, pretending your debts are not there. It's a fact of life. You need money for all these fancy, expensive things you surround yourself with.'

'You're treading on dangerous ground, Monsieur.'

'I think not, Madam. It is you who are treading on dangerous ground. It's a wonder you haven't been hauled in front of a magistrate and jailed.'

'It will never come to that. I will soon have every-thing under control.'

'I hope for your sake you do.' He must tear himself from her influence. He would leave London.

'I am not a fool,' Amel said quietly.

'No, I am the fool. You are what you've always been. For a long time I just didn't know it.' Gone was the glint of admiration. His dark eyes were cold and piercing. 'Now, if you'll excuse me, I'm leaving. I think perhaps I've over-stayed my welcome. Go back to your so-called friends with their damaged reputations. I'm going home where there's some normality.'

'Don't worry, Monsieur, I have no wish to detain you.'

She continued to gaze at him with her ice-cold blue eyes until he took his top hat, white silk scarf, and cloak from the highly traumatized maid, who turned away immediately they left her hands.

Luke raised a hand to stop her. 'Wait!' The poor young girl froze on the spot. 'I almost forgot...' He felt in his inside pocket, his hand closing around what he was searching for. What he said next set the girl trembling with shock.

'Your mistress was born without a conscience, but has a greedy heart that keeps her legs apart. I'm not sure how much it costs these days...' On saying this, he passed the shaken girl a handful of bank notes. '...but, here, this should just about cover her services.'

The poor dumbstruck maid! So shocked was she, she looked as if she was about to fall to the floor in a dead faint. But Amelia Duprez was unabashed. The insult fell on stony ground. She never as much as batted an eyelid. She simply held out her hand to the tremulous maid, who seemed to have lost the power of speech. The distressed girl lowered her eyes in humiliation and, with unsteady hands, passed the notes to her mistress.

'Good night! Have a safe journey. You think it all over but you hunger for what I can give. You'll be back. We are tied to each other, you and I.'

Luke walked out into the cold night air and without as much as a backward glance left by the stone steps at the front door, climbed in to a waiting carriage that was driven out of the courtyard and away down Piccadilly. But long after he had gone the great Saloon still resounded to music and laughter until the candles guttered and the cold dawn light showed the carriages and the groups of weary footmen in the courtyard.

THIRTY-TWO

On the 15th of September the Liverpool and Manchester Railway finally opened - 31 miles long and consisting of a double line of rails of the fish-bellied type, laid on stone and timber sleepers. A gala occasion that included a procession of eight locomotives, including the Northumbrian, the Rocket, the North Star and the Phoenix, and graced by no lesser personage than the Prime Minister himself, the Duke of Wellington, accompanied by other distinguished guests. Sir Robert Peel, Minister of State, was there, and Charles Poulett Thomson, Treasurer of the Navy. Also John MacAdam, Surveyor-General of Metropolitan Roads, Lord Palmerston, Secretary of State for Foreign Affairs, Lord Wilton, Count Batthyany, Prince Esterhazy, and Count Matuscenitz, George Walker, scientist and mechanic, and William Huskisson, Member of Parliament for Liverpool itself.

When the Duke became Prime Minister in 1828, Huskisson refused to serve under him and resigned from office. But Huskisson had championed the cause of the new railway, helping to get the Bill for its construction through Parliament, linking the port of Liverpool with the manufacturing centre of Manchester. It was partly to conciliate his opponents that the Duke had been persuaded to come at all. With Huskisson also to be a guest at the railway opening, here was an opportunity to effect a rapprochement that even the Duke could now see to be necessary.

Unless he could get on good terms with the reformers in his party his government would surely fall.

The Liverpool & Manchester Railway was on a grand scale and so was its impact on the nation. This was the initiation of another era in which the railway train with its ability to carry people and goods at amazing speeds from one part of the country to another would play an enormously powerful role. For days there had been such an influx of people, all come to witness the great event. There was not a bed to be had at any hotel, lodging house or tavern. It was evident that not only were the people of Liverpool going to enjoy this great day, this splendid moment in the history of their town, but that folk from elsewhere were determined to enjoy it as well. It seemed everyone was out on the streets, all the local inhabitants and those from every village within walking distance.

Working men, women and children dressed in the fashion of years ago, those which endured for decades; Sunday clothes; dark colours, of course, since they were practical, worn only once a week or on special days such as this. Tall silk hats, ostentatiously beflowered and befeathered bonnets mingled with cloth caps, bowlers and the more discreetly ornamented and outdated bonnets of the lower classes. For this railway era belonged to them all no matter what their status. And who could resist the excitement of it?

Banners and flags decorated the shops and houses, streamers flying across streets that were packed with folk of every age, shape and size doing their best to get to the station. The streets were jammed solid with the press of carriages: coaches, tandems and horsemen, striving to curb their fretting mounts to walking pace, causing a continuous blockage. Streams of equipages were lined up, with their occupants in gowns of variegated colours, giving the impression of a brightly patterned carpet outspread for a giant's stride. Among the bustling crowd souvenir-sellers did a brisk trade in mugs, glasses, handkerchiefs, even snuff boxes, all crudely decorated with images of railway works and locomotives. And above all the clatter and clamour a brass band was playing, a grand procession doing its best to force a way through the assembly, and children were swarming everywhere, unsupervised and in danger of being trampled on.

Passenger trains started at the Crown Street Station in Liverpool and after passing Moorish Arch at Edge Hill, terminated at Water Street in Manchester. The grand occasion attracted a large number of important people, a great many of which were men of eminence in the political and scientific world, drawn by the excitement of these stirring times. The Home Secretary, Lord Melbourne, whose late wife once scandalized London society by having an affair with Lord Byron, the poet - the most celebrated young man in the whole of London. He had been irresistible to all kinds of women, who smothered him by their advances. A most fascinating rebel, he was embroiled in scandals without number and fled England for the Near East. He died young, disillusioned and splenetic, fighting for Greek independence.

Now rumours were circulating about Melbourne's relationship with Caroline Norton, the editor of La Bella Assemblee and Court Magazine, and a married woman. George Norton had heard these stories but as he hoped he would benefit from his wife's friendship with the Home Secretary, did not intervene. When he lost his seat in Guildford, Lord Melbourne arranged for him to be appointed as a magistrate in the Lambeth Division of the Metropolitan Police Courts.

Also present was Sir Richard Owen, the brilliant anatomist and palaeontologist from the Royal College of Surgeons, and John Walten, the proprietor of The Times newspaper, Archer Horne, a prosperous wool trader, William Ewart Gladstone, the fourth son of Sir John Gladstone. Immediately next to him, George Hudson, who controlled the selling of Railroad shares, was conversing with Luke Sheridan, who had had the good sense to purchase over £30,000's worth of shares himself.

Samuel Courtauld had turned out for the big event, an arrogant conceited man that Luke did not much care for. Courtauld had his own silk mills. One in Braintree, Essex, one in Halstead and another in Bocking. In 1825 Courtauld installed a steam engine at his mill in Bocking. He also invested heavily in power looms and had well over a hundred of these machines in his mills, making him extremely unpopular with the weavers. John Blenkinsop, the manager of Middleton Colliery stood right next to him, the proud owner of his own locomotives for transporting coal from the colliery to Leeds. They were expensive to use and heavy wear took place between the driving gear wheel and the horizontal rack. But despite these problems, the four Blenkinsop locomotives were still in use at Middleton Colliery.

Isambard Kingdom Brunel was amongst the crowd, chief engineer of Bristol Docks and well-known for his part in the work on the Thames Tunnel - the formation of a passage for carriages and pedestrians under the Thames, which would, when finished, be one of the most extraordinary and stupendous works of ancient or modern times - a great feat of engineering.

There were also a noticeable number of elegantly dressed ladies present. The notorious Madame Duprez, for once without a male chaperone, but accompanied by the disreputable Duchess of Kingston - both exquisitely attired, dazzling women. Luke had deserted her. The glory, which had encircled him as her lover was departed now; yet occasionally some good quality of his would return to her memory and stir a momentary throb of hope that he would again present himself before her. Ah, yes! She knew when her spell was weakening, when the current wanted, as it were, renewing. But calmly considered it was not likely that such a severance as now existed would ever close up; in the heat of their argument too much had been said. Or perhaps not! She would wait and see what the future brings.

The delectable Lady Wilton, Mrs. Huskisson, and the gracious lady - the Duchess of York were in attendance, and leading actresses Ellen Kean and Fanny Kemble …to name but a few. A motley parade of fashion, leaning on the arms of their escorts, promenaded to an incessant interchange of chit-chat, greetings and women's tinkling laughter. Fanny Kemble had a sparkling personality and had several elderly admirers including George Stephenson and Thomas Macaulay, who had invited her to the opening of the Railway. Macaulay regularly contributed his articles to the Edinburgh Review, a journal formed by Whig politicians. Elizabeth Fry, a well-Known personality for her charitable work in Britain was amongst the crowd, accompanied by her brother, Joseph Gurney, the celebrated author of several books and essays on religion and morality. Although prison reform was Elizabeth Fry's main concern she also campaigned for the homeless in Brighton and London, for improvements in the treatment of patients in mental asylums, and promoted the reform of workhouses and hospitals. She was a remarkably courageous woman. All rubbing shoulders with not only the ordinary inhabitants of Manchester and the gentry of its vicinity, but the elite men and women in the county who came from all parts of it.

Luke was beginning to get agitated. The smoke and the noise alone, not to mention the vast volume of people was bearing down on him, almost suffocating him. What kind of taste must these people have, who really preferred the adulterated enjoyments of this God awful City with its wall to wall noise, to the genuine pleasure of a country retreat where you could breathe in the clear, unsullied air and enjoy refreshing sleep? Sleep which was never disturbed by constant noise, nor interrupted, but for the cheerful twittering of birds outside your window of a morning.

A sweet and honest country face suddenly came to mind. It was between pretty and beautiful, with a bloom upon the cheeks, posing in a riot of glorious chestnut curls. He recalled the grace of the delicate throat curve, little tricks of expression, the sweetness of her energy. An artist might object to the strength of the chin and then relent at the soft fullness of the rosy mouth parted as though waiting for a kiss, wholly in keeping with the tenderness of those remarkable eyes, brilliant and sparkling like two precious emeralds, forming a picture of irresistible charm. A blend of strength and tenderness that baffled him.

With him he carried a vision of her, young, ardent, all fire and flame. All the freshness of the heather-sweet, wind-swept uplands was in her countenance - a true daughter of the fells. But it was the merry laugh that so long dwelt in the memory - nothing so thoroughly enchants one as the woman who laughs from her heart in the joyousness of youth. And that merry, genuine, unaffected smile - clearly delighted to see you and not in the least ashamed to show it. Loving, wild and undisciplined. He respected her independence of spirit but at the same time her behaviour sometimes maddened him. At the drop of a hat she would involve herself in any cause that caught her attention, voicing concern over the plight of the homeless, the jobless, the down and outs - a lot of bloody spongers in his opinion.

She was impossible, but at the same time funny and overflowing with passion, the invincible strength of its countless threads bound him to her fast. He supposed he was fond of her in a detached unsentimental way and had to admit he missed her. During the last two months he had seen very little of her, but she was always there, closeted as she was in the depth of Cumbria - her personal concept of Heaven. He sighed in deep contemplation - he must soon return home.

He straightened up and his bleak eyes came to rest on Courtauld whose voice was still droning on and on. He had just about had enough of the man's constant bragging. He excused himself and moved about the crowd in search of his old friend, George Cayley, a most interesting man to talk to. He had said he would be here. Cayley was a Yorkshire man who had spent most of his life experimenting with flying machines, the first to define the principles of mechanical flight. Luke couldn't find him in the immense throng, but did come across another familiar face - Richard Trevithick, another extraordinary, brilliant man. Delighted to see him, Luke shook his hand vigorously in greeting. With him was Lord Morpeth - the Whig candidate for Yorkshire and William Whitehead, the banker who was also an acquaintance of Luke's.

The event, which began promisingly enough, was to end in tragedy. On the meadows by Sankey Canal thousands gathered from an early hour to see the trains and their noisy engines, with their pennants of smoke billowing proudly back from their tall commanding chimneys, steam briskly across the viaduct on their way to Manchester. There were seven of them.

A volley of cheers and a discharge of cannon heralded the setting off of the first train from the grand creation which was Crown Street Station - a central booking hall of towering splendour, grandiose office buildings and spacious waiting rooms for all classes of traveller, and impressive wide platforms; the whole protected with an immense roof held up by massive wooden arches made up of segments screwed and safely bolted together.

The Duke and the rest of the VIP's - the directors of the railway and a large party of gentry occupied the first train, consisting of 33 carriages, hauled by the Northumbrian and driven by George Stephenson himself, which had one of the two tracks all to itself. Other favoured guests began climbing aboard the splendid carriages, accompanied not only by an ear-splitting crescendo from the band and the surging clamour from the crowds, but a great deal of whistling and deafening shrieking from the engine. The novelty of the sight, the strangeness of the sounds, the marvellous velocity with which engine and carriages gradually disappeared, and the dense columns of sulphurous smoke were altogether too much for simple folk to take in.

On the other line, following in procession at regular intervals, came the rest of the trains. The most intense curiosity and excitement prevailed and though the weather was uncertain, enormous masses of densely packed people lined the road, shouting and cheering, waving their hats and handkerchiefs as the train flew by them, travelling at 35 miles an hour - swifter than a bird could fly. The power, the speed and the grandeur of these great locomotive engines was looked upon with such wonder and admiration. Mesmerized by the dramatic spectacle before them, it was doubtful that the passengers spared much thought for the unnamed navvies whose sweat laid the rail tracks, built the embankments and dug the tunnels through which they passed.

The engineers and the architects tend to receive most of the credit for designing and having built the structures and earthworks that went to make the railways, but without the special skills of the contractors in assembling the men, the materials and the bank credits to carry the paper plans to completion, the drawings of the engineers and architects would have remained on paper only. The contractor was often viewed by his established social superiors as a gatecrasher, portrayed as vulgar in satirical magazines, yet courted and cultivated by engineers, financiers and others who stood to gain by his acquaintance, through those skills of man and money management, which the best of them possessed, together with that manic energy which enabled them to control a huge and fractious work-force operating in many parts of the country.

Directing their labours with flamboyance, daring and sometimes more than a touch of deception. But the hardest and most brutal life of all was that of the navvy and quite often the shortest. They worked with picks and shovels, crowbars and wheelbarrows and their bare hands; the only other aid they had was the blast of gunpowder; everywhere noise, dust and smoke fills the air. Contractors generally worked to deadlines, and if - as sometimes happened - the navvies were on piecework; both groups had a vested interest in going faster, which was when accidents happened.

Men sometimes lost an arm or a leg; maiming and mutilation came with the job. Navvies were lucky if they escaped with nothing more than the loss of a limb. Men were sometimes blinded by explosions, others buried in rock falls. If anyone was injured, neither they nor their families would get compensation unless the contractor happened to be particularly benevolent or there was a sick-pay fund. Rough-looking gangers drove their butty gangs to ever-greater feats of earth-moving by threats, promises and, at times, well-aimed kicks, for the pay of the gang depended on the efforts of the team as a whole.

All led a life of hard, grinding physical toil, tramping from one construction site to another in search of work. Where it was difficult to recruit local labour, shanty towns sprang up around the more remote rural railways workings, isolated encampments, closely crowded together, housing the social outcasts. They were frequently made scapegoats for local disorder in which they were only marginally involved. Did anyone give them a thought?

At Parkside, 17 miles out of Liverpool, the Duke's train stopped while the engine took on water. This is when the frightful tragedy took place. To get a better view, several of the gentlemen in the directors' carriage alighted to stand between the tracks and look about; Lord Wilton, Count Batthyany and Count Matuscenitz, including Mr. Huskisson. All were deep in conversation when an engine on the other line, which was parading up and down merely to show its speed, was seen coming down upon them like lightning. The locomotive was not fitted with a whistle to provide an audible warning of its approach.

The overriding concern of the locomotive builders was to ensure that their machines would go and go reliably. Bringing them to a halt, especially in an emergency, was far from their minds. After all, they would stop frequently enough of their own volition. Use of the regulator and the reverser were sufficient to control a locomotive in normal conditions. In terms of braking power, all that was considered necessary was a handbrake on the tender to prevent movement after coming to a halt.

The Rocket was coming in the opposite direction and was about to pass the Northumbrian on the line on which the men were standing. It was almost upon the group before they observed it. In the hurry of the moment all attempted to get out of the way - a sudden conversion of a scene of gaiety and splendour turning into one of sheer horror and dismay. The most active of those in peril sprang back into their seats. Lord Wilton and Count Batthyany saved their lives only by rushing behind the Duke's carriage, and Count Matuscenitz had just leapt into it, with the engine all but touching his heels as he did so.

Poor Mr. Huskisson, less active from the effects of age and ill-health, bewildered too by the frantic cries of the onlookers that resounded on all sides, completely lost his head. He looked helplessly to the right and left and was instantaneously prostrated by the lethal machine that dashed down like a thunderbolt upon him, passing over his leg, smashing and mangling it in the most horrendous way.

Mrs. Huskisson, who along with several other ladies witnessed the accident, uttered shrieks of agony that those who heard will never forget. A doctor attempted to stem the bleeding, but it was of no use. Stephenson used the Northumbrian to take the badly injured man for further treatment, but despite these attempts to save him the unfortunate man died later that day - the first railway fatality.

It did not end there. Further trouble was to come. The Duke and his party continued their journey, steaming at last into Manchester many hours behind schedule. They were greeted by the vast concourse of people of the lowest orders, assembled to witness the triumphant arrival of the successful travellers - among whom great distress and a dangerous spirit of discontent with the government at that time prevailed. Shouts and hisses greeted the carriage full of influential personages, in which the Duke of Wellington sat.

High above the grim and grimy crowd of scowling

faces a loom had been erected, at which sat a tattered, starved-looking figure of a man, evidently set there as a representative of the weavers, to protest against the triumph of machinery and the gain which the wealthy Liverpool and Manchester men were likely to derive from it. Unpopular even in his own party for his implacable opposition to parliamentary reform, the Duke was hated in the north for the Peterloo massacre eleven years earlier, for which the cotton workers of Manchester had never forgiven him.

It had been a holocaust of wounded, dead and dying, a storm to fan indignant outcries in a blaze that threatened to demolish a generation of Toryism. Now he was being carried in state to their city on this highly publicised steam train. They pelted passenger carriages with stones, the whole lot of them booing and hissing. While they surged around the carriages, Stephenson used the loop-line to get his engine to the other end of the train and start hauling it back towards Liverpool. Needless to say, the banquet arranged was cancelled, if only to save the Duke from being lynched.

Huskisson's funeral was attended by a great multitude, showing every mark of respect and feeling. The loss of his economic experience and wisdom was deeply felt.

As for the Duke, he was deeply affronted by the way he was booed and hissed at by the mob, an experience that made him hostile to the railways and he warned that cheap travel might result in revolution. However, he was soon to change his mind, after he developed a close relationship with George Hudson, who helped him make a great deal of money by advising him when to buy and sell railway shares.

THIRTY-THREE

Within a month of opening, the railway carried over 1,200 passengers a day, which was 500 people more than the mail and stage coaches had managed to carry between them. First-class carriages were enclosed and upholstered; the doors of which were kept locked while trains were in transit lest any passengers should escape without paying for their tickets. But second and third-class carriages had only wooden benches seating four abreast and were open at the sides, providing no protection from the weather or the pollution created by the Locomotive.

Soon after, along with passenger service the railroad carried mail and freight, and in the county goods and services into remote areas. The total quantity of goods passing between Liverpool and Manchester was estimated to be one thousand tons per day. The average length of time taken by canal was thirty six hours, and the average charge 15s a ton. By the projected railroad the transit of goods between Liverpool and Manchester was four of five hours and the charge to the merchant reduced by at least one-third. The most striking result produced by the completion of this railway was the sudden change, which has been effected in ideas of time and space. What was slow is now quick; what was distant is now near.

What Stephenson launched was not just the first major public railway, but the idea that through some form of mechanical propulsion people would be able to do what had never even crossed their minds - travel safely and comfortably at speed across land wherever they chose to go. Until now most people's horizons had been limited by how far they could conveniently ride on horseback or in a carriage. After the success of the Liverpool & Manchester Railway, business people based in Birmingham began to consider the advantages of having a railway.

Birmingham had seen rapid economic growth and was now sending one thousand tons of goods every week by canal to London. Many were hostile to the disruption caused by railways. Most opposition to the railway came from vested interests - bridge owners who would lose revenue from tolls, canal and stagecoach companies that would lose trade. Farmers near London opposed it, fearing competition; on the other hand, country farmers were delighted with the prospect of the new markets that would open up with a more efficient means of transport. Canals were notoriously unreliable. Quite apart from the slowness of horse-drawn barges, frosts, winter floods and summer droughts caused great delays. Once people realized how much money was to be made from the new railways, hostility began to diminish.

The Liverpool & Manchester railway was a great success, with profits topping £71,000. Shareholders were regularly paid out an annual dividend of £10 for every £100 invested. Travelling by train was faster and cheaper than the coaches; there were no hidden extras in the form of tips and meals at the inns *en route,* and it was fun.

The age of the railway was upon them. Even when the Liverpool and Manchester Railway was under construction, another railway was opened in

1828, which was to connect with it - this was the Bolton and Leigh Railway, incorporated in 1825 to link Bolton with the Leeds and Liverpool Canal at Leigh. Wherever railways were being considered and plenty now were, promoters wanted Stephenson; just to have his name on the prospectus was enough to draw investors. So when business interests in Birmingham joined with those in Liverpool to connect their two cities by rail and carry the line on to London, Stephenson saw himself in overall charge of what would be the first trunk line across the country.

During the earlier part of 1831 the current topic of conversation everywhere was the political crisis. As soon as Lord Grey became Prime Minister he formed a cabinet committee to produce a plan for parliamentary reform, details of which were announced on the 3rd of February. The bill was passed by the House of Commons, but despite a powerful speech by Lord Grey, the bill was again defeated in the House of Lords. The defeat of the Reform Act resulted in Lord Grey calling a general election. The Whigs were popular with the electorate and after the election had a larger majority than before in the House of Commons.

The Tories were in disarray and in no position to survive a critical vote in the House for they were hopelessly divided. There were by this time three broad groups within the party; the remaining ex-Canningites, a more progressive group on the left, who did not, however, always act in unison; the centre, which followed Peel and Wellington and accepted the inevitability of moderate and reasonable change; and the Ultras who opposed change of any kind. So large was the group of Ultras that it constituted a party within a party. It had the sympathy of the King and the Tory press, and was attempting to convert the all-inclusive Toryism of Liverpool, Peel and Wellington into a narrow, coherent, well-organised and popularly-supported anti-reform Tory party. However, those on the Tory side who had up until now opposed parliamentary reform were losing their cohesion. Whilst the bulk of the party rejected any change in the electoral system, some believed that a more representative House of Commons would have never allowed the passage of Catholic Emancipation and were therefore prepared to support a moderate measure of reform.

The General Election that returned the first Whig Ministry for 23 years, had resulted in a general combustion. The United Kingdom thundered with the repercussional effects of the fight between the Tories and the Whigs, while the future of Britain hung in the balance to make of democracy the triumphant emergence of enduring liberties, or the most colossal blunder in the history of politics.

Lord Grey tried again to introduce parliamentary reform but the Lords still refused to pass the bill. When people heard the news, riots took place in several British towns. A large mob protested by looting and burning down unpopular citizens' houses, including the Bishop's Palace and the Custom House. Nottingham Castle was burnt down and in Bristol the Mansion House was set on fire. The Dragoons attacked the crowd and hundreds were killed and severely wounded.

Early in April Lord Grey asked the King to

dissolve Parliament so that the Whigs could secure a larger majority in the House of Commons; this would help the government to carry their proposals for an increase in the number of people who could vote in elections. William agreed to Grey's request and after making his speech in the House of Lords, he walked back through the crowds to Buckingham Palace. The monarch's near-madness was a problem for all who had to deal with him. But after the reign of George 111 and George 1V it had become natural for the people to regard madness as almost part of the kingly office.

THIRTY-FOUR

Numerous jars of cream and bottles of perfume, mostly imported from Paris, cluttered Amel's dressing table, and yet she used simple lemon juice to cleanse the skin and brighten the complexion. She preferred to wash the rest of her body with a sponge dampened in milk and to freshen up with a vanilla-scented eau de toilette, which was fashionable in Paris. She dabbed on a light touch of powder over her face and the faintest hint of rouge on her cheeks, studying the result in the mirror, tweaking a curl into place and biting her lips to redden them. She stood up then and turned sideways, running a critical hand across her perfectly flat stomach. At this point in her life her health was not at all good. She not only suffered from the usual fits of dizziness, which affected her during menstrual periods, but from constant headaches and severe stomach cramps.

'A quart of spring water, boiled and allowed to cool. Beat the white of an egg, lemon juice and half a cup of white wine together and stir in the boiled water. Take the mixture once a day. That will help keep the fever away,' was what the Doctor recommended. That, and as much fresh air as possible and frequent walks to improve the circulation. 'Exercise is unquestionably one of the very best means for the preservation of health, but its real importance is too lightly considered by the majority of females. It has extraordinary power in preserving the vigour of the body, in augmenting its capability to resist disease, in improving the freshness and brilliancy of the complexion, as well as an influence in prolonging the charms of beauty to an advanced age. If women would shake off the prejudices by which they have been so long enthralled, their health would be essentially improved,' was what he alleged.

And so Amel took regular walks in Hyde Park, just as the Doctor prescribed. Parades between four and six in the afternoon, revealing society in all its glory; the long unbroken stream of brilliant equipages and lovely horses, and fine ladies with their glaring coloured silks, standing gossiping under the chestnuts trees. Whiskered gentlemen with their silk top hats and silver topped canes lolling on the grassy slopes or leaning over the iron railings to chat with elegant, long skirted, veiled equestrians. Open alike to the rich and the poor, elegant as an opera and as merry as a fair. From an old man of seventy to the young child in its mother's arms, from a duchess to the gypsy, listening to music played in the bandstand or feeding the ducks, taking the dog for a walk, stopping for tea or simply promenading around - all very civilised.

Whatever the true nature of Amel Duprez's illness, the fresh air and gentle exercise seemed to be doing the trick. Her health gradually improved. But her troubles were not yet over.

At thirty-one Amel Duprez's life was filled with misery and frustration. Her "heads" and vague feelings of being unwell had now crystallized in to something solid. She was frequently physically sick, spending the best part of each morning in her bed, withdrawing into herself. After her late-morning bath she would wander about the room with nothing on, examining every part of herself in the numerous long mirrors that lined the walls.

There were creams and powders to apply, then the feet and hands had to be cared for and finally the face, neck and shoulders. She often became impatient and unreasonable, expecting her maid, Bridget, to know just where she had left things, but her vivacity seemed inexhaustible and in a moment or two all irritation turned to laughter. While Bridget brushed her hair, she polished her nails. Afterwards, Bridget scurried about removing the debris of the earlier stages of madam's toilet, before leaving the room.

The last illness came upon Amel suddenly. First, she was seized with the most agonising cramps, the feeling of burning in her stomach - much worse than before. Then she had a touch of diarrhoea. Although now recovered, she felt thoroughly drained, worn out and utterly devoid of conversation. Her complexion, fair as it was, appeared yet fairer from the effect of two darkly shadowed eyes.

She broke the silence by giving a low groan, laying a hand on her chest. 'Oh, you'll … you'll have to excuse me.'

'What is it now?' Luke asked, with impatience.

She motioned him away with the wave of a hand. 'It is nothing. I'm just having another of my off days.'

It was true. She felt sick again, slightly feverish and was all of a tremble. Everything danced before her eyes as she fought to catch her breath. Feeling too weak to stand and fearing she might fall, she had to sit down. She closed her eyes for a moment, hoping if she closed them it would all go away.

'Here, drink this,' Luke suggested quietly after some minutes.

She opened her eyes. 'What is it?' she asked in a tremulous voice.

'Coffee. It might help you feel better.'

The black coffee steadied her some, but she did not have the strength to stand. She reluctantly stayed where she was, as lifeless as a statue, gripping onto the chair so that her knuckles turned as white as her face.

'I think this has gone on long enough, don't you? I'll arrange for you to see another doctor for a second opinion. Trust me! We'll have you well in no time,' Luke said resignedly, without any real concern.

Although perplexed by her lack of movement, he seemed to be incapable of any strong emotion. 'In the meantime, I suggest you cancel any arrangements you might have and rest in your room for a few days.'

'All on my own?' The thought of being left all alone struck terror in her mind, followed by an emotion she instantly recognized as panic. 'You won't leave me again, will you, Mon amour?' In her moment of need she used the term of endearment ... my love.

'I'll see you're well taken care of. And I'll never be far away.'

Anxious as regards to Amel's ill health, which was interfering with his own enjoyment, Luke arranged for a Doctor Arnold Cleland, who had an excellent reputation, to call at Burlington House. Arnold Cleland began practising medicine in Reading and later moved to London where he became a fashionable physician, consulted by the upper classes. He followed a demanding program of study and was up-to-date on new discoveries.

It was said, he was extremely knowledgeable and that he was far more than a healer of physical ills. He was a counsellor and helper to be relied upon in any emergency, as useful and faithful in his profession as he knew how to be.

The doctor called to visit the sickbed of the presumptuous sinner, offering a show of comfort. His first impulse had been to refuse, but principle was overshadowed by his curiosity to see at close hand this beautiful, well-sought-after courtesan and the surround-ings in which she lived.

Madame Duprez hardly fitted the bourgeois ideal of a domestic angel ...he thought to himself, although he would never dare to voice such an opinion. In his eyes she was just another victim of male lust, who had used her ill-gotten gains to live in splendour, a high-class courtesan who could pick and choose who to take as a lover, and being a better class of prostitute perhaps, but nevertheless a prostitute ...was no doubt paid well for her services. And he in turn would be paid well for his. That he could be sure of. First he enquired about her symptoms.

Amel complained to him of bad heads, recurrent attacks of agonising pain to the chest accompanied by difficulty in breathing, a sore throat and occasional queasiness of the stomach. He proceeded by taking her pulse, and then peered down her throat. He listened to her chest with a stethoscope and finally made a thorough examination below the waist. He was impassive as he examined her, cloaking his repugnance and agitation. When he had finished he advised she stay in her bed and. prescribed a tonic which made her drowsy, compelling her to rest. It was his belief that the patient was on a downward spiral of her own making, destined for an early grave, keeping herself alive by the very over-indulgence that was slowly but surely killing her. Hell was where she was headed.

THIRTY-FIVE

It was late April. The countryside was calm and peaceful. The clear air seemed to quiver and sparkle with light. Fields of whispering grasses were speckled with daisies and cowslips, stone walls a perfect mosaic of colour, and the hillsides crowned with bracken, heather and ferns. The lakes were spangled with silvery light, and by the roadside, primroses, violets and wood sorrel flowered. The great towering oaks were in their first foliage of golden green, a number of sycamores already in full leaf, and the birches greenish here and there with a little purple on their twigs. And beneath those trees life flourished in abundance: glorious foxgloves, wild Canterbury bells and daffodils bloomed, hiding the dull brown of the earth beneath and providing a breathtaking blanket of vivid colour, as they tossed and danced in the breeze that sighed across the fells. Spring in all its glory!

But in London it was gloomy and dark, a light drizzle falling throughout most of the day, accompanied by an atmosphere of the constant vibrating clatter of traffic. The evening brought fog to blanket the streets, putting out its clammy fingers. It was not a good night to be out in and wasn't helped by the evening darkness, which was more of a screen than Luke cared for, hiding the ruts where feet were liable to slip.

'I think it would be wise to stay home tonight, my darling. We could share an intimate dinner together,' he suggested.

But Amel was not interested in savouring the simplest of meals in the privacy of her own home. Rosy lips took up a sensual pout as she fluttered long, gold-tipped lashes and used all her feminine charm to have her way. She had been looking forward to this all week and would be crushed if he disappointed her now.

'But you've been promising me this treat all week,' she said with obvious displeasure. 'Don't you want to go out on the town with me? Oh, Mon amour, please …don't make me beg.'

Luke indulged her by taking her to a concert at Druary Lane Theatre, held in the aid of Charing Cross Hospital. With neck and shoulders bare, Amel ventured forth into the damp and chill air of the night, in a gown totally unadapted to guard the body from the influence of cold. She had on flimsy silk stockings and slippers of a scarcely more substantial material, arriving at the place of their destination shivering.

The music was by Handel, one of the greatest composers who ever lived, but it was long and drawn out, and Amel quickly grew tired. She tried to ignore the dull throbbing in her head, but it only grew worse. Her wretchedness was most acute on finding herself obliged to return home. Except for some desultory conversation, the journey was undertaken in silence, each wrapped in their own very different thoughts, each with their own subjects of reflection, of anxiety and of hope.

In the peace and warm security of the bedroom, Bridget stood brushing her mistress's hair. Amel dismissed her as Luke came in to the room. He held out his hand to her. She placed icy fingers in his and he covered them possessively.

'You look a great deal better, my darling. The colour's come back to your cheeks.'

And yet she seemed somewhat remote, almost unaware, he thought as he bent to kiss her cheek. A strange eerie sense that something was wrong came over him. Something unpleasant. He had breathed its pungent air more than once these past weeks.

When she spoke her voice sounded hoarse. 'I have such a misery in my throat.' She began to cough. She couldn't breathe. Her blue eyes looked into his beseechingly, filling with helpless tears. 'I …I can't …can't breathe. I …I'm going to die,' she murmured feebly.

'Come now, what flight of fancy is this? Do they have a name for what's wrong with you?'

Doctor Cleland was sent for and when he arrived he looked down her throat, and listened to her chest with a stethoscope again. 'Well Madam, I suspect, like so many ladies of fashion, you neglect to protect your body with sufficient clothing when out in the cold and dampness of the external air. Who can be surprised that the consequences of such imprudent exposure are affections of the throat and lungs, attended with a cough and hoarseness?'

Amel retired from the public eye for the next few days, laid up with an indisposition that kept her confined to her room. Luke spent much of his time at his club, White's Club, situated at the spot where St James's Street junctions with Piccadilly, next to Holys, the royal boot maker. A club where women were forbidden, except on the first Saturday of each month when each member was authorized to bring a guest at his own discretion.

The club had flourished since the eighteenth century, founded by a group of businessmen, no more than half a dozen members to start with, but now numbered over seventy. The annual fee was high, but once a member, food and drinks amounted to very little. But woe betide any member who did not abide by the rules, for his membership could easily be dissolved. In its pillared halls gentlemen met to talk over the changing topics of the day, do business, smoke, drink, dine and to gamble. Politics were vehemently discussed, arguments robustly phrased and barbed with wit, as they, the gentlemen members' drank and played cards. Luke's opinion carried weight and his judgement was respected, particularly when it came to business.

Amel Duprez had become a victim of her own extravagances. The household often ran short of food and on one occasion the water was cut off, because the bills had not been paid. The workmen flatly refused to reconnect the pipes until they were paid in full ...in cash ...not empty promises.

She owned no other residence out of London now, having long sold the property she had once possessed in France. She began to cast about for a means of raising more money. Those she approached were all wealthy and mainly married men, but she - the "other woman" had suddenly become less desirable to them. A fair skin and rosy cheeks are calculated to excite admiration, but if it is discovered that they are entirely produced by paint, that admiration becomes disgust, or if owing to disease as in Amel Duprez's case, it is changed to pity. Unkind tongues begun to wag. Was whatever she had contagious? Could you catch it by merely being in her company?

Amel was not by nature spiteful, she seldom bore malice, but when Archer Horne had the effrontery to offer her a ten-pound banknote, she was more than just a little miffed. She was outraged and gave him a piece of her mind.

Once more alone, she had nothing to do but think of the past, of the wonderful times she had had and of her past lovers. George Romney, who had painted numerous portraits of her, had been the first. She had been initiated at the age of sixteen. Then she became mistress to Pierre Duprez, who gave her a son and had eventually married her - and taught her the facts of life, opening her eyes to the weaknesses of men. How naive she had been! But she had survived her brutal apprenticeship. The relationship she had with Francis Gordon, a gentleman farmer, had been stormy to say the least and had ended abruptly.

Then there had been Lord Cavenish, Lord George as she always called him, who had installed her in a lavish apartment overlooking Hyde Park. Alexander Westmore, a wealthy banker, and not forgetting the handsome and charming Francois Belard who had turned her head, but dumped her for a younger and much wealthier woman. John Walten, owner of The Times, Archer Horne, the wool trader, and Charles Jersey, who had come to her seeking relief from the relentless monotony of marriage and his clinging young wife.

Horace Twist - dear Horace with his quick wit and those remarkable pale eyes. Their attempted coming together had been disastrous, but they had found other ways to satisfy his appetite and had stayed friends, close friends. He had been good to her, supportive and loyal. And her melancholy Captain of the 91st Argyllshire Regiment of Foot, Rubin McLachlan - dazzling her with his exotic tales; such a pleasurable distraction. Albert Moore, the cotton manufacturer, who had given her one of his Rembrandt paintings in payment for her services. And many more, numerous others, whose names she had forgotten.

But it was Luke she thought of most. He had character, integrity, and such energy - the qualities needed for worldly success. A wonderfully powerful rogue who knew exactly what he wanted and went all out to get it, whatever the cost. And he was so attractive, his whole physique long, slender and graceful, the wide shoulders to exquisitely narrow hips. The nose straight, the cheekbones high and pronounced, the hair thick and as black as night, curling at the nape of his neck. Brows, lashes and eyes just as dark. A man with a strong, vigorous mind, always immaculately turned out - a man who lusted after pleasure. That was why she was so drawn to him. It was this very need that made him weak. And as for money, she had always understood he had plenty.

From time to time he paid generous amounts into her private account. She didn't have to twist his arm to get it either. There were other ways, much more effective ways. As a lover he had filled her life with radiance, knowing just what she enjoyed, putting her pleasure before his own, which led to excite him. She thought of the long, tremulous nights they had passed together and the languor that lulled them to sleep in one another's arms. The rapture of brief stolen moments when their passion overwhelmed them and they surrendered to its call.

She lamented the emptiness of her life when as must happen he left her, but they ended with a cry that all she had to suffer would be worth it for the absolute bliss that for a while had been hers. She distinctly remembered when she had first met him. He came just when her own bitterness of disillusion was hardest to bear, when her faith in life had been shaken and her soul had felt lonely. She thought it would be an affair of a few weeks, a few months even, but although their happiness was precarious, miraculously it had lasted for years.

Perhaps it was owing to the irregularity of their meetings that their passion had retained for so long its first enchanting ardour? Those who approached her were wealthy, privileged men, with two social lives; one shared with their wives and the other independent of them, in the company of the alluring Madame Duprez.

She was very good at what she did and not only earned a living at it, but also enjoyed it immensely. She had been dealing with men like these all of her adult life and knew exactly how they ticked. There is in men, when once they are caught, a fund of gullibility that their lordly wisdom little dream of, and in virtue of which the most sagacious of them are seen often as dupes. It was clear that, in its crudest form, the male sexual urge was basically a desire for possession and that the act of physical penetration was an act of aggression. What these men most lacked was will power.

When the pain began again, she knew what it meant. Her superstitious dread was justified. She had survived a brutal apprenticeship at the hands of George Romney and Pierre Duprez, the turmoil of the French Revolution and the terror of the Napoleonic wars, and now if she was not mistaken she was terminally ill. She suffered from severe stomach cramps, headaches, and sore eyes were constantly prostrating her. She took small doses of opium to ease the pain, spending many long hours alone since Luke had gone. Her handsome Cavalryman continued to call on her, helping to soothe her melancholy, but it didn't last; his visits come to an end when he was called away.

So weary and miserable was she, she slept for hours, seeking any kind of relief from the relentless monotony. This life was no life at all. It was a dull existence. It was not to be borne. How she longed for some gaiety. It would be different if Luke were here. She would write to him and ask him to come.

THIRTY-SIX

Maggie brought in the newspaper and the morning post, handing them to the master. There were several letters. Jessica watched her husband's face as he glanced through them one by one, turning pallid when he came to a certain envelope. He always turned pale when a letter came, but quickly recovered. Judging by the effect they had on him, they must be associated with some sentimental secret.

She felt a premonitory chill - justified by the sight of the letter. A letter from a woman, another vulgar case of entanglement no doubt. Just seeing it there in his hand she could sense the threat, and an inexplicable pain buried itself deep in a hidden corner of her heart. There were times when the present filled her with a new dread of the future.

She hadn't realised how brief happiness could be. She had grown afraid to take it for granted. She had believed that if you love someone long enough and hard enough, they would love you in return, but how wrong she had been. Even if she had not actually seen the mysterious letter, she would have known it had come by the change in his face and the look in those dark brooding eyes. What troubled her was a subtle fear that crept insidiously through her veins like a shuddering cold - a terror lest something, to which she could give no name, should separate them. For the psychic lines of attraction between two human-beings are finer than the finest gossamer and can be easily broken and scattered, through some recklessness or folly, either on his part or her own. She couldn't go on like this. The strain had become intolerable.

Luke sighed, unaware that he had done so. Putting the envelope aside with the others, he opened the newspaper and began to read.

'Anything interesting?' Jessica asked casually.

'No! Just the usual, business letters.'

'Aren't you going to open them?'

'I can't be bothered right now. They can wait.'

'Shall I open them for you?'

'No! I think not. What interest could they possibly be to you?' he said hastily, lowering the paper and looking at her thoughtfully.

Her morning gown was the colour of golden corn, a beautifully draped but very simple style in which she looked quite glorious. She was very quiet this morning. Of course, she had been more subdued since her father's horrendous death, and he knew that in the seclusion of her room she still wept for him, despite the brave front she put on for the rest of the world to see.

He folded the newspaper and gathered up the letters, bending to kiss her on the forehead in passing, as was his habit, and went out of the room.

'I'll deal with them in my study.'

Evidently, he wanted to be by himself when he read it. Shortly after, she followed him and stood just outside the study door, shivering with the premonition of something inexplicable, intolerable to be faced. She longed to open the door to his study and steal in, but remembered what he had said of her getting between him and his work. She would have no peace until she found out, and then her gnawing uncertainty would be over. The alternative was to question him, but that would be difficult.

Luke sat in his study reading a letter from Doctor Cleland, an invitation to call at his surgery. There was no urgency. When he was next in London would do. The doctor had not mention what for. It was most likely over the matter of an unpaid bill, he wouldn't wonder, which he would settle of course. The man had won his respect for his medical skills.

Amel's letter was mostly full of gossip about the celebrities she had met at the theatre, with a note of melancholy creeping in. Frederick Rolleston had been found on the floor of his study, after a serious stroke that had left him very frail. She said she felt she ought to call on him, but as she was no good around sick people could not bring herself to do so, but she had sent him flowers accompanied by a note of condolences. Also her young friend Richard Parkes Bonington the artist was apparently very ill, although what with she didn't state.

To lift her spirits she had been on a shopping spree and had purchased two beautiful new evening gowns, with slippers and the necessary accessories to wear with them. And she had given a dinner party, with music and dancing afterwards, omitting to invite Elizabeth and Charles Jersey, or Catherine Gurney, but inviting her newfound friends from the theatre. Also Ellen and Charles Kean, very good friends that had never let her down, people she could rely upon. And dear Horace, of course, who always managed to cheer her up. But both Lord George and John Walten had refused her invitation. Also Albert Moore had made his excuses. Nevertheless, it turned out to be a very pleasant evening, although she had only danced the once. She ended the letter by saying she had decided to go to Paris for a month, but would be in London until the end of the week and was longing to see him before she left.

Luke felt a suffocating surge of anger. Entertainment and travel cost money ...his money. He held his hands up in mock horror, wondering what other debts would emerge from the woodwork. He knew Amel to be a compulsive shopper, often buying things on impulse, things she might never wear, but hoarding them possessively. She was unable to pass a jewellery shop without buying what she referred to as a little trinket: a ring, a brooch, perhaps a tiara or a diamond hair comb. God knows she wasn't his responsibility. Do leeches ever let go? People left her out and refused her invitations because she was no longer part of the "in group". She only had herself to blame for what was being said about her.

Thus, for reasons touching on hostility and distaste mingled, he put off his return from day to day. Instead, a sharp reply was sent in a very explicit and bluntly worded letter, his writing slanting with haste and the intensity of his anger.

THIRTY-SEVEN

So long as the first illusion that each understands the other is supported by the thrilling delight of ever-fresh discoveries, the sensations lived through are so joyous that the lovers do not realise that there are no firm foundations of real mutual knowledge beneath their feet.

While even the happiest pair may know of divergences about social customs, politics or religion and opinions on things in general, these, with patience and goodwill on either side, can be ultimately adjusted, because in all such things there is a common meeting ground for the two. Yet so often things come up, which causes a pain that covered up at once would not have amounted to much. But the more these things are bottled up inside, the bigger they seem to become, things best forgotten, but when held up to view and brood over, they seem to grow before your very eyes, and those very differences which drew them together begin to work their undoing.

Jessica had been given a sufficient allowance: silks, velvets and laces, necklaces, earrings, and all sorts of various pleasing little trinkets had been lavishly heaped upon her and yet, with all this, she was far from happy. There were stories circulating about Luke. And there were the letters. Doubts rankled in her breast, a plague that corrupted faith and hope, love and trust, all she held most sacred and most dear. It fed upon itself, threatening to unbalance mind and reason. Her thoughts became too terrible to express themselves; they were but grim and monstrous impalpability's that evolved from out some secret pit and darkened her very soul.

When her husband was unaware he was being observed, his eyes had a distant look as if he was thinking about someone else, but as soon as he became conscious that she was watching his face, he smiled.

Head to toe in butter-coloured muslin and lace, she looked positively charming. But Luke detected the unease, a sense of disharmony and unrest that dispels the peace and the air of restful security which is an essential feature of a true home. His agitated state made him concerned that she might make herself ill.

Dark eyes looked into green, the green a brim with unshed tears.

'I know you're always under pressure. But this is different. You seem distracted.'

'Jessica, why must we struggle so? I'm imploring you not to get into this. It is past history.'

'Oh no, it's the here and now.' She sprang to her feet, pacing towards him, having a hard struggle to conceal her emotions. 'And don't tell me again that I'm imagining all this.'

'I'm just saying she was no...'

She raised a hand. 'Stop! I know just what you're going to say. You're going to say that she's no more than a friend.' She went to sit back down again, fidgeting restlessly in the chair. 'I know you better than you think.'

'You won't be happy until you dig into it, will you?'

She was up on her feet again, moving towards

him. 'I need to know. If I'm not good enough for you, then say so. I won't be pointed at when I'm out and whispered about behind my back.'

He sighed with exasperation. 'Don't talk such nonsense.'

'I want to know who she is.'

'Was,' he corrected. 'Who she *was* is of no importance.'

'What did you talk about?'

'I don't remember. We just talked.'

She glided up and down the room, as was her habit when upset, her hands moving nervously against the skirt of her gown. 'You must've talked about something.'

'If you must know we talked about everything.'

'How do these things get started? Did you receive a special engraved invitation?'

He sighed again. 'Stop behaving like a petulant child.'

'I want to know,' she returned with fierce determination. 'Why this particular woman?'

'You'll wear a hole in the carpet. Sit down and I'll tell you. That's if you're not too exhausted by your tantrum.'

She did as she was told, her jaw set defiantly.

'Why her?' he repeated thoughtfully. 'I suppose because she had different interests in life besides the usual every day mundane things. She talked of politics ...travel ...places I've never been, about books I've never read, and she asked questions I had to think twice about before I could answer,' he explained reluctantly.

The blood pounded in Jessica's head. To hear it put into plain words was like a knife through her heart. 'And tell me ...did she make you feel things you don't feel with me?' she asked in a quiet, hurt tone. 'Was that it?'

'I'm not going to tell you what you ask. There are certain things that should be left unsaid. You're too young to understand.'

'Understand what? Betrayal?' she cried.

'It did not last.' But a lie has no legs, thus it requires other lies to support it. Tell one and you are forced to tell others to back it up. 'I never see her now, as God is my witness...'

Sharp words rushed to her lips. 'Don't you dare bring God into this. You're worse than the devil himself. You with your lies. The devil has many tools, but a lie is the handle that fits them all.'

'That's enough! Don't talk such nonsense,' he warned her angrily.

'There's nothing I hate more than being lied to.'

'I've told you ...it's over!'

But she could not stop. Her anxiety turned to dry-mouthed, heart-fluttering panic, her mind a turmoil of questions, running round and round in her head until it throbbed with the pain.

'If I left you, would you go to ...to this refined, educated woman?'

'Why? Are you thinking of leaving?' he asked, his dark brows rising inquiringly.

'Don't make fun of me, Luke.'

'You're the one I married. Isn't that what counts?'

'I want to know. Would you go to her?'

'She was content with her life as it was,' he told her, careful to use the past tense.

'But if she would have you now ...would you go to her?'

His answer was firm, 'No.'

She looked surprised. 'No? Why not?'

'Because I belong here with you.'

'Here with me? Is this where you belong? In this house with a woman who hasn't read the right bloody books? I would laugh if my heart wasn't so heavy.'

'Jessica ...I said that's enough! Damn it!'

But trust is a very fragile thing and when it's been broken it's so hard to repair. The hurt showed clearly in her eyes, and for just a moment he wanted to take her in his arms and make her forget, but her voice rose to a pitch and that moment of weakness passed.

'A woman who sleeps in your bed and gives you all her love, but doesn't know the right bloody questions to ask. A woman you don't care for.'

'Now, you know that's not true,' he said quietly. 'I agree I married you for all the wrong reasons, but you're wrong when you say I don't care for you. I do care.'

'But you can't say you love me.' The tears would flow in spite of her efforts. A single droplet escaped and rolled slowly down the pale check. She quickly brushed it away.

'I admire you. Your looks, your spirit...'

She shook her head miserably. 'Then I don't think you belong with me.'

'If I felt that I would have left months ago.'

'So you stayed be because she wouldn't damn well have you? Is that it? Well, aren't I a lucky bitch? I got some bargain ...did I not?'

'Now stop this at once! You'll only make yourself ill.' He was angry now, his patience at an end. ''No matter what you may or may not have heard, you'll just have to accept my word that nothing is going on.'

He realized he was shouting and immediately lowered his voice. 'Now then, let's have an end to this. Why are we fencing anyway? The affair ended months ago.'

'So that makes it right, does it?'

'No, it doesn't make it right, but it doesn't do to dwell on the past either,' he said edgily.

'Oh ...I …I'm so angry ...so hurt by your bloody selfishness ... I could scream.'

'Then scream and have done with it.'

Jessica came into the room without him hearing. They did not, either of them, refer to the events of the preceding evening. What had been said appeared to have been forgotten, by Luke anyway. But for Jessica, the unspoken accusation remained, to chafe and harass whenever leisure gave room to remembrance.

'How are you feeling?' he asked in polite concern.

'Well enough thank you,' she returned with equal courtesy. Beside her plate lay a long, blue velvet box tied round with a gold ribbon. 'What's this?'

'A gift for you.'

'You mean a peace offering, don't you?' she said tartly.

He was grinning, his self-satisfied grin. 'Call it a gesture! I thought they might cheer you up.'

She untied the ribbon and pressed the spring of the box without any feeling of pleasurable curiosity and beheld - pearls. A single string of pearls that must be worth a small fortune. But she disliked pearls regardless of their beauty, although she did not say so. She had been led to believe that pearls signify tears and were therefore, not good omens of a happy marriage, but she thanked him with a forced show of gratitude.

'I also have something planned for the end of next week. If you feel well enough you might care to accompany me to London. One night we could go to a play, then dinner. Another night we might go to the opera. And if the weather is warm enough we could take a boat trip along The Thames. What do you think?'

She made no effort to hide her delight. The best gifts are tied with heartstrings. 'Oh ...Luke!'

'In 1814 the Thames froze over, you know. They actually held a fair on solid ice. The Wheel of Fortune, stalls, skittles, swings, roundabouts, the lot.'

'That's amazing.'

'There'll be plenty to see. You'll enjoy it.'

There was more. The most exciting of all. He was to take her to the Druary Lane Theatre, where she had always longed to go.

Laughing and eager, she tumbled in to his arms, pulling his face down to cover it with kisses, which he accepted without comment and was curiously soothed.

THIRTY-EIGHT

To travel in, Jessica wore a carriage dress of dark blue satin with matching blue spencer and bonnet, each elaborately trimmed with black braiding, creating a subtle sense of elegance. A little pink reticule echoed the pink ribbon and roses of the bonnet. All other clothes had been laid in folds of tissue paper and stowed carefully in two large domed trunks.

The steaming splendour of the horses and the grand, glittering black and maroon-coloured stage-coach was something to see. They were called stagecoaches because they ran in stages - from one coaching inn to the next, where fresh horses were harnessed to the coach whilst the passengers took refreshment. Lamps hung on the four corners of the bodywork and the windows were large and square allowing plenty of opportunity to see out. The rear platform was taken up by the trunks, which were well strapped down. The hatboxes Jessica took inside. In addition to passengers, they carried news-papers, letters and parcels. A middle aged man wearing the traditional top hat and waist length scarlet jacket, held open the coach door, then climbed up to sit on the box. Luke settled himself on the wide leather seat beside Jessica as the driver flicked the reins and the coach jerked into movement. They were off.

There were four other passengers. Two men and two women, all elderly and soberly dressed. Jessica smiled at each of the two women in turn, but they just looked at her solemnly and then looked away. They sat in cramped discomfort for what seemed like hours, creaking, lumbering and jolting to the drum of hooves and the crash of coach springs, travelling at a good fifteen miles an hour, showing no sign of slackening the reckless pace. Everything outside sped by so fast it made Jessica feel quite dizzy.

She craned her neck out of the window as the drum of hooves suddenly altered to an undulating clatter and rumble on cobbles. The noise was like thunder, making her head throb. It was absolute chaos, each street a bedlam of rattling carts, gigs and hackneys, cracking whips, catcalls, curses and cries and barking dogs. The coach slowed to almost a crawl and made a sudden left turn, rumbling into some sort of courtyard.

'Whoa!' They came to a sudden jerking halt, but so disorientated from the constant jolting, Jessica felt she was still moving. The driver let in a hurricane of wind with the glad tidings that they had reached the destination of the inn where they could have half an hour grace for refreshments. The courtyard was a frenzied turmoil of activity; with the rattle of wheels, clip clopping of hooves, jangling of harnesses and shouted commands. Such noise! It was quite deafening. Grooms stood by with leather buckets to give each of the horses a drink. Jessica gazed with distaste at the cloud of flies competing for what was left of, what appeared to be, a decomposing body of a cat, lying in the gutter through the middle of the yard.

Shortly after climbing back into the coach, she must have nodded off, because when she came to Luke told her they had reached the city - London, with its tall and impressive buildings; not only the administrative, commercial and financial capital of the country, but also Britain's centre of manufacturing. A city richly endowed with statues of the great and the largely forgotten, the earliest dating from the seventeenth century. Where else could there exist so many miles of square and crescent? Where else were there so many two-storey houses of dirty brick, their ledges and woodwork never cleaned or painted?

The innumerable houses of the suburbs sunk in a heavy atrocious boredom of their own, where, in the drab and airless stillness of their rooms, smothered behind dusty faded curtains, a sigh turned to a groan. Here, in the mazes of brick, where spring came for a few days once a year, with an unutterable beauty of its own, loading them with its most fragile and honeyed treasures that seemed to bring the sky right down into the streets, Streets that were crowded with passenger coaches, post chaises, and cheerfully painted wagons with the owner's name prominently painted on the tailboard.

Loaded carts and wagons, their wheels churning up the filth, the massive horses that pulled them surrendering their great strength to the carter's will, their commander who was always ready with the right word of encouragement. Then there were the noisy groups of foreigners, strangely dressed, with beards and the most peculiar hats, chattering in different tongues and waving their arms around theatrically - and the Londoners themselves thrusting through the crowds with the impatient authority of the native. To add to the confusion there were hawkers with baskets and barrows stacked high with fruit, musicians, drunks, urchins and beggars. All   strange sounds mingled together, foreign to the ear.

Jessica threw herself with enthusiasm in to the whirl of London life. The Londonderry Hotel in Park Lane where they stayed, stood big and rambling, a warren of rooms and passages, with all the comforts of home. Every day was crammed with excitement and activity, the evenings booked ahead. Luke took her to just about every musical concert and ballet, every theatrical event the city had to offer. The boat trip on the Thames he had promised her had to be postponed due to the fog. Jessica hoped they would be more fortunate the next day, and her wishes for fine weather were answered with a beautifully dry, bright morning.

They took a cab west through sprawling country-side all the way through the city of Oxford - the playground of the wealthy, and down to the riverside where they boarded one of the gaily coloured double-ended long boats hired out for day trips. There were long benches to sit on and a small cabin in the stern for shelter should the weather turn wet.

The River Thames is the longest river in England and the backbone of an extensive waterway network. A grand and majestic tideway controlled by locks, most of which are set in spots quite isolated from towns and villages. Leaving Oxford behind, the boat headed south towards Iffley, known for its famous Norman church, with a massive tower and a doorway richly decorated with chevron and typically Romanesque stylised animals and birds. Iffley Lock was one of the oldest locks on the river.

Flanked by distant hills, the river took a route

along a wide valley, swinging in great loops past the woods of Nuneham Park, and round Abingdon - the wealthy wool and oldest thriving market town in England, and one of the major monastic centres on the river through its great abbey founded in the seventh century. Past Goring and Pangbourne where the hills close in, forcing the river into a dramatic tree-lined valley that carries it through the Chilterns. There the riverfront was dominated by an old mill, a grand brick building whose colour echoed throughout the villages, continuing downstream through Caversham to industrialised Reading, with its engineer-ing works and breweries, and a fine church whose battlemented tower dominated the town.

Farther on were a number of grand sixteenth and seventeenth century stone houses with gables and mullioned windows, standing proudly near the river's edge that was dotted with boathouses, decorative structures with balconies overhanging the water. The river wound its way through a delightful countryside that held so many attractions, following a quiet route across a low-lying landscape of fields broken by bridges with elegant arches, cut from lovely soft stone battered by time. Winding past stony, lichen-crusted country churches standing in delightful isolation among whispering grasses, generating a remarkably peaceful atmosphere. Drifting on past a Lock keeper's cottage of golden-grey stone, over-grown and half-hidden by trees. The Lock keeper stood outside keeping an eye on things.

Jessica lifted her hand and waved. The scene was enchanting. Long stretches of steep woodland filling the narrow valley and sweeping down to the water where geese bobbed joyfully and swans glided majestically on the surface, in perfect harmony. The water lapped quietly under an old bridge of soft red brick in the warm sunlight, and dappled trees by the riverside, captured the spirit. On past Hurley, Marlow, Cookham and towards Maidenhead, where the valley and landscape open out and the Thames becomes a truly regal river as it approaches the great towering bulk of Windsor Castle soaring up to the heavens …a royal residence since William the Conqueror. Impressive and massively built over centuries.

There the river twisted and turned, the path curving along the Windsor quayside, past Eton and on to the Palace of Westminster and Westminster Abbey standing together, church and state united, in every way a landmark structure, adding farther magic to that already engendered by the magnificence of the castle. Jessica was overawed. The view was breathtaking. An unrivalled landscape. A magical spot, especially in the soft light of early evening. They drifted on past Staines, approaching London by the quay on the northern shore of the Thames where the trees shaded the riverside promenade and the stench was pungent. Jessica covered her nose and mouth with a delicate lace handkerchief, as Luke took her arm to steady her and help her back on to dry land.

Millions of tons of cargo were brought from every corner of the world, making London's docks that flanked the Thames among the busiest in the world. The coming and goings of hefty cargo ships and sailing decked boats, employed in trawling for all manner of sea fish, crammed the river with continual traffic. Boats were hauled upstream by teams of magnificent horses and big brawny men; bargemen whose trade depended upon the flow of the water.

There were old smoke-stained warehouses: factories, slaughter houses, tanneries and mills on either side, with their vast brick pilasters, their decorative window arches and old cranes and hoists, rise above the dense mass of roofs and gables, frowning sternly upon the water too black to reflect even their lumbering shapes. Little groups of houses randomly built, filled the gaps between the commercial structures; owned mainly by ship's captains who returned from long and hazardous voyages to spend brief periods with their families. Built right on the waterfront, these houses kept them close to the river's turbulent life.

The early evening light turned the riverside industrial clutter into a random assembly of abstract shapes, a strange geometry of rectangles, triangles and cones made more dramatic by the strong shadows thrown by the setting sun.

That night they were going to the Theatre Royal in Druary Lane to an opera - La Traviata - an expiration of a love affair that turned sour. Jessica kept wondering about the details, with something of the simplicity of a child who wants to have its anticipated pleasures described beforehand. She talked about what she should wear, with an unsettled anxiety that amused Luke. Without any force at all, she found herself led and influenced by his will.

The gown he chose was simple, a beautiful powder blue moiré silk creation. She had had no call to resort to frezettes and scalpettes, the popular hairpieces that women of fashion added to their coiffures. Jessica was blessed with a thick, healthy abundance of hair, russet stresses, which were obstinately curly and long enough to be braided and pinned up for the evenings, with two superb hair combs handset with tiny stones and accented with pearl seed beads in the centre. She needed neither chain nor bracelet he told her, no ornament other than the pearls resting on the swell of her breasts. She looked very young and vulnerable.

The pleasure of setting out with her husband in the snug comfort of a carriage on a chilly but fine night, and the sight of the stars twinkling in the sky as they rolled along, held a peculiarly exhilarating charm for her. She supposed people who went regularly to places of public amusement could hardly enter into the fresh gala feeling with which an opera or a concert enjoyed by those for whom it was a rarity.

Jessica caught a glimpse of a face under the flickering, uncertain light of a lamp - the face of a woman, bloated and distorted, by drink she wouldn't wonder. She felt a momentary shuddering sense of what humanity might sink to when life was lived apart from the sweet, health-giving influences of open green fields and flowers, of art, music and books, of the stimulus of interesting activity, the gentle amenities of happy hours and contact with the educated and the cultured.

The whole theatre was lit up in a rich blaze of radiance. They alighted under a portico amongst a great bustle, in a place that hardly reflected the poverty around it. Jessica clung to Luke's arm as she glanced about with a mixture of wonder and excitement. He smiled at her indulgently. They mounted a majestic staircase, wide and easy of ascent, deeply and softly carpeted with crimson, leading up to great double doors.

She found herself in a grand hall, wide and high with sweeping circular walls and a domed ceiling of gold, hung with a wondrous treasure of dazzling crystals, sparkling with facets, all ablaze with what seemed like hundreds of twinkling stars. Ivory and gold mingled in wreaths of gilded leaves and lilies, and wherever there were drapes and carpets the sole colour employed was deep burgundy. At some turn she suddenly found herself in a softly carpeted compartment with a balcony in between two pillars, furnished with four gold and burgundy regal chairs that commanded a good view of that vast and dazzling hall filled with a splendid assemblage. Jessica was all eager delight, her eyes darting here, there and everywhere.

The stage, raised above the pit and auditorium, was hidden by an enormous heavy burgundy curtain. A continual buzz of voices rose from the audience as they settled in their seats. There didn't appear to be an empty seat in the theatre. The auditorium was packed, stalls, pit, balcony and gallery full, and yet they continued to admit party after party, until the semi-circle before the stage presented one dense mass of heads, sloping from floor to ceiling - everyday people in velvets and satins, plumes and gems, flowers and feathers. The gentlemen were stiff in their sombre dark suits and the ladies beside them, fluttering their fans like nervous colourful peacocks.

'Luke ...that woman...?'

'Which woman, my pet?'

'The one sitting in that box with the man in uniform.'

Luke turned his head, looking in the wrong direction.

'No, over there, opposite,' Jessica said, pointing straight ahead.

The lady in question was no other than Amel Duprez with a companion - her latest admirer, the fair and handsome Captain McLachlan, in his full dress coat of scarlet and gold. She was attired in a vibrant, midnight blue gown with a low décolletage, her golden hair curled on the top of the forehead with small thick curls, separated with what appeared to be, a band of sparkling diamonds crossing the forehead and continuing round the head. Indeed, Amel Duprez did love anything that gave a hint of the exotic. One could not help but notice her.

She sat in full view of all eyes, a magnetic influence of glance, cold and beauteous as the ivory columns that rose at her sides. For a moment, Luke was stunned, feeling a tinge of resentment mingled with anger. To women such as Amel Duprez, an opera box for her own personal use at all times was not just a necessity, a showcase or shop-window, but a fashionable rendezvous where she held court. The price was high. A box for the season was two hundred guineas. He should know. He had paid for it.

She held tiny gold binoculars up to her eyes, levelling them across the house, looking directly at him and then moved them slightly, to scrutinize the woman at his side. A minute or two later she lowered them and laughingly whispered something to her escort. Luke couldn't stand to look at them a moment longer. His dark, brooding eyes were immediately returned to their former direction.

'Don't point. It's bad manners.'

Jessica noticed the fleeting look of anger, and presuming it was meant for her, immediately went on the defensive. 'But it's just as rude to stare. She was looking right at us. Do you know her?'

'Not personally,' he lied expertly, 'But I've heard she's one of the most popular hostesses in London society.'

'Really? How interesting. She's certainly beautiful and so elegant. And the soldier's handsome. They make a striking pair, don't you think?'

'I can't say I noticed,' came the reply.

'Well, you're about the only one who hasn't. Everyone seems to be looking their way. I do like the way she has her hair. Do you think I could wear mine in that style?'

'You look perfect as you are, my pet. I wouldn't change a hair on your lovely head.'

'Oh Luke, you can be so wonderful sometimes.'

'Did I not promise to devote all my time and attention to you, to make you happy?' he said cleverly, in an unguarded moment.

But a slow anger was burning inside him, kindling and growing. The prospect of sitting through a long, tedious evening was no longer appealing. He sat in silent suffering, a melancholy man. But Jessica was brimming with her usual exuberance ...the woman forgotten.

'Oh, Luke, I'm having a wonderful time. Enjoying every minute of it. I'm so glad you brought me.' She scanned through the program. 'Have you read this? The opera is divided into three acts, with two twenty minute intervals in between.'

'Yes, I know,' he said impatiently.

'Oh look, all the musicians are taking their

places,' Jessica went on excitedly. 'That man with the stick must be the leader.'

'That's the Concert Master with his baton.'

'Baton ...stick ...what's the difference!' she mumbled to herself. She opened the program at the front, glancing down the page. 'According to this the orchestra consists of 24 violins, 13 violas, 12 cellos, 9 basses, 5 flutes, 2 piccolos, 4 oboes, 5 clarinets, 4 bassoons. What may I ask is a bassoon? Luke, are you listening?'

'What is it?' he answered rather sharply.

'I asked what a bassoon was.'

'It's a wood-wind instrument.'

'Just listen to this. There's also 5 horns, 5 trumpets, 5 trombones, a tuba, a harp and last but not least ...a timpani.' She frowned. 'Whatever a timpani is. I've never heard of it.'

'Bowl-shaped drums, part of the percussion group. They're made of metal, the tops covered with stretched skin.'

She smiled with wonder at her husband. He seemed to know all about everything that had ever been printed. 'Oh, you're such a mind of information. You seem to know just about everything.'

'If you look you can see them at the back of the pit.' He pointed out, in an effort to take his mind off Amelia Duprez and company, struggling to keep his eyes from wandering in their direction.

'Yes. I see them now. The musicians are so huddled together. They certainly pack them in. It must be going to start soon.'

'They have to warm up first,' he explained half-heartedly. 'The curtain won't go up until they've played the overture.'

It was a tragic plot, dramatic entertainment in which nearly all the dialogue was sung to orchestral accompaniment. Shifting and wriggling about in her seat, scarcely able to contain herself, Jessica ooed and aahed at each new sight, constantly tapping her fingers to the music. When the curtains dropped at the first interval there were roars of appreciation and tremendous applause from the audience.

'It's stifling in here,' Luke said, rising with sudden impatience. 'I'm going for some fresh air and a smoke.'

Jessica started to rise from her seat. 'I'll come with you.'

'No …stay where you are. I won't be long.'

The interval between was one of relaxation and the pleasantest imaginable stir and commotion. The whole hall seemed to be in a whirl, alive with energy and movement …people rising and remaining standing, some walking about, every one talking and laughing.

Out in the vestibule with a distressing sense of faintness and a throbbing brow, Amelia glanced briefly at her reflection in one of the gold-framed mirrors that lined the walls. Just for a second she had a perfectly ghastly feeling that she was looking her age.

She swung round theatrically to face Luke as he approached her from behind, the vibrant, midnight blue gown she had on flowing with sophistication and class. Men turned covertly to watch her, for there was no denying she looked absolutely radiant and knew it. Besides the diamonds she wore in her hair, there were diamond pendants hanging from her earlobes, and in her cleavage a gold and diamond cluster that was certainly the most expensive looking piece of jewellery Luke had ever seen on a woman.

She spoke with a soft calm-like politeness, in spite of his grave expression. 'Good evening, Monsieur. That look on your face is not happiness to see me, is it?'

'Try surprise.' He reached for her arm, taking hold of it and guiding her farther along the packed vestibule to a less crowded spot. 'I thought you were going away?'

Amel closed her eyes momentarily. 'I was not well enough to travel.'

'But well enough to flaunt yourself to half of London with that young scoundrel at your side? What kind of a man is he to leave you out here alone?'

'It just so happens he has gone to fetch me a drink. My throat is so painful I can hardly swallow.' She lifted her small chin and held his direct gaze, as she tried to pull away. 'Now, kindly let go of my arm.' Her tone had turned frosty, her voice dropping to just a hoarse whisper. 'Don't be so demonstrative or I might faint and you would have to carry me out. If such a burden were laid upon you, how would you explain to your companion?'

He released her arm. 'I make no apologies. You deliberately led me to believe you would be away by the end of the week.'

'And you, Monsieur, specifically told me in your letter, a very abrupt letter I might add, that you were too swamped with business matters to have time for frivolities … as you put it,' she retaliated, speaking in a clipped tone. 'And here I see you with another woman.'

'It just so happens that woman is my wife.'

Amel fluttered long, golden lashes. 'Your wife! Well, that is a surprise! I must say she looks quite enchanting. It's so selfish of you to bury such a pretty little thing in the country.'

'My wife prefers the country. She feels ill at ease in the city. Is your curiosity quite satisfied now?'

'But I'm sure she would enjoy it here, given the chance. You should bring her more often.'

'Had I known you were to be here, I would never have come in the first place. It could have proved very embarrassing.'

'Only for you, Monsieur.'

'Why are you behaving this way?' He had no understanding of woman's emotions. Like a pendulum they could swing any way.

'You seem to forget I am a free woman, accountable to no one. Free to do as I please, when I please.'

'Just answer my question,' he said, with the nervous irritability that comes from worrying perceptions.

'I'll answer your question willingly, Monsieur, but you're not going to like what you hear. You're no longer the one magical person who can make my life wonderful. I have a life to live. After all, I cannot be expected to hide myself away from the outside world until you have a mind to put in an appearance, when the mood suits you.'

'Then go to hell!' he retorted, with as much dignity as he could muster.

In spite of his rudeness and the soreness of her throat, she laughed gaily. 'I dare say I will, but not just yet. There is so much to be enjoyed first. Now, do excuse me. I must go. My companion will be looking for me. I will be in our favourite restaurant tomorrow, Monsieur. Between twelve and one. Should you be free and have a mind to, please do join me. I will look out for you.' And with that she turned and glided away.

Back at her side, Jessica was conscious of her husband's change of mood. He leaned back in his seat with a slightly listless air, pretending to study his programme intently, and appeared half asleep, owing to the way in which his eyelids drooped and the drowsy sweep of his lashes. Desirous to rouse him from it, she drew his attention by asking him whether he was enjoying the opera.

Luke started and gave her a weak smile, answering her very briefly, saying that he was, but invariably relapsed as soon as she ceased to speak. His thoughts still lingered moodily on the exquisite Amel Duprez, on how she still affected him. There had been times she had made him believe he was the only man in the universe that mattered to her and yet now, she openly turned away from him, treating him as if he meant no more to her than all the others. The truth was there was something sadly lacking in her. The inert force of the love she bore herself could only be surpassed by her proud impotency to care for any other living person. He would make a point of going to see her tomorrow, if only to tell her what he thought of her.

La Traviata had the most disastrous ending. The heroin, Violetta, achieved high B flat and then collapsed, while the orchestra raced on towards a cadence that was reached six bars later when the doctor pronounced her dead. The opera concluded, and the curtain fell. It was all very emotional.

Jessica discreetly dabbed at her eyes with a clean

linen handkerchief her husband passed to her. Luke glanced across the hall. Amel Duprez and her companion were no longer to be seen.

THIRTY-NINE

The ardent lover was now an absent husband, off on business somewhere, so Jessica decided to explore the city on her own. A walk through the central districts of London revealed such wealth. A circumference of nearly a mile round the country-like parks of the West End was filled with grand houses, mainly built in the Italianate style, for the residence of the upper middle merchants and professional classes, all of which kept private carriages.

The area of Mayfair, bounded on the north by Grosvenor Square, on the south by St James Park, on the east by Bond Street and on the west by Park Lane, was where many of the great family mansions were situated. Phaetons skimmed about the streets like so many glittering, brilliant coloured insects, their line and carriage work triumphs of the carriage-maker's art. St James's area was predominantly a masculine preserve, the side streets packed with bachelor lodgings and expensive shops.

Heads turned wherever she went. She had on a dress the colour of the moss that grew under the Lakeland trees, simple and beautifully cut, made of a material known as bengaline silk - a wool fabric with threads of silk interwoven, chosen by her indulgent husband. It had an untrained skirt of ankle length with a slightly flared hem. Over it, she wore a matching pelisse with an ivory lace ruff at the neck, and puffed sleeves that ended at the wrist with a lace frill. She had on a silk bonnet to match, with an ivory frill beneath the rim and elaborately decorated with ivory silk roses and ribbon ornamentation, tied in a neat bow under the chin. A little silk reticule echoed the ribbon and roses of the bonnet, while the ivory lace ruff and bonnet trim drew the eye to the startling fresh beauty of her face. Her gloves were ivory too and so were her high-heeled, kid ankle-boots. Her polished-chestnut hair fell from the back of the bonnet to her waist in a thick, curling cape. The whole was an ingenious picture of elegance that brought an appreciative gleam to each male eye that fell on her.

Beyond the turnpike at Hyde Park Corner lay open country dotted with the villages of Chelsea, Brampton, Knightsbridge and Kensington. St Paul's and the city lay outside the fashionable perimeter. They were for merchants and lawyers, just as the rookeries of St Giles and Seven Dials were breeding grounds for prostitution, pick-pockets and other petty crimes, where press gangs struck terror, seizing men for forced service in the navy.

Oblivious to the scandalized glances of passerbys little accustomed to seeing a young woman of her class unaccompanied, Jessica wandered into the tumultuous city where one could get lost or worse still, if she was not careful. Crushed by horse's hoofs or the wheels of the great coal-wagons and other loaded carts, vehicles of every sort, passing too close to the crowded pavements. It was a shoppers' paradise, full of markets, shops with large windows of plate-glass set in massive brass frames, and arcades.

An Aladdin's cave of beautiful and costly treasures. Gentlemen's clothing: top hats, boots, umbrellas and walking sticks, leather goods, hand-somely bound books, and for the ladies; bonnets, parasols, gowns, shawls, boots, shoes and beaded slippers, perfumes, cosmetics, jewellery, and décorative fans. There were all manner of fancy wares to adorn the hair: artificial flowers, feathers, ribbons, bejewelled combs, turbans and tiaras. The accumulation of things were absolutely astonishing.

The sidewalks were swarming with men and women, hurrying this way and that, to goodness knows where. One was struck by the number of faces that exhibited a type of cold determined will, a multitude of individuals, pale complexioned and rigid looking, walking straight with a geometrical movement, without looking in either direction but straight ahead.

Farther on there were innumerable hawkers and salesmen of one sort and another. One man stood on the street corner turning a tune out of a barrel organ. Another, occupying a doorway that looked gloomy and forbidding, invited her to step inside the Chamber of Horrors, where, for one penny, you could see all the celebrated murderers of bygone years. The pressure of the crowd seemed to be increasing and there was such a din.

'Sprig o' 'eather, lady? Tis scented.'

Jessica shook her head and mouthed 'no thank you'.

The noisy dusty sprawl of the city held little attraction for her. It was the general effect that was overwhelming. She walked down Rose Street past the Lamb and Flag Ale House that dated back to 1623, turning the corner into Kings Street where piercing voices screaming abuse could be heard.

At the bottom of Kings Street was Covent Garden. Here, the crowds were even denser, partly because it was so narrow and partly because so many inhabitants of the hovels nearby were glad to get out in to the street for a breath of air. It was no easy task to squeeze ones way through. There was a momentary block ahead, a little mob that had gathered round an almost lifeless looking figure beating out with a couple of quills, what he presumably thought to be music, from a sort of homemade dulcimer.

A few yards farther on, a boy without any legs was the object of attention, and nearby, was a skin and bone dog scratching for something to eat in the evil smelling rubbish that had accumulated in the gutter. Jessica stooped to give the poor boy a coin. The pavement was narrow and the few feet of the roadway was occupied by a continuous string of stalls, each attractive from some specialty - an assortment of leather goods, rolls of materials, kitchen-ware and candles, second-hand clothes and boots, an array of cheap jewellery: tools, crockery, hats and bonnets, and no end of curious things - all going cheap. A pie man was selling everything from meat pies to fruit tarts, iced-buns and gingerbread, and hot liquor of a crimson hue sold in small glasses …and roast chestnuts that gave off a particularly pungent aroma.

''Ot chestnuts. Penny a score.'

Busy hands were at work displaying the merchandise, selling whatever would raise a few shillings. Everything from jams and eggs, artificial and fresh flowers, fruit and vegetables, to plucked chickens no bigger than sparrows, and various meats and fish. All were laid out on display and buzzing with flies. The cries of the vendors was deafening. Round every stall were eager women, poor mothers who must use every farthing sparingly, bartering with the salesmen. The meat must be bought, and so must a pair of boots for her young son, his old ones so worn that they no longer kept out the wet.

Just ahead, groping in the slushy mud was a neat little woman with tears running down her cheeks. She had lost half a sovereign, all her husband's earnings for the week, and she had bought nothing for to-morrow's dinner, but there were sympathetic hearts close by. A gentleman stooped to slip something into her hand, an example that was instantly followed by two decently dressed working men. There was no doubt of her gratitude, although protestations of it were absent.

Jessica wandered around looking bewildered, staring about as though she had been lightly stunned, ready to be taken in by any genial rogue who would give her a kind word or a friendly smile in this alien place. It was then that she caught sight of him, Luke entering the door of a grand restaurant. She pushed through the crowd and went in after him.

The reverberation and bustle and vivacious laughter, the bright colours of the ladies gowns, all in the very height of fashion, swirled all about her and she felt she was in the centre of a swiftly moving kaleidoscope. She glanced dazedly about for her husband and spotted him. Wonderfully tall and long limbed, with powerful shoulders. A white cravat emphasized his dark hand-some features, his hair as black as night, thick and curling about his ears. All other faces faded into insignificance.

She lifted a hand to draw his attention, but he obviously hadn't noticed her for he turned away to speak to someone. She leant slightly sideways; just enough for her to see who it was he was talking to …some business colleague no doubt. She could feel the jump of her heart, that jerk of something which quickens the blood and sets the pulses racing when you are afraid, that leap of alarm, that flutter of tension, and her eyes widened in disbelief.

A sound escaped her lips, a sound somewhere between a gasp and a moan cut off suddenly. The person her husband was talking to was a young woman with a pale complexion and blonde hair arranged into fashionable Grecian curls. The very woman they had seen at the opera. She was so fine …so beautiful, perfectly groomed and impeccably dressed.

Jessica stared in stupefaction at the scene, Luke leaning towards the woman, intimately close and whispering something in her ear, something that must have been very amusing, for the woman threw back her golden head and gave a gay tingling laugh.

In the split second it had taken for her to recognize the two of them and for her mind to acknowledge what it was she was seeing before her very eyes; her husband bending his head with evident affection to another woman, something happened. All the strong feelings, which had been scattered over her existence since she had discovered what love was, seemed gathered together into one pulsation now. Her heart was racing and she felt she would suffocate.

He was hers. Hers! She loved him. She had always loved him. In all her sufferings, there never was a time when she suffered in an absolute sense what she was suffering now. But this was the mood of a few instants only. When the momentary blow had passed, her expression changed to a silent imperious anger, her eyes narrowing to brilliant green slits like those of a cat.

She drew back to herself again by a strenuous effort of self-command, sinking gratefully in to a chair. Quickly taking up a magazine from the pile on a side table, she set about the pretence of reading, a myriad of thoughts whirling around and around in her head, filling her heart with fear, turning her cold and making her feel physically sick.

Voices buzzed around her, getting louder and louder and the shocked core of her was still as a mouse cornered by a cat. He had lied …deliberately lied …again. He had blatantly told her he didn't know that …that woman, yet here he was before her very eyes, standing familiarly close and whispering intimately in her ear. It was all there to see; the intimacy, the easy touch of two people who know each other well.

Excuse it as she might, they were lies flapping their black wings like a fiend. Was she the one? The refined, educated woman he had had the sordid affair with? Was it still going on? If it was, she didn't know what she was to do about it. Should she go to them, openly challenge them and find out the truth? No, she felt she could not let them see her. It would only humiliate her further. She must bear it alone, though how in the name of God she was to do that she could not imagine.

She felt lifeless, and yet her body pulsed and the blood ran in her veins. She found herself quivering with silent anguish - a victim of betrayal; seeing them together was too much for her to bear. It was not to be borne. She had to get away from there. Though it cost her every shred of strength and will power, she rose shakily to her feet and crept out through the door like a thief.

Jessica's spirits underwent a complete change; she became silent and distracted. How life could change in a few short moments. Nothing so hurts the heart than to find out the person you have opened up to, made yourself vulnerable to, has deceived you and given himself to another. She could remember the desolation which had claimed her when she had come across her husband and that ...*that* woman talking so intimately together.

She could no longer conceal the bitter discovery from herself; the truth could not be denied and she was forced to accept her husband no longer cared for her. A new mockery on the part of Fate. She was drowning in the depths of her own despair.

FORTY

Luke entered the gaming room where the atmosphere was heavy with the aroma of tobacco. He found Amel seated at one of the tables, looking dazzling in a gown of brilliant poppy-red muslin, trimmed with gold, the bodice edged with vandykes in the military style, and a turban of poppy-red and gold to match. The gown really did embrace her superb shape. Pearls dangled from her ears and hanging from her wrist was a beautiful peacock fan. Luke sensed by the slight slump of her shoulders and the tiny beads of perspiration glistening on her brow, that she had had a run of bad luck. Underneath a thin veneer lay a compulsive gambler, gradually spiralling out of control.

Several club members sprawled around the green baize table, watching with intensity the game that was taking place, men who gambled huge amounts, winning and losing hundreds of guineas on the turn of a card. It was a weakness that many could not control, an affliction from which some would never be cured, taking hold of their lives in a way which spelled disaster, destitution and heartbreak. One of these was Henry Thackeray, known to be heavily in debt.

At last Luke caught Amel's attention and beckoned by tilting his head, trying to discourage her from gambling further, his look urging her to stop this madness. But Amel merely scowled at him. Resentment flooded in a wave of indignation. Did his meddling know no bounds?

Luke consulted his pocket watch, then moved around the table and stooped to whisper close to her ear. 'If I were not here to keep an eye on you, you would soon have nothing left. It's time to go.'

She had in fact - he was to find out later - lost a great deal more than she could afford. With the shake of the dice, she had flittered away a little under two thousand pounds in the one night at the tables.

'But it's still early.' Time held no meaning for Amel Duprez. Why should she hurry over what was her chief pleasure?

Luke found his patience becoming over-stretched. He had a gruelling schedule ahead. 'I've a heavy day tomorrow.'

But Amel obstinately stood her ground, rolling her eyes expressively. 'I will not be dictated to,' she hissed under her breath

'But you're throwing more and more of your money away. You'll only end up in trouble,' he whispered. 'I cannot stand calmly by and see you run your head blindfold into a noose.' He straightened up.

For a full two minutes Amel met those dark, burning eyes without speaking, then said shortly, 'Why should that concern you? It is *my* money, after all.'

It was the irritation that he heard in her voice that prompted him to walk away. Never let it be said that he couldn't take a hint. Never in all his life had he met a more capricious, self-indulgent woman. Well, she could find her own way home.

For the next four days Luke was tied up with business matters, the evenings spent leisurely at his club. On the fifth day a note was delivered to the hotel. He opened it and read it through at once.

My dearest devoted friend, when I think I might never see you again, I feel quite wretched. My mind dwells upon nothing else but you. Absent from you, I feel no pleasure. My poor pen cannot describe such feelings. I cannot do without you. I beg you, do not desert me in my time of need. Please ...please forgive me and come to me.

Your Amel

Her message brought him instantly to her side. She was dressed in a froth of ivory silk and lace, with her golden hair hanging loosely down her back. With a glance, he saw her face was unusually pale and bore the mark of recent tears. He had never known her to shed tears, not Amelia Duprez, who had never feared anything in her life, save the vanishing of her youth.

But Amel had been increasingly worried over the past few weeks, under a strong emotional strain, quite sufficient to account for her distress. It was the strain of presenting a smiling face and a pose of imperturbable confidence, when she was up to her neck in debt, in fact, right over her head with debts she was too frightened to acknowledge to anyone, not to mention the unspoken fear that lurked in the back of her tortured mind.

She went into his arms with tears spilling from her eyes. 'Mon amour, I've been truly afraid. Afraid that you might not come.'

'How could I stay away? You've been foremost in my thoughts,' he said smoothly. It was not his choice to be here today. It was high time he headed home. It was only her obvious distress that had brought him.

The dreadful whiteness of her face troubled him profoundly. 'What have you done to yourself? You look positively ill.'

'That's because I have been ill.' She blew her nose on an incongruously delicate lace handkerchief.

He lifted her bodily and placed her gently down on the bed, against a pile of soft pillows.

'You may do what you will with me?' she said softly, nestling her hand on his crutch, moving her fingers expertly.

'Not now, my darling. I think you should rest.'

She smiled weakly. 'But you know I can't bear to stay in bed.'

'It's only for a short while,' he assured her. 'You're not about to push up the daisies. Only the good die young.'

'Oh, how I wish I didn't feel this way. I used to have such energy.'

'And so you will again. Oh, I almost forgot.' He drew a long blue velvet box from the inside pocket of his jacket. 'I have something for you.'

He opened it. Inside was a two-row pearl choker. Amel's smile widened. It was absolutely exquisite. Just the thing to make her feel better. The choker was enhanced with three oval pearl-set ornaments, dropped with leaves and baroque pearls. It was a beautiful piece of jewellery, costly too.

'Oh, Luke, you have raised my spirits already.'

'I know how fond you are of pearls. I had it made especially.'

Her tenderness grew with the sense of his eagerness to make her happy. It was in this region of thought and imagination that she had dreamed of a lasting hold over him. 'Oh, how generous you are. Do you know, I think before all this you'd began to truly care for me.'

Luke detected the note of regret in her voice. Amel was elaborately tactful. She waited, kept silent, leaving him to his emotions, but no poignant response came, so she carried on. 'I know I …I'm not an easy person to feel affection for. Nor is it easy for me to give affection, but I must confess I …I've developed a true fondness for you,' she murmured, gasping for breath as she struggled a little farther up the pillows.

The truth was, she simply adored him with a woman's passion, but was too much the realist to imagine that he would stay with her forever. She knew the tie between them depended only on their pleasure - the sensual tie that binds men to women.

'I sometimes think you're the only person I … I'm capable of really caring for.' She raised delicately fine arched eyebrows. 'Perhaps this is what they call love?'

Luke listened with genuine surprise to this unexpected declaration. It was no more in her nature to talk of such emotions, than it was in his. But was it this thing called love or a dependency? Not emotionally, but financially?

'I do not begrudge you looking elsewhere for what I am unable to give you at this moment in time, Mon amour.'

'That's the last thing on my mind.' "That" being what he craved, but denied himself. 'I need you to get well again,' he said kindly, trying to calm her frayed nerves.

Amel Duprez had no time for the weakness that had taken her over, a series of minor complaints, one after the other. There was money to be earned, appetites to be gratified, and accounts to be paid. After all, wasn't she all the rage? All fashionable London aspired to be her lover, for a night or two, or her protector for longer.

She suddenly cried out as a fierce pain shot through her stomach.

'What is it?' Luke asked anxiously.

'I have a pain ...right here,' she complained, dropping the pearls on the bedcover and laying both her hands on her stomach. 'Ca fait mai.'

'What?'

'It hurts.'

She felt so unwell, she could hardly think. She was beginning to panic, fear attacking her. There began an extreme heaving of the bosom, resembling the panting of a dying bird. 'Mon ...mon la vie ... vie je veux ...veux ça l'arrière.'

'What is it you're saying?'

'My life ... I want it back,' she repeated, the pearls forgotten.

FORTY-ONE

Dark eyes blinked appreciatively at the grace and beauty of his hostess as they sat over a quiet dinner together in the dining room of Burlington House, her trim, subtle loveliness glowing in the fluttering candle and firelight. She looked wonderfully in tone with the setting of elegant décor, the rich warm colour of claret and the superbly fashioned Jacobean furniture. On Luke's lips was a hovering smile of happy expectancy of what was to come.

'I've been gravely embarrassed?' Amel complained quite suddenly, shattering the restful silence of the room.

'Embarrassed by whom?' Luke asked.

'By Elizabeth Jersey. She and Charles are having a party to celebrate their wedding anniversary. I have not received an invitation.'

'Then you must deal with the rejection. You've become the object of common gossip.' In short, Amel Duprez was forgotten.

'Huh! Common gossip by common people.' She was bewildered and hurt by the disloyal behaviour of her society acquaintances. 'I am the victim of a foul conspiracy. Elizabeth's poisoning my life. What a mediocre person she is. Even in the society of her most intimate friends she frequently confesses that she is bored to death. And what pretensions to airs and graces! She's the kind of woman who always wants to be the centre of social interest. Is it my fault that Charles prefers my company to hers? So little bonhomie penetrates through her dignity that few feel sufficiently attracted to induce them to try and thaw the ice in which she always seems bound. She is most definitely not liked.'

Amel was a lamb for the slaughter, gradually falling from fashion. Invitations had stopped coming. Luke wasn't at all surprised. Not in the least. Two or three times at the table, on various occasions, he had overheard a brief interchange of remarks between Catherine Gurney and Elizabeth Jersey, which were cruelly cutting to Amel, who they were ridiculing. They had not disguised their contempt. He saw nothing in these people's remarks but a tendency to disparage everything and was shocked by it.

That bitch Catherine Gurney, after the suicide of her lover, Waldoff Huskissson, had moved from Paris to settle in London permanently. She was a brilliant but acid and dangerous woman whose wit was lethal. For a while she and Amel had been close friends, but all that had changed. She seldom missed a chance now to diminish Amel's charms. He could have brained the woman with her fan. She was jealous and unscrupulous, a regular creeper; meaning by that, she had a flattering tongue and was ready to make a doormat of herself when she saw it would be to her own advantage. A scheming seductress who was constantly trying to acquire Amel's more spectacular conquests, and sometimes succeeding. And as for Elizabeth Jersey, her tongue wagged far too easily. All this affectation and bitchiness made her thoroughly unpopular, even with her own husband, who had in recent months taken to visiting Amel regularly.

Luke gazed in to the sparkling blue eyes. 'Never mind. At least you have your health back. You seem to have made a complete recovery.'

'I have.'

'What do you think triggered it off?'

'I really have no idea,' she answered softly.

They sat in silence for a short while.

'Mon amour...?'

'Yes, my darling?'

'I've been thinking we might go away together. Just the two of us.'

'I've commitments that keep me tied up at the moment.'

Amel felt disappointed and vexed. 'Oh Luke...'

'You'll just have to wait, my darling. I need to concentrate on making money to keep you in the style you're accustomed to. Also, I've made arrangements to call on Frederick Rolleston. He hasn't recovered from his stroke.'

'Poor Rolley.'

'I've only just heard he resigned from his position as President of the Board of Trade. He's confined to a wheelchair.'

'Then of course, you must go to see him. When you do, give him my fondest regards.'

'I will. Give me, say three or four days, then I'll be free and all yours.'

She brightened. A successful mistress has much more fun than a mere wife. 'That will be marvellous.'

'Where have you in mind?'

'There is no better place than Bath in Bristol at this time of year, where the wealthy go to the Spa to relax and take the waters as a medicinal cure. It is extremely pleasant there. There will be a great deal going on, plenty to amuse us. A kind of general indulgence prevails so that everybody does what they like best.'

'Then Bath it is, my darling.' He listened to her describe her new gowns that she would wear. 'Why not try them on? Give a little fashion parade?'

'What now?'

'If it pleases you.'

A coachman, and an armed guard to deter any attack made by highwaymen, manned the black and maroon coach pulled by a team of four smart black horses. In addition to the passengers' trunks - of which there were many, shoeboxes and hatboxes, all constructed from the finest of hide, the coach carried packages and letters. At each inn, fresh horses were harnessed whilst Luke and Amel took light refreshments.

Bath is a magnificent city, alive with history and containing some of the finest architecture to be found anywhere in England; next to London it is the most fashionable venue for the cream of society. The coach was driven along the course of streets between extensive buildings, sticking to the centre to avoid the steep camber at the sides, amidst the dash of carriages, rumbling carts and drays, and the shouts of vendors - noises that belonged to the winter pleasures of Bath.

Over the centuries many local figures designed developments to improve and enhance the city. The Royal Crescent is a perfect example of the Palladian style of architecture that took the country by storm during the eighteenth century. A magnificent sweep of thirty terraced three-storey-high houses with basement and wrought iron railings, each exactly the same, built in an arched street forming a grand and majestic facade, enhanced by the golden glow of the brickwork. Designed by John Wood in the 1760's, a design contrived to make individual houses appear as a single great long mansion.

The River Avon lends much charm to the city. Sir William Pulteney built an area on the east bank, which is the epicentre of upper-class living, dominated by grand residences along carefully arranged streets, avenues and parks. Pulteney Bridge, with its three picturesque arches was created by a young Scottish architect by the name of Robert Adam, constructed in the 1770's as a link from the development on the east side to the city centre on the west.

The healing properties of the springs were reputed to have been discovered around 300 BC by the father of the legendary King Lear, Prince Bladud, who, suffering from leprosy was banished from his own court and became a swineherd. One day he noticed that his pigs' skin diseases appeared improved and even cured by rolling in the mud and puddles created by the springs, so he decided to try it for himself. He was cured of his leprosy and returned to court, where he eventually became king.

It was the Romans, however, who first turned Bath into a famous spa town, constructing a number of grand buildings to house the baths. After the Romans left Britain, these magnificent structures were left to decay and only saw a revival in fortunes at the turn of the eighteenth century, when visited by Queen Anne, instantly becoming a fashionable attraction once more, drawing the rich and famous to take the waters.

There were three pumps in the city that collected water from the thermal springs through faults of rock below the surface of Bath. The buildings themselves remain an awe-inspiring sight, a complex design of pillars and walkways, with rooms for bathing and cooling off, and many other wonderful relics of the Roman era.

Amel took a regular dose of mineral water from the most favoured of the pump rooms, King's Bath, together with the gentry that assembled every morning between the hours of seven and ten, to drink the water whilst listening to the music playing. After a morning visiting the pump room, a promenade in Sydney Gardens followed, where tea and cakes were served to the accompaniment of a band, and the afternoons spent shopping, among the squares and crescents.

Bath had its own code of conduct, privileges and round of events. Cooks, ladies and gentlemen bargained in Bath's food markets that were the centre for gourmets in England, for Regional specialities such as sturgeon from the Severn estuary, turbot and sole, a splendid variety of cheeses, Scotch beef and Welsh mutton. Visitors initially came seeking the waters as a cure for various ailments… and to wash away their sins, but the city also offered an enormous array of fashionable shops. The three principal shopping streets being Bond Street, Milson Street and Bath Street, where elegant gowns, trimmings and the most exquisite of accessories were available in abundance.

Stores boasted the most excellent linen, the smoothest of silks and the most delicate lace from France and Italy, the finest of hosiery, shawls, bonnets and footwear, high quality china, superb Italian urns, vases and figurines of every description, elaborate gilt clocks, an extensive choice of dazzling jewellery, first-class stationery, perfumes, combs and brushes. And as one might guess, prices were astronomical. Amel bought Luke a gift of a superb walking stick, the top in the form of a hare's head carved in ivory.

They had not been there three days before they fell into the debauch of drinking that threw Luke into a relaxed, carefree mood, and although he had counted on staying away no more than a week at the most, decided to stay the two. The hotel was just the kind of hotel he enjoyed, with the dignity of a house with tradition, excellent food and drink, and the sort of fundamental peace that at times he feared had altogether vanished from the world, apart from in the countryside of course. And he had to admit, Amel was not only lovely, with her golden hair and vital charm, but was the most excellent companion. They had an exciting and immensely entertaining time.

There were two sets of Assembly rooms - the upper and the lower. Dancing was held in the main ballroom of the upper rooms, wonderfully illuminated by nine chandeliers of Whitefriars crystal, for those who wanted to dance or simply sit and watch or listen to the music. There was the addition of card playing available in the anteroom adjoining the ballroom. Also backgammon and anagrams were popular, but none of these superseded cards for an evening's diversion for the men.

A concert was held in Sydney Gardens on Tuesday evening, with fireworks afterwards. But the theatre was Amel's favourite entertainment. Luke secured a box for Saturday evening at the Theatre Royal near the abbey on Orchard Street. It had only opened in 1805, a most splendid theatre with its elegant, gold and crimson interior.

Bath, with its visitors from all walks of life was, also an irresistible target for the caricaturist's wit. George Cruikshank, a member of a family of highly successful caricaturists, made a good living from illustrating the foibles of fashionable life, selling his drawings, some of which included attacks on the royal family and leading politicians, to over twenty different print sellers. These prudish elements of society sometimes complained about the bawdy nature of some of illustrations.

His latest target had been the ill-fated Waldoff Huskisson, once Catherine Gurney's lover - the so-called Albanian Prince. Ill-fated because he had been apprehended for gambling debts incurred at the tables in London, debts which Catherine Gurney had refused to settle. He had been imprisoned for debts on two separate occasions before. The humiliation of this blow was no doubt a factor of his eventual suicide; he hung himself in prison.

Cruikshank's most recent target was Madame Duprez, stating in The Times newspaper that her beauty, elegance and wit were to be admired, but she lacked sense and had no principles. Illustrating her as a comical figure with very little on, but dripping in glittering jewels, with a line of well-dressed gentle-men, literary style, that exaggerated certain features and mannerisms for satirical effect, queuing up for her favours ...down on their bended knees, in a begging position, all holding a wad of bank notes in their hands.

Madame Duprez was an integral part of a wealthy society where privilege, arrogance and leisure flourished. This was a courtesan's natural background; if these things disappeared, particularly the wealth which leisure implies, the courtesan would be doomed, falling from fashion.

Amel Duprez was not rich in comparison with the company she kept, and could only just afford to sustain her role in society, a society that put so much emphasis upon status, where advancement was the motive for so many of the parties. She had borrowed money at a high rate of interest. The modifications to Burlington house and the furnishings, together with her collection of treasures, had come to well over twenty five thousand pounds. She was piling up debts she had no certainty of being able to settle. And yet, she thought nothing of buying vast objects abroad and arranging for them to be shipped back, to ornament her house. The new carriage alone had cost six hundred guineas.

Also, a fashionable lady needed numerous morning dresses, walking dresses, afternoon dresses, as well as evening gowns of various grandeur. One could not possibly wear the same garment again and again. Hats were obligatory and so were gloves, different for every possible permutation of the social scene. Then there were pelisses, opera cloaks, reticules, scarves and parasols, shoes, boots and dancing slippers.

Amel always went to the most fashionable and most expensive milliner of the day, spending much more than she could afford, thinking nothing of paying a hundred guineas on one evening gown alone. Of course, she refrained from giving her suppliers any idea of just how thinly she was stretched. They naturally assumed she had money and she let them assume so. If she abstained scrupulously from telling outright lies, she also abstained and equally as scrupulously, from revealing the complete truth about her affairs. The total cost of her debts was staggering, sums that meant nothing to her.

There was only one way to raise money. She had learned a few tricks over the years. Once you found out what a person wanted, all you had to do was provide a means by which they could get it. As simple as that! There were those who would gladly pay her any sum she named, enjoying her for a night or a season in circumstances of anonymity or in the full glare of publicity. But for that she needed time and right now time was the one thing she did not have. There were those who wanted their money now, right away, but she just did not have it.

Luke leaned back in the chair and relit his cigar, looking at her as if she had taken leave of her senses. Knowing him as well as she did, she gave him time to consider, not asking for an instant decision from him. She had a devilishly cunning way with him; an easy charm. He would eventually relent and she knew it, but not before he had had his say.

'Eight thousand pounds?' he repeated. 'You want me to loan you eight thousand pounds?' He drew on his cigar, removed it from his lips and slowly blew out the smoke before carrying on speaking. 'You can't be serious?'

Amel fluttered long, gold-tipped lashes. 'But I am serious.'

'But that's incredible, unbelievable.'

The love of money, which was with him a very

ruling propensity, and the gratification which it has received from habits of industry, sustained throughout a successful life, had taught him the value of sobriety during those seasons when a man's business requires him to keep possession of his senses.

Amel had been having a good ride at his expense and he knew it. She thought herself frugal and well-ordered about financial matters, but he knew differently; she was absolutely hopeless with money, wasteful and immensely extravagant. He felt that she was in some way making a fool of him and was tempted to get annoyed at this, but presently he realized that if he was a fool, then he was a self-made fool.

'I wouldn't loan you eight hundred, let alone eight thousand. I know for a fact you would gamble it away before the ink was dry on the bank draft. I also happen to know you have already borrowed all over town. And borrowed against the house.'

'Just how do you know that, Monsieur?'

'I have my means. You've not yet settled the bill for the carriage. There's still two hundred and eighty pounds owing on that alone, not to mention what you owe for the new lamps and fancy embossed door handles you recently had fitted. I'd say you are in debt to the tune of over thirty thousand. That's not counting what you owe the club.'

Her look was indignant. 'You've no right to check up on me. You are not my keeper.'

She could have bitten off her tongue the moment the words left her mouth. An open show of her annoyance would achieve nothing. It wouldn't do to vex him. She needed money desperately. She was unable to pay the trademens' bills.

As it was, Luke was willing to ignore her sharp words. She wanted money. He had it. As simple as that! He had her just where he wanted her, right in the palm of his hand. 'If I agree, how and when would you pay back the money?'

'I'll manage. I'd say you will have it back by the end of next month,' she said with confidence.

'That's optimistic!'

'You have my word on it.' It was, after all, only half a lie. She had other sources she could raise money. Rob Peter to pay Paul, so to speak.

'It will take more than that.' Her eyes met his, in a look of disappointment. 'All right, let's compromise! I'll loan you two thousand pounds, to be paid back by the end of next month...'

'But…'

He held up a hand to silence her. 'Let me finish. Besides loaning you the two thousand, I'm also willing to pay off the balance owing on the carriage and whatever you owe the club, but nothing more.'

'What I owe the club is the least of my worries. That can wait. They can go and whistle for their account.'

'Waldoff Huskisson said the very same thing and look what happened to him.'

Amel gave a slight shiver. 'Oh, it doesn't bear thinking about.' First Huskisson committing suicide, and then her friend and confident, Richard Parkes Bonington had died at the early age of twenty six. And then poor Rolley had a stroke and was now confined to a wheelchair. It was all too depressing.

'Gambling debts are sacrosanct and have to be paid at once. By the way, you won't be allowed any further credit at the tables,' Luke said, breaking in to her morbid thoughts.

Amel simply shrugged. What did it matter? There were other clubs.

'Accept the offer. It's a good one,' Luke encouraged.

'Unquestionably.'

'Two thousand pounds is not to be sneezed at.'

'But there's more of a jingle to guineas,' she suggested skilfully. 'I have not yet paid the servants' wages for the last quarter.'

He threw his head back and laughed. She drove a hard bargain, but she would pay for it …every penny. 'Only if you're incredibly grateful.'

'Have you ever known me to be anything but, Monsieur?'

'Then guineas it is.'

Her faint smile showed satisfaction. She went in to his arms. 'Merci, Mon amour,' she said sweetly, holding on to her feeling of triumph, glad to get any amount she could lay her hands on.

Debt was a way of life, a matter only of juggling credit.

FORTY-TWO

All thought of Amel Duprez fled while Luke sought in vain to discover the reason for his young wife's sudden change. He had the feeling that she could follow his moods, that her eyes could see him everywhere, as cat's eyes can see in darkness. That feeling had been with him, more or less, ever since their visit to London. When they came back she had altered.

It was curious the way she had unexpectedly and quite unreasonably rejected him. He had explained the chance meeting with Madame Duprez and had thought she accepted that it was purely coincidental, but to his infinite grief and surprise the gay, open-hearted girl was rapidly assuming the form of a gloomy, morose young woman, her manner abrupt and sometimes harsh. There was no hint of her former merriment and mischievousness, of her bold opinions, her rebellious behaviour or her impertinent curiosity. Whatever it was, her spirits had sunk and her temper soured. All sweetness and light had vanished from her eyes. Women were known to be capricious, but how could one be expected to know what was going on inside a woman's head?

He tapped lightly on her bedroom door, opened it and stepped inside. She was sitting in front of her dressing-table mirror, brushing her vibrant hair that lay in a coppery cloud about her proud head and shoulders. She had on a soft, gauzy thing, the colour of ripened wheat, trimmed at the edges and cuffs with wide ivory lace. His eyes narrowed speculatively, for she really looked quite splendid, and at once he forgave her the annoyance she had caused him in the last few days.

'Would it be reasonable to presume you are in a happier mood?'

Jessica turned on the stool and threw him a bitter look. Dear sweet Jesus, Luke and another woman! She could not bear to think of it. She would not think of it. But her mind had a will of its own and the pictures it showed her were cruel. Bitterness filled her. Desolation showed in the line of her jaw and the steeliness which shone from her usually kindly eyes.

'Hardly. You've destroyed whatever there was between us.'

'Hell's teeth! Not this again! Stop being so melodramatic,' he countered with irritation.

Luke's eyebrows dipped swiftly and ferociously into a frown, a look so familiar to her she felt her heart crack agonisingly against the wall of her chest, but she would make no apology for challenging him. He deserved none.

'What would you have me do? Fall into your arms and tell you of my undying love? I think I'm entitled to feel hurt. For months now I've been living with a stranger, not knowing what mood you're going to come home in. That's if you come home at all.'

'Please, spare me the tantrums. I've told you everything. I happened to run into Madame Duprez in that restaurant purely by chance. We were simply discussing the opera. I mentioned we had seen her in the theatre and told her how much you admired her hair. That's the truth,' he exclaimed with impatience.

'You wouldn't know the truth if it hit you in the

face. For your information, I happen to know you've seen *that woman* frequently and quite recently. Martha Roebling broke her neck to tell me. She couldn't wait to see my reaction. Naturally, I told her not to believe all that she hears. Didn't I do well, defending my husband like a good and dutiful wife?'

'I'm surprised you believed the likes of her. A gossiping acquaintance who indulges in scandal should be avoided as a pestilence.'

'At first I thought she had made the dreadful thing up, just to spite me for refusing her son, George. But then she asked me if I had seen the newspaper,' Jessica added after a short silence, in a voice that every moment became more charged with emotion.

'What newspaper?'

'The Times.' She stood up and walked across the rich, thick carpet to the occasional table, picked up a paper and practically threw it at him. 'Here, see for yourself. One thing is certain, the whole bloody neighbourhood knows about it now.' She pressed her lips tightly together in mute anger and cast fury filled looks at him.

Frowning with annoyance Luke stooped to retrieve the newspaper and glanced at the illustration of Amel Duprez as a comical figure. Even if her name hadn't been printed below, there was no mistaking just who it was meant to be. There she stood, larger than life, in a state of undress and covered from head to toe in glittering jewels, with a line of well-dressed gentle-man with exaggerated features, each clutching a wad of banknotes, waiting in line for her favours. The one at the very front of the queue, on bended knee, vaguely resembled him. Or was he imagining too wildly? As luck would have it, it was a ridiculously poor imitation, in his view.

He was astounded that John Walten, the owner of The Times and also one of Amel's ardent admirers, had allowed it to be printed in the first place. Of course, Walten himself was not on display to the public, to be made a laughing stock of. It would certainly create a stir amongst those who were.

'Just look at it! Grown men fighting over a whore like dogs over a bone. Can you imagine the humiliation I felt? Can you? No. I doubt it,' she cried hysterically, shaking her head from side to side.

'Calm yourself! You are doing yourself no good.'

But she would not be silenced. 'Calm myself! I don't want to bloody calm myself,' she screeched, out of control now, her fierce pride holding back the tears. 'I just had to look at the likeness to see it was you. Everything fell into place then. You've obviously been living two lives.'

A curtain fell across his dark eyes and his face became unreadable. 'This could be any number of men.'

She laughed without amusement. The gossips had not omitted to give her full information about her husband's activities. 'Oh, spare me your lies. I wasn't born yesterday.'

'Stop yelling at me.' Her passion for outspokenness was something with which he was all too familiar. He himself hated the whole conversation, but was keeping incredibly calm and cool.

'I can't help it. For weeks I've lived with the fear, praying it wasn't true, hoping the rumours would stop. No more whispers, no more innuendos or visits from that ...that gossiping old windbag. She couldn't stop crowing about it. When she's got something to crow about, the whole damn neighbourhood knows. Then, just yesterday morning, who should come calling but that …that Dent woman.'

'Dent woman?'

'You know very well what woman. You've met her often enough. She and Mr Pendle...'

'Oh, Elizabeth Dent! What could she possibly want here?'

'What do you think? She's never liked me. "Guess who has been seen having dinner with Madame Duprez in the Pulteney Hotel"…she said. "The very same hotel where Mr Pendle stays. And not just the once either, but three times in a week."'

'People are quick to jump to conclusions.'

'More lies! It just shows what our marriage is like. A marriage doomed by secrets and betrayal.'

'It's true, I saw Madame Duprez last week, but not for what you are thinking.'

Jessica's eyes narrowed. 'When have you ever been interested in what I might be thinking?'

'She's gone to Montmartre,' he continued, ignoring the sarcasm.

'Montmartre?'

'Paris.'

'I know where Montmartre is. I'm not as stupid as you seem to think,' she said, with a bluntness she had inherited from her father.

'I've never thought you stupid. And as for Madame Duprez, I saw her for the last time to bid her bon-voyage,' he answered guardedly.

'Huh! Always the perfect gentleman, presenting the best side without showing the real you,' Jessica sneered. 'It must have been a long farewell from what I've been told. You were seen leaving together.'

'We might have left at the same time, but not together. I meant what I said. It's over!'

'If only I could believe you, it might make a difference. There was a time you could make me believe black was white, but not anymore. You've told too many lies. Truth to you is no more than a mouthful of bloody words.'

'You're using bad language again.'

'I have good reason, don't you think?' she cried, her eyes glinting dangerously. 'To think I've defended you and ...and all the time you've been deceiving me, cheating on me, sleeping with that ...that *whore.*'

The very notion of him, her own husband, the love her heart beat for, offering that exclusive intimacy to another as well, doing to some other that which he did to her in the privacy of the bedroom, contaminating what had been so sweet and pure, was too appalling, too earth-shattering to contemplate.

'If, when you see her next ... tell her she can damn well have you, for all I care.'

With a look of weariness he laid his hand over hers. 'Now, you know you don't mean that, Jessica.'

She snatched her hand away. 'I damn well do!' she screeched, seeing no reason to curb her inclination to curse when she felt like it. 'Oh, you've been so damn smug with my love of you, haven't you?' She waited to hear a denial, but none came.

'So, what do you want to do?' he asked resignedly.

'What do I want to do?' she cried, white faced and trembling, probing herself in the chest. 'What do I want to do?' she repeated, on the edge of hysterics. 'You have an affair and I'm left with the choice of ...of forgetting about it or ...or living alone for the rest of my life?'

Her husband, who had submitted to her cross-questioning with a sort of contemptuous composure, as though he were humouring an unreasonable child, suddenly turned on her with a look of antagonism. 'Oh, for goodness sake, stop dramatizing,' he said in a clipped, furious tone, raising his hands in a frustrating gesture. He wished she would stop her forever-prattling tongue. 'I didn't have to tell you anything, but you just couldn't leave it alone, could you? I've closed the door, forgotten it! But not you! You have to dwell on it. Indulge yourself. I'll be glad to get away again if all I am to get here is hostility.'

'No gladder than I'll be.' Her lips twisted with bitterness. 'Do you know, you're so weak. I never expected to get through a lifetime without you ever touching another woman, but …but caring for her, doing with her what you …what we do together, is something I can never forgive.' She was shaking with emotion now.

'That's enough! Why are you behaving like this? I had an admiration for her, but no thought beyond. Nothing at all.'

'Is that supposed to make me feel better? Just leave me alone. Go! Get out of my room.'

'Your room! You'd do well to remember just whose house this is.'

'Oh, I know whose house this is. You've hardly let me bloody forget it.'

He threw up his arms in frustration. He had been genuinely concerned for her after the tragic loss of her father, and during the last few weeks of their estrangement, but he did not like being spoken to like this. 'Why must you always exaggerate about everything? Blow things up out of all proportion? Pull yourself together. Deal with it. And I'd advise...'

She cut him off there. 'I don't want your damn advice. At this point I wouldn't care if someone cut your bloody heart out, if they could find it, that is,' she cried with fierce hostility. 'In fact, I sometimes doubt whether you ever had a heart at all. You've never cared for anyone but yourself.'

'I said ...that's enough!' he bellowed. He had had enough. It had to stop right there.

But Jessica wouldn't be warned and couldn't be stopped. 'I will *never*...*ever* forgive you for this.'

'I admit what I did was wrong. I only lied because I didn't want you to turn against me. Now I've told you the truth you're shutting me out.'

'You're damned right I'm shutting you out. Sleep where you bloody well want, but not next to me.'

'Do I have to remind you of your duty?' he asked between gritted teeth.

She stuck out her chin and pursed her lips, and then did the unforgivable ...she deliberately turned her back on him, knowing full well it would infuriate him even more.

'Don't you dare turn your back on me. It would be a grave error on your part if...'

'Oh ...go to hell,' she screeched, cutting him short.

'What did you say?' he asked fiercely.

'I said ...go to hell,' she repeated, her tone biting.

'You dare to speak to me this way?' he yelled.

His voice could be heard throughout the house. Cook and the maids stopped what they were doing and froze in their tracks.

Jessica swung round to face him, her heart thumping wildly. She tossed her head, her stare ice-cold. 'Yes ... I dare,' she hissed with infinite loathing. 'All my life I've been taught things like dignity and principles ... believing in them. But just what kind of principles does a man who cheats on his wife have? You ...you bastard!'

'Guard your tongue, Madam!' His rage was out of control now. He lifted a hand threateningly in her direction, forming a fist and for a moment she thought he was going to strike her.

She flinched involuntarily, steeling herself to receive the onslaught he was about to inflict, but he breathed in deeply and lowered it again, his fist still tightly clenched and his lips that had snarled in temper, folded into a rigid line of restraint. He spoke through them as though they were stuck together.

'You best watch what you say to this bastard, since he's the one who keeps you in the style in which you've become accustomed. Just remember, there's nothing ...nothing you possess that I can't take away.'

This was met with a steely refusal to be beaten down. Jessica stood her ground, with hands on hips. 'Oh ...do whatever you damn well please. I don't care anymore.'

The bedroom door opened then banged shut after him.

'I don't bloody care. Do you hear?' she screamed after him. 'I don't bloody care.'

Desolation flowed over her. She could not bear the pain, the misery, truth in all its rugged harshness. The avalanche of her emotions drove her towards the great double bed where she thrust her face in to the pillow, pressing it to her mouth to still the terrible sound of her weeping.

In the kitchen Mrs Osborne and Cook both stopped what they were doing and looked up as they heard him bellowing.

'Mrs Osborne …Mrs Osborne.'

'Well, I never! What's all that about, I wonder?' Dora Osborne mumbled half to herself, as she practically flew out the door. She was back within seconds.

'He wants dinner served in his study,' she told cook. 'Maggie can serve him. I'll send her t'you when I find her. I don't know where that girl could've got to.'

'Making herself scarce I shouldn't wonder,' was cook's reply. 'Look in the dining room.'

'I don't need you t'tell me where t'look, thank you very much. I'll send her t'you, then I'll go up t'see if the mistress needs anything.' She knew the mistress hadn't been herself since returning from London and wondered what could be wrong.

More like to find out what all the shouting was about, thought Cook, as she picked up the heavy pan, the silence of the kitchen broken by her placing it noisily on the stove to start heating the soup right away. It wouldn't do to keep the master waiting, the mood he was in.

FORTY-THREE

'Women! Their styles may change, but their designs remain the same,' Luke said with a sigh. 'I'll never understand them. There are those who work so hard at making a good husband that they never quite manage to make a good wife.'

Justin Courtenay put out his cigar and glanced at Luke sideways. 'The measure of a man's real character is what he might do if he knew he would never be found out. Now Jessica has discovered your secret, what does she say?'

'She says whatever I want her to say. There would be no point in her arguing. The only choice a woman should have is whether to have the lamp on or not.'

'Obviously, success in marriage is much more than just finding the right person. She won't be the first to turn a blind eye to her husband's infidelity in order to stay together. It happens the whole world over. Evidently scruples and being rich doesn't mix... in your case.'

'I see no fault in committing that which you yourself have surely committed at some time or other,' Luke said in his own defense.

'Entertaining more than one woman, you mean?' Justin asked.

'If you want to call it that.'

Justin chuckled. 'That I cannot deny, but there is a difference, my friend.'

'In what way?'

'I'm not a married man, therefore am free to do as

I please. Marriage is a serious commitment, hard enough to make work without adding problems to it.'

Justin Courtenay had known and loved many women, but was able to erase from his memory the relics of past affairs, the frustration of multiple farewells, the jealousies, deceptions and disasters of other relation-ships, giving himself without guilt to his next brief passion. His experience had not come from pathetic embraces with squalid whores. He prided himself on never having had to pay for pleasure because women of varied station, from the humble chambermaid to the arrogant countess, gave themselves to him un-conditionally.

'Just whose side are you on?' Luke asked.

Justin held up his hands. 'I make it a rule never to take sides, my friend.'

'Then tell me where is it written that a man must lay with only the one woman all his lifetime?'

'It isn't as far as I know. But the only problem with that is one must be absolutely certain one's brain is completely alert before engaging one's mouth. It must be very embarrassing to be caught out. The only way to settle a disagreement is on the basis of what's right, not who's right. Nonchalance, my friend, is the ability to look like an owl when you've acted like a jackass.'

'The bonds of matrimony are not worth much unless the interest is kept up. Pleasure is like a poppy. You seize the flower and the bloom is shed. It's much more exciting making love to someone you're not married to. Especially someone with no inhibitions.'

'I've no doubt it is. But tell me, how did Jessica really take it?'

'Oh, she was just hurt at first, but things have got much worse. She's been quite impossible of late. A real bitch in fact.'

'How can you speak of her like this? You are the one who's been selfish.'

'All men are selfish. Nature did that for us.'

'True, but surely, if you are the one in the wrong you should make the first move? Clinch the argument by taking your wife in your arms?'

'This is more than just an argument. Besides, your compassion is misguided. She's the one who closed the bedroom door in my face. I don't know why she's behaving like this. It doesn't achieve anything.'

'You can hardly blame her, Luke. With all due respects, if you make a mess on your own doorstep, you are bound to slip on it.'

'Oh, she'll get over it soon enough. She's resilient, strong. And in the meantime, if one won't the other one will.'

'Personally, I think you're making a big mistake, jeopardizing your marriage over a scandalous liaison with the likes of Madame Duprez. All you are to her is a means to obtain money. By all means, have your affair until it's over, but don't destroy what could last the rest of your life.'

'Do you think this is any ordinary affair? It's more than that. I've never known a woman with greater or more pleasing a talent. I must add that I've never seen a woman behave so outrageous either, like the heart-less whore that she is, but quite fascinating, irresistible for all that. People are afraid of the rawness of passion. They sugar coat it by calling it love. Have you never felt real overpowering passion?'

'Of course I have! But eventually it wears off.'

'Contrary to popular belief, everything in life doesn't come to a clear-cut conclusion. Life is barely long enough for a man to fully understand women.'

Justin took out a cigar case from his pocket, selected a cigar and snapped the case shut. He lit it and placed it between his lips, drew on it then turned his head away, releasing the smoke. 'In my experience it doesn't do much good to worry about why a woman does what she does. Women are a whole different breed than us men. They don't think like us. They seem to have a whole other language. And they've all these rules that they don't tell you about until after you've broken them.'

'The man who does understand women is qualified to understand pretty well everything I shouldn't wonder,' Luke replied. 'How does that saying go? The one about a woman worrying about the future?'

'A woman worries about the future until she begets a husband, while a man never worries about the future until he begets a wife. Is that the one?'

Luke grinned. 'Yes! That's the one.'

'You're right there, my friend. Women are necessary evils. We can't live with them and we can't live without them. As far as Jessica's concerned, sit tight, wait it out. You knew she was an independent, strong-minded woman when you married her.'

'Oh, she'll come round. She always does.'

That was the last Luke was to see of his good friend, Justin Courtenay - alive. Two weeks later he was struck down by an epileptic fit, which left him speechless and suffering from dizziness in the head and spasms in the chest. Three days after the first fit, he was seized with a second and fell into a comatose sleep. He died four days later without ever regaining consciousness, aged thirty-nine years.

FORTY-FOUR

Jessica was impassive now, dry-eyed and silent in her self-induced calm; rigid of mind and body. She took her time to bathe and dress, coming down to breakfast late, hoping that Luke had already left the house. She selected a closely fitted morning dress of soft, ivory cashmere, with a small collar of white muslin, its sleeves short at the wrist to display the full puff of muslin around each hand. It had a row of gimp embroidery on the collar and at the hem of the skirt. She entered the dining room to find her husband still sitting in his usual place, at one end of the long table.

'Ah, here you are, my pet. How are you feeling? I take it you've fully recovered?' he asked and then, before she could answer the questions, he added another. 'I thought perhaps you might care to accompany me to London? Spend a few days seeing more of the sights. What do you say?'

The maid's knock kept them both silent. 'Shalla fetch fresh toast, Madam?' Maggie asked timidly.

The atmosphere could be sliced with a knife.

'No thank you, Maggie. I'll just take tea.'

Luke turned his gaze on the uneasy maid. 'That'll be all for now. You can go.'

Maggie curtsied. 'Thank you, Sir ... Madam.'

'Thank you, Maggie,' Jessica said quietly. She didn't speak at once, but sipped the tea while watching him.

'Are you going to say something or am I to get the silent treatment?' Luke asked patiently. 'There's nothing to be gained by sulking.'

She would always readily forgive the hurt he inflicted and all would be well again, but not this time. She sat there all rigid with bitterness and indignation, looking at him as if he had grown horns and a tail. 'It's far too early to look upon the devil, let alone speak to him.'

He threw his head back and laughed, deep and loud. Those busy in the kitchen stopped what they were doing and looked at each other, giving a sigh of relief. Surely, the master laughing like that must mean the terrible quarrel he and the young mistress had had was over and done with?

'You certainly have a way with words, my pet.'

Her anger could not be stemmed. 'Laugh all you want. There'll be no laughter in hell.'

'That's the spirit! You sound more like your old self.'

'I've always been myself underneath, even when I've been trying to be as you want me to be. You've spoilt everything between us. All I have left is my memories.'

'You really are a sweet, silly creature,' he said with a wicked grin. 'Such a romantic.'

'Can we put an end to this charade? The truth is, you would like to be rid of me, wouldn't you?'

'Now, you must stop this. You're not in command of your senses,' he said, scolding her like a child. 'I'm concerned for your health. You look quite worn out.'

'I'm no longer the naïve, trusting girl you married. You're just going to have to deal with this bitch that has taken her place.'

A draught of cold blew right between them and his

light-hearted mood abruptly changed, his features assuming their usual impenetrable arrogance. 'I'm getting more than a little tired of your attitude. Why can't you get past this? For your own peace of mind, let's pass the peace-pipe and have done with it.'

But so tormented was she, Jessica could not stop. She felt sick to her soul at the thought of him in another woman's bed. 'I know you want rid of me so you can have that ... that *whore* here,' she cried, her jaw clenching.

All of a sudden he clamped his hand down hard on the table, making the cutlery dance and Jessica wince. His voice cracked like a whip. 'Just shut up!'

But all she could think about was his betrayal and the lies, which had trampled and crushed out the very thing that her heart had ached for. It was eating away at her mind, turning it into a breeding ground of paranoia. What blindness! To think she had worshipped him. She wanted to hurt him, just as he had hurt her. If she could turn her love into contempt, how much simpler it would be to cut him out of her life. Then, instead of loving him she could treat him with indifference.

'I wouldn't care if I never saw your evil face again as long as I live,' she said with contempt, torn by a raging conflict of emotions.

That made him dangerously bad-tempered. 'Be careful what you say, you vain little fool,' he warned, his voice icy cold.

She looked so wretched, so miserable that he felt sudden regret for losing his temper and for having been so insensitive to her feelings. He might have asked her pardon, but the next words she uttered changed all that.

'Do you know what you make me feel inside? Revulsion.'

'You'll get over it,' he said briskly, the moment of regret gone.

His temper could be ugly. Jessica would be wise not to test it too far, his expression said. He would not be spoken to like this. By God, he wouldn't, especially as he had been doing his best to let her see that he was willing, eager even, if he was honest, to resume the pleasant relationship they had known before she found out about Amel. But she would have none of it, her ice-cold, narrowed eyes, cat-like and dangerous, told him so.

'I shall go and stay with your mother and Dorothy.'

'Not without my say so, you won't!'

'Why? Are you afraid I might learn something about you that I don't already know? Some other dark secret you have hidden?'

She had made the mistake of asking him that very question once before and his reaction had been aggressive, to say the least and she had never dared ask again. He was unnaturally silent upon the past that related to his mother and Dorothy Hawell. She wondered for the umpteenth time just what had happened to set him against the women, one his very own mother.

'I don't owe you anything. Least of all, explanations,' he said abruptly. 'I'm not in the habit of accounting for my actions to anyone.'

'Of course, you're right. I tend to forget, I'm just part of the household. One of the servants, at your beck and call.'

He got to his feet and thumped his hand down

hard on the table, which caused her to flinch. 'Oh ...for heaven's sake! All this hysteria.' He was so irate he could hardly mouth the words.

'If you're so obsessed with this ... this *whore*, why don't you damn well go back to her for another helping and leave me in peace?' she jeered, finishing on a defiant note. She just could not help herself. 'Don't let a silly little thing like marriage stand in your way.'

'I might just do that, if I so choose,' he said cruelly.

His face was expressionless and his dark eyes told her nothing of what he felt. She could scarcely believe what he said next.

'Besides, divorce is out of the question. I might appear well off in your eyes, but divorce can only be obtained by the extremely wealthy, and even then, requires an Act of Parliament.'

Then, turning on his heel, with his composure held tightly about him, he strode from the room.

FORTY-FIVE

Faults are thick when love is spread so thin. The discovering of his indiscretions had triggered off in his young wife a sudden bewildering change. She was in a condition of high nervous tension. Overwrought, as he termed it. Both were to blame for the disagreements that followed. Both were stubborn, both obstinate. Talk, what little talk there was, was of trivial things, to avoid any further arguments. The spontaneous laughter that used to bubble between them was now replaced with oppressive tension. They would sit in silence and if he spoke at all, it was usually some criticism, and then, he would simply get up and depart before she had time to respond. An appointment - a business meeting - always something to take him away from her, leaving her baffled and fractious. So many times she had wanted to reach out to touch him and yet could not; an impenetrable wall seemed to have risen up between them.

It was curious that instead of becoming tearful and more clinging, as he had expected, she suddenly and quite unreasonably shut him out, pushing him away, rejecting him; she who needed to love and cosset. But her refusal only served to arouse his longing. What point was there in building one's life, stone upon stone until the edifice was sound, if there was no one to carry it on?

Isolated in his own thoughts and broodings, he felt a strong need to feel warm arms about him, welcoming and comforting. He was a man of avid appetites to the desires which addicted his life, the most obsessive of which was that for his mistress's body, but not having the means to quench that hunger drove him for relief to the next person. By God, he would not be rejected tonight. He had been patient with her, realising how one crushing blow after another had devastated her, but really, they couldn't go on like this for much longer.

Somehow, he must break through this carapace she had erected about herself to shut out the pain and sense of betrayal into which, first her father's death and then his own infidelity, had flung her. He would not be denied what he wanted, needed, that which he believed to be rightfully his. He had been used for most of his adult life, to his own way and could be perilous when it was blocked. A son is what he needed, a child for whom all this planning and work would make sense. If she needed to be reminded of it, and of his mastery over her, then he was perfectly willing to refresh her memory. She would bend to his will, fulfill her obligation to him, or he would break her to it, toss her on the bed and put her to the use she was intended for.

He climbed the stairs and went quietly into his dressing room where he stripped off his clothes and lowered himself into the waiting warm bath. It was about fifteen minutes later that he slipped into a quilted dressing gown of burgundy brocade, with a twisted gold belt and edging that reached right down to his ankles. Padding barefooted across the passage-way to her bedroom, he found the door locked against him.

'Jessica, unlock this door.' He waited as patiently as was in his nature.

'Go away. I want to be alone.'

'Open the damn door,' he bellowed like an enraged bull, after only a few moments, rattling the doorknob fiercely. 'I said open the damn door.'

His voice carried to the far corners of the house, and into the yard where Ned Miles, and Tom Saunders, who was giving the old man a hand sawing the wood and chopping logs, both lifted their heads and stared at one another in silent amazement.

Luke heard the key turn in the lock. Gripping the handle he pushed the door wide and strode into the room. She had lost none of her defiance. She swept back her glorious cloak of hair that hung loosely about her shoulders, turning to look at him with eyes narrowed and flashing, her face flushed with indignation. The tension in her crackled like a living thing.

Luke eyed her appreciatively, his expression softening, but he did not move. She was always at her best when in a temper and yet quite unconscious of the full brilliance of her loveliness. In fact, she looked quite magnificent in a shimmering silk, ivory wrap with wide sleeves that fell back to expose white ruffled lace at her wrists, the tantalizing roundness of her breasts crowned with the sweetest buds of beauty; a splendid parade of feminine charm. He felt a strong stirring in the pit of his stomach, a perpetual strain that nature imposed on him.

'Very presentable. Very presentable indeed,' he said approvingly.

Something in his manner gave him away at once. Nothing was more calculated to inhibit all desire for a union in a sensitive wife than the pre-knowledge of what her husband wants. He only came to her room when he had some demand to make upon her, using her as a passive instrument for his needs, making her that and nothing more. Those thoughts were so depressing, so bitter to one who had other causes of complaint, serving only to increase the damage already done. Was she a toy to be set in motion just as her master chose? Had she no say on the matter? Had she no choice? Since the trauma of the miscarriage she had felt no true urgency for physical contact; it was as if that part of herself was in profound, permanent slumber. The dread of finding herself in that condition again was stronger than the impulses of youth. Besides, he had put her through hell and back by his betrayal.

Jessica faced him rebelliously, with hands placed on her narrow hips, but deep inside she was secretly afraid, without a precise notion of why. 'I'm not looking for company tonight,' she said as steadily as she could, willing her voice not to waver.

Luke came to stand in front of her, gently tracing the contours of her face with the very tips of his fingers, her jaw, then her neck; signs of amorous intentions. There was a light of faint wonder in his eyes, as he spoke. 'But I am, my pet. And you'll do nicely.'

Something in her wanted to upset that poise, that certainty of self, and when he took her hand in his to touch it with his lips, she snatched it away and turned her back on him as though she was no longer concerned with his trivial tyranny. 'Well, I'm not!'

It was a rebuff so cutting his mouth whitened. All of a sudden, his hands were on her shoulders, gripping them brutally and spinning her round. Pure cold, murderous cruelty shone in those dark eyes and reddened his face.

'Never … never turn away from me again, do you hear, or I'll make damn sure you regret it,' he warned her fiercely as he released his hold. Seeing him with the mask of good manners and courtesy torn away made her shiver. 'It would be in everyone's best interest if you were to be more agreeable tonight.'

'Everyone, meaning you, of course?' she scoffed audaciously.

'Let's put it another way. Inject a little reminder. If I remember rightly, the agreement was, I provided you with a country house and showered you with everything your little heart desires. Your idea of Heaven, you said, and you in return would present me with a son. Well, my pet, I've shown you what Heaven's like, albeit there are no golden stairways or silver clouds. That's just a figment of your imagination, I fear. You were put on this earth for one thing, one thing only. To breed. There never was a more utterly idle and nonsensical creature in the world than a childless woman.'

There was mockery in his tone and the look he gave her was as if he saw her as a doll tricked out in garments, labelled soulless. He was so self-assured, completely certain in his muscular world that he would have his own way, arrogantly believing that it was a wife's duty to do as her husband wanted.

Jessica's spirit revolted with such turbulence and the blood so throbbed in her that she could hardly stand still. How dare he think of her like that, a nothing, a bundle of soulless sensuality to be used? It was he who was the soulless one, the cold, godless one, who, in his sickening superiority thought he could use her!

'You have had more than enough time to recover from your ordeal. Your health has returned and the time has come for you to keep your side of the bargain. You have taken all and given nothing. It is time now to pay the piper. And for this, I require complete surrender.'

He seemed more than just a little affronted that she only presented her cheek to receive his kiss, a mistake that he immediately corrected by taking hold of a handful of her glorious hair and forcing her head round, pressing his lips down brutally hard on hers, bruising them. She moaned in objection in the back of her throat, managing to bite down spitefully on his lip, drawing blood. He released her abruptly, his face twisting with rage. His hand went to his lip, examining the blood on his fingertips.

'If you want it rough, then I'll give you rough.' His fierce, knife-edged anger rippled across the room.

Jessica flinched involuntary at his malicious words. Leaving her just long enough for him to fasten the door on the inside, he returned with doubled eagerness to his prey. When he lent toward her she strained away from him, averting her face.

'Please ...I don't feel up to it,' she implored.

'It's not open to discussion, my pet.'

He pulled her to him, but she refused to give in and struggled to break free, which unleashed the rapacity and ruthlessness in him that had been waiting to emerge. He was unable to accept defeat in any form.

It all happened so swiftly. He began to lose control, showing her a side of him she had never seen before, a peculiarity of taste he had, a streak of cruelty. She fought him, hammering with clenched fists on his chest, almost taking him off his feet. He was amazed at how strong she was. But she was no match for him; she had no defense against his male superior strength.

Everyone has his sadistic streak and nothing brings it out more than in the knowledge that you've got someone at your mercy. A little squeal of fright escaped her lips as he sprang back at her and was upon her, his dressing gown flying open in the struggle, revealing his nakedness beneath.

His face carved in lines of brutality, as he panted and cursed, holding her in a steel grip she could not break.

'Bitch!' he hissed.

'Bastard!' she returned just as severely.

'Surrender!'

'Never!' Her answer was fierce. 'I …I'll scream.'

'Sometimes I have … have that effect on women,' he replied breathlessly, with an evil grin on his lips. 'You remind me of a horse I once had. A magnificent creature, stubborn and …and spirited. A lot like you. Just needed to be …be broken.'

Jessica seethed inwardly, her face flushing with righteous anger 'And you remind me of …of the devil.'

Desperate times call for desperate measures. Seizing one of her hands he brought it to his pride of nature, already grown to a prodigious stiffness, rock-hard and grandly erect, a column of white ivory, demanding of her what it meant to have. She snatched her hand away as if it had been burnt, fighting him like a wildcat, but she had not a chance. She was fully at his mercy. A sudden fit of trembling seized her and she began to sob uncontrollably.

'Don't ...please don't do this,' she cried frantically, as they wrestled.

Luke slapped her hard across the face then, twice, viciously and accurately, his palm first against one side, then the back of his hand to the other, hard, so that her neck muscles wrenched in agony as her head whipped from side to side, spreading heat like a scald across her cheeks, the shock quietening her.

He didn't want to hurt her but it was the best thing to do in view of the fact she was becoming hysterical. She was dazed for a moment, Luke's maddened figure whirling round and round in a blurred circle. Then, as it cleared, without hesitation her nails reached for his eyes, like claws of an enraged wild cat. He saw them coming and strained back from the attack, his hands locking about her wrists, and with the ferocious strength of his rage flung her onto the bed.

Her nightgown was suddenly up above her waist. With all the means at the disposal of an animal that had been forced into a corner, she defended herself to the very last, refusing to unlock the twist of her thighs, still pleading with him to leave her alone, insisting she was not well. But he was beyond any consideration for her female weakness that struggled against him. Ignoring her pleas he shoved his knee cruelly between her clamped thighs, forcing them roughly apart, his male strength dominating her.

Jessica was innocent in the ways of the world, having no knowledge of the terrors of sexual abuse, the dark side of pleasure, but was about to find out. There were no tender, whispered intimacies, not the least grain of gentle persuasion, none of the sweet glory of active delight that crowns the enjoyments of passion when two bodies tenderly unite.

To her utter horror, he took hold of her legs, gripping them like a vice and in pure wantonness kept them stretched wide apart. She grew rigid, her shock genuine as she felt the forced, painful insertion, thrusting unmercifully at the most tender part of her body - making his entry triumphantly, taking away her very breath. She wanted to scream, but instead gritted her teeth, afraid of being heard by the servants and of the humiliation it would bring.

Trapped in the morass of passion with no link to reality, no longer his own master but caught up in a tornado of madness, the need to possess, he snorted with lust as he exerted himself with a kind of fierce rage. Impotent to all restraint, his thrusts became more and more furious, cruel and merciless, crushing and almost suffocating her, jolting her body with the very force of it, putting her through the most intolerable pain in this hideous orgy of agony.

All her resolution deserted her, as pain put her beyond all regard of being overheard. Only then, wide-eyed with shock, did she scream out just as he gave one last violent plunge, taking away what little breath she had left, followed by a long agonising shudder, drowning himself in sheer pleasure and cooling the fever in his blood; then he collapsed on top of her. At once the tension of his whole body relaxed and his muscles fell into gentle, easy attitudes of languorous content. In a few moments he was sleeping like a child.

Tick tock. Tick tock. The clock ticked away in the silence of the room where she lay recovering from what had been a battle, brutal rape, exhausted and trembling in every limb through the force of it, with the taste of blood in her mouth where she had bitten her lip. She was dry-eyed and broken-hearted, but finally she gave herself up to the arms of blessed sleep.

Jessica awoke first. Observing her husband sleeping by her side, she carefully disengaged herself from his outstretched arm spreading across her chest, scarcely daring to breathe for fear she might waken him by the motion. She pulled back the covers with great care, displaying his nakedness ... and *that - that* which she could not without some remains of fear, fix her eyes upon. That which was no longer an instrument of love, a thing of delight, but that which had, with fury, torn the most tender part of her body which had not yet done smarting from the effects of its rage. With the supple softness of its shaft shrunk into his body, above the sprout of dark hair, it looked to all appearance, incapable of the mischief and brutal cruelty it had committed.

She shuddered with distaste. Shame kept sweeping through her; shame and rage. It was strange that she had felt no shame in their lovemaking before, but things had changed. How different things seemed. What could be worse than this? She felt used, humiliated, violated. How dare he? A woman should have domain over her own body. But she knew he dared because her body and person was no longer her own property. She belonged to him and therefore, since she was his possession he could do as he pleased with her, and there was nothing, nothing at all, she could do about it. That thought was more than she could bear. She was a woman trapped and sinking, knowing not where to turn, what to do, where to look for help or counsel.

Jessica had covered the bruising to her cheeks as best she could, with a dab of light powder and by wearing her hair loose about her face. Aching and in shock, she sat motionless, her spirit drained of life. The languid chill of her eyes turned upon the cruel object: the man who had satisfied his carnal urges, yet had subjected her to so much pain and humiliation.

'You once said you would never force me,' she said at last, burningly flushing with her present feelings as much as with shame.

'That was before you become my property.' He sounded cool and unconcerned, as if nothing unusual had happened.

'Indecent assault. That's what it was.'

'I think not! A husband has the right under common law to correct his own wife by chastisement.'

'Just what a man would say.'

He grinned. 'I am a man, my pet.'

'There is such a thing as decency,' she said sullenly. 'And I'll thank you not to call me your pet. I am not your anything.'

'You will be what I want you to be. And for Heaven's sake, pull yourself together. Where's your taste for excitement?'

'I cannot surrender myself to things as you do.'

Ice cold eyes fixed on her. 'Well, you best get used to it. You've had it far too easy and don't even know it. I have allowed you far more freedom than most husbands allow their wives,' he answered quietly, his voice calm but authoritative.

'You mean you actually have a conscience? Your guilt was so strong you allowed me to do as I please, allowed me to roam the fells? How noble of you,' she scorned.

'You can think what you like. But I have something to say and I want you to listen, because I'm only going to say this the once. These constant rows must stop. And you must remember your duty. As long as you live in my house and sit at my table, you are subject to my will.' His voice was cold and arrogant, sending a prickling sensation over her flesh and making her shudder.

She was looking at him with a startled air of confusion which trembled on her face and he did his best to appear unconcerned.

'In future, I expect you to make yourself readily available whenever the mood suits me. It is a wife's duty to concur with her husband's wishes at all times. That is your function in life and you must accept it. That's all I have to say on the matter. Consider yourself warned.'

Each day was as bad as the last. There was no gladness in her heart, nor any pretence of it, only a tired realisation that it was futile to struggle against what must be her fate in life. Never did he attempt to mend matters. Every sound of that slow, smooth step as he came to her door seemed to strike her heart like a tread of doom.

Under subjection to those arbitrary tastes that now ruled his appetite for pleasure with an uncountable control, he came to her again and again, taking her by force, placing her in all variety of postures imaginable. Abusing her in so unworthy a manner it stripped her of all remains of bashfulness and modesty. Sometimes standing against the bedroom wall, with her petticoats up, going to work with an impetuosity and eagerness bred very likely by changing his system of battery.

Sometimes leading her to the bed like a victim led to sacrifice, stripping her stark naked whilst saying the most incredibly cruel things, humbling her, diminishing her sense of worth, his so-called love-making taking on a bizarre unnatural course that seemed to give him an added physical delight. His hand entwined in her lustrous hair, painfully forcing her head back, the other gripping her fiercely by the thigh - liking to a dog mounting a bitch - pounding away at her body, heaping every indignity upon her, violating the very laws of decency, leaving her bruised and traumatized. It was abnormal.

In a few minutes he was in condition for renewing the onset, scarcely giving her breathing time from the last barbaric attack, driving the same course as before, treating her no better than a common whore, with unabated fervour, as she lay beneath him with her face averted. So detached was she from the whole procedure, it was as if she did not exist. Such were the rewards of love.

FORTY-SIX

Jessica felt sick at heart. She was caught up in circumstances she did not understand and could not control. She lived in a fine house, had money enough for whatever she might need, and yet no longer led the charmed life, married to her knight in shining armour. The man she had married was holding her happiness in the palm of his hand.

After every assault she was left shattered in both mind and body, wakeful and nerve-racked, so on edge that hours would escape before she could sleep, often remaining awake the whole of the night. In the cold light of day she struggled to calm her anguish, putting on a brave face, but so wretchedly unhappy was she, locked fast in a nightmare from which there was no escape, the pain of it tore at her vulnerable, loving heart. She spoke to no one but Dora and was scarcely to be seen. Gone was the ignorant, love-struck girl who in her naivety had imagined being loved in return. In her place was a woman who had no dreams, no illusions.

Mornings, she waited until he left the house before going down to breakfast. Not that she was eating enough to keep body and soul together. Dora was that worried about her. She could not fail to notice there was something badly wrong with the young mistress. Dark circles shadowed her eyes, evidence of her pain.

Dora smiled at her with affection. She felt anxiety grow at the fraught state into which the young mistress had fallen. She had always been such a cheerful, light-hearted soul. As for the master, she had a fair idea what had caused all the friction in the first place. But discretion was too ingrained for her to speak aloud any suspicions she might harbour.

'How do you feel?'

'Much better, thank you, Dora,' Jessica replied, in barely a whisper.

'I don't know how t'say this.'

'What? What could he do to me that he's not already done?'

Dora told her the ill tidings that he had gone - indefinitely.

'That's so damn predictable of him.' Jessica's voice shook with emotion. He had humiliated her even further by leaving her as easily as he had gained her. That fact rendered her inconsolable. 'I'm so unhappy, Dora.'

'I know he's difficult.'

'Difficult! You …you've no idea...' Jessica trailed off, too ashamed to speak of what had taken place.

'Oh, I've a fair idea what he's been putting you through,' Dora said sympathetically.

'I just don't know him anymore. He's a monster.' Jessica's mouth sagged and her brow crumpled as she burst into tears, hiding her face behind trembling hands and shaking with racking sobs.

'Oh, my dear! Don't let him distress you. He seems t'have the same streak his father had.'

Jessica took a deep breath to steady herself, wiping her eyes with a delicate, lace handkerchief. 'Did …did you know his father?'

'Yes. It was my misfortune t'know him. A vicious, cruel man he was. Treated Mrs Sheridan, the master's mother, that is, very badly. Fortunately, he was away most o' the time.'

Jessica blinked away a stray tear. 'He died in an accident, didn't he?'

'Yes, when Luke was quite young.'

'Oh, Dora, why is nothing ever straightforward? You fall in love, marry, have children and are happy ever after. That's how I thought it would be.'

'No life is without its regrets, my dear, yet none is without its consolations…' Dora answered, her voice trailing away as she relived some past event, some treasured moment. 'Happiness is a very complex issue.'

'Well, he can go to hell for all I damn well care,' Jessica cried bitterly. 'I must get away.'

'Oh no …no, my dear! Don't say that.'

'Then what am I to do?'

This was not the first hint dropped by the young mistress that the sorry drama of her marriage was played out. Nevertheless, it came as a shock to Dora, who had seen and deplored the increasingly bitter hostilities between the two, whose frequent savage quarrels had bled the young mistress of her love. Her account of these brawls presented her as an angel, and him as a monster whose physical cruelty and brutal assaults she displayed in minor bruises about her body.

'Well, since you press me for a personal opinion …I think you shouldn't make such an important decision in a hurry.' The girl was so much to be pitied, but to leave would be foolish. 'It would be putting your head int'a noose, so t'speak. You have everything you want here. A blind eye would serve you better.

Jessica was momentarily taken aback, quite

appalled by Dora's words. 'But you've no idea what he puts me through. I have my pride.'

'Swallowing ones pride seldom gives one indigestion.'

'I refuse to be humiliated any further,' Jessica cried with indignation.

'But at a heavy price. You must hold fast t'love.'

'I don't think he's capable of loving anyone.'

'Now, don't let him harden you. Be the first t'forgive. It'll all come right in the end.'

'That's what my father used to say. Be the first to forgive.'

'He was right. You can conquer by forgiveness.'

'I wish he was here now. I miss him so much.'

'I know you do, my dear. I wish I could say something t'make you feel better.'

'Dora, I'm truly touched by your concern. How do you put up with me with all these complications?'

'Your sadness affects us all.'

Not wanting to betray the aching emptiness she felt, Jessica turned away then, her breast heaving with the effort of holding it in, but it was no use, a sob escaped her lips and the tears came again. She could not seem to stop them. Lifting her hands to cover her face, she wept. She wept for the child she had carried and lost, for her beloved father who had gone out of her life forever, for the loss of Alice who had been her friend, and for the man she had known and loved, the man that had abused that love, a love that had turned to animosity, until there was no more weeping in her.

For a few seconds, when Jessica first opened her eyes

from the healing wings of sleep, everything seemed fine, but then it hit her, that ugly feeling of betrayal. Drawing the covers more closely about her she lay there in the bed trying to convince herself that what had happened hadn't really happened at all, pushing those tormenting thoughts aside, banishing the pain that came when she relived those moments of discovery. Luke had promised her heaven and shown her hell, crossing the line by insulting her in a measure that was past all endurance.

Nothing was the same. Nothing would ever be the same again, the house, this very room …it was all so different, cold and unfriendly. She had given herself unwittingly into a loveless marriage and could see no answer to the dilemma in which she now found herself. As a woman she had no rights. He had complete control over her body. It was his entitlement.

Her mind went over all that she had suffered at his hands, which had caused the breach to widen. She winced at the memory of those nightmarish moments when lack of self-control had led him into acts that were unforgivable, and a fresh wave of humiliation flooded over her. She had been pushed to the limit by the barbarity of his treatment. Something in her had died the night he raped her, taking over her life like a shameful secret.

This was no way to spend a life. She couldn't live with such a high level of aggression. Her brain was in a whirl, her thoughts, tossing to and fro like straws in a storm-filled brook, were without design or purpose. She was a prey to many emotions, vacillating between love and hate, doubt and certainty, time and again there passed before her mental vision the events of the previous hours. One and all were stamped upon her consciousness with a clarity that time itself could never efface. So she believed; for youth has little knowledge of the gentle alchemy of passing years.

Time and time again, amid the beauty and the solitude of the sunlit heights, by babbling brook and in the scented stillness of the pinewood, Jessica sought solutions to her dilemma. Tears had drained her of her rage. Her mind was now a turmoil of indecision, caught between wanting to do something about it and yet, being afraid too, desperately trying to fix on the future and not on the man she loved.

Realisation came to her as if a blindfold had been removed from her eyes, recognizing with despair that the love she had for him was gradually being destroyed by the lies, the pain and humiliation he inflicted upon her. She could no longer submit meekly to this ...this degradation. For that was what it was, degradation, viciousness, sheer brutality. The torment that she must go through seemed to her too brutal and undeserved! It was not to be borne, this wreckage of her happiness, this horror that had come crashing down on Heaven.

If she could turn her love into contempt how much simpler it would make her decision to cut him out of her life. There was no plan, just the instinctive reflex for flight from the pain she was in. She was afraid to remain with him, fearing complete mental collapse if she stayed. She must get away.

PART FOUR

FORTY-SEVEN

Joe could hear April clattering pots and pans in the kitchen below, as she prepared the men's breakfast. He gazed out of the bedroom window. A veil of mist hung about the yard. It would soon lift, he reflected as he pulled on his clothes. Today was the day he was to help Jessie move to the cottage. By the time he drove over to pick her up it will have cleared to another fine, sunny September day.

Bracken, who had taken to sleeping on his bed of a night, stood up and stretched, then leapt to the floor and padded after him down the stairs. April stood humming to herself as she stirred a cauldron of porridge over the fire. Joe mumbled a good morning as he stretched to ease his aching back, before seating himself down at the table that was already set with a bowl of steaming porridge, a flat dish of fried eggs and crispy bacon, and a plate of buttered bread. Bracken sniffed at the air and sat patiently at Joe's feet, looking hopeful.

'Where is everybody?'

'Been an' gone. Yer've just missed them by about five minutes or so,' April told him.

Just as she spoke, the door latch clicked and Miles came in, a tousle-haired lad of eleven now. A fair, slim youth, with the extraordinary eyes of his father and the smiling kindness of his mother. April's gaze rested on him affectionately. She doted on all her children, but had a special soft spot for her eldest. And quite clearly, Miles had a strong affection for his mother, but his attachment to his father, in spite of his early death when he himself had been only eight years of age, was expressed in a wistful remembrance of him in some words he wrote in a book: "The thought of earlier days brings my father into my heart which shows itself in my eyes."

Joe nodded his head in greeting and gave the boy his tasks for the day. 'You're t'help O'Malley muck out the cowshed. Then clear up the yard.'

The boy's expectant expression fell. 'But I thought I was t'elp move the rest o' Aunt Jessie's things t'day?'

'No lad. There's little left t'move. Just some bits an' pieces. We'll manage well enough. You best get on with your chores. You've school t'morrow.'

April spooned steaming, thick porridge into a bowl and placed it before her son. The poor lad, he had been forced to grow-up fast after his father's death, finding it tough. Life had only got easier since Joe had taken her on as housekeeper and housed them all in one of the farm cottages.

She could not understand why Jessica was to leave Wildacres where she had everything a woman could desire: servants, fine clothes and a wealthy husband to pamper her, to move into an isolated, run-down cottage. The girl needed her head examining, in her opinion.

'I don't know why Jessie refuses t'move in 'ere. Yer've plenty o' room.'

'I don't know either, April. Mind, I've never pretended t'understand you womenfolk. You refused the same offer yourself, if you remember.'

'Ah, well, that's different. Jessie's your own flesh an' blood. Besides, I'm perfectly 'appy in the cottage. 'Tis what I'm used to an' 'tis close t'the farm anyway.'

'Just as you like. It's your decision,' Joe ate the rest of his breakfast in silence, feeding the rind off the bacon to Bracken.

The dog leapt to her feet as Joe rose from the table, lifted his hat from the back of the door and placed it firmly on his head at a jaunty angle. 'I shouldn't be long. I'd say I'll be back by ten at the latest, if anybody wants me.'

He looked down at the boy. 'Megan'll be down shortly. Keep an eye on her, will you lad?'

Miles nodded with resignation. He had made a companion of Joe's little daughter, Megan, who was slowly teaching him to laugh at his vexations. She followed him about the farmyard like a shadow while he did his chores, driving him mad with her questions.

Bracken inched forward, lest she be forgotten. 'Stay!' Joe ordered.

The dog hated that command. Her tail dropped immediately, almost concealed by her legs except for the upward tilt at the tip. But trained to obey, she did as she was bid and obediently settled back on the floor, her head down on her paws and her sharp eyes watching the door her master had just left by.

'Why do I get all the worse jobs?' Miles asked

sulkily, once Joe was out of earshot.

'Now then, lad, yer can't complain. Yer want fer nothing,' his mother answered crossly, although a smile was not far from her lips. But she would have nothing said against Joe. He was their saviour. They owed him everything. He had given them a home, a cosy cottage, when they were at their lowest, having lost her Owen to the mines, and two of her precious children to fever. No, she would have nothing said against Joe Greenward.

'Now, cheer up. Yer've got a lot t'be thankful fer. There's mutton an' potatoes fer supper t'night, followed by a nice home-made apple pie, with cheese t'finish.'

Joe shaded his eyes against the rising sun. The dawn air was sweet with the scent of freshly picked apples and the new mown hay that was already stored in the barn. As he had foreseen, the sun's rays had dispelled all trace of the morning mists by the time he had reached the high rise of the crossroads. Pulling the horse and cart to a stand-still, he paused to look back as he always did, to survey the land …his land, with jubilation, feeling a surge of quiet pride.

He could see the farm spread out between the dry stonewalls that marked off Chapel House Farm's boundary from Courtenay land. The old substantial farmhouse, overlooking lush meadows and meandering streams, in a rich undulating valley crowned with woody hills that swept abruptly down into the green enclosures. A series of buildings: stables, the carthouse, cowshed, granary, barns and cottages.

His ten acres looked comparatively small alongside Lewis Courtenay's vast spread, but he felt no envy, no envy at all. Both he and Lewis Courtenay alike, shared the same dedication to hard work and pride in their labours. It had taken a lot of back-breaking labour slaving on the soil, and personal sacrifice, but he had done it. He had become an enthusiastic farmer, a thriving farmer, pursuing his labour cheerfully with a calm trust in the future, emerging from the house in the grey of dawn and returning only when the last of the dusk was gone. Reading exhaustively on farming methods and hiring reliable hands.

Under his frantic efforts the land had grown fruit-ful again. While not rich, he was not pressed for cash. He kept a great many milk cows now. The luxuriance of the pasturelands had always been proverbial and consequently, his cows were some of the finest and most productive in the area. His milk and butter the richest and the sweetest, bringing the highest price at every market at which he offered them for sale. He was filled with an inexpressible confidence, noting, with a practiced eye, the stock in his fields below, his sheep scattered far over the fells. There would be a gathering in soon for mating and dipping. He needed no great gifts. He drew his inspiration from the soil.

If only Rose Bradley was here to share it all with him. Her leaving, and Kitty's tragic death soon after, had left him devastatingly miserable, restless, with a gnawing discontent that had tried to eat his heart out, and had he not been blessed with an inborn love of the countryside, would have succeeded.

He had slowly learned to listen again, to the stimulating quiet made wonderful by tiny sounds; whispering grasses, the soft choir of a multitude of grasshoppers, a solitary lizard scuttling to its hole or the splitting pods of the gorse. And his wondering eyes learned to see again, wonderful things, quaint and curious, colours marvellous and surpassing the imagination of the cleverest paint brush in the world. A kestrel overhead, almost motionless, with just a tremble in wings and tail, soaring and sailing into the blue. The play of shade and light across meadow and wood, shafts of sunlight over spring-green copse, glowing as though the glory of the light of the world dwelled within.

Light, be it sunlight or moonlight, pierces the soil, awakening the sleepers, stirring the languid and healing the wounded, and behold, leaf and blossom spring from the darkness, and one stands dumbfounded before the magic of new life.

He took a deep breath of the pure air, filling his lungs and squaring his shoulders to counteract the effects of the past week, trying to juggle several jobs at once and preparing the cottage in time for Jessie to move in.

Giving one last glance at the two-storied farmhouse, whose dilapidated doors and windows formed a melancholy contrast with the wealth of green fertile fields, he clicked his tongue and pulled at the reins, turning the horse and cart about in the direction of Wildacres.

The early mist had left the trees dripping, on every leaf hung a tear and in Jessica Sheridan's eyes too. She wanted to turn and take a last look at the house; the house that she had grown to love, the house in which she thought she would spend the rest of her days. Where she had come as a new bride, full of expectations and love, a love that had never been returned, but she was afraid that if she did look back she might weaken and stay. It was possible to perceive now that the childish impression of permanence as a thing in itself, was false. How hard it was to see a dream die!

All she had brought with her was plain, sensible clothes and shoes, all her books and a few personal belongings. In her departure, Joe provided her with a haven of refuge, where her ever-throbbing heart might find perfect rest, in the cottage "Little Tarn", a circular little structure with a slate roof. Situated amid trees and half buried in creepers, it looked like a nest. The very same place he and Rose Bradley used to secretly meet, the "love-nest" where they had lain in each other's arms, out of sight from the eyes of the rest of the world.

The garden was a mass of tangled weeds and crammed with birds, whole broods of blackbirds, thrushes, tits and finches. The cottage that had been made into a habitable state was almost round, taper-ing off at the top. There were two rooms downstairs, a parlour with a low window, and a fireplace with a wall-oven to one side. The other, a small back kitchen, no bigger than a walk-in cupboard really, but both had been freshly whitewashed and the stone floors cleaned and polished. The one good sized room above was a kind of loft with a sloping ceiling, furnished with a double bed, a cupboard and a chest of drawers, a washbasin and jug, and other necessary objects, all donated by Joe from Chapel House Farm.

He had brought her two upright chairs, a small gate-legged table, which, unbeknown to her, or she wouldn't have accepted them, had once belonged to Kitty. A quaint old corner cupboard of oak that had been scrubbed to a snowy whiteness by April Ramsey. The rocking chair Joe had rescued from the fire, a creation that had been lovingly fashioned by their youngest brother, John, for their father, which he placed close to the hearth, thinking Jessie might find comfort in it. And outside, he stood a great round barrel to one side of the door to catch the rainwater.

There was an oddment of bed linen and towels, crockery and kitchen utensils, and even an old tin bath. Jessica had brought with her two candleholders, a clock, a wall mirror, and her brush, comb and hand mirror - all she needed really. By the end of the week it was all over Uldale and Branthwaite and even as far as Caldbeck - the servants' grapevine saw to that - that Jessica Greenward, or Jessica Sheridan, as she was now known, had left her husband who had not only brazenly taken himself a mistress, but had supposedly beaten his poor young wife again and again. As if she had not had enough heartache in her young life. Mind you, wasn't it what Luke Sheridan deserved? - was the general opinion. That kind of behaviour would always find its just deserts. You couldn't do that sort of thing and still expect to be called a gentleman, could you? He was a proud, powerful man, but this would bring him down a peg or two; by leaving him she had made a right fool of him.

FORTY-EIGHT

The weather turned foul, with rain and high winds, and on top of everything else, the fire wouldn't light. Again and again, Jessica set twisted paper sticks and faggots of wood in the grate, just as Joe had shown her, until at last, just when she was about to give way to despair, it caught.

There were days when that which had driven her to her life of solitude closed down upon her soul afresh, times when she seemed to move in a dream. Her attempts to harden her emotions had failed. Instead, she seemed to have become more vulnerable to the hurt. Her self-esteem had so many wounds to sustain. She just could not seem to clamber out of the dark hole into which she had fallen. At first, she tried to fight it behind closed shutters and a locked door, sometimes lying lifeless like a mummy, in warmth and candlelight, the emotional struggle raging, trapped within. Shutting herself in for days on end, rarely going out, other than to bring water from the barrel, which she heated in small quantities over the open fire. Never seeing anyone, apart from Joe who looked in on her from time to time to check if she was still breathing, always bringing her gifts of some kind: vegetables, flour, eggs, bread, cheese and butter, and milk in abundance.

Joe's visits were the only relief. He brought with him a sense of life beyond those restricting walls, a life whose threads she would soon have to pick up again, but for the present she was unwilling to face the outside world and preferred to just let herself drift.

Joe's weatherworn features crinkled in concern. He was doing his best to understand, but hadn't been prepared to see her looking so white and lifeless, like one of those marble figures on a tomb. It alarmed him.

'I'm not going t'ask how you are right now, because I can imagine it's not good.' He brought her a mug of water and placed it in her trembling hands. 'Here, drink this. It'll do you good.' Taking the empty mug from her, he set it aside. 'It's all right t'let it out, pretty lass.'

'What's happening to me?' she cried despairingly, putting her arms about herself, sobbing as she spoke. 'How naive I was, expecting happiness to …to come like a gift. I tried being who he …he wanted me to be. One day I looked in the mirror and I was gone. He took my soul and shattered it, making me feel so …so worthless.'

'The bastard!'

'There's not a day goes by when I don't think I should ...should kill myself and be done with it.'

Joe turned on her fiercely. 'Don't talk like that. You just need time t'heal. If I could take the slightest part o' your pain away, I would.'

'Oh, Joe, I know you would. But some wounds never heal.' She wiped her red-rimmed eyes. Crying only made her head ache.

'They will, given time,' he answered quietly.

'But I feel so …so lost. With him I felt alive. Now, it's as if part ...part of me has died.'

'Just listen t'yourself, pining over a man who's simply not worth it. Cruelty isn't the attitude o' someone who cares for you, now is it?'

'I suppose not.'

Joe took her hand in a firm grip. 'You've been through a lot. You've put up with more than anyone should put up with. But life has a way of working out. Yours isn't over. A new chapter's beginning, but you're still in shock over the loss o' father, an' on top o' all that feel utterly betrayed after having sacrificed your freedom for that bastard. He simply fell under this sophisticated woman's spell. You're going t'have t'deal with it, Jessie. Start t'rebuild your life. Things can only get better.'

'I long to be myself again. When I was younger my feelings were never troubled like this.'

He saw bewilderment in her face and gentled his tone. 'You will, lass. Give it time. When Rose left I felt much the same, like the bee after the first sting, as if about t'die.' He shrugged his broad shoulders. 'But I didn't. Life goes on. I went on living, even after the sadness o' Kitty's…' he trailed off.

Jessica gazed up at his face. Although smooth and taut with good health, there were visible lines about the mouth where it had turned down in sadness and his eyes were no longer the warm, brilliant green they had once been, but faded as though some of the colour had drained away with his spirit. Seeing the sorrow in those dear eyes, she quickly forgot her own agony.

'Joe, it's about time you put down that burden. You were not to blame for Kitty's death.'

'I know that. It's just that I sometimes feel I should've tried harder,' he said regretfully. 'Father's horrific death almost brought me t'my knees, but grief becomes mitigated by wearing itself out. I wouldn't say time flies, but it no longer drags. The secret o' being miserable is t'have the leisure t'bother about whether you're happy or not, which is something I don't happen t'have ...leisure t'dwell on things.'

'Oh, Joe, hold me. I feel like I'm dying.'

FORTY-NINE

Luke slouched in the great leather chair in his study in the dark. He did most of his serious thinking after dark. On his desk lay the unopened gift he had brought home from London for Jessica. A musical clock for the bedroom, an ornate creation, the case finely chased with wheat-sheaves and geometric patterns, raised on splayed feet, the front slide opening to reveal a maritime scene with little sailing ships. The engraved back-plate was signed "Henry Borrell, London" the maker of musical clocks and watches. He had chosen it with her in mind, as it was similar to the one she had once admired in the Plumgarths Hotel restaurant, Kendal, thinking it would amuse her, please her even to have such an unusual piece. But she was not here.

He felt a growing unrest, unable to comprehend the abruptness of her leaving. True, he had treated her badly, but hadn't he given her everything a woman could wish for? To leave it all behind didn't make sense. This was just one in a series of blows to his personal life that made him look back with dismay. Life was an endless uphill struggle that one had to make continuous effort to see any meaning to it. She had thought him invulnerable, that he sailed through life untouched by the battering of fate. First, he had lost his father, and in the past few years, his Grandfather Penrose, who had been the one person that meant everything to him, his wife Annie and the child, and Justin Courtenay, his one true friend. Also,

Daniel, the man he had always trusted and relied upon, and now, with Jessica gone too, all his purpose in life.

Fate had shown her teeth with a vengeance and he found himself viewing the years ahead totally alone. He had great difficulty in coming to terms with it all. A nightmare he could not wake up from. Jessica was too damn impulsive by half.

Women! They were all alike, expecting a man to be a tower of strength but then, when they find he had a few weaknesses - in his case the only weakness, concerning the needs of the flesh - they desert you. He knew he was not unique; it was rooted in the very nature of a man. It was a craving, a chase after beauty and life, after his own youth!

He was warm, comfortable and had splendidly cooked meals, just the same as always, but he had no appetite and was continually sending his food back untouched. In fact, he was as well looked after as ever, but none of it compensated for all the deep regret on his loss of her. Her leaving had affected him like nothing had ever done before; life had grown strange and empty. He felt completely alone, a prisoner of his own melancholy, alone with no one to hold, with no interest in anything.

His heart had never been touched by any woman, not in the way he had heard others speak of and yet he had to admit, Jessica had brought something to his life, something that he had not experienced before. He could only describe the feeling she had aroused in him as... as contentment, gratification, bringing a kind of comfort into his life. It had been like holding Springtime in his arms, her moods like the Lakeland weather, unpredictable, forever changing, warm and meek one moment, rebellious and fiery the next. In some ways she was a child still, spirited, with a great sense of fun ...sensitive and vulnerable, so easily hurt.

He had been so sure of himself, so certain she would always be here, a friend upon whose constancy he could depend, waiting with open arms for his return. So confident that he had her right where he wanted her, in the palm of his hand and yet, had let her slip through his fingers like melting snow. Here one minute, gone the next. At first he had felt indifferent, not in the least concerned, positive she would soon stop playing the martyr and come running back with her tail between her legs, begging him to forgive her foolishness. But then, as the days turned in to weeks and she had not come back in to the fold, the tide had turned, leaving him shaken and withdrawn, with a deep aching loneliness within.

He shut his eyes to rid himself of her image, but instantly she became ten times more visible, his feeling ten times stronger. God, what power a woman has over a man, he thought as his mind fell into a mercifully numbed state. But she must never know. She must never know the full ferocity of his agony. He must have some shred of dignity. She was out there somewhere. But where? He had made discreet inquiries, but without success. It seemed she didn't want to be found.

The atmosphere of the house, which was certainly oppressive, weighed heavily on Dora Osborne's mind. It had been a frightful time for everyone, with rumours of the most dreadful kind being whispered. A deep sense of sadness affected them all. Even the dog went about with his tail down. The master looked haggard and defeated, as he sprawled in a deep armchair in the drawing room, drowning his sorrows over a large glass of brandy, not in the mood to listen to anyone, but determined to say her piece, Dora stood her ground.

'She might not've been born a lady, but you'll be hard pressed t'find a more caring girl.'

'This is not your quarrel,' Luke answered sternly, pouring himself another brandy.

'But it affects us all. At least when you spoke t'the young mistress you knew you were heard. She always took the time t'listen. We had more in common than I would've suspected. I'm her friend an' count myself fortunate t'claim it. She brought joy t'all who knew her,' Dora said in a monotone, which spoke of her distress.

Poor girl - she thought - so desperate to be a lady and do the proper thing, but letting herself down so often by such volatile emotions. The master, she felt, was cruelly severe on his young wife and totally lacking in under-standing.

'Jessica touched all of us. Each in a different way,' Luke said sullenly.

'I don't know what you did t'the poor, sweet lass. She seemed so detached, no joy in her face. Torment-ed she was.'

'She's overly-sensitive. Feels things too much.'

Just at that moment he was allowing himself the weakness of regret, draining the cup of misery to the very dregs! It was torture. He was afflicted by a series of nervous ailments, brought on by over-work and worry. Chief among these was a persistent, terrible insomnia, accompanied by the utmost depression of spirits and anxiety of mind. His system was strung up by slow degrees to such a high tension, both physically and mentally, that the quietest and most soothing of friendly voices had no other effect upon him than to jar and irritate.

'She must've been desperate, the poor lass, near the end o' her tether t'leave her home this way, t'give up all she holds dear. I never even got t'say goodbye. It was my afternoon off,' Dora said, her voice tinged with sadness.

'She'll soon miss it all. Then she'll be back. Such foolishness can't last.'

'Well, don't hold your breath.'

'I just don't understand the girl. Within reasonable limits I tried to do my duty by her,' Luke rationalised.

'Ah, well, when a man says he doesn't understand his own wife it's because he won't take the trouble.'

'What do you mean?'

'Well, lots o' things really. Did you know the portrait o' your late wife in your study upsets her?'

Luke shrugged. 'I hadn't given it a thought.'

'Exactly! Don't you think it insensitive keeping it there?'

'Why? Has Jessica mentioned it?' he asked.

'She did say the eyes seemed t'follow her about the room, making her feel she was being watched.'

'Superstitious girl. She should have told me she wanted it removed.'

'She shouldn't have to. It should've been taken down before you brought her here as your bride,' Dora said disapprovingly. 'An' another thing, did you know she always spent most o' her allowance on little treats for the children here-a-bouts? She bought Iris Gower's brood a pair o' boots each.'

'Iris Gower! Do I know her?'

'I doubt it, but the young mistress does. It was Iris Gower's husband that drowned along with that Greenward woman. The mistress's brother's wife. There's a lot more t'that young wife o' yours than you ever had the gumption t'see. She's perceptive, thoughtful, just an' generous, an' possesses more compassion than I've ever known. She puts everyone before herself. Do you know, she even sorted out the servants' quarters? Put in a few bits an' pieces. Made their rooms more comfortable an' cosy like. She likes t'see everyone happy.'

'It seems she's obsessed with helping the down-trodden.'

'She's well thought o' by just about everyone.'

Luke leaned back in his chair and looked at Dora reflectively. She knew more about his wife than he did.

'You seem to know an awful lot. What do you think she feels for me?'

'Why should that worry you? After all, you're not in love with her, are you?' There was no response, so Dora carried on, 'You may know the pains o' possessing an' dependency, reducing a person t'an object, but that's not love. Love takes the bad with the good an' makes it all very special. You know how it is when it happens, like a search that's ended. An' the wonderful relief at having found someone t'come home an' talk to, who knows an' understands you. We all need love, but I doubt you deserve it. You can be cruel sometimes.'

Luke tutted impatiently. 'All this talk of love!'

'Why don't you go t'her before it's too late? Ask her forgiveness?'

'I told you I don't know where she is. Have you any idea where she is?'

'No, but that brother o' hers will know.'

'Oh, he knows all right, but he's not letting on. Even if he did, I have my pride.'

Dora saw the torment that lay beneath his disguise of stiff dignity. His pride was an obsession, stupefying the real good in him, which was considerable. Under its dominion he would break his own heart in this imaginary grievance.

'Too proud t'open your heart an' too blind t'open your eyes. Seems a lot t'lose for pride's sake...'

She stopped speaking abruptly. There was a silence filled with awkwardness. Luke fidgeted, uncomfortable with his housekeeper's evident emotion. For politeness sake he had allowed her to say her piece. She managed the house efficiently and with style, kept impeccable accounts and never bothered him with minutiae. But now she was taking advantage, going much too far.

'That's enough. You'd do well to remember your place,' he told her brusquely, breaking the stillness of the silence.

The sharpness of his tone made Toby lift his head and peer up at him as if offended by his attitude. The dog then sighed and lowered his head on to his paws again.

'Oh, I know my place well enough. But boy an' man I've known you, an' I know what a fool you can be,' Dora returned with fierce determination.

Luke's dark eyes narrowed threateningly. He sat up so abruptly he spilled his drink down his shirt front. His voice was heavy with menace. 'I'm warning you ...vex me not!'

'Some things need t'be said,' she went on un-waveringly

'You've said enough, damn it!' he roared. 'Keep that tongue for the servants.'

His voice thundered through the warm calm of the room and the dog leapt to his feet and with tail down between his legs, made a hasty retreat. As for Dora, she had not yet finished.

'This is not easy t'say, but needs t'be said, all the same. You think you're a gentleman because you were born int'money, but the truth is you're no better than your father. He was cruel t'your poor mother.'

She had gone too far this time. His temper cracked and he hurled the crystal glass at her with a precision of aim that astonished even himself. It came straight at her, catching her on the chest, causing her to flinch with pain.

Dora Osborne, who had been the housekeeper at Wildacres for well over twenty years, gave no notice of her instant departure, saying that no consideration would persuade her to spend another night in the house with him - a man made in the devil's image.

FIFTY

Lifting his head, Luke breathed deeply, the air slipping like sweet white wine down his throat and into his lungs. The little terrier tore after him, out through the front door and round and round the garden, as though the devil himself was biting his behind, leaping and barking his excitement and delight at this escape from the confines of the house.

Everything was astir. The bird music was especially lovely. In those quiet expectant minutes the blend of their voices had the quality of many-stringed instruments. It was the self-same music that had always lifted Luke's spirit, ever since the days when he was a lad.

The quiet decay of autumn was spreading, the dying vegetation beginning to rot, ready to turn itself into the nourishment needed for next year's growth. Occasionally, a withered, yellow leaf detached itself, fluttering from the branch like an exhausted, starving swallow left behind in the ebbing tides of migration, twirling through the still air till it came to settle on the earth.

Toby raised his nose to sniff at the air, the breeze just lifting his floppy ears. His bright, curious eyes followed the movement of his master. He ran on ahead, his sensitive button of a nose to the ground, blissfully sniffing and breathing in the exhilarating scents of the forest in the quiet stillness, darting off the path into a sea of copper bracken, disappearing from sight.

A chestnut fell with a dull thud, striking twigs and branches in its fall, rattling noisily and sending more leaves fluttering down, and the stag resting quietly on a bed of dying leaves started and twitched its nostrils. Then into the peaceful calm came the distant sound of blundering footsteps, without doubt, the footsteps of a human being. The stag bounded to his feet and thrust his antlers in among the branches and brushed them vigorously to and fro, his movements the outward manifestation of a growing restlessness within.

A whistle was heard and a voice calling. The nostrils of the red stag twitched anxiously as a mixed scent of dog and man - the enemy - reached him. The dog came into view, a tiny scrap of a thing, a streak of brown and white furry.

Toby saw the stag and halted, looking back as though to reassure himself his master was not far behind. Then, with a cheeky yap of self-importance he dared to scurry forward, his little stump of a tail quivering with sheer, ecstatic excitement. The stag loomed gigantic, standing perfectly still as it peered with huge liquid eyes at the insignificant creature.

Yapping and barking, the bold little animal approached the deer, which tossed its head and tapped impatiently with its powerful forefeet. Had Luke been closer he would have seen those signs and called off the foolish little fellow. As it was, the stag bounded forward in a sudden rush with the huge head lowered and the wisp of dog-flesh turned to scuttle frantically away on its short little legs into the sanctuary of the brush, but he was too late in turning. Luke heard the dog's agonized yelp, followed by a long hoarse bellow from the stag.

A mile away some nibbling hinds heard it too and

lifted their heads with swift, excited movements. It bore to them the message of their kind, the announcement of the wild, the challenge of one stag to all others for the right to seek and hold the hinds. And not only the hinds heard it. Another big, fully grown stag was cropping the grass at the edge of the forest. He too was alone and as the bellowing roar rang through the stillness, he threw up his massive head and with nostrils dilated, stood with one forefoot lifted from the ground, a very statue of grace and strength and poised expectancy, releasing a responding raucous bellow, full of menace and meaning.

This time the challenging stag pawed the ground as it bellowed again, yet did not move from where he stood, but gazed in the direction the rejoinder came from. No sooner did he hear the answer to his call than he tossed his magnificent head, shook his powerful antlers and dug them into the ground so that they came up with earth and dead leaves hanging on to them, then set off on a lumbering trot towards the edge of the wood to meet his contender. From a distance Luke watched the flight of the magnificent powerful beast - the slayer of the brave little terrier.

FIFTY-ONE

Jessica felt nauseated and was beaded with sweat. It had been a tremendous strain to get back to the cottage. After a few minutes she hurriedly got up from the chair to stoop with her head over a bowl, retching her heart out. When she finally straightened up, she wiped her face with a towel, wandering shakily over to the mirror on the wall. It shocked her to realise that the face in the mirror was her own, ashen and hollowed-eyed. She knew for certain now that there was a life growing inside her, a life born without the least grain of love, but of cruelty and lust.

Ever since that fateful miscarriage, which she thought she had at last put out of her mind, her body had gradually settled into its regular rhythms, which none of the many changes and upsets she had encountered had disturbed until now. There was, too, an unfamiliar feeling, a tingling in her breasts, and there had been this strange, gripping spasm in the lower part of her body, as if her womb was fighting to retain its new burden. But it was none of these physical symptoms which convinced her that she was pregnant. She just knew it was so, that she carried another life in her, and was horrified. Nothing, not even the fact that it was Luke Sheridan's child, the child he had longed for, could make this baby welcome. Full of wretchedness, she sank back onto the chair. She must have dozed then, for the next minute Joe was bending over her.

'Oh, Joe, it's you. I must've dozed off,' she said,

all bleary eyed.

'There's been another message.'

'What does it say?'

'I've no idea. I burnt it,' he replied.

Her lids flickered with despair. She looked to be almost in tears.

'Are you all right?' Joe asked with concern. 'You look so pale,'

'Joe, what am I going to do? There's something I haven't told you.'

'What is it? What is it that weighs on you so heavily? Spit it out before you choke.'

'I'm going to have a child,' she cried, wilting in to hysterical tears.

'God Almighty!'

'I didn't want to speak of it until I was certain.'

'An' you're certain now?'

'I have no doubt.'

'Well, you can't go on like this.'

'But what can I do? I don't know if I can get through this on my own.'

'I'm here. I'll do anything I can t'help. You know that. No one would guess you're carrying a child. You're as thin as a blade o' grass. I don't like t'see you like this.'

'I can eat nothing. Besides, it's dull cooking for oneself.'

'Why don't you come back with me? At least until you're feeling better. April will see that you eat an' you'll have the little'uns t'take your mind off things. Being among other people sometimes helps.'

'I don't want to be with other people.' She could not put into words her need for peace and privacy in which to do her grieving. She begged her brother to understand. 'Please try to understand, Joe, I need to be alone.'

His eyes clouded. 'All right! I'm only trying t'do what's best for you. Give you a few words o' comfort.'

'I know. I'm sorry. I'll be all right now.' She smiled sadly through the tears, a smile to melt even the hardest of hearts. 'It's just that it needed to come out.'

'Should I send April over?' he asked anxiously.

'No! Please don't! She has enough to cope with.'

'Then promise me you'll try t'eat properly. If anything happened t'you I'd never forgive myself.'

'I will. I promise.'

'An' I think you need t'find something t'do, something you enjoy. You can alter life by altering your attitude o' mind, you know. It's going t'hurt for a while yet, but you're strong, you'll pull through. One o' the great arts o' living is the art o' forgetting.'

'Have you?'

'Have I what?'

'Forgotten Rose?'

His voice was hoarse with regret when he spoke, his words slowly uttered. 'No, not really, but time has deadened the pain.'

Jessica searched his face. Never had she seen such sorrow, such mournful dignity as was in that dear face. Despair had curved deep furrows in his brow, making it look as if he was in pain. He was physically fit and yet gave the appearance of a man with the worries of the world upon his shoulders.

In return for the supplies Joe brought her, Jessica

started to bake in the old but still useable wall-oven to one side of the fireplace, heating it by burning dried heather bents, brambles and faggots of wood. When the oven was hot enough, she raked out the glowing embers and slipped in the bread, pasties, or an apple pie. Another day a mixed fruit cake or a rolled jam pudding, whatever it was she had prepared, filling the cottage with the fragrance of cooking.

She knew that whatever she made would soon be greedily devoured by her forever-hungry brother and the farm hands. It was tiring work, but it passed the time and she actually enjoyed it. It somehow satisfied something in her that had been stifled for so long.

Long days and even longer nights, she lay awake listening to the foxes yapping under old oaks, as she wrestled with her torment. She would ask herself a hundred times whether she had had a chance to flee from the overwhelming passion that had warped her life. Whether maybe she could have turned away and saved herself? But every time she asked herself that question she concluded that her fate had been determined since the beginning of time - there had been no escape. When she did sleep, bad dreams came again and again, like unwanted visitors. It proved a long struggle that ended through sheer weariness of mind, replaced by a savage determination to fight it.

As the weeks passed she sought relief by tramping the heather, scrambling up the slopes to shake off the depression that had taken hold. Now she was free and away from the rules and restrictions with which her life had hitherto been bound, at an hour when golden shafts of light pierce and irradiate the cloud-wraiths on the heights, she climbed the grassy slopes. She wore an old jacket and cord breeches that had once belonged to her beloved brother, John, who had lost his life in the mines.

Free from the clinging follies of absurdly fashioned, modern garments to restrain her movements, she laboured up the scree where parsley fern and bramble clumps clung in seeming precariousness which helped to bind shifting stones, in full consciousness that a sudden slip meant worse than death.

Beauty lay all about her, but she paid no heed. A curlew called, a raven croaked, sheep bleated, a multitude of sounds: squeals, wails, chuckles and cries, splashings and rustlings, whispers to tell of the comings and goings of unseen bodies, but she barely noticed. Her ears were deaf as her eyes were blind to the treasures of living beauty.

Under the high vaulting of the old beeches, their pillars grey like smoke, down the steep uneven paths that lay deep in leaf-mould upon the rocky side of the hill, Luke stood alone in the shadows, watching her climb slowly up the steep acclivity. Because she was on higher ground he could not fail to see her. Even in her manly disguise there was no mistaking her, her very movements, the way she had of swinging her arms and swaying her narrow hips. The way her glorious hair, as it always did, broke free from its restraint and took to the air like a forest fire out of control, when the wind tugged at it.

Sudden distress at the sight of her affected him, affected him deeply, and through his wretchedness stole the unbelievable awareness of something so over-whelming he was afraid to take it out and study it for fear it might slip through his fingers and be gone again. But love and passion know no master.

They win their way regardless of the human will. The strength of a man is but a jest before them, his intellect a snare that trips and throws him when he thinks he stands most firm. His dark eyes were full of grief, for he had seen joy pass him by and knew that it was lost to him.

Her name sighed on his lips, but he made no sound or movement to betray his presence.

FIFTY-TWO

When Jessica ventured out the dawn was breaking, the cold, pale light coming slowly as the leaden clouds raced before the wind and ragged wisps trailed like smoke across a sky that was neither grey nor blue or copper-tinted, but a blend of all. Shrill cries seemed to come from every quarter, yet from no particular place at all, and though for a moment, she was startled, she soon realised it was but the wind that wailed, her playfellow, sweeping her up into the heart of the wild. She spent much of her time in the open - weather permitting, with peace and beauty all around her and only the sheep that graze those fells for company.

The ancient parish of Uldale covers a great diversity of terrain, from the gentle vale of the River Ellen in the north and west, to the rolling hills of the Uldale Fells in the south and east, ideal pasture for sheep. From Uldale they stretch for many miles across the Northern Fells, extending even to Skiddaw and Blencathra in the south. Skiddaw and the Uldale Fells are best viewed from Green How on Aughertree Fell, a short walk from Uldale onto the grassy, open and wind-swept common.

From there a panoramic view opens up, with Skiddaw and Ullock Pike rising majestically to the south, the far north-western fells forming an impressive background to the west, and the distant Pennines just about visible to the east. The hills fall gently away and an ocean of green fields and twisting stonewalls spread out before her, eventually disappearing out of view. The peace and serenity was intoxicating.

For the first time in weeks, Jessica felt herself relaxing. It is the sudden sense, keen and startling, of oneness with all beauty, seen and unseen. Something of that beauty and the constancy of Nature entered into her soul during those hours of loneliness and sorrow; they were as an anodyne to her.

A small dark figure rose, a black scar amid the greenness of the bracken-decked slopes, a mere floating dot that wavered and circled, mounted and grew bigger until it showed itself to be a buzzard, its brown wings wide-spread and flashing. Its body tilted slightly as each graceful sweep carried it higher and ever higher in to the upper heavens where it was suddenly lost. It was only then she was moved to wonder.

The marvels of life were not exhausted. Her heart, which had been so long overloaded with anguish, began to dilate and open to the least gleam of diversion, with intervals of surface contentment. One sight after another came to gladden the eye, provoking a familiar excitement in her, giving the day a brightness, a spark so small yet brightly seen and cherished, smoothing the jagged edges of her soul.

Heightened tension then glorious, triumphant sound everywhere, rhythmic, throbbing, advancing to crescendos, retreating to diminuendos, faint in the distance, yet close at hand. With intricate shades of light and dark that filled her with sensation until there was no room for any more and she wanted to cry out. She wept a little, her tears giving relief and her countenance grew, if not cheerful, at least more composed and free - as she found her identity, strength and self-respect again. It was only then she come to realise that spilled on this earth, before her very eyes were all the joys of Heaven, here in the Lakelands where she lived,

Gazing across its lakes and bracken valleys to its deep woodlands of oak, hazel, beech and rowan, and beyond, far far beyond, in a most lordly vision, across mile after mile of rich land. There was so much to love in the country side …those wonderful majestic oaks and green grasses, the sleek, lowing cattle, the smoke curling up from cottage chimneys in a mysterious and blended sea of tender abundance, the strong, kindly hard-working men and women who were so at home among its familiar scenes. The country houses; slow talk of land and timber, sheep and crops, of sport in clandestine and by river, of sitting in the saddle among the heather, of the smell of meadow hay, of the full moon, of parties and croquet on smooth lawns, of familiar faces and childhood memories - all taken for granted and accepted as a whole.

Just before she reached the garden gate to the cottage she glanced up and saw a dark figure standing in the doorway. With a sick dread in the pit of her stomach she slowed her pace unconsciously, all other things for-gotten. It was only when he spoke, she recognized who it was.

'I heard you'd moved out,' he said quietly. A voice from the past.

Jessica was so taken aback she could not speak. She just stood gaping at him, her mouth slightly open.

'Well, that took courage. Courage has power and magic to it, you know.' Still no word from her. 'So what're your plans?' he asked, ignoring her dumb-founded air.

She blinked. 'I have no plans,' she managed to say at last, smiling with surprised pleasure and relief. 'You gave me quite a start. I didn't realise it was you until you spoke.'

'The trouble with you is you've always had your head in the clouds.' There was something in his tone that made her smile fade and she wondered why she was allowing this man to speak so freely, so person-ally to her. She pressed her lips tightly together, but made no reply. But he still went on, undeterred by her silence. 'You aimed too high. You need to keep your feet more firmly on the ground.'

Jessica drew in her breath, her small chin jutting out as it always did when she was about to disagree. 'I don't have to listen to...'

'No, but you will...' he interrupted, with what looked to be a gleam of humour in his eyes. 'Because you know it's the truth.'

She shrugged then, relaxing and lowering her eyes. 'I suppose you're right,' she replied sullenly. 'I just don't like to admit I was wrong. It must be the Greenward stubbornness.'

'You've got a brain in that pretty head of yours. Use it. Life's too short to dwell on what might have been. Wake up. Start a new life. What you can do or dream you can, begin it. Be your own person, just as I am.'

'I thought I was doing just that,' she said bitingly 'Anyway, enough about me. What are you doing in these parts?'

'I drop in on Joe from time to time. He told me the news. So...' He shrugged, tilting his head sideways.

'…here I am. I decided to pay you a visit to see if there was anything you want.'

'That's kind of you, but there's nothing, thank you. Joe provides me with all my supplies. But come on in. I'll make a pot of tea and you can tell me what you've been doing all this time.' She spoke in the soft, well-modulated voice she had acquired, without realising it, from the wealthy and privileged person she had married. It was by this her background could be detected.

He followed her into the cottage, glancing at the faded drapes at the window that permitted very little sunlight to enter the room, but it seemed cosy enough. There was an old corner unit with a few pieces of crockery, a pile of books on the floor by a comfort-able looking, oval-backed cushioned chair and a brightly coloured rug by the fireplace, odds and ends on the mantel and a mirror on the wall above. He peered up the narrow staircase that led to the bedroom. 'It's a proper little paradise you have here. Considered to be well furnished by some standards.'

'It can get a bit lonely sometimes,' was all she said.

A blue chenille cloth covered a small gate-legged table and a pot of red geraniums stood in the very centre. His eyes come to rest on the two huge pasties over-hanging the sides of a plate with a cheerful aspect of abundance. 'They look good.'

'They were left over from the baking.'

'You look as though you could do with a bit of feeding up. You're as thin as a reed.'

'One of the disadvantages of living alone is it leads to a neglect of meals. One is apt to make do with a few scraps or even do without.'

'Oh, is one?' he mimicked in his very best voice.

'Don't make fun of me, Mathew. I'm not in the mood.'

'Sorry. It's just you sound so …well …different.'

'I am different. I've grown up,' she said, her look steady. 'Tell me what you've been up to, whilst I brew the tea. Oh, and do help yourself to a pasty.'

'Eating without sharing would be unthinkable.'

'No, really! I have no appetite. Please, sit yourself down and tell me all about what you've been doing.'

He did just that, sat down at the table with his hat still perched jauntily on the back of his head and without bothering to remove it, pulled the plate towards him, picked up one of the inviting looking pasties and attacked it vigorously.

Mathew Robinson had never married. Jessica smiled sadly, yet felt obscurely flattered and vaguely guilty, all at the same time. He had once confessed to loving her and she had turned down his proposal of marriage, to marry the man who had stolen her heart and promised her heaven.

Mathew wore a working man's jacket with a pullover beneath and a pair of dark cord breeches. His face was bronzed through working out in the open air and his eyes were clear, untroubled, blue like the autumn sky and shining with good health. Apparently, he owned a wagon with his name painted in large bold letters on the shaft, and a horse to pull it along, all bought and paid for, so he said. He allowed his mind to ramble back, telling her of how he lived, a week here, a week there, sleeping as he could, drifting around the countryside, dabbling in numerous things, trying to make a living in a world where big fish eat little fish.

'Ribbons, buttons, cottons, needles, pincushions, scissors, workbaskets, soaps, knitted scarves and gloves, and penny novels. You name it, I sell it. Beer for the men and damson wine for the ladies. And all the usual things popular with you women. Candles, lamps, the odd clock, silverware maybe and costume jewellery...'

'Costume jewellery? What would ordinary folk want with costume jewellery?'

'You'd be surprised. I sell all sorts of little tempting things. Fine handkerchiefs and the odd bottle of perfume. That little bit of luxury to treasure. The wagon's loaded with hardware. There's a great demand for saucepans and buckets, hammers, nails and saws. Then there's the rugs, the odd chair or two, boots and shoes from time to time. Tea, sugar, vegetables, and when I can get it, meat, and bread of course. I do well in some of the smaller villages where there's no baker or butcher. Oh, and I've a knife-grinder's wheel. That earns a penny or two. And I collect the odd halfpenny for passing on letters. Always ready to serve the needs of not only the local community but also the far-flung neighbours living on isolated farms, that's me! With guaranteed delivery that's not only sure but swift,' he informed her, singing his own praises as he now strutted before her with excited self-importance.

'I'm a man of independent means. Known to all who know me, as reliable and honest. Anyone can labour, but selling takes brains. Being able to talk to people, that's the thing, no matter what you're selling. It's not the product, it's the salesman,' he said cheerfully, slapping his hands and rubbing them together.

'That's the good news. The bad news is, I'm off to the weekly Monday market in Cockermouth. I always make quite a few sales there and a tidy little profit. But I'll be back before you know it. I don't know where the time goes. It goes by so fast it makes my ears whistle.'

He was standing quite close to her now, with his hands stuffed deep in his pockets, jingling the silver. The smell of stale sweat was unpleasant, but Jessica tried not to let her distaste show. He might be a rough diamond, but he was kindly.

'I'll be counting the days,' she heard him call, when he finally went on his way, reluctant to leave so soon.

FIFTY-THREE

Believing Jessica to be starved of human contact, living so isolated, Mathew came to her rescue frequently. He would rap at the door of the cottage and ask after her health in the gentlest tone, never forgetting to accompany such inquiries with some small gift, a piece of ribbon, writing paper, a pen or a book of some kind. There was nothing to pay, it was a gift, he would say. Jessica insisted on paying and a few coins changed hands, but she was not sure that she liked him well enough to endure his perpetual company.

Somehow, he seemed different to how she remembered him. He gave the impression of being a rather lackadaisical, a run-of-the-mill sort of man, the type to be content to go on plodding through life without aim, without ambition to better himself. Besides that, his teeth looked to be in bad condition and his breath was fetid, which she found repulsive, making her wonder what she had ever seen in him in the first place. And on top of all that, he was self-righteous, so sure that he and everything belonging to him was perfect. He had little to recommend him except kindliness and good humour.

'What an earth do you find to do with yourself out here all alone?' he enquired quite suddenly.

'Oh, I have my drawing,' was all she could say.

'Drawing?'

'I've taken to drawing plants and the animals of the fells. I quite enjoy it.'

He lifted the edge to a sheet of paper amongst a pile on the table. 'Are these 'em? Why haven't you shown me?'

'I didn't think you would be interested.'

'Well, they might be worth a glance. Do you mind?'

'Not at all. Be my guest.'

His interest surprised her, as he had given her the impression that he had no interests whatsoever outside his own affairs. Each time she attempted to converse about the book she was reading, or the countryside, or perhaps the flowers she had found, it was never long before he brought the conversation back to himself.

Mathew gave each of the pages a fleeting glance, his eyes widening as he did so. The illustrations were quite exquisite, all of which showed true-to-life images of animals, birds and various wild flowers, each with a description written in a neat hand beneath.

'Why, these're rather good. You seem to have the magical ability to draw. I didn't know you had it in you. What're you going to do with them? I'll take them if you don't want them. They might bring in a penny or two.'

'By all means, take them. It's my first attempt. I suppose in time, if I improve, I might gather my work into a book.'

The sun had gone down in constant glory, the honey-coloured west full of soft, grey-blue mist hovering beyond the bordering hills. The delicate traceries of the trees stood tenderly dark on the illumined sky.

One lone minstrel thrush chanted to the dying light. Soon the silence of sleep reigned supreme over the woods, the stillness broken only by pattering drops of moisture from the branches overhead and the soft no-coo-co-coo from the doves settled amidst the foliage. Millions of bright twinkling stars sprinkled the great violet dome, casting a radiant silvery glow over the hushed sleeping fells, revealing a new marvel.

Jessica sighed with the wonder of it, feeling strangely comforted. There was no time for crying. It was better to have loved and lost than never to have loved at all ...she told herself in the silence. She had ceased to wonder what each day had in store, but took as a gift whatever it brought forth, and had learnt that the gloom of the world was but a shadow, that behind it, yet within reach, was joy.

It was as she stood gazing out into the radiance, with those very thoughts restoring her to calmness that a dark shadow suddenly crossed the little window. Her insides lurched with sudden fear as the door to the cottage slowly opened and there, framed in the doorway stood a tall, faceless silhouette, with a mop of dark hair gleaming in the fading light.

She emitted a sound that was something between a gasp and a sob. He took a step into the room and for a full minute they stood and stared at one another, frozen in time, he holding her eyes like a magnet. His face was set like granite, although as he stared it seemed as though a ray of inner light gleamed from those sombre eyes, which gave him a somewhat sleepy look. His gaze moved from her unwelcoming features to the crumpled dress she had on, then back again to her face.

Jessica broke eye contact and moved slowly

around the table to put something between them, gripping the back of a chair for support. The alarm in her was deep, but she held it in, forcing herself to stand still, to stay calm as she faced him. He was dressed in a casual tweed jacket and cord trousers, the legs pushed into the tops of his knee-length boots. In one hand, she saw he held a walking stick, the top in the form of what looked to be a hare's head carved in ivory, his other held stiffly by his side.

She felt she must say something to break the heavy, boding silence between them, and came abruptly to life. 'What're you doing here, creeping around in the dark?' she asked with obvious contempt. 'I don't recall inviting you. How did you find me, anyway?'

'I followed your brother,' he replied with no display of emotion, striving to speak lightly, doing his utmost to restrain some inner tumult.

He hadn't wanted to come. He had had a bad day. A contract he had been counting on had been snatched from under his nose by a competitor. 'I came only because you haven't answered my messages I left with him. I take it he passed them on?'

'Yes, he passed them on.'

'Then why did you not reply?' he asked directly.

Her response was blunt. 'There was nothing to say.'

Luke made a move toward her and she immediately stepped back. He stood before her in an uneasy, half-hesitant manner, suppressing a flicker of feeling deep inside his breast, but said nothing. He was completely silent which was all the more unnerving since always before, his rage had been loud and explosive, strident with his temper.

'Just what is it you want?' There was a slight tremor to her voice as she swung round, looking for a way to escape, but there was none.

'What the hell do you think I want?' His expression was stern, but he held his temper. 'Do you know, you really disappoint me.'

'Why does that not surprise me?' she said flippantly.

'Don't you think you've taken this a bit too far? All this time you were right here, under my very nose,' he said, pointing a finger at the floor. 'Why here, of all places? This was the last place I expected to find you.'

'Exactly! That's why I chose it.'

'But aren't you nervous?'

'Should I be?'

'I mean being out here all alone, after what happened to Alice?'

Jessica shuddered at the reminder of the horror of the poor child's death, for that was all she had been, an innocent child of sixteen.

'The brute was caught.'

'It was evident Cartwright murdered your father and stepmother, but you can never be certain he was the one who raped and killed Alice.' Luke sighed heavily. 'Anyway, what an earth can you find here that you can't find at home?'

'Something you wouldn't understand.'

'You'll soon come running when you run out of money.'

'It might come as a shock to you to know that your money can't buy everyone.'

'It bought you, didn't it?' he said callously, raising

a brow.

He glanced about the room, taking in the faded drapes at the window, the old corner unit, the few pieces of crockery and the pile of books scattered carelessly on the rug by what looked to be the one decent chair. The table decked with the blue chenille cloth, with a vase of green foliage set in its very middle. There seemed hardly space enough to move.

'Well, all I can say is you've more courage than you have common sense.' His eyes came to rest on her again. 'I had a call from the Parson. From what he had to say, you've obviously been complaining about me.'

She threw him a bitter look. 'There was no need. News of your...' she could hardly bear to say it, '...your indiscretions, reached him soon enough.'

'You had no damn right to discuss our private affairs with a stranger.'

'Parson Appleby is no stranger to me.'

'I never thought you of all people would turn against me.'

'How the hell did you expect me to react?' she cried heatedly, her eyes narrowing with indignation, anger and humiliation flooding through her at the thought of how he had treated her.

'I see your tongue has lost none of its sharpness.' He was so controlled, with a lifetime of self-discipline behind him.

'Who in the hell do you think you are?' Maddened that he could affect her so, she took in a deep breath to calm herself. 'What ...what if the shoe was on the other foot? What then? Would you not have turned against me? Perhaps you should think about it.'

That brought the question to the back of his throat,

choking to get out. 'What is he to you?'

She looked puzzled. 'Who?'

'The young man that paid you a visit?'

Her voice broke into a cry of accusation. 'Don't tell me you've been spying on me?'

His face was an expressionless mask. 'Not at all. I just happened to be here at the same time.'

'Then why didn't you show yourself?'

He pursed his lips and shrugged 'I've no idea. I didn't want to cause a scene I suppose. Won't you answer my question?'

'He's a friend. A very close friend.'

The words silenced him, jolting his brain. He didn't take kindly to a rival. The muscles in his face quivered and his look suddenly became dangerous, threatening, a look that came close to being murderous. 'You're a married woman. You remain tied to me.'

'Thank you for reminding me.'

'I meant he is getting too familiar.'

'Oh, I know exactly what you meant. How dare you of all people talk to me about right and wrong. You might see yourself as the centre of the universe, but as far as I'm concerned, what I do with my life has no longer anything to do with you.' She held her breath, fearing she had gone too far, letting it out slowly.

'Everything you do is my business,' he stated, guarding his emotions zealously, hiding behind the high wall of protection he had built around himself. 'Now listen, I don't have time for your silly games. If I find you have been...' he trailed off, not able to bear naming it, but a twist of doubt struck him in the gut and teased his mind, though he did his best to ignore it for it was …was unthinkable! The very thought of it sent his brain into a spin. He steeled himself to ask the question, calling himself a fool, for his mouth had gone dry and his heart was hammering quite furiously in his chest. He hated her for having this effect on him and when he spoke his voice was almost a snarl.

'Have you?'

'You should know better than to ask,' she replied with bitterness.

'And you should know by now that I share nothing of mine. You would be wise to remember that. Nothing! No one takes what belongs to me, not until I have done with it.' He was completely self-possessed now, his strangeness gone.

'Not only do you insult me, but you do my friend a great injustice. He has been nothing but kind and supportive.'

'Oh, I bet he has.'

'Those in glasshouses shouldn't throw stones. Besides, I don't care a damn what you believe anymore.'

'You and your silly sayings!' He held her with his dark cold gaze. 'Now, I'm going to talk. What I have to say will be brief.'

'I think you've said enough,' she replied acidly.

'Don't think! Just listen! And it would be best if you didn't interrupt.'

'Oh, just say whatever it is you've come to say and go,' she snapped angrily.

'As you wish. Firstly, I would remind you that you're still legally my wife. In leaving you have broken the law.'

'Then the law is a foolish one.'

'I said don't interrupt,' he barked, making her

flinch. 'Secondly, you should know I could have you physically returned to the house, if you won't come willingly. Do you understand?'

Jessica had listened reluctantly and her answer was short. 'Perfectly.'

His eyes narrowed menacingly. 'And you can be sure that I will. Do I make myself clear?'

'As a bell.'

'Is that all you can say?'

'What would you have me say?'

'That you take what I say seriously.'

She blinked momentarily, opening her mouth to reply, then realising the futility of further argument, closed it again without speaking.

'Oh, you might care to know that Toby has gone.'

'Gone where?'

'It was an accident. In the woods. He was killed by a stag.'

She closed her eyes momentarily in remembrance of the plucky little fellow. 'Poor little thing. I hope he didn't suffer.'

'I don't think so. It was over very quickly.'

Quite suddenly he was there beside her, sliding an arm about her waist in a strong possessive grip, taking her by surprise. He could see her stiffen quite visibly.

A panic began in her breast, which was hard to suppress, her face turning ashen with fear. The thought of what he might do made her feel physically sick.

'Don't! Don't touch me! Get away from me,' she cried, trying desperately to break free, but he only tightened his hold. Her softly opened lips, almost colourless, quivered with her uneven breathing.

He thrust his face close to hers. 'Just remember …you belong to me. You belong to me in every way. I'll never let go of what is mine. The sooner you come to terms with that the better.' Although he was smiling when he said it, it wasn't a pleasant smile and there was absolutely no warmth in his voice. 'I shall have my way. You can depend on it.'

He released her just as suddenly as he had grasped her and left without another word, going off in a bitter mood of indifference concerning the past and reck-lessness for the future. The harshness of his words seemed to jolt her out of her self-pity. She was trembling so violently after he had gone she had to sit down in a chair or she would have fallen. There in the cottage she had found peace and he had destroyed it. No. Interrupted it …she told herself. Peace would come again.

FIFTY-FOUR

Madame Duprez had once been one of the most sought-after courtesans in London, but fate had not been kind, the illness she had been struck down with now rendered her incapable of leading a normal life. She had let Luke go without a word. What could she have said to him? That she had a serious health problem and he might be carrying the infection? It was a sticky situation. She never knew she could be so afraid.

In financial dire straits, she was now completely dependent on him for every penny. She longed, if not for conquests, for some link with the world of gaiety in which she had once lived, but all invitations had stopped. She had attended her last social gathering, had danced her last dance. Most of her friends avoided her and, everyone who had business with her, considered it terminated. No longer able to go out in public she withdrew from the outside world and gradually faded.

A slight rash appeared on her chest, which by the end of the day had travelled up her neck to her face that, quite frankly, gave grounds for alarm. Her legs became swollen and she was often stupefied by laudanum, taken to ease the pain, all revealing the seriousness of her illness. Her wretchedness was most acute. She could not relieve the irksomeness of imprisonment. But there was worse to come; something far nastier awaited her.

She sat at her mirror, gazing at her reflection.

What a different face she saw. The faint smile on her pale lips seemed to mock the rosy vision of the other Amel Duprez. The skin was flushed with the rash, which she presumed would fade in time, but to make matters worse there were visible bags under her eyes, extinguishing her hopeful faith that ageing was only for others. She could not pinpoint precisely when she had began to fade.

Pain never left her now. And she was amazed at the effort even the smallest of movements took. She sat in a trance-like state, staring down at the comb tray that was full of hair - her hair. She felt alarm tinged with exasperation, filling her mind with fancies. She feared she was going bald, every woman's nightmare. She would have to resort to frezettes and scalpettes. What other miseries were in store for her?

Amel Duprez's nerves were in a critical state. She pulled persistently at the bell cord, but the staff were beginning to show signs of deafness as her illness progressed. With the kitchen in the basement, water had to be carried up three flights of stairs to fill her bath and then carried down again, by the maids. And who could blame them for their deafness? Money was owed to them. They had not received a penny piece for their services rendered.

Long before the onslaught of bills and writs from tradesmen, the servants had lost no time in lining their pockets. They had ample opportunity for cheating her, their employer. Several little treasured trinkets, small items easy to dispose of had noticeably disappeared from the rooms and some valuable books had been removed from the library. Bridget was the only one she could trust, the only one in the house who cared for her and stood by her. She had her sell the odd piece of jewellery, to buy quantities of laudanum. And Horace Twist, her dear friend, called on her regularly, bringing her gifts of flowers, and fancy boxes of sweetmeats that lay untouched on a table beside the bed.

Then came the crippling bouts of melancholy. It got to the point that without drugs she never slept at all, but shuffled slowly back and forth in her room, reeking with malevolence. Was she losing her mind? Those around her could do nothing to alleviate her distress during the last months it took her to cross the red line of death that had been lurking there all the while. She slowly succumbed to the malignant thing inside her. There was pain and more pain, fear and isolation. No one could have anticipated the dreadful change that had taken place. She had been made white-lipped and helpless by shafts of pain, struggling with an illness that she wanted no one to know about.

Conscious only of anguish of mind, agony and utter lonesomeness that stirred every fibre of the emotions, she constantly took laudanum in ever increasing quantities to dull her suffering, drawing a veil over her mind, a veil that shuts out the world and grants privacy, complete as darkness. Such privacy might one-day be too complete.

FIFTY-FIVE

To Jessica's utter surprise, Mathew Robinson had sold her sketches to some farmer who intended framing and hanging them in his study. With the money he had bought her more paper and pencils, hoping he had done the right thing, he said. She had been so much on her own that at first the stories he had to tell of his travels had been most welcome, but now, his constant droning chatter began to get on her nerves. She felt she had to get out, out into the fresh air where she felt free, liberated from the claustrophobia of the cottage.

'Come and walk with me,' she suggested politely, hoping he would decline and be on his way, but it wasn't to be.

They walked in silence, watching the clouds passing overhead, great galleons of piled-up cumuli, they floated in the heavens, their shadows racing with them. In the hedges the blackbirds feasted on the red and orange berries, leaning forward on their perches to reach one after another, which they swallowed greedily. The trees were still a blaze of colour from copper to the palest gold, almost the appearance of the sunlight that filtered through the branches in soft golden bars that danced with dust.

The last of the autumn days were growing shorter and chillier. Winter was close at hand. The birches showed their silver bark half hidden in thinning leafage, the mountain ashes pure yellow, the horse chestnut too, and the oaks towered above all, smouldering in their russet dress. The sweet sound of rustling leaves was as soothing as the rush of falling water. Bracken on the slopes was beginning to turn from green to brown and the heather from purple to amber - nature's forms of loveliness.

Jessica felt a slow change of mood. Her boredom waned and she forgot her frustration. The day was so perfect that it left no room for discontent.

'I love the trees. I used to scramble up them when I was a child. It all seems such an age away now,' she said distractedly. 'Autumn's so colourful, but I think I love spring best of all, when the primroses bloom. Did you know primroses open only at dusk, so swiftly that they can be seen and heard? The buds sound like popping soap bubbles as they burst.'

'Do you believe in fate?' Mathew asked quite suddenly, breaking her trial of thought. 'That things are meant to happen?'

She gave him a perplexed look. 'What do you mean?'

'Well, you and me, for instance ...here ...now. It's as though everything has been waiting for my return. Is it luck, do you think?'

'Just to be born is said to be lucky.'

'Well, I think it's more than luck. I'm convinced it's fate. All along we were meant to be together. Why else should all this have happened?'

It was strange how life tosses up possibilities, moments to grasp. He wanted Jessica's love for himself, and now she had seemingly turned away from her husband, it was the moment to step in.

'My mother used to say love only brings heartbreak,' Jessica said. 'I know now that she was right.'

'I remember warning you he was one for the...' he

started to say.

'It all seems a lifetime ago,' she interrupted. 'I recall my answer was not too kind.'

'So I remember. But one thing about memories, you can always make new ones.'

'My mind's full of memories, things I would sooner forget. But that's not so easy. Luke somehow got into my head. I felt like one of his possessions. As long as I played the obedient wife everything was fine. But he was so...' she floundered for an acceptable word, '...controlling, so manipulative. Forever adjusting me; my speech, my hair, and my clothes. He was continually telling me what to wear, what to do and what not to do, what was acceptable and what was not acceptable.'

'A person should be loved for who they are. Isn't that what everyone wants?'

'I suppose it is. But at first it didn't seem to bother me, but it got so I couldn't think straight, let alone think for myself. He told me who I could see, what books I must read, and I was never allowed an opinion of my own. Oh, I could go on and on, but don't want to bore you.' She pulled her cloak closer about her, lifting her hair to twist it back into a knot out of the way. 'What a sight I must look with my swollen eyes and mess of frizzy hair.'

Mathew caught at her arms and drew her to him, tightly, trapping her arms helplessly within his. She turned her face away.

'You have beautiful hair. It should be left loose about your shoulders, not bundled up and contorted into some frigid style that doesn't really suit you.' His fingers touched one loose wisp that escaped her grasp.

'It's from habit I suppose. My hair was a constant irritation to him. I strove to keep it neat and to his liking, but...'

She trailed off as Mathew put one hand under her chin and turned her face towards his. His kiss was light, a butterfly touch, his mouth resting lightly upon hers in a touch that was the very ghost of passion.

For the life of him he could not stop himself. This time his kiss was not meant to comfort, but more forceful, more demanding and infinitely more reckless.

Jessica's skin prickled, setting off bells of alarm ringing in her head. She stiffened and pulled away.

'What is it? Is something wrong?'

'What do you mean?'

'You seem uncomfortable, if I might say so.' His look was soft with adoration, his eyes pleading. 'Jessie, just let me hold you.'

'No, don't!' Her cry was tremulous and her eyes wide with something like fear.

Startled by her reaction, he reluctantly stepped back, waiting for her to recover. 'A little jumpy, aren't we? What the hell did that bastard do to you?' he asked ferociously, tearing her composure to tatters.

He studied her closely. Her lips were compressed by thoughts, thoughts that were obviously distressing her, her eyes betraying the feelings she was trying to keep under control.

Jessica was determined not to weep. Her lips parted to speak, but not a word came from them. Speech was impossible. She simply shook her head helplessly and her breath came in shuddering gasps.

'Don't tell me nothing!' Mathew said fiercely 'When I look at you, all I see is sadness. A smile never reaches your eyes.'

She let out her breath she had been holding, in a long, quivering sigh. 'All forms of humour have been squeezed out of me. You can know nothing of the nature of my life with him. There's no words to tell you what I went through.' Her voice was clearly anguished.

'I just have to look in your eyes to see the fear. What the hell did he do to make you so afraid?'

There was a fragile calm, the recipe for disaster. Inside she was over-wound by suffering. 'It's not something I can talk about. But the torture, I assure you, was acute. In the end, he crushed my spirit. He …he didn't leave me with any …anything …pride, self-respect …nothing.' She yielded to a preliminary sob.

'My God! I could kill the swine.'

'Don't! Don't say that! As much as I hate what he did to me, deep inside I …I still love him but just couldn't go on …go on turning the other cheek,' she said weakly. She bowed her head like a dying creature that has drawn its last breath. 'I don't know who I hate most. Him for making me … me love him or myself for needing him so. I thought I had it all. Now, I sit alone and listen to the quiet of the night. Oh, Mathew … I'm so lonely...'

Sympathy and, indeed, a feeling of understanding radiated towards her. In the face of his compassion the sorrow in her heart was hard to bear. She stood with trembling hands clasped over her mouth, blinking rapidly, doing her best to control her distress but the tears spilled over her lashes and glided down her cheeks. He went to her.

'No...' She made an effort to thrust him away, but

his arms were tight about her and he held her against his heart. Her weeping broke out afresh, her eyes closing against the pain, her anguished cries muffled against his chest. She really thought her heart would break.

Jessica wept frantically for that other young girl as much as she wept for herself ....the girl who had dreamt of Heaven and experienced Hell. So naive she had been, so much in love and had longed to be loved in return.

Mathew could feel her warmth through his clothing. His love for her touched him anew through her nearness, but the situation needed careful handling. He gently stroked her hair, but longed to kiss away those tears, whisper his undying love and take her away from there. Her eyes came up to his, swollen and weary, all the sparkle gone from them.

'When two lives touch they ...they can never again be separated. He was the man I ... I chose. The man I vowed to cherish all ...all my days.' She sniffed loudly. 'Oh, Mathew, I ...I'm sorry.'

'Now then, it's all right, my love. Dry your tears. I never knew a woman had so much water in her.'

Mathew found her vulnerability highly desiring, a desire difficult to hide. First love was like smallpox - it leaves its scars. Oh, he had had different affairs, wallowing in female flesh like a pig in clover, some as sweet as a peach, but he had to admit none had touched his heart as Jessica Greenward had. He placed his fingertips gently on her wet cheek, not daring to do more for fear she would shrink away.

'You know, Jessie, people are only lonely because they build walls instead of bridges. Bad memories're like corks let out of bottles. They swell and no longer fit. Lick your wounds and make a fresh start. We could go away together, you and me. Just the two of us. Take a room and live respectably.'

'Oh, Mathew, I don't know what to say. I ...I'm speechless.'

He let his hand drop to his side, feigning shock. 'Speechless! That's impossible.'

A weak smile shone through her tears. She wiped her eyes as she spoke. 'I'm flattered, real ...really I am, but this...' She shook her head from side to side. '...this can never lead to anything. There's some ...something I haven't told you.'

'You're with child. I know,' he said, his tone matter-of-fact.

Her swollen lids widened. 'You already know?'

'Joe put me in the picture. But it doesn't matter to me.' He took both her hands in his. 'Jessie, let me take care of you and the child. Let me put the smile back in your eyes.' Even before he had finished he could see by the look on her face that he had made a terrible mistake, that he had been too rash, too impetuous.

'But don't you see it matters to me? I'm still a married woman. A wrong choice in marriage is impossible to undo.'

'Then we'll go where no one knows us,' he suggested hopefully.

She cringed at the very idea and shook her head. 'No matter what the outcome in the future, I will always be his. He has my heart.' That was where her soul was - with him - bound by blessed bonds that bind husband and wife. 'Just because you can't see the chains doesn't mean they're not there. I long for him and yet fear him, all at the same time. He still stands beside me you see. He always will. I'm sorry, Mathew, truly I am. I could never go with another.'

Now she had made plain what her feelings were, he let go of her hands and stepped back, stoically putting away his private dreams.

'There's no need to explain. The look on your face says it all.'

'But you don't understand. Things are complicated. Nothing prepares us for the feelings we have. I think I finally understand how much I meant to you,' she added remorsefully. 'If he had the suspicion ...the slightest suspicion that you wanted to be more than just a friend, there's nothing he wouldn't stop at.'

'I gathered that.'

'The pain of loving a man who loves not me, but another, is so sore that I pray to God to deliver me from it. And to make matters worse, I have to be pregnant. A child is the last thing I want right now.'

'Don't talk like that, Jessie. Think what you're saying. It has to be seen for the gift it is. You'll only do yourself harm by being bitter. Let go of your hate. It will all come right in the end, you'll see.'

'Do you think so, Mathew? Do you really think so?'

'I'm sure of it. It may not seem like it now, when you're drained of hope, but you'll feel differently in time. Blame only keeps wounds open. Only forgiveness heals.' He smiled reflectively. 'Do you know single men live longer?'

She wiped her eyes with the back of her hand. 'Really? I can't say I did.'

'It's a fact. I read it somewhere.' He took in a deep breath and let it out in a long sigh. 'Oh, well, I think it's about time we were turning back. I don't want to be on the move in the dark.'

They fell silent for some time, but the silence between them was not at all awkward. It was only when he brought her to her door that he decided to speak.

'Jessie, it's time you got your life back together again. Gather your strength and go to him.'

'But my head says forget him.'

'Forget your head and listen to your heart. You can't go on living in the past forever. You have a choice. Keep hiding or build a new life, lick your wounds and try again. You said yourself he wants you back.' Before she could think of a reply, he stooped and brushed her cheek lightly with his lips. 'Goodbye, Jessie. It's time to move on for you and me both. Be happy. No more sad eyes now. They always give you away.'

The man watching from a distance was almost urged to desperate deeds by the sight of the younger man standing so close to her. He did not care to see his wife handled. A great surge of emotion swept over him, choking him, a mixture of longing and, if he was to be honest, jealousy. He wanted to take the young pup by the throat and choke the very life out of him. But a sense of shame at the possibility that his young wife, who already despised him, should despise him even more, by discovering him there. He was vexed beyond measure that his sentiments should have led him to dally about the cottage in this way. But the truth was, he was afraid of her losing her heart to some other lucky bastard.

FIFTY-SIX

It was hard to believe that she had been in the cottage almost two months and was now into the third month of her pregnancy. Time had slipped by with no disturbing influence save those of her husband's visits that still persisted in her memory. Heaving off the burden of those thoughts, she concentrated her energy to a better purpose …indulging in the dream of becoming a naturalist - studying the animals and plants of the fells, the beauty of even the smallest wild flower, making her talents a source of usefulness as well as pleasure. Looking forward to anything but loneliness and misery, hoping that, in time, to render herself happily independent. For if the supersensitive germ of an idea be watered and tended, then surely all its ripe beauty would be ready to burst upon the world?

He came again two weeks after the first visit, settling himself down on an upright chair at one end of the table. The man who sat before her, the man whom she had loved with a passion which had almost overwhelmed her, had become her bitterest enemy, and the force which stretched between them was sharp and hard to bear. More often than not, tall in the company of most men, he now looked somewhat stooped, emaciated even, and his person showed marks of neglect.

He had on a dark grey, single-breasted jacket, which had three buttons but was fastened with only the one and sloped away from just above the waist, showing a rather crumpled waistcoat underneath. The collar of his shirt was high against his cheeks and turned up all round, with a lawn cravat wrapped about his neck and tied in a small knot at the front; neither looked very clean. The trousers he had on were tight-fitting, tapered and tucked into leather boots that were in need of a good polish. In his hand he held the cane which he gripped firmly.

Jessica's eyes shifted from the clothes to the face of the person who wore them. His hair was unruly and a good deal longer than he usually kept it. Red lips peeped through a profusion of dark stubble that covered the lower half of his face which had a strained look about it, the eyes unusually dim, some-how making him look older. She couldn't believe it was really him. To be at all times absolutely impecc-able had always been an obsession with him.

He made no excuse and gave no explanation, but he was polite. 'Do you mind if I smoke?'

'I don't care if you burn,' she said maliciously.

For a minute he seemed unable to speak, revealing his wounded feelings fleetingly. Collecting himself with an effort, he spoke quietly. 'There's no need to be unpleasant.'

'I'll be as unpleasant as I want. What were you expecting? A tearful reunion?' she tried not to let her voice reveal her heart's anxiety.

He lit a cigar and placed it between his lips, drew on it and twisted his head away to release the smoke. Then he turned to look at her, meeting her startling eyes. There was so much going on behind those eyes. He could see the pain in them now, the bitterness and the hurt. Her lips were red and dewy, her cheeks rosy, flushed with obvious indignation. She didn't want him here, he could tell. She had screwed her long, thick hair into a firm bun on the back of her neck to keep it off her face, but stubborn curling tendrils had escaped to hang down the side of her cheeks. She was clad in a drab grey day dress, tight at the bodice and done up at the high neck with a brooch.

His eyes rested on the gentle swell of her breasts that gave promise of the arrival of rich adult years. He felt the heat flame in his belly. How he longed to cup one in his hand, and to kiss that sweet spot at the back of her neck. He drew on his expensive cigar again and released the smoke, before finally speaking.

'I've come to ask you to give our marriage another chance.'

Jessica's reply was sharp. 'After what you put me through? You can't be serious?'

Not a glimmer of his thoughts showed in his eyes as he puffed serenely on his cigar and released the smoke slowly, deliberately taking his time.

'You have a right to feel used. You were! But it does no good to dwell on the past. There are other things to consider. Why can't you make allowances? God knows I made plenty for you.' His manner, his flippancy was no more than an armour against hurt, but Jessica never saw it that way.

'Which only goes to prove I don't belong in your world any more than you belong in mine.'

He sighed wearily, his hand going to his head. 'Please, don't let's quarrel. I just want to say I've been hoping you could find it in your heart to let bygones be bygones and come home, back where you belong.'

Some strange emotion passed over his face, an expression of sorrow, of regret, the emotions mixed together, come and gone so fleetingly Jessica wondered if she had seen them at all. He still had that power of affecting her and deep down he knew it. The truth was, she still loved him, but her wounded pride would not allow her to forgive him. She took a grip of herself and managed to speak a little more calmly.

'You're not the person I thought you were. I don't even know you anymore. But I do know I don't belong with you. We lived totally separate lives. When you were home, all you ever did was take. It was all one way. You never gave anything in return.'

'I can't agree. I think I gave more than enough. You wanted for nothing.'

Her face stiffened into a strange, hard expression. 'Dear God! This is so typical of you. What have I done that I must endure...? I meant affection, not possessions. You gave me everything except what I needed most. Not to mention, the pleasure you took in constantly pointing out every little flaw I have. But none of that matters now, because I no longer care. There is nothing you might have to say that holds the slightest interest for me anymore.'

He pushed his hand, which had a curious tremble to it, through his thick hair. 'Well, it seems I am just wasting my breath.'

He rose to his feet and went to the fireplace, throwing the cigar in to the embers, and as he turned back he took out his watch from his waistcoat pocket and glanced at it.

'I should be on my way. I'm already late and I need to bathe and change before I leave,' he said quietly, revealing nothing of his inner turmoil. 'I will be in London for the next week...'

Jessica's fury rekindled, bringing fire to her eyes.

'With that whore, no doubt?'

'Now, Jessica, that remark is beneath you. You're being offensive.'

'We both are. The difference is I'm trying to be but you just can't help it.'

He tutted impatiently. 'For your information I haven't seen or spoken to Amel ...Madame Duprez for some weeks now.'

She would not suffer in silence. The presence of Amel Duprez constantly between them embittered her words with scorn. 'Well, then, don't let me detain you.'

'I am only going to visit because she is not at all well. And I have other appointments, important business appointments to keep.'

'How dare you have the nerve to come here to ask me, your very own wife, to come home when you're still associating with that ...that *bitch*. Just you remember, a man who chases two sparrows catches neither.'

His eyes closed briefly in exasperation. 'Hell's teeth! I really don't have time for this. I have more important things to do than play your silly games. I should be home again by the end of the week, Sunday at the latest and expect to find you there when I get back.'

'Don't expect anything, then you won't be dis-appointed.'

Luke sighed dramatically. He stood there for a while just looking at her, his face set in a dreadful rigid mask.

'You know, it took a lot for me to come.'

He wanted to go to her, put his arms about her, tell her how badly he missed her, needed her even, but he could not do it, of course. She had wounded his pride and self-esteem by leaving, damaged his standing in the community and he could not forget it.

'Either you knock the self-pity on the head and we make a fresh start or it's over. As simple as that.' He spoke with listless resignation. He made for the door and clasping the latch, turned to gaze on her one more time, pointing the cane at her. 'I'm warning you, I won't come again.'

Jessica went to close the door, staring mournfully after his retreating rigid back. Desolation savaged her battered spirit. Don't despair, she told herself, but, dear God, it was hard. She knew she would weep again that night.

FIFTY-SEVEN

It had been raining since before dawn, a thin icy rain that slicked London with a grey sheen, moving across the country like a fine net. It dripped dolefully from the trees onto the greasy pavements beneath and sent the chill striking through to the very bones. The waiting-room to the London surgery was carpeted and soberly furnished, something like a country parlour. Luke paced the floor restlessly

The surgery door opened and Doctor Cleland came through, greeting him with a handshake. 'Ah, Mr Sheridan. I had almost given you up.'

'My apologies. I haven't been in London for some time. I've been extremely busy.'

'Well, you're here now.' He gestured toward his office. 'Please, do come on in.'

Luke walked past him. The room had worn, unpainted floors, but there was a look of winter comfort about it. The doctor's flat-top desk was large and well made, the papers in orderly piles under glass weights. Behind the stove, a wide bookcase with double glass doors, reached from the floor to the ceiling. It was filled with medical books of every thickness and colour. On the top shelf stood a long row of thirty or forty volumes, bound all alike in dark mottled board covers with imitation leather backs.

'Take a seat.' The doctor motioned toward a chair, he himself perching on the side of the desk, his hands gripping the edge.

Luke sat down. He smiled, but would not have

if he had known the surprise fate had prepared for him. 'What was it you wanted to see me about?'

'May I speak plainly?'

'Yes, of course,' Luke replied.

'It's to do with Madame Duprez's illness. It is against my principles to divulge information to do with any of my patients. However, in this case, as it was you who hired my services in the first place, I feel it my duty to warn you there are things you should know.'

Luke raised dark eyebrows inquisitively, wondering what the deuce was coming. 'I'm listening.'

'Syphilis, or The Pox, as it is more commonly known, is a contagious disease...'

'Syphilis?' Luke echoed with genuine shock. 'Are you telling me Madame Duprez is suffering from syphilis? Syphilis?' He repeated yet again in sheer disbelief.

'I fear it is. Without a doubt. Syphilis is prevalent among such women. Promiscuity spreads the disease rapidly.'

Luke felt a fearful constriction of the heart. He took in a deep breath to steady himself. 'I can't believe it. There must be some mistake,' he murmured, reasoning with himself, denial taking over. 'I thought it was some woman's complaint, just a passing phase. She's unwell one minute and the next, as healthy as ever.'

'Don't be misled by what is only a temporary improvement. Change is not always visible,' the doctor warned. 'How long is it since you last saw Madame Duprez?'

'Just a little over three weeks ago. Why?'

'I must warn you, you are in for a shock. Madame

Duprez's health has deteriorated rapidly over the last weeks.'

Luke met the doctor's steady gaze. 'I know very little about syphilis. Enlighten me.'

'I did not want to alarm you by going into details, but since you ask, I will tell you all I know. Syphilis is a disease, a contagious disease of slow development, contracted in adult life by sexual contact with an infected person, as you no doubt know.'

Luke was rendered speechless. He merely nodded.

Doctor Cleland continued. 'There are a number of different forms of the disease, one of them being G.P.I.'

'G.P.I?'

'General Paralysis of the Insane, in which progressive mental deterioration is a prominent feature. Mental derangement and sometimes fits.'

'Good God!' Luke drew in his breath.

'Another form affects the spinal cord, first manifestation of the disease occurring soon after infection. The early stages of the disease are mild, but years later the effects can often be ultimately fatal.'

'You mean, it can lay dormant for years?'

'In some cases, yes! Of course, in the second stages it can affect the skin and mucous membrane, ulceration speedily comes on, and yet, in other cases showing little more than a slight skin eruption. Thirdly, the bones and muscles and eventually the brain.'

Luke tried hard to overcome his shock and find his voice. 'Are you saying what I think you're saying?'

'I am saying the disease can eventually affect the brain and nervous system.'

Luke fidgeted in his seat. 'But is there no cure?'

'The disease may be arrested by treatment, but not reversed. Treatment consists of applications of mercury ointment, which hopefully, suppresses the symptoms of syphilis, but in turn can cause kidney disease and painful burning. Do you follow me?'

Luke shuddered. He felt as though an icy hand had touched his spine. 'I'm ahead of you.'

'Cases vary of course. In Madame Duprez's case, she is extremely ill. In the third stages I fear, making treatment virtually impossible.'

'What will happen to her?'

'As I have said, she will go insane. Progressive mental deterioration is a prominent feature,' the doctor explained gravely.

Luke met his gaze. 'Tell me, what is the first sign?'

'The usual sign is a chancre, a very small ulcer, usually in the genital region. In some cases, it may be very inflamed or it may well be so small that it goes unnoticed. It's during this stage that the person is highly infectious. A few days after the ulcer has appeared, glands all over the body become swollen and hard. This condition lasts for several weeks as a rule, then the sore slowly heals and the glands subside. I expect you'll agree with me, Mr Sheridan, when I say that you yourself need to take control over your ...err ...sexual impulses.'

'Reluctantly, I do,' he lied expertly.

'Allowed to go unchecked, the bacterium that causes syphilis can invade and destroy the inner organs. Of course, you might well have been fortunate enough to escape the infection.'

Luke's response was eager. 'Do you think so, Doctor?'

The doctor held up his hands and shrugged. 'Who can tell? As I have explained, it's during the early stages that the person is highly infectious. Madame Duprez might well have been carrying the infection for years without even knowing of it. I suggest you arrange an examination and then we will see.'

He turned and picked up a small box off the desk. 'In the meantime, if you intend visiting the …err …lady in question, perhaps you would be so good as to pass these pills onto the nurse. To be given to the patient four times a day and into the night if she's unable to sleep. It's written on the box. They will help with the fever.'

Luke took them from him. 'Fever?'

'Yes, Madame Duprez is burning with fever again.'

'Again?'

'Yes. It is quite common. Undoubtedly, the patient would have suffered fever at an earlier stage. After a variable period, usually about two months from the start of the infection, the secondary symptoms appear which resemble an ordinary fever in so far as they include rise of temperature and feverishness, loss of appetite, vague pains throughout the body and usually a faint rash, seen best upon the front of the chest.'

'She has already complained of pains in the back area and the abdomen.'

'So I understand. The pills will help ease the pain also.'

'Thank you, Doctor. Tell me, how long will the fever last?'

The doctor pursed his lips and shrugged. 'The duration of this stage can vary. Sometimes a week or two, sometimes longer, that's if the patient has not already departed from this earth.'

All hope for Amel faded. 'Merciful God!'

'I'm afraid it gets worse.'

Luke ran his hand nervously through his hair. 'How could it possibly get any worse?'

'In untreated or inadequately treated cases, manifestations of the tertiary stage develop.'

'The tertiary stage?'

'The third stage. This can happen after the lapse of some months, even years in some cases. These consist in the growth, here and there throughout the body, of masses of granulation tissue as hard nodules in the skin, or form tumour-like masses in the muscles. They may even develop in the brain and spinal cord where their presence causes very serious symptoms.'

'Just how more serious can it get?'

'Oh, still later, effects are apt to follow. Mental failure. Also certain nervous diseases.'

Luke shuddered with dread, holding up a tremulous hand to draw a halt. 'Please, stop there! I've heard enough!' His hand then went to his forehead. 'Tell me, what are Madame Duprez's chances?'

'I'm afraid Madame Duprez is past help. Time is a luxury she does not have. Her future could be measured in weeks, days even.'

Luke glanced at the doctor enquiringly, his face deadly earnest. 'Then wouldn't it be wise to move her to a hospital?'

'She'll receive far less attention there. There's not much they can do for the dying. The emotional strain of her situation must be taken into account. At least, in her own home we can make her as comfortable as possible until the end comes.'

'Yes, of course.' A stab of fear made Luke's heart lurch. There was something he had to ask. 'One more thing, Doctor. There's something I must ask. Can this …this disease in any way affect pregnancy, an unborn child?'

'Indeed it can. The infection can be spread to the foetus before birth by an infected mother even, a condition to which the unborn child is infected through the maternal blood stream, leading then, as a rule, to miscarriage or a stillbirth.'

This at once opened Luke's eyes, which had been shut in downright stupidity. The tragedy of his and Jessica's stillborn child. The shock drained the blood from his face contorted by the pangs of conscience, in a choking sense of disaster, making him look quite hideous. In that moment he surrendered all hope for sons of his own.

'However, should the child survive, the effects appear in infancy, tertiary syphilis affecting the brain and nervous system.'

'Merciful God! Stop! I think you've said enough,' Luke said brusquely, not meaning to sound so curt, only trying to hide the guilt and sadness the doctor's words had caused, words that burnt themselves ineradicably into his mind. Thank the fates that such a melancholy truth was discovered before it was too late. There could be no more pregnancies, no son that he had longed for.

As it was, the good doctor did not take offence, but carried on regardless. 'Madame Duprez ought to be speedily enlightened.'

Luke's look was one of surprise. 'You mean you have not yet told her?'

'I will be calling on her later today, but how does a stranger tell one as young and beautiful as Madame Duprez that she is to suffer a slow and agonising death? But she has to be told. She needs to settle her affairs.'

'Indeed!'

'Any person suffering from this disease forms a source of infection and should take precautions not to spread it.'

Luke stood up. 'Thank you for your advice, Doctor.'

'Oh, before you go there is one more thing. The question of an outstanding bill.'

'That's not a problem. I'll settle it.'

'Thank you, Mr Sheridan. Remember now, the disease may be arrested, but not reversed by treatment. I suggest you're examined thoroughly right away. Salvasan organic compound of arsenic is used in the treatment of syphilis. But that treatment must be instituted as soon as possible after infection is acquired. One must never take anything for granted. We must prepare for the worst and hope for the best. Health and time are most important. Make the most of the second, whilst you have the first.'

'I just hope it is not too late,' Luke said with trepidation, feeling the full terror of the thought. 'One must tremble when one thinks of just what can take place.'

FIFTY-EIGHT

A person protects himself from fright, by anxiety. And Luke certainly felt uneasy. Who could blame him? If the doctor, who seemed to be a man who knew what he was talking about, had meant to scare the living hell out of him, he had succeeded. He was so overcome that he walked around the streets until late into the afternoon when it started to rain again, but a drowning man is not troubled by the rain.

The dark firmament and keen cold air suited one who had little need of aids to emotion--one who had, indeed, but the single wish to get rid, if he only could, of the terrible sensation in his head. Without thought or intention he drove his legs along; not running, because he knew that he would have to stop the sooner, but striding on, blindly following his footsteps where they led, along Park Lane into Piccadilly and past the market gardens of Old Brompton. A desperate walk in the heart of London, keeping always in the dark; not a human being spoken to or even clearly seen, not bird or beast, just the gleam of the lights, and the hoarse muttering of the traffic. All the time he was wondering how he could tell Amel what Doctor Cleland had told him. Over and over again he brought to mind the doctor's words.

'I suggest you're examined thoroughly, right away. Treatment must be instituted as soon as possible after infection is acquired.'

Taking a hedged lane to the left he came to Chelsea embankment where the voices of half-naked urchins mingled with the plaintive mew of gulls flying inland from the sea. He stood watching the brown-sailed skiffs and heavy barges trailing their shadows in the pewter-coloured water. A foetid stench of sewer refuse came to his nostrils; he felt the panic in his mouth and did desperate battle with it, mastering nausea and his stunned thoughts, crowding so close upon him that he seemed plunged in a confused state of semi-consciousness.

He gazed across the expanse of river, soothed by the wistful charm of the hazed distance wreathed in scarves of mist about the farther shore, where graceful mansions shouldered a mushroom growth of warehouses, stark against the fading sky; progressive present nudging elbows with the past.

A shocked awareness filtered through from the lifting curtain of his bewildered mind, a fragment of memory coming to taunt him, sending a shiver down his spine. He could see Amel that evening, standing before the mirror in a shimmering creation, her cloud of golden hair about her shoulders …asking him if he noticed anything different, anything unusual about her. He shrugged the idea away. It was too ludicrous to contemplate.

There had been nothing to indicate disaster. Nothing more than an occasional headache, a tossing restlessness, a faint glaze in those incredible blue eyes. She had also complained once or twice of numbness in her hands. Nothing more. And yet she must surely have known? Why else would she have asked? Like a man tied hand and foot, he was swept by such a feeling of exasperated rage as he had never known. That woman! Let him be free of her and the passion, so that his brain might work again!

A couple of sewer rats were edging up to him; their little, old pinched faces smeared with a mildewy slime. He dug out of his pocket a handful of coins and flung them at their bare, filth-crusted feet and hurried away.

The afternoon had dwindled into evening; the sky was dark and overhung with clouds, and a creeping fog to chill him. Majestic houses that lined the road stood solidly behind brick walls and great iron gates, concealed by trees and shrouded in their conservative silence. Luke stood brooding in the dwindling light, outside Burlington House, staring up at its grey front through the trees, the shadows of whose trunks, in the light of a street lamp, were spilled out along the ground like the spines of a fan.

If Amel Duprez were dead, would he really care? Should he not be almost glad? If she were dead her witchery would be dead, and he could stand up straight again and look his wife in the face! He shivered a little, feeling cold and then hot. The rain had stopped long ago, but his clothes were damp and the cold struck through to his bones. He had eaten nothing since breakfast and it was now past six o'clock. He should have gone back to his hotel and changed in to dry clothes.

Inside, a deadly silence had fallen on the great house. It was hard on those servants that still lived under its roof. They hovered about the place like ghosts, their voices hushed, moving to and fro virtually on tiptoe, the frightful sight of Madame Duprez day after day getting on their nerves, sometimes driven to exasperation by the plaintive sound of her voice and the sudden inexplicable moments of rage. Her life was now spent as a bedridden recluse, a syphilitic outcast, living in a profligate and extremely expensive world, trapped like a bird in a gilded cage …every day a torment to her.

Bridget was the one who informed Luke that the doctor was with the mistress now, as she accompanied him up the stairs. Doctor Cleland had arrived before him and was already on his way out. They met on the landing, the doctor telling them that Madame Duprez's condition was much the same; but she was now passing urine the colour of burgundy - his frankness causing Bridget's face to flush scarlet. She hastily excused herself and went on in to her mistress's bedroom.

'Madame Duprez requires complete rest to reserve her strength,' the doctor informed Luke, speaking with no trace of pity. 'But she needs to know the truth. She must be told that there is no hope of recovery.'

Doctor Cleland knew the intricate mechanisms of the human body, procedures for treating the early stages of Syphilis, cooling fevers, hastening the expulsion of mucus from the chest, soothing babies' colic and inducing relaxing sleep. Calming earache and toothache, lancing boils, setting broken limbs, easing haemorrhoids and inflamed skin, and stopping the flux of watery bowels, and he could give warmth to those who suffered the cold of approaching death. He was doing his best, but for Amel Duprez it was already too late. She had sold her soul to the devil and the devil was waiting to collect.

After the doctor departed, Luke stood stock still just inside the door of Amel's boudoir, arrested in his tracks, shuddering a little against the scented heat of the atmosphere and screwing up his eyes until he grew used to the dimness. He could not abide the atmosphere of illness, the hush and the whispering. The sight of the nurse gliding around the bed was enough to make him feel ill at ease, bringing flashes of times past to his mind. Inside him the tremble of fear returned and he felt his courage ebbing. A second's hesitation and it might have failed him. He felt like two men, separate and distant, joined in uneasy alliance. Willing himself, he trod silently across the expanse of carpet without knowing quite how he moved at all, until he was standing next to Bridget, beside the bed.

'Please, don't stay too long, Sir. The patient needs her rest,' the nurse whispered on her way out.

Luke wasn't really listening. The sight of the frail outline beneath the covers made him feel physically sick. It was not Amel Duprez that he looked upon, not the woman he had known, the exquisitely beautiful goddess he had watched charm and entice men round her with one glance from astonishingly sparkling, blue eyes. Those once startling eyes were now slightly inflamed, wide and unblinking, as she tossed and murmured unceasingly. The golden hair, which had been her pride and joy, her crowning glory that had bounced so enchantingly on those smooth white shoulders, now lay dull and lifeless in a wispy mess about her head. The face was marred and disfigured with angry red blotches that spread across the cheeks and down to the once creamy neck.

He was astonished at the infatuation that had rendered him possessed, thus thoughtless and careless of the fate of another, his young, innocent wife. But now the spell was broken. He gazed at her with distaste and remorse. On first seeing her one felt a sense of shock at so much beauty spoiled, a dreadful travesty of the woman she once was. No longer was she that alluring person, the sensuous Amel Duprez with her quick wit and intelligence …and capacity for lying. He shook his head in horror and passed a trembling hand over his eyes as if to brush this nightmare from them, and turned away to face Bridget who stood right beside him, staring down at her mistress with a look of such misery on her face.

'Monsieur Sheridan, I have been meaning to speak to you. I have a diamond ring, a solitaire that belongs to Madam. She wanted me to have it, but I couldn't possibly keep it. It is too valuable. What should I do with it, Monsieur?'

Luke shrugged. 'If Madam wanted you to have it, then keep it.'

'But Monsieur...'

'I gave that particular ring to your mistress. It's of no use to me. You have my permission to keep it. Do what you will with it. Sell it if you wish.'

'Merci, Monsieur.'

'If there is anything else you would like, take it. It will only be seized by the bailiffs.'

'Oh, no, Monsieur, I couldn't. Madam has always been good to me. The ring is more than enough. I will treasure it always.' After a few minutes of silence, she spoke again. 'Is there anything I can get you, Monsieur? Some refreshments perhaps?'

'No. No thank you, Bridget.' He looked thoughtful for a moment. 'But there is one thing that's been on my mind … something I've been meaning to ask.'

'Monsieur?'

'My letters to your mistress. Would you happen

to know where they are kept?'

'Oui, Monsieur.'

'You would be doing me a great service, Bridget, if you were to reclaim them for me. Can that be done? Discreetly, of course.'

'Oui, Monsieur. I will see to it personally.' She curtsied and went from the room.

Luke glanced round in the gloom and heaved a weary sigh. Crossing to the fireplace he pulled at the bell cord. It was some time before a maid put in an appearance.

'It's too gloomy in here. Bring more candles for the lamps at once,' he ordered.

It was then that he felt her eyes upon him. He moved to the side of the bed, peering down at her in the fading light, this woman who had always had first claim on his time. Endurance and despair, composure and the pallor of death, all mingled weirdly in her face.

'Is ...is that you ...Luke?'

'I'm right here,' he answered softly.

'Stay ...stay by my side.' Her voice was flat, scarcely above a whisper.

'I'm right here should you need me.' Involuntarily he put one hand out to her but she had not the strength to take it.

'Merci.' She closed her eyes again as she drifted away into sleep.

That was perhaps the most awful moment of all. For the life of him he couldn't tell her. But surely she knew? It seemed cruelly unfair that a body that had housed such a zest for life should have to surrender to decay and premature death. Remembering her sweet fragrance, her spun-gold hair and the smoothness of her skin, aroused in him a pity that kept him by her side. That night was spent sitting in a chair.

Troubled by the patient's irritating cough and her erratic breathing, the doctor bent low, lifting the sufferer's chin, taking a good look at her face. There were angry-looking encrustations at the corners of her mouth.

'Lord preserve us,' he murmured.

The good doctor had won Luke's deserved admiration, as much for his personal loyalty as for his medical skill and discernment. He wanted to tell him so, but his mouth was so dry, he couldn't speak the words.

'There's little I can do,' The doctor whispered against his ear. 'It's out of my hands. I fear the death struggle has begun. The clock is ticking.'

The disturbance at such a moment was more than Luke could bear. His anxiety found no outlet. He desperately needed to return home to be with his wife. He cleared his throat to find his voice.

'How …how long?'

Doctor Cleland shrugged his shoulders. 'Who can tell? She might last a day, maybe longer. The fact of the matter is, her strength has gone. If God is merciful He will let her die soon rather than later, without further suffering.'

Only a ghost of what Amelia Duprez had been remained, her feeble grip on reality had shattered. She lay in a strangely delirious, dark world of unreality that precedes death, her life hanging on a gossamer thread, her lily-white hands outstretched and moving from side to side with a regular unchanging motion as if to clear away the darkness that was closing in on her. A soul in torment; on the brink of hell.

Revulsion mingled with Luke's terror. Should he go? No …he could not bring himself to leave. The night drained away in tumultuous dreams and nervous insomnia. Wide-eyed and restless, he paced the floor. If he did manage to sleep, he awoke exhausted. Although he found it offensive and he shrunk from her, his conscience tormented him. Dutifully, he stood alone in the room of silence. She could not live much longer. She was literally wasting away. And yet, it seemed impossible that a woman with such a fierce love of living would give up the struggle and cease to breathe. It was a tragedy! An outrage!

In the room where she lay, this person who was a stranger to him now, a ghostly-pale, shrivelled woman who refused to die, this quiet was most marked for there her breathing was so faint it was scarcely perceptible. He stood by the side of the bed, his muscles in a grip of iron, looking with wondering curiosity upon the form of death, the body of a presumptuous sinner, who, with contemptuous ease had wound men around her little finger. She had welcomed many rather than be owned by one, the willing creature of every satanic impulse, the repulsive sport of demoniac possession.

When would death deliver her from that body of corruption? A lesser woman would have flickered and died, but not Amel Duprez. Only once did she falter. Her lips moved in one of those little, soft hurrying whispers that unhappy dreamers utter, the words all blurred with their wistful rushing. In those desperate moments she opened her eyes to beg, murmuring something about a loaded pistol. It had wormed its way into her tired brain... the idea of ending it all... to be spared the agony of such a slow, painful death.

All the while Luke was filled with an almost physical anguish that rose in him to the point of nausea, so powerfully that he thought he was going to vomit up all the horror that this spectacle had aroused in him. He could not for the life of him touch her. He lowered himself into a chair, listening to the slow wind moaning about the house, as he sat stiffly erect and motionless beside the bed. As the minutes crawled past, his thoughts turned to times gone by, of the very first moment he saw her, of those very earliest months, when he had been like a man possessed. Convinced she had been the woman for him, he had offered her marriage, a means of escape from the precarious life she led, which she had flatly refused.

The attachment, although it went beyond attachment - it had been more of a fixation - might have ended there had they not encountered each other again and developed an uncontrollable passion for each other. He had not expected her to exercise such power over him, but she had drawn him back to her like a pig to a trough. Smitten he had been by her beauty, infatuated, all over again. For she was ...had been lovely, absolutely exquisite. No other words would do.

He felt a sudden stab of guilt over Jessica pierce him, an innocent victim of circumstance, giving birth to a stillborn child. He had been too blinkered to see that he might be sowing seeds of his own, possibly her destruction. Mistakes are part of the dues one pays for a full life. Her moving out had only served to fuel the guilt. How he longed for the peace of mind he once had. He needed her and hadn't realised just how much. She had got to him somehow, touched him on the inside, but he had acted like a complete fool …worse than that - a raving lunatic. He had expected tears and anger, but instead there had been coldness and contempt. Jessica was a vivacious young woman with a strong sense of fair play.

For a moment his iron control shattered and he threw back his head, dragging his hands through his hair, pulling at the roots and the flesh of his forehead in despair. Seized with fury, he jumped up to go, but stopped in his tracks to gaze on the face he had so passionately desired. As far as he could tell in the soft gloom she betrayed no consciousness …but tears lay still upon the cheeks and her lips constantly moved, yet no sound broke the silence, no words came forth from those lips that had only a short time ago been so warm and so kissable. He knew exactly what she wanted of him and it struck as cold as ice against his heart. It was not anger so much that he felt, nor horror or dismay, though he was dismayed and he was horrified, but utter bewilderment. Breaking out into a sweat he began to suffer from a series of panic attacks that were to bring him to the edge of a nervous breakdown. He had to get away.

FIFTY-NINE

Madame Duprez parted this world on the 26th day of November in this year of 1831, in her London home. Her troubles were over; she was now where laudanum was no longer necessary. Her death caused something of a sensation and was viewed with some suspicion by the police, but they eventually concluded that it was nothing more than suicide. Being afraid of burglars, Madame Duprez had been in the habit of keeping a loaded pistol in a drawer by her bedside, and in a fit of deep melancholy had shot herself in the head.

Luke was to wonder for some time after, just who had granted her final wish. Amel could not have shot herself, for she had not the strength. Had it been the devoted Horace Twist? Or the loyal Bridget perhaps?

The servants rifled her possessions and made off with all they could carry. Through Bridget, Luke managed to retrieve the letters he had sent Amel, and he purchased the Louis XV needlework table carpet that hung on the wall in the dining room, which he had always admired.

Madame Duprez had been recklessly extravagant, borrowing money from her banker and as the mortgage had never been paid off, her debts, which totaled more than £60,000, pursued her beyond the grave. Her prized four-wheeled carriage and two matching white horses were the first to be seized. The bailiffs gained access to Burlington House, impounding it on behalf of her creditors and the bank, seizing all the valuable French furniture - the great exotic canopied bed, the magnificent Roman marble bath and the washstand fashioned in the shape of a castle. They claimed the gilded chairs, elegant sofas and a chaise lounge of equal elegance, the billiard table, cues and score-board, and the pianoforte. The Jacobean sideboard and all the side tables, a set of twenty four rococo chairs, silver ware, and the fine china and sparkling crystal.

A multitude of hangings were removed, French, Italian and English arts, embroideries and gilt framed mirrors. Clocks and oil lamps of all shapes and sizes. Anything that was removable was taken - absolutely everything - the magnificent carved doors, marble fireplaces, crystal chandeliers, even the drapes and carpets - all in perfect condition. Gowns, furs, boots and shoes, hats, tiaras and all other jewellery and millinery they could find.

All was to be sold, of course, at the much talked-about auction of her belongings, all her possessions and treasures, even the precious canaries that chirped away in their elaborate ornate cages, in order to pay off her debts.

Had it not been for the generosity of some of her closest male friends, Madame Duprez would have died in a debtor's prison, and it would have been entirely her own fault. Luke himself, together with Horace Twist, had provided for her in the last few months of her life and, strangely enough, although all too late, Frederick Rolleston, who had no surviving relatives, had ironically left her, not only his London property, but also its valuable contents, together with over £30,000. He had been found unconscious from a stroke on the floor of his study some months earlier, and had resigned from his position as President of the Board of Trade, living on as a feeble invalid until the day of his death, just two days prior to Madame Duprez's.

Had she survived, she could have sold the house and its contents, and together with the £30,000, cleared all her debts and lived comfortably, if she had moderated her extravagant life style. But for her, death had come too soon …as published in the newspapers:

> *Madame Amelia Duprez, one of the most beautiful young popular hostesses of London society, a woman who transgressed with such panache and died at the early age of thirty one years, breathing her last on the 20th day of November, in this year 1831. It is believed that Madame Duprez took her own life while the balance of her mind was disturbed. No foul play is suspected. Verdict: Suicide.*

The funeral was such a modest affair that it attracted little attention. The mourners numbered only nine… Luke himself, Horace Twist, whose acute grief caused him to weep like a girl all through the service, Charles and Ellen Kean, Bridget - Amel's personal maid, and three of the housemaids, whom Luke had paid to attend. Catherine Gurney, the Duchess of Kinston, had the nerve to put in an appearance, although the service was already half way through. Luke wondered how she dared show her face.

They drove to Bow Cemetery at two o'clock and in less than an hour it was all over.

Luke could not allow Amel's memory to fade and

her last resting place go unmarked. He arranged for the erection of a monument that suitably commemorates the life of a most beautiful, remarkable woman - a life-size angel - of stone.

The traffic rolled past the entrance of the great house in Piccadilly and filled the air with the roar of wheels on stone, but never did a carriage turn in through the great gates to the courtyard. A house shrouded in shadows, grey as a forgotten grave, like a tomb. All was empty and still - not a breath, not a footfall! Nothing to move the emotions, nothing to dispel the deafening sound of silence. What secrets must have been confided to Amel Duprez within those walls, from the many voices that had echoed there. No more was there the gaiety and the laughter. It would never know such brilliant days again. Gone were the eyes that had looked with gladness and the feet that had walked there …gone forever.

SIXTY

The door began to close, but Luke put the flat of his hand on it, preventing it from closing entirely. Jessica backed away as he stepped inside.

'I've come to tell you Madame Duprez has passed away.'

Jessica blinked. 'Passed away? Did you say passed away?' He simply nodded. 'But that's just dreadful. What an earth happened? Was there an accident?' She asked, her eyes wide with genuine shock.

'No, not an accident. She died in circumstances too distasteful to speak of. But she's at peace now. That's the way to look at it. Now she's gone, nothing stands between us.'

Her eyes narrowed, slits of frosted emerald glass beneath the long curve of her lashes. 'My God, you're so bloody callous. How can you be so cold?'

'It's what keeps me in control.'

'No, it's what keeps you alone.'

Luke shrugged, silently cursing the arrogance he had inherited from his grandfather. He had not meant it to sound that way. The beginning of a headache gripped like a vice at his temple, and his hands shook like poplar leaves before rain. He searched for words, not knowing where to begin, wary of saying the wrong thing again.

'I don't want to quarrel. I've had time to think about the past. I've been stupid ...completely selfish.' His dark eyes seemed to beg forgiveness, but still he did not apologize for his weakness. That was not his way.

Jessica was startled by the change in him. He was casually dressed in an old tweed jacket and beige breeches, his face unshaven and his hair a careless tumble of waves. He looked a sorry sight, gaunt and hollow-eyed, his flesh a peculiar colour likened to unbleached linen and he was bathed in perspiration. In fact, he looked positively ill. She felt obliged to ask him to take a seat.

Luke moved woodenly, as if his limbs resisted the dictates of his will. One hand went to his throat, the other feeling behind him for the back of the chair. He had not had much sleep for forty-eight hours and had driven himself through the long day by sheer power of will, but now exhaustion was finally catching up with him. He sat down heavily, fumbling in his pocket for a handkerchief to wipe the perspiration from his brow.

Under his impassive mask she knew he suffered. His eyes were unfocused, glazed with a deep, dredging unhappiness, and his mouth seemed to droop.

'There's something I want to say ... need to say.'

At last comes the apology, she thought silently. He was surely about to extend the olive branch, to speak of a reconciliation, an end to this terrible estrangement which existed between them.

'Do you know ...when I was growing up I was most always alone? My mother was always gone and...'

'Oh, please, spare me your sad story. None of that interests me now,' she ridiculed, jabbing the table top with her finger, allowing him no further drifting into self-pity. 'You seem to forget you physically attached me ...again and again.'

'Does that make me such a terrible person? The house seems empty without you, Jessica. You were always there. That was everything.'

She broke eye contact then, lowering her head. 'You'll get used to it. Our union was a disaster from the beginning. I see that now. I was naive and blind. In time you will thank me for having made the first move.'

'What's to be gained by our talking to each other in this way? I'm as capable as being in the wrong as any man,' he admitted reluctantly. 'I'm willing to give this another try.'

She lifted her eyes and met his defiantly. 'Are you now? Well, I don't want another try. I'm much happier without you.'

Deep inside him something moved, some emotion that grasped tightly about his heart. 'Now, you can't mean that?'

'Oh, but I do!'

'Those words are like a knife in my heart.' He heard himself say.

'You have no heart. If you want to know the truth, I found you not the rock on which I thought to build my life, but weak …like straw. I can't bear even to look at you. You disgust me,' she cried, with such contempt in her voice that he actually flinched.

Only then did his shoulders slump, despair drowning him. 'Then there's nothing more to be said.'

He got up and stood there as though he had been struck by a bolt of lightning. There must have been something wild in his eyes then, something of the feeling that was stinging his heart, for her voice had died away and there was silence. A feeling of nausea overcame him and he wanted to crouch and give way to it, but knew he must not. Only a weakling breaks. He placed both hands on the table to keep them from trembling and swallowed hard, the muscles of his throat painfully contracting.

'I'd   I'd be grateful for a glass of water. As soon as I feel well enough I'll leave,' he said shakily.

She saw the shocking whiteness of his face, the rigidity of his body, as though death hovered above him, waiting to snatch his soul. She disappeared for a moment, but was soon back, placing a mug of water on the table between them, and reluctantly sat down opposite.

Luke drunk gratefully. Putting the mug down, he met her steady gaze with a sad smile. One compassionate look from her then, one touch and he would have clasped her to him. For one human moment of indulgence he needed to feel warm arms about him, to blot out his cares.

With little but his indomitable will to support him, he got slowly to his feet. For half a minute he stood in controlled exasperation, then stepping shakily around the table, reached for her hands, grasping them tightly.

There was something menacing and desperate in the way he seized and crushed them. When he attempted to bring her hands to his lips, she wrenched them away from that too fervent grip, hardening her heart against the bewitching trick of his smile.

'Hell's torment! I see you really hate me. How can I convince you that I've changed?'

'Not by all your play-acting.'

'But my life is bound indissolubly with yours.' Some strong emotion stiffened his spine, a kind of torment. He had never felt like this in his life. No torture could wring the humiliating secret from his lips. 'I came to tell you I'm going away. Perhaps when I come back, I can call on you?'

Jessica waited for an opening to tell him what she wanted to say.

'Or you might prefer to come to the house? Whatever suits you best.'

'There's really no point. I have no wish to see you again,' she said, her tone as cold as her gaze.

The finality of those words made him start involuntarily, but he suffered the crushing defeat quietly, giving only a long weary sigh. Using every scrap of strength he had, he turned his back on her, and walked through the door out in to the rain, with an ominous heaviness of heart. His going made her weep.

Luke sat for hours in meditation, in total immobility, sinking into the void and silence of his own spirit. Only a week had passed since Amelia Duprez parted this world, but it seemed much longer; a tragic loss of the woman with whom he had shared so much fire, so much passion. All through the liaison he had been aware of the fragility of the tie that bound them, but still he had been enormously traumatized by her death. Did he miss her? Indeed he did and yet, strangely enough, he experienced an incredible sense of freedom.

Even death seemed to him quite tolerable; now that his head was clear and he had come to grips, death passed out of his mind like the shadow that it was. Sanguine by nature, he had the power of eluding grief by simply adjourning it. Other issues had reality;

death none. He could put off the consideration of any particular spectre till the matter had become softened by time. No sorrow could survive the smothering of time. He supposed she would become a distant memory, a closed chapter of his life.

His mind turned to the bewitching sweetness of manner that one prized in Jessica, and the playfulness, the loveliest combinations of youth. He did not see her with the same indifference, because something in him had changed. He never ceased to be saddened at losing her, and feared that she may have thought the loss not unwelcome to him. It was as though the light had gone from out of his life, bowing him down with anguish. But she must never know the full ferocity of his agony.

Trembling and weak, he wandered in the diffused light from one room to another, scarcely knowing where he was. The house seemed silent, alien and somehow frightening. In a curious moment of forget-fulness, he was about to pull the bell rope, wanting Mrs Osborne. But then, remembering she had gone from the house, he pressed his hand to his forehead in an attempt to collect his wits. He had for the moment forgotten Dora had left.

Dora Osborne had always been there when he returned home and could always be counted on to keep everything as it should be, knowing immediately what he needed. Always behind him with his interests at heart, supporting him in whatever he did and above all, she had tolerated his moods, but now she too had left him alone. Alone - few men were more solitary! It was something he sadly missed, someone whom he could turn to, someone he could count on to listen. He had seen the silent criticism in the other servants' eyes. They looked at him as if he had grown horns and a tail, as if he was the devil himself.

He reached the front door and stepped out into the cool clear air of the evening. There he stood for several minutes, watching the twilight swiftly deepen as the winter sun dropped down behind the pines, whose topmost pyramids took on a richer colouring from its glowing rays.

When he finally came back in to the house, he sank down on a chair, staring in to the flames of the fire, melancholy tightening its grip. He had only the quiet ticking of the clock to keep him company. Oh, he was the cause of his own suffering, he knew that. He felt a deep remorse for his soiled past. Unwisely, he had tried to have it all ways, to keep a mistress and still retain his wife's affections, hurting and wounding her; something he deeply regretted. He was truly sorry, really he was, because he did care for her. He was mourning the loss of her all over again, the sweetness, the delights and irritations, the laughter, qualities of every sort which made up the whole complex structure of Jessica ...his Jessica. All that variety in her alone, which he had sought for in a number of women ...the fondness, the tenderness and comfort and so much more.

An emotion tugged at his heart, a sensation that he had never felt before, opening every door to his mind. He started to think of all the things he should have done differently, about a thousand and one things he needed to apologise for. Of all those simple moments they had shared, those moments of happiness he did not deserve, moments taken for granted that now she was gone had become precious memories to him.

Settling into the luxury of remembering, he

brought forth again and again to solace his empty hours, comfort his doubts and banish the dark enclosing fears, her lovely face, those warm, eager lips that he must have kissed more than a thousand times. That tingling laugh of hers and the most wonderful of all ...the tender love and sparkle that had shone from those remarkable eyes with such impulsive sweetness. He had not then known the treasure he had, never stopped to think just how happy he had been. He should have cherished her, but had failed, handling it all wrong. God - he missed the girl with every fibre of strength in his body. He needed her nearness, but it appeared they were never to be together again.

He had to get a grip on himself, do something positive - start building bridges. He would start by renovating the cottages that he knew she felt so passionate about ...and any others that might need improving. He would make a point of seeing Edward Morley first thing in the morning, to get things underway. Then he would take himself off to Charing Cross Hospital for the next stage of treatment to free him from the hold this social disease had on him. But before anything else, he must right the wrong he had done his young wife.

In a letter he would transform himself into the perfect lover, tell her of his true feelings in words such as no other woman had heard, melt her frozen thoughts and lead her to look on him with toleration, if not with love. And he would write an apology to Dora, ask her forgiveness. The past had its place. They all had to move forward.

He eagerly fetched pen and paper and settled down in the leather chair at his desk. He wrote the letter to

Jessica in an agony of anxiety, fears for his young wife's health, despair for his own future and regrets for his past mistakes. But by the time he had finished both the letters his spirits had lifted. Fear disappeared to give rise to the jubilation of his emotions.

Jessica turned the folded sheets of paper over and over in her hands, staring at her name written in a flowing familiar hand. She placed them against the vase of wild flowers that stood in the middle of the table. It was some time before she could bring herself to open the letter.

Jessica,

I won't call you my pet, as I know it will only serve to infuriate you further. I will address you as My Dearest, for that is what you are to me...my Dearest, my Beloved, my Heart, the most important person in the world to me, the centre of my universe, the reason for my very existence.

I know I am not the ideal husband, far from it, and I am not proud of my behaviour. I have done things I am ashamed of, breaking all the rules. After seeing myself through your eyes, I didn't like what I saw. And if I have shown no feeling it's only because I have been taught well by my Grandfather Penrose and my father before him. My heart and senses were put on ice from the day I was put into that lonely maelstrom of a boarding school. The stern schooling was sheer hell. There, I was taught to keep a stiff upper lip at all times, and in self-defense, learnt to keep my emotions to myself. I saw anyone who tried to get close to me as a threat.

I deeply regret the hurt that I caused you. Truly, I cannot apologise enough for my conduct. When I first saw you that day in the woods, my heart was captured then, only I did not know it. You were everything I never knew I wanted.

An individual that stands out, a special person, like a beautiful living flame, a light whose beams shine through the lives of those around you. I just didn't know what I had. It has taken me all this time to recognize the feelings in my heart were there all along. Feelings I tried to strangle, feelings I did not want. I had begun to feel I belong somewhere before you left, here in this house, my sanctuary, with you, and nothing else truly mattered. As long as you were here, waiting with open arms, I felt safe. But now, the house is empty without you, no longer like home.

The worse thing is having all these feelings and no one to give them to. I should have come after you right away. I wanted to, but I let my foolish pride get in the way. Now I am experiencing a terrible loss. Only you can fill this aching gap. I feel these words as if their naming were a weight lifted from me, knowing that you will read them, know my heart and share my burden. You are all that I want in the whole world. I am prepared to hear your refusal and have fixed my resolution if that should happen, but pray you may never know the pangs that at this instant tear at my heart. My poor pen cannot describe how I yearn for you - my heart is with you now as you read this letter. My mind dwells upon nothing else. There is no waking hour of the day when you are not far from my thoughts. For the first time, I feel time like a heartbeat, the seconds pumping away in my breast like a reckoning. Absent from you, I feel no pleasure, my Dearest. You are everything to me. Like a lovely breeze that swept through my life, changing the way I see things, without me even knowing it.

Through ill health, I will be spending a short spell in a London hospital, but God willing, hope to be home in time for Christmas. Let this be a new beginning. Never again will you have to do anything you don't feel good about in the years ahead. We can have separate rooms if you so desire or I will move out of the house all together if you so wish, but please ...please, my Dearest ...my heart, come home. Wildacres is yours. I shall never take it from you and I could not live here without you. Life is not worth preserving without happiness, and I care not where I may linger out this miserable existence.

Your devoted husband
Luke.

In the most feverish language he had told her what he did not dare in person, out of pride and reserve.

She read the letter three times, slowly, then with deliberation, tore it up into tiny pieces and dropped the fragments into the fire. But her inner turmoil increased, and her weeping echoed about the little room of the lonely cottage, as it had done so many nights before.

SIXTY- ONE

Jessica rubbed at her skin to restore the circulation to her numbed limbs. But cold and numb as she was, she was content to stay where she was for a little while longer, surrounded by all she loved best, amongst the joys of Heaven. Unseen a curlew whistled, a raven croaked, and sheep cried from somewhere in the distance - the true voices of the fells, but all was somehow hushed in the stillness of the swirling wraiths of mist.

The cry of a cock grouse came faintly on the wind, breaking the silence and the solitude where the heather grew dense and rugged tufts of grass quivered in the chill blasts that swept over the fells. There could be no mistaking the cry of a red grouse. She spotted it flying but a few feet above the brown bents of heather, in which the wind whined, searching with diligence for something to eat; backwards and for- wards it glided on seemingly motionless wings. Of all the birds of the highlands, eagle, hawk, plover and curlew, there was none so fine as the red grouse. A handsome bird with red-brown, speckled plumage on a rich chestnut chin and throat, and grey-white feathers on its legs.

The sky was suddenly heavy with racing clouds and the wind began to roar, chasing away the mist. Jessica rose to her feet and started back to the cottage, gasping for breath as a hail of leaves and dust met her. Despite her exertions and the layer of clothing, she was cold to the very marrow. It made her realise in the most immediate and physical way, her vulnerability.

Outside it froze, and it was freezing to almost the same extent inside too. No sunshine had penetrated the windows for days and although there were shutters at the windows, the frames had shrunk with age and fitted poorly, chill shuddered round every corner and many a keen draught whirled through the room. Jessica sat by the fireside, staring into the glowing heart of spent embers. There was a sinking feeling in the pit of her stomach, a coldness about the ribs and a general weariness.

She rose shakily from the chair and went outside to get more wood from the supply of logs stored in a narrow lean-to at the side of the cottage, out into the velvety blackness of the night. The death-cry of a rabbit in the grip of weasel or stoat caused the skin to prickle at the back of her neck and a shiver to run down her spine. She was not yet accustomed to the creatures of the night and their startling ways and eerie, nerve-shattering noises. The branches of the trees swayed in the wind, casting ghost-like shadows on the ground, the last of the rustling leaves shining with pale reflection from the light of the moon. She stooped to pick up four of the larger logs, struggling with the weight.

The sudden sound of dry brush crackling made her freeze. She stood quite still and listened. A few minutes went by but she heard nothing more. Then the silence was shattered by her mighty sneeze, and whatever it was took fright and scurried away. A cloud came upon the moon, like dark fingers across her face. She hung on to the logs tightly and hurried back through the door, pushing it shut behind her. Quickly disposing of the logs, she went to slip the latch bolt in place on the door and closed the faded drapes across the window.

Her head started to throb and her throat felt tender. She flopped lethargically in the chair. There was only the sound of the fire. She closed her eyes and listened to its music. She was deluged by a wave of nostalgia for those she had loved and lost, dear Adam and John, her mother, young Rufus and his sweet little sister, Holly, her new-found friend, Alice, and then, the loss of her beloved father, Clara and the child. How she yearned for Betsy, her long lost friend. She could see her standing in the kitchen, round and rosy, smelling of soap and freshly baked bread, always with a wooden spoon or a rolling pin in her hand, and a pot boiling on the stove …like an affable witch.

She had come to terms with many ghosts in the time she had spent alone, was even free of the ghost of her mother at last, putting away the memory of all those who, though cherished in her heart, were gently laid to rest. But she could not come to terms with her father's horrendous death, the cruellest of recollections, the most appalling shock of her life. It had shaken her to the very core. She didn't want to feel that kind of pain ever again. He had been her idol, her rock, and she had thought he would live on forever. Little incidents of her childhood, those she thought she had forgotten, presented themselves one by one in the faithful recording cells of her brain. Fond memories flashed through her mind, impressions passing like dark shadows, which only time would erase. What was it Parson Appleby had said, when she had gone to him to unburden her soul, as he put it - comforting her battered heart?

'The winds of life may bend us, but cannot break us. Disappointment and suffering is the supreme test of character. God will never put us through more than we can bear. You have your whole life ahead of you. Embrace every part of it. You must learn to be patient, live one day at a time, letting yesterday go and leaving tomorrow until it arrives.'

She hadn't understood when he had spoken of the soul; she could not differentiate it from the whole of her person, but now she was beginning to glimpse of what it was - the immutable part of her being.

It was the long silences that were hardest to bear, when she fought against the encroaching shadows of the past - old lost dreams and hopes that came flocking and clung in the corners of her mind, as cold as snowflakes. Yet when sounds came: a burst of bird song, the rain on the window or the wind through the eaves, she envied their melodies and rhythms. They reminded her of when she too had had the power to lift hearts and raise spirits. Into her weary mind came all manner of recollections. Some, in themselves, pleasant. The time she had spent at Hawthorne Manor, of tea parties and croquet on smooth lawns, and the new gowns she had worn.

A yearning filled her for those past sounds, those haunting tunes, triumphant rhythmic sounds that went on forever, and those gentle waltzes rising and falling, one.. two.. three, one.. two.. three. Forms and faces, long vanished from her life, closed about her in drifting colours. Like the links in a chain those memories came flooding back in such profusion, leading her on to other times …those first exciting days she and Luke had spent together, happy, carefree days in Windermere …the brilliance and the beauty of the most mundane objects. The joy of loving and seeing his eyes smile. Reliving all those wonderful moments, the sensation that there was nobody in the world but the two of them, huddling together for shelter under an umbrella long after the rain had stopped, laughter over nothing, shared across a candlelit table.

The thoughts darted into her head, like minnows beneath the surface of water. She didn't want them but there seemed to be nothing she could do to stop them. One did not just remember the flowers or the compliments, one remembered standing at the upstairs window watching the evening shadows while waiting for him to come home to her open arms.

The dying embers of the fire shifted their position, bringing her out of her daydreams. She gave a long, quivering sigh of despair, wrapping her arms about herself, rocking backwards and forwards in a way women do when they have reached the boundary when sorrow becomes unbearable. Even now she could feel him all around her. She could not help recalling those soft evenings in summer when they had sat in the garden where the sweet scent of lilac and roses mingled in the air, watching the twilight fade, sharing the last of the light together. So many magic moments of quiet anticipation - a smile in passing, a touch of his hand on her shoulder - expressions of love. Times past came gliding across her reluctant mind, lulling her into a happy serenity and, when lucky, she would fall asleep before they faded, a sleep of weakness and exhaustion.

She was no better the next day and the following day she was worse still. Fever crept through her body. To the anguish of her soul her head throbbed and there was a pain in the back of her neck, banishing sleep and holding its sweet oblivion at bay. She wheezed and gasped the dark hours away, feeling queasy and exhausted, trembling in every limb, depressed in body and spirit. Sometimes the sun found the window and gently warmed her, but its visits were rare - not long enough to ward off the cold and the damp. The silence had become more oppressive. The new life she had built up like a wall between her and the rest of the world was beginning to crumble. Days all the more restless and unhappy because it was almost Christmas, when all others except for herself would be carefree and jolly.

SIXTY-TWO

Plagued by memories that surfaced so irrepressibly at times, Luke withdrew yet farther into his shell. His health was suffering seriously from anxiety and want of rest. In five days it would be Christmas and still she had not come home, and there had been no response to his letter. He put his hand to his brow and rubbed it, remembering what she had once said... *'Feeling rich is born of simple things, good health and laughter, along with being loved.'*

Everyone needed someone in their lives whose face lights up when they walk in the room. He knew that *now*. Love had gradually unfolded, naturally, out of a companionable friendship. He had loved her unconsciously. His slow mind had not known it, his slow tongue not spoken it. Now, too late, he understood. It could certainly spin your head around. It was no use; he could not stay away from her. He was a fool - he knew. She had rejected him not just the once, but twice. She had her father's strength, and he had his pride. He had let that very pride divide them and condemn him to a lonely, empty life, but pride was no antidote for the longing and the need he felt deep in his heart. He would swallow his damn pride and go again, the third and last time, with hat in hand and ask – no ...*beg* on bended knee like a lovesick adolescent, if it became necessary - beg her to forgive him and come home.

Luke stood within the belt of tall elms and soaring birches, immobilized by misery at the thought of rejection, looking out across the wild sweep of bracken slopes, a silent, friendless world where nothing moved except the shadows of the clouds, and an appalling loneliness like a dense fog fell upon him. The last of the reluctant leaves were dropping in the lanes, wavering and rocking like boats from side to side. The brambles, which retain most their leaves throughout the winter, were still green, and in the hedges the hips and haws glowed a vivid scarlet, a feast for the birds in the bitter days to come.

As he walked on he disturbed a grey squirrel that despite the cold was active on the ground, searching for acorns that it had buried. But predominating the evening was the caw of rooks, not yet starved by cold and forced to work all day on half-frozen ploughed land, they took their ease, sitting in the oaks and elms, their glossy backs shining like metal. They did not stir as he went by beneath with uplifted face, but cocked their bright heads sideways and cawed all the more. For just a few moments their presence gave him a sense of companion-ship. He picked up a stick, holding it fast in his hand and walked on, nearing his destination.

Joe was busy digging among the roots with a hoe. He wore an old knee-length coat of brown whipcord and a brimmed hat that had faded with weather from black to slate grey. His breath made little white puffs in the cold clean air as he worked and the coat flapped about his shanks. He heard the rustle of leaves in the lane and straightened, a mite stiffly. When Luke approached, he stared at him with suspicion, his greeting as expected - aggressive.

'Who let you out o' your bloody cage?' Joe was amazed at the change in the man.

His face looked emaciated and there were dark shadows under his eyes and an expression of strain. The dark hair was flecked with premature grey and hung over his forehead like the forelock of a shaggy pony.

'What the hell're you doing round these parts? If you're wanting another message passed on, you're wasting your bloody time. It'll go straight int'the fire like the last.'

Luke snapped the stick and throwing the two ends away, thrust his hands deep in his pockets for the want of something to do with them. 'No, there's no message. I just wanted a word with you.'

'What would we have in common t'talk about?' Joe was not in the best of moods to listen to other people's troubles, particularly not this man's.

'The person we both care for. This situation is tearing me apart. Without Jessica in my life I'm lost.' It was an embarrassing admission to have to make. 'The whole of my errors or whatever harsher name you choose to give them, are all in the past. Love has come into my heart and has so completely changed me. I've a different view to life now.'

'What a crock o' shit. Don't pretend t'walk the path o' bloody righteousness when you strayed from it. If you want something say so an' stop the bullshit.'

'I thought …hoped you might help me talk some sense into her. Make her come home. It tears at my heart to see her in such a state.'

Distress and concern were written on a face that normally revealed neither, but Joe wouldn't be taken in.

'Well, now, is that a fact? Your concern is a bit late, you son o' a bitch. I heard you went off t'be with your whore, when your own wife was on the edge o' a breakdown. Nothing you say'll make any difference now. She doesn't want anything more t'do with you. Can't you get that int'your thick skull? Stay away from her, you self-centred, bloody coward.' Joe held up a hand in warning, his colour high with anger. 'Don't go where you're not wanted. Understand?'

Luke stooped to pick up another twig. He snapped it again and this time threw the pieces violently from him.

'You seem to forget that Jessica's my wife. Whether I go near her or not is none of your business.'

'Then why're you here asking for bloody help?'

'I hoped we could speak with calmness.'

Joe hit back, sympathetic as well as indignant, on his sister's behalf. 'How can I speak with bloody calmness when I know my sister suffers?'

Schooled to betray no emotion, Luke stood in rigid immobility, straining every nerve to be agreeable.

'There's nothing to be gained by arguing. I'd never have come if I'd known you would take offence. But it will soon be Christmas. I can hardly leave her in that cottage alone. I'm worried about her.'

'I've persuaded her t'come t'the farm over Christmas an' the New Year. Hopefully, she'll stay permanently.'

'What is to happen in the meantime? She's so thin. Aren't you concerned for her health?'

'What kind o' bloody question is that? O' course I'm bloody concerned. But whatever Jessie's suffering, she'll throw it off. It's not in her nature t'go under. Just keep away from her. That's all I ask. An' if you ever raise a hand t'her again, I swear I'll break your bloody neck. '

There was a limit a man could take and Luke had reached it. 'That's big talk coming from a man who drove his own wife to drink. You've no right to judge, you self-righteous hypocrite. I suppose the rumours about you and Miss Bradley were completely un-founded?'

'Why, you no good...' The shuddering growl that Joe emitted in his fury was clearly heard. He let fly the worst of his temper, punching Luke straight in the mouth, splitting his lip.

Luke stumbled backwards but managed to retain his balance to stand straight and rigid, taking the punishment without retaliation. To fight back would only make matters worse.

'Fight you bastard,' Joe yelled, hitting him again and again, harder each time, giving him the thrashing he so richly deserved.

It was only when Luke felt the air explode from his lungs that he staggered backwards, landing against the trunk of a tree, side on, with such force he injured his shoulder. He slid to the ground and stayed there some minutes, then struggled slowly to his feet and just stood there swaying, suspended in painful agony. His left shoulder was throbbing madly and pain shot through his ribs like a sharp knife. He winced and moved shakily towards Joe, clutching at his arm for support, blood trickling from his nose and upper lip.

'I think I …I have a …a dislocated shoulder and a couple of bruised ribs.'

'Well, you asked for it, you sadistic bastard. One thing I can't stand is a man who forces himself on a lass. '

'You're right. I'm a bastard and a s..sorry one at that. I handled things badly. All wrong.'

'Christ! You look like hell.'

'I feel like …like hell. I was a little run down, but nothing drastically wrong …until now.' Luke forced a grin. 'You hold a …a hell of a grudge.' For a moment he lifted that calm sardonic mask to reveal himself. He looked a broken man, on the brink of a physical collapse. 'Mind you, there's worse injuries, but they are invisible ones. I think we create for ourselves our own Heaven and …and Hell. What a cursed situation. It seems we are …are two of a kind …you and I. Quite a pair, aren't we? The only difference is you …you weren't caught out. But Miss Bradley leaving in such haste leaves little room for …for doubt of your guilt. Not to mention ge..getting the innocent girl with child.'

'Hell's teeth! I had no idea,' Joe cried, his weathered face suddenly ashen. He stood there like one stupefied

'Do you know, I …I believe you're telling the truth.'

'Why didn't she let on?'

'What good would that have done? You were not a free man.'

There was silence between them now that every-thing had been said. Luke suddenly winced, his face white and twisted with pain as he hung onto his left arm.

'I fear this is a job for a doctor,' Joe said with sudden regret. He should never have allowed his anger to determine his actions.

'I've no wish to see a doctor. A sudden jerk will do the trick. Perhaps you would be good enough to get me home before I make a bigger fool of ...of myself and pass out. I will not detain you ...oh, hell...' He drew in his breath as the pain shot through him. '...longer than I can help.'

'Stay where you are. I'll get the cart.'

'I'm not going anywhere.' Luke felt absolutely drained, his limbs leaden.

The journey in the jolting cart was a painful one, but he made no complaint.

'Dora, pour me a large brandy.' Were the first words he uttered as he walked unsteadily in the door.

Sitting awkwardly in an upright chair, he downed the first in one swallow. 'Give me another.' He swallowed that back too and also a third. He turned stiffly to Joe who stood hovering beside him. 'Right, I think I'm just about ready. If you will do the honours?'

'Right!' Joe braced himself as he placed one hand on Luke's shoulder and gripped his arm with his other hand.

'Ready?'

'As ready as I'll ever be.'

'Well, take a deep breath. Here we go...'

Joe gave a sudden jerking tug with all the strength he could muster. Luke screwed up his eyes and a deep moan left his lips as there was a clunking sound of bones slipping back into place. Then there was silence, nothing was said. Dora waited until Luke was sufficiently re-covered before asking just what had happened.

'It was an accident. I stumbled against a tree,'

Luke informed her.

'Oh, a tree was it? Dangerous things trees. I suppose it blackened your eye an' split your lip too, did it?'

'Something like that, Dora. Now, bring the decanter and another glass, will you? I dare say Joseph will join me in a drink.'

'I wouldn't say no. It's been a strange sort o' a day all in all.'

They sat quiet while Dora placed the tray holding a crystal decanter and glasses down on a small table beside Luke's chair. 'Have Mrs Miles mix me a potion, will you, Dora? I must sleep tonight or I'll be of no use tomorrow.'

'I'll see t'that right away, Sir.'

'Thank you.' She went out of the room and closed the door. 'Mrs Osborne's been with me all my adult life. I don't know what I would do without her,' Luke said, when she had gone. He gestured to the tray. 'Help yourself and pour me another, will you?'

'It's good t'have someone you can rely on.' Joe lifted the glass and handed it to Luke, then sat back down again. He sipped the golden liquid slowly, savouring it. Lowering his glass, he studied Luke's face. He looked somewhat older than his years, strained and haggard; a changed man. 'I dare say that shoulder'll be painful an' stiff for a day or two. The ribs too. There's nothing you can do but rest.'

'I've no time for rest. I've important things to attend too. Arrange the rest of my life. I must make Jessica see sense. I no longer seek to conceal my state, which is not just sorrow but sheer anguish.'

'That's natural t'one who's been humiliated such as you have. There's enough talk about you t'fill a book.'

'What do I care what people think? Jessica is all I'm concerned about. She's wasting away. Oh, I'm not saying I haven't my own selfish reasons for wanting her back. I miss her, truly miss her and want her to come home. I need her. She's become my whole life.' The anxiety in his voice was unmistakable.

'When I first made advances towards her I was influenced by no romantic feelings. I chose her solely because she was young, strong and spirited, and would give me fine sons. We were happy at first. She made an agreeable enough companion. But lives take shape in ways we cannot always predict or understand. Somewhere along the way she became more than that to me. She became a friend, but I took that very friendship for granted. As long as she was here to welcome me back with open arms, I lived my life just as I pleased, as I always had, without thought or consideration for her, forgetting how sensitive and vulnerable she is.' He wrung his hands in anguish. 'I was never here when she needed me most. I think I have killed the love she bore me, and cannot blame her in the smallest degree.

'I gave her every cause to distrust me, knowing that I was all to her that she ought to have been to me. And my sin in marrying her thus was nothing to what came afterwards, for I treated her unkindly, brutally, when I neglected her openly for that …that enchantress whom, all too late, I saw in her true colours. I abused the very person that I should have cherished, not realizing just how important she was to me until it was too late. It gives me no pleasure to come home now.'

'In all the years I've known you, this is the first time I've realized there's a human being underneath all that poise an' pageantry,' Joe said solicitously. 'I've always hated that smug attitude o' yours.'

'Don't waste your energy hating me.'

'That sister o' mine's so full o' passion an' spirit she's touched you hasn't she? An' all this time I believed you t'be a hard bastard. The first thing you must do is apologise. Tell her you miss her, that you love an' need her.'

'I've said all that in a letter.'

'Ah, well, that's not quite the same. Jessie has a flare for drama. You must do it in person. She needs t'hear it from your own lips. Those magic words are what she wants t'hear. First, the apology an' then speak o' the love you feel for her.'

'But what if she won't listen?'

'Make her listen. Don't take no for an answer. You're right. She needs t'come home. For her sake you must make her see sense. Persuasion's better than force. Jessie's lived through more dramas an' traumas o' women twice her age. She's deeply traumatised. If you don't mind a little advice...'

'Anything ...I just want her to come home.'

'Well, when you eat humble pie, eat every bit o' it.'

Joe emptied his glass of brandy and got up to pour himself another. When he settled back in the chair, he looked his brother-in-law directly in the eye and what was said next was to make Luke all the more determined to bring Jessica home where she belonged.

'There's something more, something I haven't told you. But before I do, you must give me your word not t'let on t'Jessie that you know. She made me swear I wouldn't tell you, but now I know your feelings t'wards her are genuine, I think it's in both your interests that I do. But I'm warning you, if she even suspects I've told you, you'll lose her alt'gether. That, I can guarantee.'

'Hell man! You have my word. What is it? Tell me!'

'Jessie's with child. She must've conceived before she left.'

Luke's hand flew up to his forehead, gripping it in his distress. 'Dear God! But she's so thin.'

'Emotion does that t'her. She'll soon pick up once she's settled an' content.'

'Christ! I hope so.' Inside him the tremble of fear returned. 'I won't forget this, Joseph. You helping me, I mean.'

'I'm doing it for Jessie. I know she loves you still an' it's eating her heart out. But if she suspects you know about the child she's carrying, she'll think that's all you want her for.' His look was stern again. 'An' I'm warning you...'

'There's no need for threats. I won't risk losing her again. She means the world to me. Do you know, you're a lot like your father. He was the best man I had working for me ...strong, loyal and reliable. I feel privileged to have known him. He's greatly missed.'

'Yes! He's missed sure enough,' Joe said sullenly. 'But not forgotten.'

'No, not forgotten. Now Joseph, since you've done something for me, I'll do something for you in return. Time is short. We must seize every opportunity. Rose Bradley earns a modest living as an employee of the British Import and Export Company in London.'

'How do you know that?'

'It was through my letter of recommendation she obtained the position. During the months she dealt with my correspondence and acted as amanuensis, she proved herself to be a clever, capable young woman. Throw caution to the wind man. Go after her. You should find her easily enough.'

SIXTY- THREE

It was the time of day when a lonely heart aches; when dusk was falling and the last sounds of day comes sadly across the meadows with a forlorn, lost music, already becoming muted under the outspread hand of night. A loud rap at the door brought Jessica awake with a start. She blinked, attempting to shake the sleep from her eyes.

'Jessica! Jessica …I know you're in there. *Please* …open the door.'

She felt her legs tremble; they could scarcely carry her across the floor. She had been propped up in the chair far too long and had no more life in her than a rag doll.

Sliding the bolt, the door cried miserably on its dry hinges, making waves through the still air. The candle flame shrank back, shivering in the draught. Neither could speak.

Luke looked upon the waxen face surrounded by a riot of chestnut curls, as if for the first time. It was expressionless, as though the life, the very warmth had been extinguished inside her, leaving behind a passive, unfeeling shell. She possessed an ethereal fragility, which was the direct opposite of the spirited, carelessly warm-hearted girl she had once been, and inside Luke Sheridan, something ached for the loss of that girl.

Before he could say anything, Jessica turned and shuffled away, staggering, almost falling, but she managed to regain her balance and sink back in the chair. She stared up at him.

Gloom and despair mingled weirdly on his bruised face. One of his eyes was almost closed and there was a cut on his upper lip. He looked worn, older than he really was. But she made no comment about the state of his appearance. It was nothing to do with her.

'You received my letter?' he enquired quietly, as he stood before her. She nodded. 'You didn't reply.'

'I didn't return. Wasn't that answer enough?'

He thought his letter might have moved her to forgive and forget. 'But I thought ...hoped...' Luke wore no mask. He looked anguished as he faced her. 'What can I say?'

'Try goodbye,' she suggested.

Her eyes had a glazed expression about them, and although her words were harsh to his ears she seemed strangely subdued, which surprised him. He thought he knew all her moods, from the lightest moment to the darkest frame of mind.

'You have a fever.'

'Your powers of observation do you credit,' she replied mordantly.

'You can't stay here alone. It's almost Christmas. Let me take you home, Jessica.'

'I am home.'

'Why are you making this so hard?'

'Do you need to ask?'

Luke sighed in exasperation and fell silent for a few minutes, his mind a turmoil of passion, which he had difficulty in keeping under control.

'How are you coping on your own?' He asked at last, raising an enquiring eyebrow. There was no reply. 'I mean ...I can see you're unwell. I don't like to see you like this.'

She knew what a charmer he could be, but she

would not be taken in. Talk was cheap. It cost nothing but breath. 'I was just beginning to feel good about myself again until you came along,' she answered more calmly than she felt, holding his gaze with suspicion. She studied him for a little while longer, their eyes locked. His attitude was definitely less superior than it had been, but he still maintained a certain poise.

'At least accept your allowance.'

She gave an indifferent shrug. 'I don't need it. I do well enough on little. Besides, Joe supplies me with all I could possibly want.'

He plunged into desperation as her look formed droplets of ice in the air between them. 'But I worry about you out here all alone. You look so tired, so thin.'

'Why this sudden interest? You didn't care a fig about me before.'

'I might have acted indifferent at first, but it was just a pose. The truth is, without you I haven't been happy at all.'

There was no response from her. He sensed that her mind was a long way off. The ice of self-command, which had gathered over him was broken and the currents burst forth and over-whelmed him. The first feverish glow of passion swept over his face, and before he could stop himself the words came out all of a rush, tumbling over each other like torrents of water.

'Please, listen to me, sweetheart. In the past I admit I never truly needed anyone. I'd grown used to being on my own. With exception to my grandfather, no one ever gave me anything without expecting something in return. But with you ...with you it was different. You opened my eyes to so much with your warmth and laughter, with your impulsive sweetness. You brought a certain richness to my life,' he uttered dejectedly.

Her silence was slowly strangling him. He couldn't bear another rejection; he had to make her see sense. In desperation, he took her hand and brushed it with his lips. It was over before she realised what he was doing. 'Jessica, do you think you could love me again?' he whispered, scarcely audible.

'I don't know that I want to. You …you broke my heart.' Her voice was a mumble of pain and despair and her eyes fled away, refusing to be captured by his.

'I beg your pardon humbly for all the pain I have caused you. I have been cruel, wickedly selfish. But I will not believe that your love is dead; it is only asleep. It will awaken at the touch of responding love. Just give me a chance. That's all I ask. Let me make it up to you. I can't seem to settle without you.'

He frowned in emotional display, for once unembarrassed to show his feelings. At first his eyes had been masked with their customary self-assured bright-ness, his whole face with its usual decorous formality; then gradually he changed. That cold decorousness melted off what lay behind, as frosty dew melts off grass. He had never shown her what was in him, never revealed what lay behind those bright satiric eyes. Now, perhaps, she would see!

Jessica regarded him with the intense absorption with which one looks at a tiny wildflower through a magnifying lens, and watches its insignificance expand to the size and importance of a hothouse bloom. He was showing her his real self, since he had no reason for armour against her now.

'If being in love means not being able to get you out of my mind, then I love you madly. Every minute, every second of the day I think about you.' His voice was soft with adoration. 'You're everywhere, even filling my dreams.'

He had never used the word "love", not to anyone. But love will not be denied, and so it poured from his lips and laid itself on Jessica's lap. Now, for the first time he understood that the door to the human heart could only be opened from the inside. He understood as he had never done before, what the poet philosopher meant by "the celestial rapture falling out of heaven" …for that rapture had fallen upon him and caught him up in a cloud of glory. He believed in love as more than just a word. It gave a whole new meaning to life, a fresh hope. At last he humbly begged her pardon for the humiliation, the pain he had inflicted upon her.

'Forgive me, dearest. *Please* …I'm begging you. Say you'll forgive me.' But still there was no response. His distress was acute. 'God damn it, Jessica, I miss you. I want you to come home,' he cried in throaty desperation.

Jessica viewed him with dispassionate eyes and what she saw was a man whose spirit was broken. His sudden vulnerability caught at her heart, awakening the old feeling he had almost driven out. There was such misery in those dear, dark eyes, such wretched anticipation and she badly wanted to reach out and hold him to her, but for the life of her she could not bring herself to do so. Her mind filled with venomous thoughts, surging in her brain and boiling over. How he had deliberately lied, time and time again. His antics had almost destroyed her. She had been taken in, but only for a moment. The unyielding spirit gathered itself into a resolution only the stronger for its momentary weakness.

Luke's sensitivity had sharpened during those last weeks of troubled thought and he was instantly conscious of a change in her expression. It was as though she was suddenly on her guard again, but he wasn't about to give up.

'That's a cross you'll have to bear.' He heard her say without emotion, as she moulded trembling lips into the faintest of smiles. She was making him suffer even more than she suffered herself and yet this did not restrain her. 'It seems my leaving has damaged your ego far worse than I thought.'

The corner of his mouth twitched nervously, as astonishment replaced his utter despair, and his stiff self-control spun away from him on waves of pain.

'You know it's more than that. Love is too important to let it go.'

'If …if you only knew how I've longed for you to say those very words.' She shook her head helplessly. 'I never dreamt that when …when you did, they would come too late.'

'But it's not too late. Believe me. I know now that life without love is no life at all.'

'But that's just not enough. Love without trust. What about that? There should be complete and unquestioning trust on both sides.'

'Jessica, don't turn me away again. I know how wrong I've been. If it is any comfort to you I absolutely detest myself. We have to make our peace, you and I. Give this marriage another chance. Live together with dignity. In time trust will come. Believe me, trust will come.' He rambled on in short quick sentences, tinged with inevitable regret. 'You're all of life to me. I know that now. I need you. You're all I can think of. I want to spend the rest of my days with you.'

'But it's too late. You must let me go.' She spoke with a strange calmness that concealed her inner turmoil.

He knew she was tense and unpredictable and took his treatment in a subdued manner, a sense of defeat sweeping over him. He felt himself slipping over a precipice, his conversation seeming to be buried at the back of his throat. His compressed lips moved as those of one in great pain. But he could not …would not give up. It was time to take back that which was his. 'I can't lose you, my dearest. You're inside my heart. That's where you are. My life is with you. The house our sanctuary. I've nothing else. We had such hopes, you and I. Do you remember that first moment I saw you? You were wearing green. The sunlight caressed your hair, touching it with gold. You affected me even then, only I wouldn't admit it. A moment in time that changed the direction of our lives for better or worse.'

He faltered, unused to laying his feelings bare in such a manner. The muscles in his face twitched with emotion. 'And …that time by the lake when we kissed …our first kiss. Do you remember? We found out that our tastes were exactly alike in preferring the country to every other place. It was quite incredible. And your determination, the way you never give up on anything you believe in. That's just one of the things I love about you.'

'Love! You betrayed me and you talk of love?' she cried bitterly.

He took a deep breath. 'Jessica ...*please,* let's forget the past.'

'It was you who brought it up.'

'I know, but I've no wish to upset you.' He fell into an abrupt silence and she was silent too. It was some minutes before he spoke again.

'Do you remember you wanted to go back to Windermere? We could do that. Do you remember the old boatman in that strange little cottage? We could visit him again if you wish. You'd like that, wouldn't you?' he said eagerly, his skill and cunning tenderness calming her tortured mind. 'I bought you that book of poems the next day.' His laughed a little shakily. 'And you even had me reading them to you. Do you remember?'

The slightest of smiles curled her lips as she relaxed in the memory. 'I remember ...everything.'

That first tiny bubble of joy fluttered in her breast, which she did her best to quench. She would never forgive his betrayal, but the edge of her fury had dulled, her restraint gradually ebbing away, melting the frosts of bitterness.

A stab of hope leapt inside him then. 'If you wish, you can accompany me wherever I go. We need never be parted,' he said, his voice suddenly a shade too loud. 'We can take each day as it comes. There's every chance it might work.'

Even conflict wears itself out; even indecision has this measure set to its miserable powers of torture, that any issue in the end is better than the hell of indecision itself. The agony of dark doubt dissolved and disappeared, and a warm feeling of certainty swept right through her.

'I could never go back to the way it was. I'm not that same girl anymore. And how do you know I …I won't disappoint you again?' her lips quivered as she spoke.

He studied her for a moment. Her startling eyes were bright with unshed tears. They were too transparent to conceal anything from him. It was as though all of her being had come to focus in them. He had never been one for endearment, but now he whispered the words she had longed to hear, telling her again and again that he loved and cherished her, beseeching her to forgive him - offering all the reparation in his power.

Her woman's heart let her down. Love is the most permanent of human emotions; it knows no limits to its endurance. He had melted her into softness that could refuse him nothing. She felt it a point of her own happiness to forgive him. Moved to tears, she shook her head mutely at him, all her resolution completely gone.

He reached to touch her cheek, very gently with the tip of one finger. 'My dearest, may …maybe you can begin to forgive me for the misery I've caused you. Not all at once, but just a little at a time.' He was weeping openly himself now, making it hard to speak without a tremor to his voice. 'We both …both have scars that will show for the rest of our lives, but we …we've still a life to live.'

Great waves of emotion rippled through her, her breast heaving with the pain of it. This was not a man playing the charmer with clever deceits and smiles. Here was the truth and she rejoiced in it. Somehow there was nothing to be done but start over again. The past was the past. All that mattered now was the future. It was going to be all right. She stared back at him through a film of tears, struggling to hold them in, aching with the strain, but so filled with love for him was she that she could no longer keep them back. The dam broke, their unashamed tears falling together as naturally and easily as snow melts in a warm spring.

She took in a long, deep shivering breath and swallowed hard. 'If ...if I come back, I want to ...to be more than just a comfort to you. You must never ...never push me away ...never shut me out ...ever again.'

The reproaches she made him were murmured in so soft a tone, expressing more languor than resentment that he could not but presume his forgiveness was at no distance away. 'I've been act ...acting a part for you. I want ...I *need* to be myself.'

Luke closed his eyes and passed a trembling hand across his face. It was some moments before he lowered it and could speak again. When he did his voice was soft with adoration. 'Whatever you say, my dearest.'

He held a tremulous hand up in front of him. 'Christ, I ...I thought I'd lost you. Just look at me. I'm shaking like a leaf. Jessica, dearest, I'll devote the rest of my life to you. You have my sacred promise.'

'You once promised me Heaven.' There was calmness about her now. 'Do you remember?'

'Yes. I remember.'

'Well, I know now that Heaven isn't riches and possessions. Heaven is under our feet as well as over our heads. Heaven's the beauty about us, the giving

…and the love. But love is a two way thing.'

To love and to be loved! A new sensation for him, as different as light from darkness. For he had never been in love. He knew it now. Just to feel! The sun was shining in a world where he had thought there was none. He dropped down on one knee before her, murmuring all the endearments of assurance, slowly warming that cold, frightened space in her heart. Then, taking both her hands in his, he kissed first one and then the other, over and over again.

'Jessica, I kneel before you as a man in love. Believe me…*I really do love you.* Having you in my life is all that matters to me. You're as vital to me as the air that I breathe.'

Those words, those blessed words that she had longed to hear, which wiped out the agonies that had stripped her soul and overwhelmed her love and joy, were linked by a thread that finally reeled her in. She felt a surge of love so strong that it hurt, wanting to burst out of her.

Luke rose to his feet and ignoring the pain in his ribs and injured shoulder, stooped to gather her tenderly in his arms, lifting her as if she was no more than a feather, blanket and all. Her arms went about those stiff shoulders, drawing him close, one hand lifting wearily to touch his dear face as she drew in a long, shuddering breath and murmured his name.

'Luke, oh, Luke …take me home...'

The Promise of Heaven
Margaret R Snowdon

A passionate saga set in the first half of the nineteenth century in the glorious Lake District of Cumbria, England, in the midst of a mining and farming community, with its wild fells, enchanting woods, its mountains and magnificent lakes; glorious stretches of country, calm and beautiful, but sometimes stormy and forbidden.

And the High Society of Piccadilly, London - "the magic mile" as it was known, with its tall and impressive buildings, stretching from Hyde Park Corner all the way along to Piccadilly Circus - revealing a glittering age in all its splendid and scandalous variety.

A story of love and unsettling passions, of the people and the land, relating to two very different young women and the men in their lives.

The alluring Madame Duprez – in her late twenties, an exquisitely beautiful and wealthy young widow with the most extravagant tastes.

And the seventeen-year-old Jessica Greenward; a warm-hearted girl that believes in love and magic, who assumes, with the optimism of youth that every cloud has a silver lining. Yet, not quite an Angel, with a streak of wildness about her that is admired by more than just one man. A true daughter of the fell.

The Edge Of Heaven
Margaret R Snowdon

The discontented Megan Greenward, who has spent all her life on her father's farm, longs for change and excitement.

Miles Ramsey, who works on Joseph Greenward's farm has known Megan since childhood and cares for her, but she's drawn to Lawrence Vincent, a young doctor from London, who came to Cumbria to recuperate from the loss of his young wife and fatigue.

In time, Lawrence declares his love for Christa Sheridan, Megan's cousin; a warm-hearted girl, wild and audacious, with a fiercely independent spirit.

This triggers off a deep hatred in Megan. She leaves the farm all together, and arranges to have Christa abducted and sexually abused.

Will Christa ever recover from the shame? Will Lawrence Vincent succeed in healing her with his love? And what becomes of Megan Greenward and her evil accomplice?

When tragedy strikes again, Christa is brought to her knees and longs to end it. But there are those who will not allow it.

The Allure Of The Wild
Margaret R Snowdon

A work of fiction - written with Nature lovers in mind, this story is about wild-life, country-folk and their way of life - set in The Lake District of Cumbria, England, where every problem in life is eased as peace and beauty shed their blessings like sunset glow at eventide.

Jake Goodwin is a young man who has a love of solitary places, the seeing eye and a sympathetic heart for all living creatures. It's a three mile tramp over the fells from the cottage where he lives with his widowed mother, to the moss-clad barn in which he works as apprentice carpenter alongside Fletcher Hopper, over in Uldale. Jake makes a friend of young Julia Furnell, whose parents have taken over Uldale Farm.

Over the years, their love of nature draws the two young people closer together. Will Hopper, Fletcher's rapscallion, dare-devil son, fights Jake over Julia. But will she turn to him? Or does her heart belong to Jake? When tragedy strikes, it changes Jake's life. Will he loose his shyness and tell Julia how he feels about her? Or is he to lead a life of loneliness?

Cockermouth Farm
Margaret R Snowdon

Charlotte Gray asks Bryan Powell, the local school teacher, to be godfather to her young son, Richard, knowing he would ensure the child gets a good education.

From a distance, Cockermouth Farm looks to be in a pleasant spot, a glimpse of mown fields, bright, translucent greenness against the purple of the moor. But to Charlotte, it was a hungry farm, needing never-ending toil. Her husband, Albert, is a hard task-master and wants more children for the farm; lads to drive cattle, load hay, sow and plough; lasses to scrub and bake, to milk and churn. But Charlotte's left weak and tormented after giving birth to another stillborn child. Young Richard becomes afraid of his mother, turning more and more to the help, Megan Godhill, who's fond of the boy and promises never to leave him.

Charlotte loses her mind after the birth of a daughter and attempts to take Richard's life. When she's shut away in an asylum, Megan takes over her duties and the caring of Richard. But Megan's father discovers there's more going on between his daughter and Albert Gray and has a plan to put a stop to it.

As the years pass and Richard is grown, he takes over the farm and battles with the land and his memories. When the lovely Ruby Kimball comes into his life, everything changes and he desperately wants to take her as his wife, but has nothing to offer but Cockermouth Farm and endless chores.

Hungry and barren the hills might be, but Ruby Kimball sees only beauty in them. Will Richard's love be returned? Will fate take a turn and enable him to marry her? Or will he go the way of his parents – toiling day in and day out until the farm wears him down and breaks his spirit?